SAMMIE & BUDGIE

a novel by

SCOTT SEMEGRAN

MUTT PRESS

Austin

Mutt Press
Austin, Texas
https://www.muttpress.com
info@muttpress.com

ISBN 978-0-9997173-3-2

Photo of Scott Semegran by Lori Hoadley
Cover by Alchemy Book Covers and Design
Chapter Illustrations by Scott Semegran
Additional Illustrations by Mia Ryan Semegran
Edited by Brandon R. Wood

Books by Scott Semegran:
Sammie & Budgie
Boys
The Spectacular Simon Burchwood
The Meteoric Rise of Simon Burchwood
Modicum
Mr. Grieves

Find Scott Semegran Online:
https://www.scottsemegran.com
https://www.goodreads.com/scottsemegran
https://www.twitter.com/scottsemegran
https://www.facebook.com/scottsemegran.writer/
https://www.instagram.com/scott_semegran
https://www.amazon.com/author/scottsemegran
https://www.smashwords.com/profile/view/scottsemegran

"Illustrated throughout by Semegran, this book is the author's best. In these pages, his steadfastly idiosyncratic style really begins to click. An unconventional, beguiling, and endearing family tale."

— *Kirkus Reviews*

"The novel's delights abound... Semegran is a gifted writer, with a wry sense of humor. Poignant, yet never maudlin, this novel will appeal to literary-minded readers and fans of magical realism."

— *BlueInk Review.* Starred Review.

"More than a story of a gifted child learning to hone his talents, Sammie and Budgie is an exposé on the inner lives of children and their parents. The writing quality is excellent and the dialogue between Simon and Sammie is immersive."

— *Foreword* Clarion Reviews. Clarion Rating: 4 out of 5.

"Though Simon's love for his children shines through as one of the novel's biggest strengths, its illustrations are perhaps the best part. Expressive, adorable, and adding a fun surprise, they are a welcome addition to the reading experience."

— *Indie Reader*

For My Wife Lori and My Kids - Mia, Sophia, Ahnika, and Colin

and

For all the loving fathers--past, present, future--who adore their children and do not get the credit they deserve. I see you, gentlemen. Keep up the good work.

Table of Contents

"The mind of man is capable of anything--because everything is in it, all the past as well as the future." Joseph Conrad, *Heart of Darkness*

***

"Every person you look at, you can see the universe in their eyes, if you're really looking." George Carlin, *40 Years of Comedy*

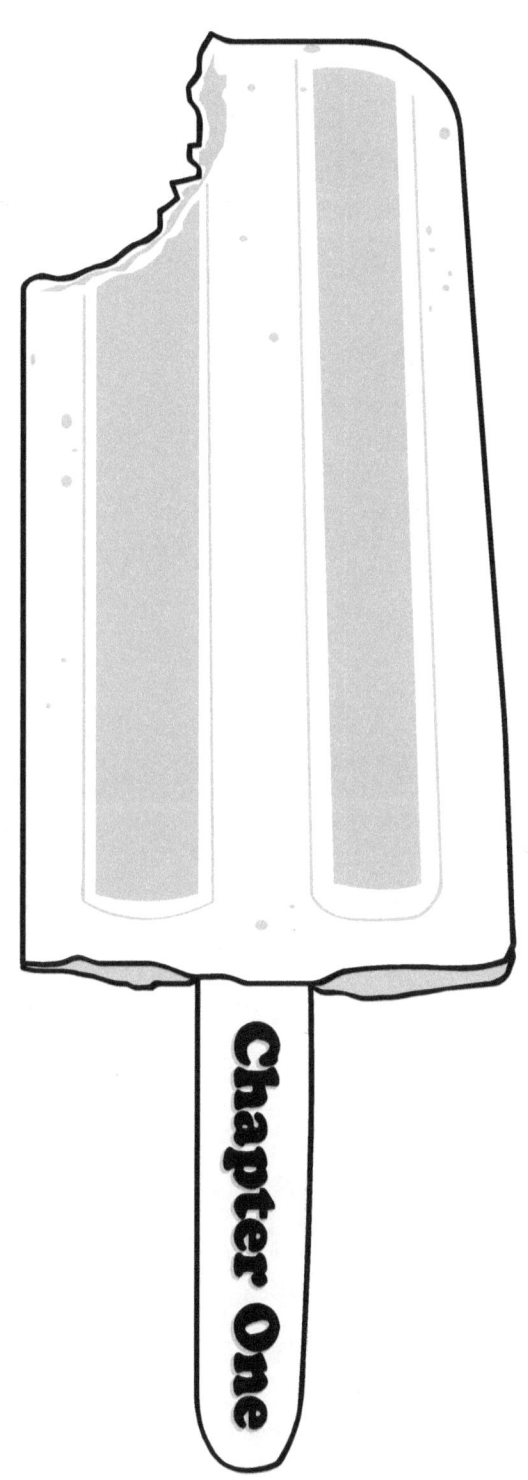

Chapter One

Chapter One

I discovered that my boy, Sammie--my son, my first child, my spawn, a chip off my ol' block, my heart and my soul--could see the future, that he could tell me what was going to happen before it happened, when he was in the third grade. I discovered this by dumb luck. Now, what I'm about to tell you, I'm telling you in the strictest of confidence. I mean, I'm telling you because I feel you need to know and I just don't go around telling everyone in the goddamn world my business because, well, it's *my business*; but I like *you* and that's all that matters. My boy, Sammie, was considered special by all accounts, not just special because I learned he could see the future, but special for two reasons: 1) he went through intensive testing and was designated as a child with special education needs by the State of Texas and 2) he's special because *I said* he's special. A father knows what a father knows, and I knew, without a doubt, that my boy was special. It's true.

Even before Sammie Boy was born, I had a feeling he was special (I call him Sammie Boy all the time--even now--because that's what I like to call him). When he was still living in the cramped efficiency apartment that was his mother's womb, he would kick and punch all over the place in a manner that made me feel like he was communicating with me in some type of fetal Morse Code. His mother would always tell me, 'Play our baby some music because I've read that playing our baby music while it is still in utero helps its intelligence.' So, I would do that. I'd get a Walkman or iPod or whatever was around, I'd put some classical music on, and place the headphones around his mother's overgrown stomach, and play the music loud so Sammie Boy could hear it. And whenever I would start the music, he would start kicking and punching all over the goddamn place, more punching when he disliked the music and less punching when he seemed to like it. Whenever I played any pop music, good ol' Sammie Boy seemed to hate it. He'd start punching and kicking and jabbing and stomping at such a furious rate that I thought he'd bust out of his mother's stomach like one of those hideous alien babies in the *Alien* movies. I played him all kinds of music to see what he would like: classical music, rock music, hip-hop music, country music, and even movie soundtracks. But the type of music that I discovered that he liked the most was jazz music, particularly John Coltrane songs and albums. He loved the shit out of some John Coltrane music--all the punching and kicking and stomping and jabbing and head-butting would cease the minute this music started. It really did, especially when I played the album *Blue Train*.

But what really made me aware of the fact that my boy Sammie was special was the day I picked him up from elementary school and he told me his after-school counselor was going to hurt herself in a serious way. I thought that to be a very strange thing for him to say, since Sammie didn't particularly have a malicious bone in his body, but was unsettling even more since my boy wasn't known to tell lies. Outside the school, out in the back where the playground and basketball court stretched beyond the portable buildings, I watched all the kids run and play while his counselor stood alone, keeping an eye on the children. It was a warm, humid day and the kids swarmed around the counselor like excited bees circling a sunflower.

I knelt next to my boy, placing my hands on his arms, and braced him gently, when I said, "What do you mean she will hurt herself?" Now, you have to understand, my boy Sammie was the cutest kid you will ever lay your eyes on, with big, round, brown eyes and a round face, tussled brown hair that never seemed to keep the style it started with in the morning, and a smile that would make a serial killer renounce his depravity and perform cartwheels in a field of daisies. Even in this serious situation, where I would have to compose myself to find answers, I had to fight the urge to pinch his cheeks and giggle. He was just that cute. "She looks fine to me," I said.

Sammie Boy looked over where the counselor stood, his sparkling, brown eyes examining her, the lids closing slightly as he peered at her, as if making out what her next move might be, and resolute sadness appeared on his cute, little face. "Daddy, can I ask you a question?" he said.

"Of course, my boy. You can ask me a question."

"Will you be *mad* at me if I tell you the truth?"

"Why would I be mad at you?" I said, firmly gripping his arms, as if to let him know how strongly I felt about expressing my true feelings to him, to comfort him. That's what a parent should do, right? A parent should be like a rock, like a sturdy thing that a delicate child could count on to protect him, and that's how I felt. I was Sammie's rock. It's true. "You should *always* tell me the truth. Always," I said.

"I don't know how I know, but I know. My brain is telling me," he said, his head tilting toward his chest, as if heavy from guilt for knowing something I couldn't quite comprehend. He wouldn't look at me.

I turned and looked at the counselor, an occasional errant kid running toward her then around her and using her as a swinging pole, she seemed fine and not in any way in danger or in a position to be seriously hurt by anyone or anything. Sammie wouldn't look at me anymore, his head heavy on the end of his limp neck. He drew imaginary circles on the ground with the tip of his Converse sneaker. I felt really bad for him because he seemed genuinely worried. I could tell.

"I think she'll be fine. How about we go get some ice cream on the way home? Would you like that?" I stood up, releasing his arms and gently placing my hands on his shoulders. He looked at me, a bigger smile on his face than I had seen in a while, since the morning at least.

"Really? Baskin Robbins?!"

"Sure, go get your backpack and tell the counselor goodbye."

"OK!"

He ran across the black top toward the counselor, who stood a few feet away from a metal bench that all of the kids' backpacks sat on, lined up in a multi-colored row of bright, pastel colors of the girls' backpacks and deep, primary colors of the boys' backpacks: ponies and unicorns for the girls, Marvel and DC superheroes for the boys. Sammie Boy waved to the counselor as he ran toward her and a sweet smile slid across her face. I could tell that she liked my son, with a look of sincere affection on her face, and she hugged him when he embraced her around her waist, waving for her to bring her face towards his. She knelt down and he whispered something in her ear, something that made her smile more than giggle. She patted him on the back and aimed him toward the metal bench where his backpack sat waiting for him. He slung his Spider-Man backpack over one shoulder and ran back to me. I waved to the counselor, relieved that nothing happened that would hurt her in a serious way, as my boy Sammie said would happen. Sometimes, kids say the weirdest things at the weirdest times and there really is no rhyme or reason to why they say these things. They just do, and what they say is like an involuntary burp that escapes your mouth an hour after lunch or a silent yet stinky fart that slips out while you're in an important meeting. It leaves an impression but doesn't mean anything at all. It's true.

I held Sammie's little hand and we walked toward my parked car when, suddenly, he tugged my arm and looked up at me, his little, round face pale and gaunt, his smile gone. An uneasy feeling tugged at the bottom of my stomach when I heard all the kids on the playground scream and, when I looked back, saw the counselor on her back, on the ground in front of the metal bench. I let go of Sammie's hand and ran toward the counselor, her body still and motionless in the dirt and grass and pebbles. All the kids on the playground came closer too, but not so close, as if keeping some distance between them and her would alleviate any blame that could come their way.

On the ground next to her, I got on one knee, touched her wrist, and knew she was still alive by the strong pulse under her skin. I didn't dare touch her head, being that it was at such a bizarre angle at the end of her neck, twisted closer to one shoulder than what seemed natural. I was in a state of shock as the kids inched their way closer and closer to their unconscious counselor, but all I was worried about was Sammie. Would it hurt his feelings that his premonition about his counselor came true? I wasn't sure at the time how he felt about his power to see the future but I did know this: he felt bad about *something*.

"Sorry I told you the truth, Daddy," he said, putting his hand on my shoulder. I was kind of sorry that I learned just how special my boy could be. Then I called 911.

* * *

Instead of buying Sammie an ice cream cone at Baskin Robbins, like I promised, I bought him a Popsicle from the cafeteria at the North Austin Medical Center, the hospital where the ambulance brought his after-school counselor. The ambulance arrived at the school pretty quick after I called 911 and I couldn't just *not* check on the poor counselor, leaving her outcome to just mere chance. Sammie insisted we go to the hospital too, even though I knew I would have to pick up Sammie's sister, Jessica (or Jessie, as I call her), from taekwondo. Luckily for me, Jessie could stay at taekwondo as long as her little heart desired because the instructor, Master Lu, taught late into the night and Jessie was never eager to leave practice anyway (she's a hardcore first-grader when it comes to taekwondo). So we followed the ambulance to the hospital and I promised Sammie I would buy him a snack if I could find him one, which we did, in the cafeteria.

As he ate his Popsicle while running laps around the table where I sat in the dining room of the cafeteria--brightly colored streams of sugary liquid running out of his mouth, down his cheeks and neck, and onto his striped t-shirt--I learned all kinds of unsavory things about Sammie's after-school counselor that I didn't know before (and wasn't quite sure I wanted to know). I learned that her name was Selena--pronounced say-LEE-nah--and that she still lived with her parents and she went to a bad high school on the east side of Austin and that she liked to drink beer and tequila together when she partied and often came to work quite hungover in her beat-up Nissan Sentra with lowered suspension and chrome wheels and that she had a boyfriend she called Big Papa (after the hip-hop song by Biggie Smalls aka The Notorious B.I.G.) but he didn't like to be called Big Papa because it made him feel *self-conscious* about his weight and he preferred to be called Stud Boy and she liked most of the kids in after-school care except for Juan and Jerome because they acted like thugs and on and on and on. Sammie could get going if I let him and, boy, was he on a roll that day while we waited to see if his counselor was OK. Sometimes, he gets a condition I like to call "diarrhea mouth" where he spews words out of his cute face at a pace that is much faster than his brain could possibly comprehend. A lot of people suffer from this condition, even adults, whether they realize it or not, what, with their bragging about the newest gadget that they just bought, or the Caribbean cruise that they just booked, or the fancy restaurant that they ate at the night before, or whatever. Adults constantly talk about the most *inane* shit sometimes. It's true. But Sammie Boy, he also seemed to be afflicted with diarrhea mouth quite often (I think he got this condition from his mother, my ex-wife) and he had a severe case of it that day at the hospital.

After a while listening to him, I grew curious how he knew so much about his counselor Selena, so I said, "How do you know all of this, Sammie?"

"She tells us stuff *every day*. She loves to tell us about her life," he said, slurping on his Popsicle until it disintegrated. He revealed the Popsicle stick to me, its soggy, wooden composition stained from red and blue food-coloring, the word 'Popsicle' etched on it. I told him to toss it in the trash can by the entrance of the cafeteria but he shoved it in his pocket instead, just in case he needed it later for something important. Kids are always doing that, stashing trash for later. "She lives a *hard* life. What's wrong with that?"

"What's wrong with what?" I said.

"Selena telling us about her *hard* life?"

"Oh, well, she seems to give you so much *detail*. It's kind of unprofessional, I think."

"Un-pro-fesh-un-uhl--what is that?!"

"Nevermind. Do you want to go see how she's doing?"

"Yeah! Let's go!" he said, as he sprinted at full-speed out of the cafeteria and back toward where we came, a set of elevators around the corner and down a hall that ran next to the cafeteria. The hospital was blandly decorated and sparsely furnished as to not offend any of its patients' family members, some of which would occupy the random couches or chairs or stools far away from the dismal environments of the small, diseased rooms of their wives or husbands or sons or daughters or partners or whoever or, in our case, my son's after-school counselor. If you really examined the patterns of the carpet and the upholstery of the furniture, they were somewhere between a Southwest Santa Fe-style and a Jackson Pollock spew-fest, pastel patterns intermingling with muted primary color splatter. It was a curious choice for a hospital, bland and obnoxious at the same time. Sammie seemed to like the pattern of the carpet and he chose to run along the pattern as if it was a crazy road map, designed by a psychotic interior decorator. He zigged and zagged all the way to the elevator, making noises with his mouth as if he was a race car or a train or an airplane or a UFO, sometimes all at once.

"Push the button!" I said, waving at him to stop and not actually go in the elevator. "But wait for *me*!" The elevator dinged and Sammie bolted inside, prompting me to run to catch him before the door closed and separated us. Once there, I held the door open with the palm of my hand then stood next to my boy. I could feel his heart pounding while I touched his shoulder. A Muzak, instrumental version of "Careless Whisper" by the band Wham! played from small speakers at the top of the elevator. "I told you to wait for me," I said, panting from being pudgy and doughy and all sorts of out of shape. I should spend more time at a gym or something, another thing to add to my lengthy to-do list.

"I did, Daddy! I did!"

"OK. OK," I said, the elevator taking us up a couple of floors. "Keep your pants on. Sheesh."

"My pants *are* on, Daddy," Sammie said. He peered out the glass back-side of our elevator car, his face and hands smashed against the clear glass, his breath fogging up his view. "The carpet looks like a rainbow explosion, Daddy!"

"It sure does," I said. It did look like a rainbow explosion from our vantage point, three-stories up, although my adult brain wouldn't have thought of it that way without him mentioning it. I think we lose some of that *creative vision* as we grow older, turning from curious children into jaded adults. Children have a way of seeing the world that is untarnished by experience or disappointment or adult's selfish bullshit. It's true.

"Daddy, can I ask you a question?"

"Sure, but you don't have to keep saying, 'Can I ask you a question?' Just ask me the question."

"OK. Daddy, can I get a pet?"

The elevator bell dinged and the door opened. Sammie grabbed my hand and we walked out of the elevator together. His little hand fit perfectly inside my hand. At some point, "Careless Whisper" morphed into a tinkly instrumental version of "Girls Just Want to Have Fun" by Cyndi Lauper.

"A pet? What kind of pet?" I said, squeezing his little hand gently.

"A bird!"

"What?! A bird?" We stopped and he looked up at me, his face shining with childish enthusiasm, his eyes aglow with sparkles and reflections from the fluorescent lights in the ceiling in his line of view above my head. He looked hypnotized.

"Yeah, a *budgerigar*! I want a budgie!"

"Birds are smelly and messy," I said, a little annoyed. We continued walking after I quickly dismissed his request.

"Budgie! Budgie! Budgie! That's what I would name it. Budgie!"

"I'll think about it."

"You always say that. And when you say, 'I'll think about it,' then that always means no."

"I'll think about it," I said, smiling.

"Daddy! Quit saying *that*!"

We found a reception counter that looked like the place to check-in but it wasn't stationed by anyone. So rather than continue into areas of the hospital we weren't sure we could walk into, we waited for someone to check us in. Sammie Boy didn't mind. He was full of life.

"Budgerigars are better known as parakeets. Do you know what a *parakeet* is?"

"Yes, Sammie, I know what a parakeet is." I looked around for a nurse or an administrative assistant or somebody but I didn't see anybody. The desk was a deserted, plywood island.

"Well, that's good," he said. "They are the third most popular pet *in the world*, behind dogs and cats of course."

"That's very interesting."

"I know! Very interesting, indeed." He drew imaginary circles in the rainbow-explosion carpet with the tip of his canvas sneaker. "So, can I get one?"

"I'll think about it."

He moaned a BIG sigh and threw his arms against his sides and exclaimed in an exasperated tone, "I'll *never* get one!" He made it seem like the world was ending, and maybe his little world was ending at that very second. Every disappointment in a child's life is always, and I mean *always*, monumental. Don't ask me why. It just is. Kids make a big deal about everything.

"Let's discuss it later," I said, then out of thin air a young woman sat down behind the counter. She was young and brunette and kind of slim (but kind of *not*) and a little irritated, apparently. The pastel cardigan she wore was a size too small; it squeezed her flesh into a succession of bulging rolls and folds, hills and valleys of overindulgence. She gave me a terse smile, part sincere and part deliberate. A name tag on her shirt said BETH.

"Can I help you?" she said. She rummaged through some papers and office supplies spread out on the desk.

"Yes, we'd like to see--what's her name, Sammie?" I said, looking at my boy. He tried to peek over the counter-top, his body stretching as high as his toes could push him, but he only could speak toward the ceiling.

"Selena! Her name is *Say-LEE-nah*!"

"Yes, can we see Selena?" I said, leaning on the counter-top with one elbow, smiling as sincerely as possible.

"Let me see if she's in our system." She typed furiously on the keyboard of her computer and as she typed, a serious look on her face, I couldn't help but think of the song *Beth* by the band *Kiss*, and their ridiculous music video with the band--in full-on makeup and leather outfits and high heels--sitting around a prissy brunette wearing a white, cardigan sweater, the drummer Peter Criss serenading her about how he was staying out late, playing with the boys in the band, not coming home soon, and shit like that. Maybe *this* Beth in the hospital was mad after her boyfriend's all-nighter, sitting at home stewing because her Peter was out late, drinking with his buddies, having too much fun, and refusing to come home to her like she wanted him to. Maybe she drank too much cheap wine from a box in the refrigerator and put herself to sleep with thoughts of a better man out there, somewhere in the world, and woke up hung-over, drank a quart of coffee before heading to work at the hospital. I bet it's true. She typed some more as we waited.

"Right, there is a Selena in our system. Are you a family member?"

I looked at Sammie Boy and he looked at me and I realized that there was a certain *protocol* to situations like this. We weren't family members. We weren't even close friends of Say-LEE-nah. For all practical purposes, we were just concerned acquaintances, or as some would say, nosey acquaintances. How strange.

"No, we're not family members. You see, my boy Sammie here, he's in after-school care. And Selena is a counselor at the elementary school. And we were there when she fell down and hurt herself. I was the one that called the ambulance."

"I see," Beth said, still pouty and unconcerned. Her boyfriend must have done a number on her the night before. I could tell. She was pretty annoyed. "Well, only family members and loved ones can go back and see patients. You'll just have to wait out here."

"OK," I said, looking at Sammie. "Let's go have a seat, son."

We found a seat nearby. I sat down and patted my legs for Sammie to sit on them. He flopped on my lap and wrapped his arms around my neck. He was a cute, little son-of-a-bitch, he was! And I say that with the deepest affection because it's true. I loved my boy with all my heart *and* his mother was an absolute bitch. But no worries, I'll get into that later. I squeezed my boy tightly.

"Is she going to be all right, Daddy?" he said, a distressed look on his face.

"I bet she'll be just fine. She's in the right place."

"All the doctors and nurses will take care of her?"

"Yep."

"They won't let her die or anything like that?"

"I hope not."

"Daddy," he said, perking up. "Maybe if I write Selena a note, then that grouchy lady at the desk will give it to her. Do you think she'll do that?"

"I don't know but you can try."

"OK!"

On a side table next to our chair was a cup filled with pens with 'VIAGRA' scrawled on their shafts as well as a pad of paper with 'PRILOSEC' emblazoned at the top. Good ol' Sammie Boy grabbed a pen and the pad of paper and earnestly wrote a quick note to his counselor--a sweet, sentimental note that said how worried he was for her and that he hoped she was all right and not hurt and how sorry he was for knowing that she was going to hurt herself. When I saw him write that, I tapped him on the shoulder and advised that he erase that part. I didn't want him incriminating himself in any way but I appreciated his thoughtfulness. He erased the 'knowing that she was going to hurt herself' part and signed the note, 'Love, Sammie.'

"Can I give this to the lady at the desk to give to Selena?"

I nodded and watched Sammie run over to Beth, her scowl turning into a sweet, closed-mouth smile. Even a sourpuss like jaded Beth couldn't resist the charms of my cute kid. Sammie gave her the note and whispered some instructions into her ear. Beth stood up and walked away while good ol' Sammie Boy returned to my lap. He was very happy and pleased with himself.

"She said she'd give it to Selena," he said, smiling, beaming with pride.

"Good. Do you feel better now?"

"Yes, I just hope she's all right."

We sat there for a few, quiet moments, Sammie swinging his legs back and forth, my arms around my little boy. He sure was special, all right, not just in the special needs way, but in a *kind-spirited* way. A lot of kids his age, kids that are in the third or fourth grade, their personalities were starting to curdle, starting to turn into something less kind, less child-like. They wanted to be teenagers. They wanted to be more grown-up. They liked to cuss, learned about sexy things from their siblings, and watched TV shows with violence and foul language and kids behaving badly and stuff like that. But not my Sammie. He was as innocent as could be, with a pure heart and pure intention. He was a really good kid. It's true.

"Daddy?" he said.

"Yes, my boy?"

"Can I draw on that paper while we wait?"

"Sure," I said, giving him the Viagra pen and the Prilosec pad of paper. With his tongue curling through his pursed lips, he hunched over the pad of paper and doodled a little bird flying through the air, a circle for a sun and three bumpy clouds high above the tiny avian creature. He drew what looked like a letter 'B' on the bird's chest.

"What's the 'B' stand for?" I said, curious about his letter choice, when Beth walked back toward us with a piece of paper in her hand. When she got to where we sat, she knelt down in front of us and handed Sammie the piece of paper. Her sour disposition was gone, replaced by a sweet demeanor that I didn't see there before. Maybe Beth didn't have such a bad night after all.

"I shouldn't be doing this but here's a note from Selena. You're a sweet boy!" She patted him on the head and went back to her desk.

Sammie smiled at me and said, "Can I read it, Daddy?" I nodded and this is what the note said:

Thank you for checking on me, Sammie. You're a good kid and my favorite of all the kids in after-school care! I have epilepsy and I had a seizure. I'm sorry that it scared you but it's something I have to deal with all the time. Please don't worry, Sammie. I'll probably see you back at the school next week. Take care and be good, Selena.

"She's going to be all right," Sammie said. He folded the note and put it in his pocket along with the Popsicle stick.

"That's good," I said, placing him on his feet. "We need to go pickup your sister from taekwondo."

"Do we *have* to?" Sammie said, whining. "Can't she just walk home?!"

"No, she can't just *walk* home."

"Why not?"

"Because that would make me a bad parent."

"You're not a bad parent. You're the best daddy, EVER!"

"Ever?" I said.

"Forever and ever!"

"That's a very long time."

"I know! Daddy, can I get Budgie on the way home?"

"No, not today."

"PLEASE!"

I grabbed good ol' Sammie Boy's hand and we walked over the rainbow explosion, leaving grouchy Beth and poor Selena behind, leaving the erectile-dysfunctional pens and the acid-reflux pads of paper on the table, and out of the hospital and back to our normal life. We found my car and hopped in, ready to retrieve Sammie's sister and possibly buy ice cream or hamburgers or tacos.

I couldn't help but think that this day would turn out like that, what, with Sammie's counselor hitting the deck, being rushed to the emergency room, and me and my boy spending an hour or so in a dreary hospital. Being a parent to a special kid leads to very unexpected things in very unexpected ways. It's true.

LIBERTY

CHAPTER
TWO

D

1980

Chapter Two

I had an evening ritual with my kids that I held close to my heart. It was something my therapist came up with to help ease the solemn feeling over dinner we experienced the first few weeks after moving into my apartment, our new home following my divorce from their mother then, later, her unexpected death. I know; sounds pretty goddamn tragic, right? I'll get into that sad story later. But it was a hard adjustment for all of us, going from living in a large two-story, suburban home to a small two-bedroom apartment in a decent apartment complex outside of our neighborhood. During the divorce, their mother and I couldn't agree on what to do with our family home. So, beyond any discussions of what would be best for good ol' Sammie boy and his sister Jessie, we had to sell our home, the solution to all of our typical procedural squabbling. Their mother moved in with her full-of-shit-salesman boyfriend. I rented a two-bedroom apartment with a full-dining room and a garage. It was the largest place I could afford and the only sane option for me after the financial disaster of divorce. The idea of being crushed under a new mortgage was not very appealing to me. An apartment was not very appealing either but it was the best I could do at the time.

Anyway, once we moved into my apartment and got used to our new schedule based on the elaborate, custody mathematics in the decree, the three of us had family dinners together in a new home with our new family dynamic. It was glaringly apparent that there were three of us instead of four and the new eating configuration was strange, indeed, for all of us. Like I said, a solemn cloud would set over dinner, which made it difficult to enjoy our time together, let alone just chew our food. It was brutal! I mean, there were no proclamations of *bon appétit* or *c'est la vie* or whatever at dinner, that's for sure. It's true.

After a few of these dreadfully sour dinners, I discussed what I could do to lift the solemn cloud with my therapist, Charlotte. She had been my therapist ever since their mother and I separated, which was something like three years before, and after a few minutes of deep reflection, she said to me, "School is a very stressful time for your children. It's a long day for kids that age. And then there is the added stress of living in a new home. And their mother is *dead*. So, rather than start a conversation like, 'How was your day?' you should ask them something more specific like, 'Tell me something *silly* that happened to you today?'"

I thought this was a fun idea! Charlotte was full of fun ideas like this one. I eventually worked this routine into our nightly dinners. One night, I turned to Jessie, my daughter. Normally, she was a vivacious kid--full of life. But her sour disposition drooped down her face and almost seemed to drip onto her plate of chicken nuggets and macaroni and cheese; she looked that sad! I felt really bad for her but I was determined to lift the mood in our apartment. I put Charlotte's fun suggestion into action.

"So," I said, plopping my palms on the dining room table-top. The sudden noise of my hands hitting the wood startled my poor, little kids. It was like they awoke from a deep sleep, groggy and limp-lidded. "Tell me something *silly* that happened today."

"At school?" she said, unsure of what I was trying to get at.

"No, on *Mars.* Yes, at school! Were you somewhere else today?" I said, closing one eye and focusing my open eye on her like a pirate peering through a scallywag's unkempt uniform and deep into her troubled soul.

"Oh, OH, YES! This girl, in my class, her name is Christina. She loves to drink chocolate milk and she was drinking it and drinking it when that boy Chris, he started telling a joke."

"Uh huh," I said, nodding while chewing my dinner of chicken nuggets and macaroni and cheese. I know what you're thinking. 'What the fuck?' I usually ate what my kids ate for dinner--peanut butter and jelly sandwiches, mac and cheese, pepperoni pizza, mashed potatoes with gravy--whatever was easiest to make. I mean, I only had enough time in the day to cook and whatever my kids were eating was what I was going to be eating. It's that simple. I looked at Sammie Boy. He wasn't impressed with Jessie's story so far. He rolled his eyes, pushing his food around the plate into new, food pile configurations.

"I know how this will turn out," he said, then shoveling mac and cheese into his mouth.

"Son, let her finish. Continue!"

Sammie harrumphed.

"It was a 'Knock, Knock' joke. It went something like this." Then she pushed her chair back and stood up, acting out the 'Knock, Knock' joke, holding her clinched fist in the air, ready to rap on an imaginary door. "Knock, knock." She looked at me to answer.

"Oh, right! 'Who's there?'" I said, perking up.

"Orange."

"Orange, who?"

"Orange you glad I didn't say banana! Then that boy Chris, he had a banana on his lunch tray so he picked it up and he put it in Christina's face, right in front of her face. Then, all of a sudden, chocolate milk shot out of her nose!"

Good ol' Sammie Boy, he started laughing all over the place, his head went back and he slapped his knee, then he held his stomach cause he was laughing so hard, chunks of half-chewed chicken nuggets shooting from his mouth. I guess her story wasn't so hum-drum after all.

"I knew you were going to say that but it's still funny, sis."

"I know!" she said, beaming from the approval of her big brother. It was sweet seeing them laughing and talking and interacting. It was a nice change from the somber dinners from the previous few weeks. She sat back down and continued eating, much more chipper now.

"What about you?" I said, looking at Sammie. He was still snickering from his sister's story. "That's a hard one to top. Anything silly happen to you today?"

"Yeah."

"Then tell us."

"Well, this boy I know, Dez, he was teaching me how to play this new game. He calls it *Thump*. It's a game you play with a quarter. Do you know it?"

"No," I said, eating more mac and cheese, which was actually pretty good, if I say so myself. "I've never heard of that game. How do you play?"

"Well, do you have a quarter? I'll show you guys if you gimme a quarter."

I reached in my pocket for some change but didn't have anything in my pockets. I had left the contents of my pockets in a bowl on the kitchen counter after we got home.

"You'll have to get one from the kitchen."

"OK. Follow me!" He leapt from his chair, ran around the dining room table, and went into the kitchen, his feet stomping on the apartment floor. He rummaged through the bowl on the counter and found a quarter. He raised it into the air like he found a piece of buried treasure. "Got it! Come here and I'll show you."

He sat on the kitchen floor then Jessie and I made our way into the kitchen and sat down with him, the three of us in a circle. He propped the quarter on its side and held it up by holding the top of the coin with the tip of his index finger, the profile of George Washington peering in the distance.

"So, this is how you play *Thump*! Two people or more sit on the floor and the first one thumps the edge of the quarter to make it spin." Good ol' Sammie Boy flicked the edge of the quarter and it spun in front of him like a miniature dreidel, spinning around in an oval path on the kitchen floor. "Then the next person has to thump the quarter to keep it spinning. Like this." He flicked the quarter again and it kept spinning on its edge, a little wobbly this time but still spinning nonetheless. "If it falls down on someone's turn or they make it fall, they lose."

Just then, Jessie threw herself on the kitchen floor and slammed her hand on top of the quarter, like a cat swatting at a moth. Sammie was horrified that his sister interrupted his demonstration.

"Heads or tails, big brother!" she said, giggling and laughing as she covered the coin, repelling Sammie's prying hands from retrieving the coin. Now, you may think that boys are stronger than girls but in this case, you'd be dead wrong. Jessie was a pretty tough cookie for her size. Sammie didn't stand a chance against her. It's true.

"Hey! What are you doing?!" he said, still attempting to retrieve the coin from under his naughty sister's paws.

"Heads or tails? Call it!"

"That's not the game we are playing right now," he said, very upset at his sister's precociousness, but unwilling to engage with her any longer.

"Please!"

"Fine! Heads!" Jessie lifted her hand and it was heads, just as he'd said. "Are you happy?"

"Again! Let's do it again!"

"No," he said, crossing his arms, defiantly.

"Please! PLEASE! PLEASE!!" she said, begging.

"If I do it again, then can we play *Thump*?" he said. She nodded. "Fine." He flicked the quarter again and it spun on its side, wobbling topsy-turvy in its unusual orbit around some particles on the kitchen floor: bread crumbs, dry cereal, hair strands, dust bunnies. Without warning, Jessie again slammed her hand on the spinning quarter, interrupting its wobbly course.

"Heads or tails? Call it!"

"Heads," he said, sighing, already bored with this game.

"You already called heads!"

"Because it is *heads*."

She slowly lifted her hand to reveal that it certainly was heads again. Her face twisted into a look of contempt and bitterness, a thing she always did when a game she started took a turn for the worse, or rather, not her way.

"This game isn't fun anymore!" She jumped up and stormed to the other side of the apartment--in their room--where all her toys were waiting for her and her brother was not. Sammie snickered.

"Dad, will you play Thump with me?" he said, begging, his hands praying for my acceptance.

"Sure."

"Yeah! I go first!" he said, returning to his ready position on the kitchen floor. He quickly flicked the coin and it spun on its side, slowly following a curved path toward me. I cocked my finger under my thumb and waited for the right time to thump the spinning coin. As it spun, it whirred and whizzed in a small circle. When the right time arrived, I gently thumped the coin and it continued to spin between us, its trajectory altered. "All right, daddy! You did it. My turn."

As he waited his turn, I watched him, his eyes on the coin like a cat waiting to pounce on another unsuspecting moth. I hadn't seen him this focused on something--anything--in a long while. But for some reason while I watched him, an image of Selena the after-school counselor appeared in my mind, her body twisted on the asphalt of the playground behind the school, and I thought of good ol' Sammie Boy telling me that she was seriously going to hurt herself right before it happened. I was curious. How did he know that was going to happen? Was it a fluke that he knew what was going to happen to her *before* it happened? Or could he see what's going to happen before it happens, even if I asked him? So, I thought, 'What the hell? I'll ask him.'

"Sammie, can you tell me what will show when the coin falls and this game is over--heads or tails?"

"Yes, daddy." He flicked the coin and it continued to spin. "It's your turn!"

"OK. What will it be--heads or tails?"

"Tails," he said, without hesitation.

Just then, I flicked the coin and it slid across the kitchen floor and slammed into the metal, oven door. It made a loud clanking noise then fell on its side, lifeless now, tails side up. It must have been a fluke. There was no way that my cute, little boy could see the future. I picked up the coin and held it between us, pinched between my thumb and index finger.

"I'm going to flip this coin in the air and you tell me--heads or tails. OK?"

"OK. Tails."

"Are you sure?"

"Yes." I flipped the coin in the air, it's metallic surface glimmering as it tumbled head over tails up, arcing in the air, then down to my hand. I caught it, then slapped it on top of my other hand. When we looked at the coin together, it was tails. "See!"

"Again." When I flipped it, he called heads and then it was heads. Again, he called tails and then it was tails and so on. We did this together like, what, 20 times and he called it on the nose every single time. He didn't even bat an eye. It was amazing! And weird. It's true. My skin began to crawl, covered in goosebumps and stiff hairs. "How do you do that?" I said, astonished. "If I keep going, then you'll know them all, which side will show?"

My little boy lowered his head, shame and embarrassment weighing it down. His excitement for playing the game was gone. He wrapped his arms around himself, squeezing his torso gently, hugging himself firmly. He was acting like I was upset with him, the way kids do when they find themselves in a jam. But I wasn't upset with him at all. With my hand beneath his chin, I lifted his head gently.

"Will you be mad if I tell you the truth?" he said.

"I won't be mad," I said. I was telling the truth. I wouldn't have been mad at all.

"I really don't know how I know. I just know."

"I see," I said, disappointed at the vagueness of his answer, his non-answer. Kids are always doing that: giving non-answers. It's their way of protecting themselves from getting in trouble. But parents are smarter than that. We know what the non-answer really means. It means they are hiding something.

"Are you mad at me?"

"Oh, no, no, of course not. But it's getting late. You know? You should probably brush your teeth and get ready for bed."

"OK. But can I have the quarter?" he said, lifting his hand, the palm side up, his arm propped by his other arm at the elbow.

"Sure."

I dropped the coin in his hand and he slipped it into his pocket.

"I'll put it with the Popsicle stick," he said, running to the bathroom to brush his teeth. He was such a cute kid. Just looking at him made my heart melt. It's true. And *clairvoyant* to boot, it seemed. Crazy, huh? I mean, I wasn't quite sure at the time if he could see the future or not but is certainly seemed that way.

* * *

The balcony to my apartment, on the second floor at the back corner of my building, overlooked the driveway to my garage as well as the property that surrounded the back of my apartment complex. It was one of those types of apartment complexes that looked pretty fancy from the street out front but once you pulled into the complex and drove around the labyrinthine parking lot, the real lives of the tenants revealed itself: windows covered in aluminum foil and the clotheslines on the balconies and the late model cars with flat tires-- lives not so fancy after all. On my balcony were only three things: a wooden bench and a wooden chair--their frames weathered and grayed and splintered and the support structure to countless spiders and their webs and their trapped meals--and an old coffee can. The seat cushions of the chairs had long-ago been tossed in the trash, victims of a malodorous assault by the old family dog who had been sprayed in the face by a cantankerous skunk then wiped her stinky dog face on the cushions until the skunk stench coated every atom of the material. It wasn't so bad sitting on the skeletal frame of the bench or chair as long as I positioned my spine or hip bones between the splintery wooden slats and not directly on them. After putting the kids to bed almost every night, I would sneak out onto the balcony, sit my boney butt on the wooden chair, and I would quietly smoke cigarettes and think about the predicament that my life had descended into. I kept asking myself when thinking about the last few years of my miserable life, 'How did this happen?' Shit, you know how these things happen. Right? They just... happen. That's life, they say. You know? That's what all the know-it-alls and the smarty-pants and the too-good-for-yous and the uppity-assholes of the world say. They think they know everything. It's true.

The balcony was my place of refuge, where I smoked cigarettes and drank cheap beer and watched the sun set as well as my anonymous neighbors walk their rat dogs or take their trash to the dumpster or chase their hyper children around or haphazardly park their cars. After my kids brushed their teeth and went to bed, I planted my boney butt on the wooden chair. It was getting late at this point so there weren't too many people to watch, just a large woman talking loudly into her cell phone--her dark, curly hair perched on the top of her head with a banana clip and her terry-cloth bathrobe struggling to stay on her stout body--telling the person on the other end of the line just how much of a bitch her boss was, which was always the case. Whose boss isn't a bitch? Silly question. As I watched her shuffle away, her whining and moaning blending with the other sounds of the night--a cacophony of cicadas, crickets, mockingbirds, and mysterious night creatures serenading the setting sun--I saw some motion in the corner of my eye. I looked over at my window, the one that looked out from the kids' bedroom. A pair of small eyes watched me, peeking through the mini-blinds, little fingers prying the blinds open, scrutinizing me, and curiously monitoring what I was doing. I knew it was good ol' Sammie Boy. He always had a hard time getting to sleep and this time was probably no different. I stood up and went inside my apartment--quietly closing the door behind me--and sat on the couch. I knew he would make his way out to the living and, sure enough, he did.

He sat with me on the couch, laying his head on my stomach, and said, "You smell like smoke, Daddy."

"I know," I said. "I'm sorry about that." I placed my hand on his back. I could feel his lungs inflate then deflate as he held me.

"You shouldn't smoke. At school, my teacher showed the class a picture of a smoker's lungs. They were *black*! Do you think your lungs are black like that, Daddy?"

"I don't know," I said, taking a deep breath, then sighing. "I really hope not."

He quickly jumped up and stood in front of me, his fists pressed into his hips like a comic book super hero getting ready to belch out his heroic soliloquy while standing over a defeated foe, and he said pointing at me, "You shouldn't shmoke those nasty shmigarettes, Daddy!" I chuckled. Before I go on, let me explain something to you.

Just so you know, Sammie Boy had this cute habit of adding 'shm' to words and changing the way they sounded, encoding them into his own form of the English language. He called it *Shmenglish*. For instance, instead of saying 'apple,' he would say 'shmapple.' And instead of saying 'television,' he would say 'shmelevision.' When he spoke Shmenglish, he would ask me for things like 'shmookies' or 'shmotato shmips.' It was freakin' adorable. I loved it!

As this new and enigmatic mode of language sunk into his little brain over time, he eventually started to recite entire sentences in Shmenglish. In the past, if me or his mother would ask him to do a chore like, 'Sammie, take out the trash,' then he would respond, 'Shmammie, shmake out the shmash!' He would stop whatever it was he was doing and run around in circles shrieking, 'Shmake out the shmash! Shmake out the shmash! Shmake out the shmash!' and continuing on in this manner yet never doing what we asked him to do which was: take out the trash. It was a diversion tactic that worked pretty well for him for a while. Most parents have a soft spot for little things their kids do that they find cute. Of course, no one else found this behavior to be cute at all--not his mother, his sister, his teachers, his grandparents, his friends' parents--nobody. I was the sole, approving, audience member of his Shmenglish monologues, his only fan, his *shmonly shman*, and Sammie knew this. Boy, did he eat that shit up, too. I soon became fluent in all things Shmenglish.

Once it was common knowledge that *nobody* liked hearing things repeated in Shmenglish but me, it became a form of communication spoken only between the two of us--me and my boy. In private, we would carry on entire conversations in Shmenglish, stopping only when one of us just couldn't take it anymore, laughing and coughing and gasping for air, or when things got serious. And I was completely aware that this was probably only amusing to me and good ol' Sammie Boy but I didn't care. I cherished these conversations with him, even if they were ridiculous. Well, mostly ridiculous. He was such an adorable kid, I tell you. It's true.

"Shmigarettes are bad for your shmealth!" he continued.

"Shmeally?" I said, the corner of my mouth tweaking upwards, straining to hold back a laugh.

"Shmes! Shmeally!" He then tumbled on top of me, giggling and laughing all over the place. He thought that was just the funniest thing in the entire world.

I put my arms around him and laughed too, even though I was a little embarrassed that I was being scolded for smoking by my third-grade son. What could I say to him? The truth of why I smoked even though I knew my lungs were probably as black as the inside of a BBQ grill just wasn't good enough for him. There was a time when I didn't smoke, which seemed so long ago.

"You're a good kid, Sammie Boy, but it's past your bedtime," I said, patting his little back.

"But I'm not *tired*!" he said, pleading, his arms and legs gesticulating as if he was running even though he was laying across my lap.

"It doesn't matter. You still need to go to bed. Do you want me to tuck you in?"

"No," he said, kissing me on the cheek then slowly walking back to his room, his head down, a sigh punctuating his exasperation. "I'm a *big boy* now. I don't need a tuck in." He disappeared into his and his little sister's room, closing the door gently behind him. But before I could compose myself enough to stand back up and sneak back onto the balcony to smoke more shameful cigarettes and drink more cheap beer, good ol' Sammie Boy flung his bedroom door open and came running back into the living room as fast as he could, a piece of paper in his little, clinched fist. He slammed the paper on the coffee table then ran back to his room, screaming, "I drew this for you!" This time, he slammed his bedroom door shut.

I stared at the crinkled paper on the coffee table, Manila paper with rough edges ripped from his spiral sketchbook (the one he carried with him *everywhere*), a drawing in black ink throughout the folds and creases of his wadded, paper canvas. I picked up the paper, unfolded it, and examined the line art of a boy sitting next to a bird--a big toothy grin on the boy's content face, the bird with a blank look, both of them sitting in a sparse world, nothing around them. Underneath the picture, the words 'Sammie & Budgie' scrawled in my boy's meticulous scribble, the drawing depicting the passive-aggressive way in which I knew he was attempting to keep his wish of owning a pet bird in the front of my mind. I thought it funny that he would even think I would forget anything he said or did or wanted. I loved being a dad and I loved being Sammie and Jessie's dad. I knew--at a very young age--that I wanted to be a dad. As far as I knew, I always wanted to be a dad. Being a dad was my calling. It's true.

❖ ❖ ❖

Sammie and Jessie went to a very normal elementary school in a very normal suburban neighborhood outside of Austin, Texas. The neighborhood was called Wells Port and the school was called Wells Port Elementary (brilliant, huh?). Built in the 1980s, the neighborhood had grown from a cookie-cutter tract development with little planning into a diverse, tight-knit, established community. Sammie was in the third-grade and Jessie was in the first-grade. The routine of getting them to school was pretty simple. It consisted of waking them up, feeding them toasted frozen waffles, helping them pick out their clothes without violating any major fashion rules (Did I even know the rules?), and making sure they brushed their teeth and their hair while I went downstairs to the garage to start the car and throw their school stuff in the trunk. Inevitably, whenever I opened the door to the garage, they would lose their little minds and run out in mid-whatever they were doing--tooth brushes in their mouths or brushes in their hair or half-way dressed and undressed or one shoe on and one shoe in-hand or whatever half-assed task they were lazily attempting to complete. The sound of the door to the garage creaking open always sent them into an impassioned, freakazoid panic. It happened every time like clockwork. Little kids are predictable little creatures. It's true.

The door would creak open and they would run out saying, "Daddy! Daddy! Don't leave yet!"

Which always had me asking the same rhetorical question. "Why do you think I'm leaving you?" Then they would stand there, dumbfounded--toothpaste dripping down their chins or hair brushes dangling in their tangled hair or their stomachs undulating along with their panting from sprinting to the kitchen--looking at me like I was severely abusing them, which I wasn't. Kids can be so melodramatic sometimes. It's simply what they do. "The whole reason for *my existence* at this point in my life is to take you to and from school."

"Oh, good!" they would always say, returning to the bathroom or their bedroom to complete whatever they were doing.

So I would drowsily descend the stairs to my garage, their backpacks and hoodies and lunch boxes in my arms, attempting to not fall down the stairs and bash my head open on the landing, opening the garage door and placing all of their crap in the trunk of my car: a white, 2000 Volvo S70. Now, there are some who would say that a Volvo S70 is a luxury car. I fully admit that there was also a time when I truly believed a car like a Volvo or a BMW or a Volkswagen or some shit like that was considered a luxury vehicle even though I knew-- after owning this car for a couple of years and surviving a few painful visits to the auto mechanic--that cars like this were really just albatrosses tied to your wallet like an anvil chained to your bank account, quickly sinking to the bottom of the deep blue, murky sea of diminishing returns. But for whatever reason, I still wanted to own a Volvo S70. My desire to own this car occupied a place in my brain that couldn't have been satiated by owning any other non-luxury vehicle; it had to be *this car*. And boy, did my wallet take a hit by owning this money pit. It really did. I might as well have set my wallet and debit card and credit cards and bank account on fire and let them burn to ashes. It spent an inordinate amount of time in the shop. More times than not, the Volvo wouldn't start or--if it started at all--it would come to life in fits and starts, as if it was going to eventually explode. Aargh! On a good morning, I would throw their school things in the trunk, start the car, and be ready to take them to school. This particular morning was pretty good; the Volvo started right up.

Eventually upstairs, the kiddos would close the door and come flying down the stairs, stomping and clomping and jumping the whole way down. With all of their ruckus I knew, if my neighbor next to us was asleep, then she wasn't asleep anymore after they came down. They were an avalanche of feet, fists, screams, and laughter. They jumped in the back seat, buckled up, and we were off.

The elementary school was across the street but, even though it was so close, they managed to have enough time to attempt to murder each other while I drove. It always started the same: Jessie would tease Sammie Boy about something, like him liking a girl in his class or something along those lines and this would always incite an angry response from him, then the shoving started, then the crying. The next thing I knew, I wanted to pull over and murder them both myself. But that never happened. They were lucky I loved them so much. It's true.

Dropping them off at school was a two-part ritual. The first part involved waiting in the car-line to drop Jessie off. She liked being dropped off in the car-line and equated it to being chauffeured around in a limo where I was her driver and her brother was her slave (not butler but *slave*). When we arrived at the curb, she would get out and wave us off, like we were free to go after witnessing her queen's wave. Then she followed it with a sincere goodbye, turned, and ran into the school.

The second part involved parking the car and walking good ol' Sammie Boy to see his speech therapist, Ms. Fox, whose office was housed in a portable building behind the main building. It seemed like most every elementary school in the United States had portable buildings behind them as a form of accommodating an ever-growing population of kids, and alleviating poor planning on the school district's part. I remembered having classes in the same type of portable buildings when I was a kid. That was 35 years ago! Crazy. Anyway, on the way to her portable building--which was the last one at the very end of a series of twelve portable buildings--Sammie would ask me some interesting questions for a kid.

He always started the questions in the same way. He'd say, "Daddy, can I ask you a question?"

And I would always say, "Sure."

Then he'd lay a question on me like, "Daddy, why do people tell white lies?" Such a simple question without a simple answer.

"That's a good question," I said, putting a hand on Sammie's back to keep him moving toward the portables. If I didn't do that, then he would just stand there, staring at me. I had to keep him moving, keep him on-task as the teachers would say. "People tell white lies so they don't hurt people's feelings."

"But isn't lying bad?"

"Most of the time, it is bad. But sometimes, a white lie is good to tell someone you love so you don't hurt their feelings."

"Why?" he said, as we walked across the same basketball court where we witnessed Selena the counselor just a few days before on the ground with blood pouring out the back of her head. We walked past the spot where she crumpled to the ground and there wasn't any evidence or remnants of what had happened, not a stain on the ground or anything, like it never happened. We didn't stop, though. We had some place to be. We had to stay on-task.

"Let me give you an example," I said.

"OK!"

"Let's say your sister asks you if you like what she's wearing--"

"I *never* like what she's wearing!"

"Hold on now. Let's say she comes out the bedroom and asks you if you like what she's wearing. And let's say she wants your *honest opinion* even though you really don't like what she's wearing. Do you really want to hurt your sister's feelings?"

Then good ol' Sammie Boy stopped in his tracks and tugged at my arm. He had a look on his face, a look of deep sympathy and empathetic pathos, a look I see on his face every once and a while when I know he has connected emotionally to someone or something in a way that he can't explain verbally but certainly understands in his heart. He was serious as all get out. It's true. "Daddy, I was joking when I said 'I *never* like what she's wearing.' I didn't mean that."

"I know, son. But do you understand what I'm saying? Do you want to *hurt* her feelings?"

"No, Daddy. I don't want to hurt her feelings."

"Then you would probably tell her a *white lie*. You would probably tell her you like what she's wearing even though you really don't like what she's wearing. That's telling her a white lie."

"Ohhh! I get it. But I thought all lies were bad?" he said, skeptical again. Something in his little brain just wasn't adding up.

"Well, lies with malicious intent are bad," I said, placing my hand on his back again and gently pushing him forward so we could continue to Ms. Fox's portable. "You know, a person intentionally telling lies for bad reasons is bad. Do you understand?"

"I understand, Daddy."

"Good," I said.

"Last one to Ms. Fox's portable is a rotten egg!" Sammie Boy said, breaking free from me and running a full-on sprint down the sidewalk that snaked through all the portables. "You can't catch me!"

Instead of running after him, I watched him race down that sidewalk, hook a left, and disappear into the group of portables. I slowly walked after him, deliberately keeping my slow pace. When I hooked the same left on the sidewalk, I saw him three buildings down, hooking a right up the wooden ramp that lead to the door to building 9A, the one with Ms. Fox's room in it. At the door, Sammie tapped a syncopated knock with his little fist. He turned to me when he was done, a big smile on his face, and said, "That's our *secret* knock. That's how she knows it's me."

Soon after, the door opened and Ms. Fox--a short, slim woman in her mid-40s with spiky, brown and grey hair and not a lick of makeup on--greeted my son with her thick, German accent, "Goot mornink, Sammie!" In a lot of ways, her and Sammie had the same haircut: unkempt and sticking up all over the place like they had styled their hair with firecrackers and glue. Her tight-fitting, blue t-shirt announced her politics. On the front, it said: Women's Rights are HUMAN RIGHTS! She was a real character.

"Good morning, Ms. Fox!" he said. He ran inside the portable, flung his backpack on a table, and sat down, ready to work. He examined some worksheets waiting for him.

"He's alvays in a good mood in zee mornink, ready to verk," she said, pleased with his behavior. How could she not be? Most third-graders are absolute terrors at this hour in the morning, just little shits, but not Sammie.

"Yeah, he's a good kid. I'm proud of him." She smiled at me--her way of saying goodbye--and was ready to close the door as I walked out when I realized, I wanted to ask her opinion about my boy. I placed my hand on the door, keeping it from closing, then I said, "Ms. Fox, do you mind if I talk to you for a minute--in *private*?"

She looked a little surprised that I wanted to converse more than just the simple, morning chit-chat. She raised her finger to me, as if to ask me to wait a moment, then she called out to Sammie Boy, "I'm goink to shpeaken to your father for a voment, Sammie. Getten yourself ready, yes?" He shuffled some papers on the table in front of him and grabbed a big, fat, green pencil, scribbling something on the paper, probably his morning assignment. She stepped out of the portable with me, closing the door enough but not quite closed, jamming the toe of her shoe in between the door and the doorframe so she wouldn't get locked out. Up above, the tangerine sky was draped with curtains of grey and white clouds, cars honking and children laughing in the distance, yet it seemed like we were alone. "How can I helpen you?"

"As you know, Sammie is a special kid."

"Oh, yes! Your son is a fery shpecial boy. A good boy. A hardverkink boy. He is one of my favorite shtudents."

"That's good. That's very good. He never causes you any problems?"

"Your son?!" she said, then bursting into laughter--a deep guttural laugh, her mouth wide, exposing her coffee-stained teeth, one of the top incisors quirkily askew. That comment really cracked her up. I mean, she was cackling all over the goddamn place. She got a real kick out of that too, I could tell, because she cackled a little longer than was comfortable for me, almost as if she was making fun of me, or as if her cackle got away from her. It was weird. After composing herself, straightening her hair and adjusting her t-shirt, she said, "Oh, no, no, no. Your son is an absolute sveetheart. He doesn't haf a *mean bone* in his body. Zat's fery rare and fery shpecial. You know, wiz most of zee shpecial needs children--"

"Yes, yes, I know you have a lot of kids with special needs but I wasn't referring to that with my boy. I mean, he really is *special.* Special--as in exceptional."

"Ah, yes, of course. You are absolutely correct. I agree vith you. But vat is it zat you vant to know?"

"Well, I don't want to sound *crazy* but, have you noticed anything unusual about Sammie? Anything out of the ordinary?"

"Hmmm, no. Vell, I don't know vat you mean. Unusual? Can you be more shpecific, yes?" she said, puzzled.

I thought about the recent events with my boy and what he said about his after-school counselor hurting herself and then it came true and the game of *Thump* that he showed Jessie and I how to play and then he went off and guessed every heads or tails without fail until I made him go to bed and I thought that no matter how I explained it to Ms. Fox--rationally, methodically, intellectually, honestly--that she would think I was absolutely crazy to believe that my boy Sammie could see the future. I mean, that just *sounds* crazy, just saying that: my boy Sammie can see the *future.* Sounds crazy, right? I thought so.

Something immediately told me that I shouldn't dare say anything at all. Because here's the thing: once you alert a teacher or a counselor or a therapist or an administrator or an advisor to an issue with your child--or something *different* about them in any way--then it has the potential to become a real problem for the school and the school district. A report has to be made and a committee has to be advised and meetings have to be scheduled and once all of this is set in motion, it is really hard to stop it. So I decided, right then and there, to keep my damn mouth shut. I just had to. What was I thinking?

"Ummm... I'm really sorry but I forgot that I have an important meeting I have to attend at work. Can I email you more about this later?"

"Uh, yes, zat vould be fine," she said, confused, quite baffled actually. I felt bad about that, kind of. I mean, starting this conversation that I initiated then cut short at the drop of a hat. It was pretty rude, now that I think about it. It was very rude. But I had to get out of there.

"I gotta run!" Then I did. Run, that is. I ran my pudgy butt down the ramp to the sidewalk, all the way to the basketball court--past where Selena the after-school counselor bashed her head on the ground--to my car which was across the parking lot and parked at the curb on the street. I jumped in my car (it miraculously started with the first try) and I tore off. I never did send Ms. Fox that email, like I said I would. In fact, I never mentioned anything to her about my boy Sammie's special abilities ever again. Something told me that it was best to keep my mouth shut and I did, if you can believe it. I mean, I have a really hard time keeping my mouth shut. Sometimes, I can just be blabbing and blabbing all over the place. And there is nothing worse than a parent that can't keep his or her mouth shut about their kid and what's so special about them. Blabbing parents are a real pain in the ass.

It's true.

SPEEDY -STOP

BEER, LOTTERY& CHAPTER THREE

Chapter Three

In some aspects of my life, I consider myself very, very lucky and somewhat successful. In other aspects of my life, I'm a dismal failure. I guess most people could chalk up their life achievements and disappointments in the same binary fashion, but I find myself particularly astute at cataloguing my successes and failures, like a professional bookkeeper organizing the wadded papers and receipts of an idiot savant, who unwittingly became successful at a business endeavor, and collating the idiot's evidence of successful business dealings into a coherent income tax return. I was constantly organizing lists of my luck and misfortunes. Once, I was told by a rather successful acquaintance that if I ever wanted to fulfill my dreams, I had to write down the things I wanted to achieve in life--the things I hoped to gain so I would consider my life a success. In other words, make a list of my *life goals*. I constantly tried to do that but the pessimist in me also had to write down the shitty things that had happened to me, too. I couldn't help myself; any success I hoped to achieve was tempered by the realization that I also thought of myself as an utter, complete failure. What a piece of work I am. Can you imagine the *frustration* I must feel? Of course, you can. Who wouldn't? We're all human. Right?

Here is a list of some of my failures in life:
1. My marriage to my children's mother
2. My career as a writer
3. My repeated attempts to make a hole-in-one in golf
4. My repeated attempts to solve a Rubik's Cube
5. Completing my list of things to achieve to have a successful life

Here is a list of some of my successes in life:
1. My children
2. My trivia skills in music, movies, and popular culture from the 1970s through the 1990s
3. That I'm still alive at age 45
4. That I can still roller-skate at age 45
5. My career as a Network Administrator for the State of Texas

I'm particularly proud of this last one--my career as a Network Administrator for the State of Texas--because I came into this career by pure, dumb *luck*. I mean, it wasn't something I went to school for or had an advanced degree in or had any real training whatsoever in doing. The job of Network Administrator just literally fell in my lap. It was a chance meeting in the hallway as I was walking to the bathroom to take a massive, coffee dump that my career path changed instantly. In a short exchange with a coworker from another department, a half-truthful statement about my experience working and configuring Windows servers would eventually turn into an opportunity to leave my position as a Help Desk Technician, and move to the Networking Department. How was I to know that the Help Desk would eventually be outsourced to a South Korean company in six, short months? I didn't know that was going to happen when I bullshitted my way through a few easy questions about Windows networking services on the way to the bathroom to release a foul, coffee turd. I couldn't see the future like good ol' Sammie Boy could, not even close. It was pure, *dumb luck* I tell you. It's true.

As I said, before becoming a Network Administrator, I was a Help Desk Technician for the Texas Commission of Employment and Benefits (where I am still employed as said Network Admin) and before that I was a writer who failed miserably (I wrote a novel called THE RISE AND FALL OF A TITAN which flopped) and before that I was a Help Desk Technician for a stupid company called TechForce (they were busted by the Feds, I believe, for falsifying test data). Now, I don't need to go into much of this because you can probably Google this stuff about me by searching for my name, Simon Burchwood. That's right, *the Simon Burchwood.* None of our lives are private anymore. Everything about all of us is just a few, simple keystrokes away from an invasion of our privacy. But it's all out there; go see for yourself. I had dreams of becoming a famous writer but those dreams never came to be. Maybe it'll happen for me at another place and time in my life. Hopefully, this is something that good ol' Sammie Boy will see in our *future.* That would be nice, huh?

When I was younger and really trying my best to be a famous writer, I was so angry at life. I was seething with rage--on the inside. I don't know why, I just was. I don't know what I was so angry about. I mean, I was mad at everyone and *everything.* It was like my thoughts had Tourette's Syndrome, what, with the cursing and the raging and the judging and the complete hypocrisy. Working as a Help Desk Tech probably didn't help either. You have to be a goddamn masochist to work as a Help Desk Tech because they are constantly being yelled at by morons who don't have the patience to just read the goddamn manual! I'm getting hot under the collar just thinking about it: the morons on the helpline. Dealing with these morons gives you an unvarnished look at humanity. It's really a shame, I'm telling you.

Anyway, when the opportunity presented itself to transfer to the Networking Department, I took it even though I didn't know jack-shit about networking, not really. I mean, I knew enough to bullshit my way through a spur-of-the-moment hallway conversation about IP addresses and data packets and how to sniff them on the network and sockets about some-such and shit like that. See? I sound like I know what I'm talking about, right? I wasn't going to pass up the opportunity to become a State of Texas employee: a state worker. When I worked at the Help Desk, I was only a contractor. But working for the Network Department, that was the real deal--a permanent, full-time, salaried position with benefits and holidays and sick days--the works! I took the position for the stability, for my kids. I always wanted to be a good dad and this was one way I could do it, by being a good provider and having a stable job. Believe me, having a stable job is one of the best things you can do for your kids. It's true.

As I was saying, the opportunity presented itself during a brief encounter in a hallway of the Texas Commission of Employment and Benefits as I was on the way to the bathroom. Earlier that morning, I drank three, possibly four, cups of extremely strong coffee and my colon was spearheading a gastrointestinal revolt. I was attempting to reach my favorite toilet stall before I shit my pants when I was greeted in the hallway by a fella named Larry Healy. Larry was the Network Department Manager and a pretty jovial dude with bright, white teeth behind a sincere, Southern smile--his hair was also gelled and his shirt pressed and his pants creased and his shoes shined and he even wore suspenders sometimes(!)--and it never failed that he always wanted to say 'Hi' to me and ask me how I was doing or how work was going, even though I didn't *know* him particularly well. When his eyes locked in with mine, I clinched my butt cheeks to repel the gastral revolt and commenced with a polite conversation of small-talk without crapping my pants.

He extended his hand to mine and said, "Hey there! How's it hanging? Working hard?"

"Oh yes. Yes!" I said, the coffee in my gut churning and grumbling. "Always busy." I really needed to take a shit. Bad! But I was trapped.

"That's too bad the Help Desk will be outsourced soon."

"What?" I said, shocked. This was news to me. "Outsourced? What do you mean?"

"Oh, boy," he said, straightening his tie as if to seal up a hole in the side of his neck which leaked this secret information. Isn't it funny how sometimes people do that? That distraction thing when they say something they shouldn't? Well, I think he said something he shouldn't have. "I guess I wasn't supposed to say anything about that... yet."

"Is the Help Desk really being outsourced? When?"

"I don't know for sure," he said, looking around as if he realized he spilled the beans about something that wasn't supposed to be spilled. Working for the government can make some people really paranoid. It's true. "But it will happen eventually, I guarantee it."

"That sucks."

"Tell me about it."

"I guess I would have to look for another job," I said, exhaling a sigh as heavy as a ton of bricks. My heart just sank. The idea of looking for another job was about as nice as the idea pulling my own fingernails off with needle nose pliers--slow and painful and infuriating.

"Another job, huh? Do you know anything about networking? We have a position opening soon."

"Really?" I said, excited, hopeful. I never, ever thought about a career in computer networking but it sounded much better than being unemployed. Considering I worked for the Texas Commission of Employment and Benefits, I knew how precarious a few months of unemployment would be for me.

"Do you have any experience with networking?" he said. And without blinking an eye, I rattled off this and that about whatever popped in my mind about networking computers, buzz words and keywords and technical jargon and whatever. I must have made some kind of sense because he didn't look at me like I was talking out of my ass--which was good--except that I *was* talking out of my ass. But sometimes, that's what you have to do to survive: think on your feet and talk out your ass. It took him a second to process the litany of terms I rattled off then he said, "Well, get your resume in order and start filling out a State app. I'll let you know the day before the position posts so you can get it in right away. I find it's better to hire from within than from the outside. Too many unknown variables from the outside. Know what I mean?"

"Sure, I get it. Let me know. I'm very interested."

"You got it, pardner!" he said, slapping me on the shoulder then walking away, whistling. Little did he know I was on the brink of soiling my pants. I ran all the way to my favorite toilet stall, my right-hand securing my backside as I ran. Fortunately for me, I made it to the toilet on time.

A couple of weeks later, Mr. Healy did inform me about the position and I did apply for it. A week after I submitted my resume and State app, I was interviewed for the position. And a few weeks after that, I accepted the job offer of Network Specialist II, a position that started at $34,521 per year with a full benefits package. To me, that was all the money and stability in the world. And it was all pure, *dumb luck*. Nothing more. It's true.

I wish I had the ability to see the future just like good ol' Sammie Boy. I mean, I tried to do the right thing. I tried to make the right choices that affected my future in the right ways but it didn't always work out that way. Mostly, it seemed to me, luck was either on my side or it wasn't. Little did I know that my fortune was about to change.

***

On the nights when little Jessie had taekwondo practice, Sammie Boy and I didn't have anything else to do. Initially when Jessie started, it was fun watching her kick the other little boys' asses. She was rather talented at taekwondo early on and her instructor, Master Lu, saw this in her, moving her up the color-scheme of mastery rather quickly-- white to yellow to green to blue to red to black with red stripes. Jessie was a black belt with red stripes, which meant she was pretty much as good and as talented as a full black belt. But because of her young age and lack of maturity, Master Lu felt holding her at the black with red stripes level was best even though she would demolish any other kid her age and up to a few years older, too--boys or girls. She kicked *any* kid's ass. Like I said, although this was fun at first to watch, the monotony of witnessing her mastery of everyone became somewhat... boring. I noticed that Sammie Boy and I were sighing with boredom while watching little Jessie kick and punch the other brats to the mat. An ugly glance from a defeated turd's mother was enough for me. I decided then and there that Sammie and I would spend our time outside the dojang--the Korean term for the taekwondo training hall-- doing much more fun things than receiving dirty looks from the mothers of the punk-ass bitches getting their asses beat by my daughter.

The dojang resided in an L-shaped strip mall across the street from Wells Port Elementary, where my kids went to school. Neighboring the dojang were a variety of local businesses--a family-owned Italian restaurant, an insurance broker, a hair salon, a nail salon, a coffee shop, a Mexican restaurant, an African-American church, a ballet studio, a Mediterranean restaurant / pizza joint, and a convenience store. The owners of the businesses were a menagerie of different cultural backgrounds and personalities. For instance, the nail salon was owned by a group of Vietnamese ladies, none of whom spoke English except for one: the youngest daughter. It seems most nail salons are owned by a similar group of Vietnamese mothers, aunts, cousins, and daughters. On the other hand, the Italian restaurant was owned by a couple who were not Italian at all but were, in fact, generic white people with a Czech background who were originally from Minneapolis, Minnesota. One time, when I was waiting for a take-out pizza that I ordered from them, I asked the wife--her name was Mabel- - why it was that they owned an Italian restaurant yet they didn't come from Italian heritage. And she said to me, with a big smile on her face, "We just like to eat Italian food so we figured we could own a restaurant serving Italian food." Well, duh. That made sense to me. Makes sense to you, right? Of course, it does.

So one night, after watching yet another brutal ass-kicking by Jessie, destroying all the little shits in her class, Sammie Boy and I decided to wander around the strip mall and check things out. He wanted to have father/son time. As we walked out of the dojang, good ol' Sammie Boy slammed the door behind us, rattling the windows around the glass and steel door. I thought for a moment that the glass was going to shatter because he slammed the door so hard. My first instinct was to scold him for slamming the door but, after seeing the cute expression on his face--his hands over his mouth in a *Little Rascals* fashion as if to say 'oopsie!'--I didn't scold him. I just let it go.

"Want to get some ice cream?" I said, holding out my hand for him to grasp.

"You mean, you're not mad at me for slamming the door?"

"Nah. Want ice cream?"

"Yes!" he said, holding my hand. He held three of my fingers tightly; three fingers were all his little hand could grip. We walked past the ballet studio (which was empty) and the African-American church (which seemed full because we could hear people singing hymns loudly inside but couldn't see anybody through the tinted windows) and the nail salon (which was full of ladies and girls yakking about stuff) and the Mediterranean restaurant (also completely empty) to the convenience store. It was called Speedy-Stop. The letters of the sign above the entrance were a bright, illuminated maroon and also the home to a family of finches--the twigs and paper scraps of their nest protruding haphazardly from the "o" in the word "Stop."

Looking at the nest as we went inside the store, Sammie said, "I wonder if those birds like living above the Speedy-Stop?"

"They wouldn't have gone through the trouble if they didn't," I said.

"Speaking of birds, Daddy. Can I still get a budgerigar?"

"What kind of ice cream do you want?" I said, pushing him gently through the door and, rather stealthily, interrupting his pet-themed train of thought.

Inside, the Speedy-Stop's aroma was obnoxious--a combination of bleach, dust, coffee brewed from the early morning hours, hot dogs roasting since 10:30am, and the smoke from Nag Champa incense sticks wafting near the cash register--yet we were kindly greeted by Himanshu, one of the owners and the cashier for the night, who was oblivious to the unusual combination of smells. He smiled a wide, bright white, toothy smile. His pitch-black hair was combed to the side and his light blue, short-sleeved, button down shirt was stained from dingy-brown hot dog water. His nose hairs were so long that it seemed like he had a Hitler-style moustache, one of those stumpy, square 'staches. It was hard *not* to stare at his nose hairs. It's true.

"Hal-oh!" he said, boisterous and pleasant. He winked at good ol' Sammie Boy. Sammie waved back.

"Hey, man," I said. "How's it going?"

"It is going! Two pack Marlboro for the price of one today," he said, pointing his thumb at the massive cigarette display behind him, a mosaic wall of a hundred tobacco brands. The cash register was entombed in cigarette boxes and cigarillo packs and chewing tobacco and electronic cigarette contraptions and their nicotine oils as well as condoms, sexual enhancement "herbal" pills, stale Moon Pies, and a plastic dish filled with dusty pennies and colored paper clips. His smile stretched a little wider until he noticed my eyes darting in the direction of Sammie then back, me quickly waving both hands in a 'No, no, no, no, no, not now!' fashion, until he got my point. His smile vanished and a serene look replaced it, a venerable look of acceptance and content. "Wrong customer. I confuse you with Tom, the accountant. You all look the same. So sorry!"

"No problem," I said, winking at him. Sammie, fortunately, didn't catch any of our awkward exchange. He was too concerned with what he was looking for, which was: ice cream! He beelined for the ice cream cooler, then he slid the glass lid open-wide. As he leaned into the freezer case--images of ice cream sandwiches and popsicles and ice cream cones and all on the side of it--his little feet raised off the ground, dangling a bit as he wiggled his way over the lip of the cooler. He knew what he was looking for and rifled through the other frozen treats he didn't want--bomb pops, push-ups, chocolate chip cookie ice cream sandwiches, Neapolitan ice cream sandwiches, Klondike bars, any frozen treat coated in nuts like Drumsticks--until he found what he wanted, a cup of Blue Bell homemade vanilla ice cream. He was a simple kid with simple taste. In the box with the other ice cream cups was a bundle of paper-wrapped, wooden spoons. He grabbed one of those, too, then popped out of the cooler, landing on his feet and sliding the freezer lid closed in one motion that looked too difficult for a man my age to do. I admired his agility like I was admiring a ninja-- an ice cream ninja!

"Daddy, can I get this one?!" he said, a big smile on his face, his cheeks flush from the cold air inside the freezer.

"Of course. Where do you want to eat it?" I said, rummaging through my pant pocket for my wallet.

"Outside in the grass!"

"Sounds good. Do you want a bottle of water, too?"

As soon as I finished asking that rhetorical question, something caught Sammie's attention. He craned his head around my waist to see what was behind me, then bolted for the cash counter. He jumped up and down, one of his hands gripping the counter, the other pointing to a plastic, clear, display case of lottery scratch tickets. He was so excited, it looked like his little head was going to explode. His face was all shades of red and the veins in his little head were popping out all over the place and spit was flying out his mouth and his hair was going here and there. It was a crazy sight to see, good ol' Sammie Boy losing his mind like that. I thought something may have been wrong with him but he was just being him, all excited and delirious. It's true.

As he jumped up and down, jabbing his little index finger at the plastic case, he said, "Daddy! Daddy! Looky! Buy that one, the one with the smiley face on it! Buy it! BUY IT! YOU'LL WIN, I SWEAR!"

I examined the earnestness of his red face then looked at the scratch ticket then back at Sammie. He was going nuts! I took a better look at the scratch ticket, which was called *Smiley Face Match*, with a cartoon picture of a smiley face emoticon or emoji or whatever you call them on the front of it, next to its $1 price tag and its $5,000 grand prize emblazoned on it with a red starburst and a fancy serif font. I felt my intuition ball up into a knot in my stomach, a nagging pull that I usually paid attention to if I was smart enough. I was skeptical that I had the luck to win $5,000. Who wins money with those lottery tickets anyway? Nobody, that's who. Lottery tickets were a scam to cheat poor people out of their money.

"Really, Sammie?" I said, setting the vanilla ice cream cup and wooden spoon on the counter. I glanced at Himanshu and he nodded knowingly, his toothy grin as white as ever, his nose-hair moustache perched above his upper lip like a bird's nest.

"We haven't had a big winner on that game yet. Today it could be you," he said, moving closer to the plastic display, extending a hand, ready to rip the next ticket from the roll.

"Daddy, I swear. On my heart, hope to die, stick a needle in my eye! You'll win!"

Feeling a smile push through my skepticism, I nodded to my boy, then looked at Himanshu and said, "I'll take one of those scratch tickets."

"The one with the smiley face?" Himanshu said.

"Yes. And the ice cream, too." I reached into my pocket for my wallet and Himanshu pinched one of the smiley face scratch tickets--bending it up and down to weaken the serrated edge of the ticket to make it easier to tear--when Sammie Boy started screaming out.

"Not that one!" he said, putting the tip of his index finger on the plastic display, the soft tissue at the end of his finger smashing against the clear plastic. "That one, RIGHT THERE!"

"Sammie," I said, placing my hand on his shoulder, constraining his excitement. "That one is kinda *way* in there. He has one ready to tear off. Does it have to be that specific one?"

"Yes, Daddy! THAT ONE!"

I looked at Himanshu, totally expecting him to back me up, and describe to Sammie the colossal pain in the ass it would be to unravel the entire roll to get that one specific ticket out. It couldn't have been allowed in the state lottery procedures to pull tickets out of order. Right? That seemed right.

But he didn't do that at all. He nodded, smiled some more with his goddamn, super-shiny white teeth and his ebony bird's nest 'stache, then said, "I can get you that *one*. Is that the one your dad should get?" he said, winking at Sammie. Sammie smiled back, thankful that Himanshu was his ally. Himanshu then pulled the strip of tickets out of the display (maybe ten of them), folding them at their serrated edges, into a neat stack, until he reached the specific one that Sammie wanted. He tore it free from the other tickets, then he shoved the neat stack back into the display, cramming them in a slot not quite tall enough for the stack of discarded tickets. He rang up the ice cream and the scratch ticket, told me the total, and said, "Good luck. $1.75."

"Thank you," I said, giving him two dollar bills then refusing the change. "Keep it."

I gave Sammie the ice cream cup and placed my hand on his shoulder, leading him outside of the Speedy-Stop. To our left, a grassy lawn stretched between the Speedy-Stop and the street. Along the side of the store was a narrow walkway with a cinder block edge. We found a place to sit. Sammie tore the lid off the ice cream cup--like a cast-away on a deserted island finding a can of food after a week without any nourishment--and tossed the lid in the grass. I examined the scratch ticket, the smiley face on the front inviting me to scratch its face off, the odds of winning a prize on the back. I leaned back a bit on my butt and shoved my hand in my front pocket, looking for a coin to scratch with. I couldn't find one.

"Lottery tickets are a voluntary tax on the poor," I said to Sammie. He had the cup close to his face, shoveling little white mounds of ice cream into his little mouth.

"We're not *poor*," he said, shoveling some more.

"That's not what I mean. Besides, the odds of us winning $5,000 are astronomical," I said. "I don't have a quarter to scratch it with."

"I have one," Sammie said, pulling a quarter from his pocket.

"Is this the quarter from the other night?"

"Yes, it's my lucky quarter."

I placed the ticket on my knee and scratched the front of it, Sammie looking on with ice cream dribbling out the side of his mouth down his chin, silver dust coming off the ticket and falling into the grass like shimmery angel's dust. After the entire play area was free of its silvery covering, I examined the exposed numbers, reading the instructions on the front of the game, and examining the numbers again. It was clear we won.

"Did we win?!" Sammie said, looking at me for a confirmation.

"Yes, looks like you were right. We won $50."

"$50?!" he said, jumping to his feet, throwing the empty ice cream cup into the air. "THAT'S A LOT OF MONEY!" In the grass, he danced a little jig, a dance only a boy Sammie's age could pull off without looking like he was insane. He was as excited as can be.

I was astonished. Even though it was only $50, I was certain now that my boy, good ol' Sammie Boy, could see the future. Our future. Maybe a brighter future. Or a darker one. Either way, he could see things I could only dream of seeing. How could he do that? Where did this ability come from?

"Will I win more if I go back in and buy more?" I said, curious.

He stopped dancing and looked at me, examining the look on my face, then looked down at the grass. It was amazing how quickly his excitement curdled into embarrassment then abashment.

"Would you be mad at me if I told you I didn't know?"

"No, of course not. But how did you know I was going to win this time?"

Sammie kept his head down, using the tip of his shoe to carve an "S" in the grass.

"I don't know."

"Sammie?"

"Yes?" I knew I was creating an environment where my boy would clam up and not talk to me. A few years before, I learned that these types of interrogations led to a self-imposed week of solitary confinement, where Sammie Boy would cram himself under his bed and not come out nor talk to me. I didn't want that to happen again and decided this seeing-the-future business was too important to risk him clamming up. So I decided to back off, for a while at least, and just not talk about it anymore.

"Will you tell me later if I stop talking about it now?"

Sammie slowly raised his head, his eyes leading the way, and nodded.

"Yes, I will."

"Promise?" I said, extending my pinky finger to him for a pinky swear. He confirmed by wrapping his little pinky around my pinky, tugging it.

"Promise! Shmomise!" His sly smile reappeared.

"Thank you, son. Let's go see who your sister has beaten up. OK?"

"OK!"

I placed my hand on his shoulder and we cashed our winning ticket together in the Speedy-Stop. Himanshu congratulated us. Then we walked back to the taekwondo dojang to see how many asses Jessie had kicked while we were gone.

* * *

As a boy, I absolutely LOVED comic books, particularly Marvel Comics, and I would devour them for hours--by myself, in my room. I loved the entirety of the Marvel Universe, all the heroes and all the villains--well, most all of them. Marvel Comics weren't perfect. They shit out a few turds here and there. I mean, the band *KISS* as superheroes? What a pile of shit! But a lot of what they published was pure gold. And my favorite was *The Amazing Spider-Man*. I loved Spider-Man and everything about Spider-Man. I collected Marvel Comics as a boy and cherished all the issues I had of *The Amazing Spider-Man*, so much so that I still had my collection as an adult. I had retained the entirety of my collection through ups and downs in my life, through thick and thin, as the value of my collection skyrocketed into the stratosphere. I had every issue from #10 - #316, all the Annuals, the One-offs, the Specials, the What-Ifs, all of them, except #1 - #9 and Amazing Fantasy #15 (Spidey's first appearance and an issue that is worth a gazillion dollars). For a brief time as a boy, I did own a copy of *The Amazing Spider-Man* #6 in fair condition, which isn't great but better than nothing. It disappeared after my friend Stanford--one of the few black friends I had at school when I lived in Montgomery, Alabama during my junior high years--came to my house to eat dinner one day after school. I confronted him about it the next day at school but he denied taking it. He denied it again years later when I confronted him about it during a trip to Montgomery on my way to New York for a book signing that went horribly wrong (I'll tell you about that later). I know the bastard took it, though. It had to have been him the way he drooled over it in my room, the thieving bastard. It's true.

Anyway, except for *The Amazing Spider-Man* #6 (I'm telling you, I know that bastard Stanford stole it. I know it!), I still had the rest of the issues in a long-box in my closet in my bedroom, each one carefully enclosed in a 2-millimeter thick, archival, polyester mylar bag with an acid-free cardboard insert to keep them straight and protected. Only a serious comic book collector would go to these lengths to protect their collection and I did it, too. To be honest, I initially was saving them as an investment and a way to keep a connection to my childhood and my love for comic books. But when I became a dad, my collection and my love for comic books was something I wanted to share with my boy, Sammie. It was something I hoped would bridge my childhood with his, something that I felt we could share and discuss together. And, man, was I right. Good ol' Sammie Boy was probably a bigger fanboy than I was. Really.

I remember the day I first showed him my collection of comic books. It was a day I will never, *ever* forget. We were still in our old house--the house we lived in before I divorced Sammie's mother and before she died--and I had come across my comic book collection while I was in my closet, thinking about packing and moving all the shit I had amassed while I was married. It was a soul-crushing realization that I would soon be moving out of the house that I swore I would never leave. As I sat on the carpeted floor--sobbing--I saw the corner of the white, long box full of comic books protruding out from behind a row of hanging blue jeans. I wiped my wet eyes and snotty nose on the short-sleeve of my t-shirt then pulled out the heavy box. Sliding on the carpet, I forgot just how heavy a long box full of comic books was; it must have weighed 100 pounds. I placed my legs on each side of the box, pulling it close to my crotch, sitting up straight, lifting the lid off carefully, and placing it to the side. The box was jammed full of comic books, the mylar bags glistening under the yellow glow of the closet light.

I randomly pulled one from the middle of the box (issue #156) and found myself transported back to the time I first saw that cover, the one that announced, "INTRODUCING: The most mind-boggling wedding guest of them all--the murderous MIRAGE!" The wedding scene depicted Spider-Man web-slinging from out of nowhere into a wedding party, their faces looking on in horror as Spidey navigated toward one of many replicas of the multiplying villain Mirage, Spidey's webbed fist punching through the mirage of the evil man, another word-bubble proclaiming, "AT LAST! The long-awaited WEDDING of Betty Brant and Ned Leeds!" I didn't remember ever caring if Betty Brant and Ned Leeds got married (What young boy cares about weddings anyway?!) but I do remember seeing Mirage for the first time and thinking, 'I wonder what this dumbass thinks he can do to beat Spider-Man that all of the other *shitheads* couldn't do!' I was, no doubt, intrigued; I still felt the intrigue as an adult looking at the cover again. I couldn't remember the outcome of the battle between Spider-Man and Mirage. I only remembered the feeling of excitement of just *looking* at the cover. I was a real sad-sack for sure, sitting on my closet floor, going from bawling like a baby to reminiscing with old comic books, when good ol' Sammie Boy discovered me in my closet. I felt his little hands on my shoulders and the warmth of his sweet breath on my neck, the weight of his body resting on my tired back.

"Wha cha doing, Daddy?" he said, leaning in to see the cover of The Amazing Spider-Man #156 comic book I held in my hands, protected by a clear, mylar bag.

"Looking at my comic book collection," I said.

"Comic books? Where?!" he said, tossing himself next to me on the carpet, propped up on his knees with an excitement he could barely contain. Who *doesn't* get excited about comic books? A no-fun jerk-wad, that's who. But my boy Sammie wasn't a no-fun jerk-wad. He was so excited he could hardly contain himself. It's true.

"Here, in this box," I said, placing my hand on the side of the long-box. "It's a collection I started when I was about your age. I've kept them this whole time."

"I didn't know you had comic books in here. Why didn't you tell me?!"

"Because I wanted to wait until you were old enough to appreciate them."

"Old enough?" he said, releasing an annoyed *harrumph*. "Old enough, shmold enough!"

"Oh shmeally?" I said, leaning forward, looking him in his eyes.

"Shmeally!"

I knew Sammie was serious about the comic books when a terse sincerity appeared on his little cute face and our Shmenglish conversation quickly turned back to boring ol' regular English.

"Can I look at them?" he said. "I promise to be careful."

"You promise?" I said.

"I promise!"

I nodded then he lunged for the comics, jabbing his fingers into the crammed-tight box. I gently placed my hand on his shoulder. He stopped to look at me and I gave him a knowing nod, as if to say, 'Please be careful.' He continued with gentle hands. He flipped through several before landing on a thick issue towards the back. He pulled it up to reveal the issue, 'The Amazing Spider-Man Annual #2.' Now, annual issues came out once a year--hence, they were called *Annuals*--and they usually had a retrospective section of things that came about in issues the year before like villains that were introduced or milestones that were achieved or characters that died and shit like that. They also contained bizarre stories that were too far-fetched for regular issues. The Amazing Spider-Man Annual #2 was no different.

"What about this one?" he said, holding the issue up closer to my face. It's bright, yellow cover obnoxiously glared through the clear plastic mylar bag. "What's this one about?"

"I don't know. Read the cover to me."

He lowered the comic book to his lap and stared at the cover, examining it. Spider-Man stood alone with nothing around him--no scenery, no villains lunging for him, no girlfriend fawning over him or his newspaper boss barking at him, no aunt begging him to be good, nothing--but the bright, yellow background and little, miniature versions of himself in various spidey poses as well as a large spidey head, floating in the middle with the mini Spider-men orbiting around it. Right beneath *The Amazing Spider-Man* title was a black banner with bold, red letters which called out: ALL NEW! "THE WONDROUS WORLDS OF DR. STRANGE!" Sammie read this banner out loud the best he could in his third-grade level reading voice, all stops and stutters and restarts. He really tried his best to sound like he knew what he was reading.

"Daddy, who is Dr. Strange?" he said, pointing at the black banner. "Is he the bad guy in this one?"

"No, Dr. Strange is a good guy. He's kind of like a wizard or a sorcerer. This is his first appearance in *The Amazing Spider-Man*."

"What's a sorce--sorce--sore--sir--err?"

"A sorcerer is someone who can conjure spells and travel to other dimensions."

"You mean, he's like a magician?" he said, scratching his head.

"Yeah, I guess you could say that, but real magic, not fake magic, like performing tricks or something. Dr. Strange is the sorcerer supreme in the Marvel Universe, the most powerful of all sorcerers. He protects the Earth against magical and mystical threats. Pretty cool."

"Wow! Can I read this one?"

"Sure, but we have to read it here together. We need to be careful with it. OK?"

"OK!"

I pulled good ol' Sammie Boy onto my lap and, together, we slid the comic book out of its clear mylar bag and began to read it. The story began with a bizarre looking character named Xandu, an evil sorcerer who possessed one half of a magic wand called "The Wand of Watoomb." He devised a plan to retrieve the other half of the "The Wand of Watoomb" from his nemesis Dr. Strange by hypnotizing two thugs and ordering them to beat-up Dr. Strange and return to Xandu with the other half of the wand. It was a whacky premise that even Sammie could see through.

"Daddy, why doesn't Xandu just fight Dr. Strange for the other half of the wand *himself*?"

"That would be too easy, now wouldn't it?"

"And where's Spider-Man?"

"He's coming. Hold on!"

The two hypnotized thugs entered Dr. Strange's lair and overpowered him, stealing his half of "The Wand of Watoomb." As they escaped to the roof of the building, Spider-Man spotted them while he swung around New York City, looking for something to do, good deeds and shit like that. Spidey approached them but they overcame him too, their spell-bound minds and bodies not tiring during their battle with the webslinger. Spidey gave up, knowing that they had the upper hand, but tagged them with a tracking device as they escaped.

"Spider-Man can find them using the tracker thingy, Daddy?"

"Yes, Spider-Man is pretty ingenious, isn't he?"

Anyway, Spider-Man tracked the thugs with his tracking device and Dr. Strange followed Spider-Man with his mystical abilities. The two heroes teamed up to defeat Xandu and Dr. Strange, with his magic powers and heroic wisdom, decided to erase the memory of what just transpired from Xandu's mind, as well as any evil ambitions he had, leaving him to wander the Earth as a mere mortal.

Then Dr. Strange grabbed "The Wand of Watoomb" and declared, "I realize now that the Wand of Watoomb is too potent, too menacing to ever fall into other hands! And so, my Mystical Amulet will drain every bit of power out of it, until all that remains is a harmless, simple ornament! The threat of Watoomb exists no more!" And with that, the powers of the wand were absorbed by an amulet around Dr. Strange's neck, and the powers of the wand became the powers of Dr. Strange.

"So Dr. Strange can now travel to other dimensions and see the future?!"

"Yes, whatever powers the wand had are now his powers. They are a part of him now, through his Mystical Amulet."

"Cool!" said good ol' Sammie Boy, jumping to his feet and assuming a super hero pose. "Daddy, can I dress up as Dr. Strange next Halloween?"

I could see on Sammie's face that the idea of dressing up as Dr. Strange was a fantastical idea and I couldn't agree more, as long as he didn't want me to dress up as Spider-Man. I wasn't about to stuff my pudgy butt inside a skin-tight Spider-Man costume. I smiled at him and said, "Sure, son. Whatever you want."

"Yeah!" he said, raising a hand above his head, his arm outstretched at full-extension, his index finger pointing to the heavens. "By the powers of my Mystical Amulet, time to disappear into the future!" Then he ran at full-speed out of the closet to a different part of the house, probably to the kitchen to get a Popsicle or something.

Chapter Four

When you go to your doctor's office, do you ever wonder who decorates the place? The waiting room at Dr. Dimes' office was a bizarre combination of kid-friendly accessories and modern kitsch decoration--things like bead mazes, stuffed animals, board books, and fish aquariums intermixed with Scandinavian furniture, wallpaper with muted patterns and colors, hand-woven Oriental rugs, and a number of plants, some real and some fake. Good ol' Sammie Boy and I were the only patients waiting to see Dr. Nadine Dimes, Sammie's doctor since the day he was born, a nice woman who seemed to truly care about her patients as well as her own kids. I decided after all the *incidents* related to Sammie's ability to see the future (and some rather deep introspection about the matter on my part) that it would be best if he saw Dr. Dimes. There had to be an explanation--maybe something medical, maybe something physiological--to why all of a sudden, he had this crazy ability. I mean, seeing the future is something you only read about in comic books or novels or see on TV or in the movies. And it usually happens to someone with *serious* issues like post-traumatic stress disorder or child abuse or a serious car accident or drug problems or a death in the family or a freakish mutation from standing too close to a nuclear explosion or some shit like that. It never seemed to affect a *normal* kid, someone like my son Sammie. Really, good ol' Sammie Boy is about as normal as it gets. Unless he *really* can see the future, then there is nothing normal about that shit at all. He would be like a real life super hero. It's true.

Anyway, after a bit of deliberation and some scheduling conflicts at my job I had to work through, I made an appointment to have Sammie see Dr. Dimes. She was a constant source of great advice as well as support in our lives, helping me figure out the right things to do as a parent. I mean, she had known Sammie since the day he was born, since the day he popped out of his mom. She examined him when he was just minutes old and watched him grow all this way. Why wouldn't I trust her? There is one thing, though. The only issue I have with Dr. Dimes is that, sometimes, she dresses a little whore-ish for my taste. What I'm trying to say is that, sometimes, she seems to be dressed like she's ready to hit a nightclub, pick up a 22-year Puerto Rican kid after downing five, double Piña Coladas, then go back to his apartment and ride him like a mechanical bull with a dildo strapped on the saddle. Whoa, right? The way she dressed could be pretty ridiculous, especially in a professional setting, but I let it slide. She really, really seemed to be a good doctor despite her horrible, *horrible* fashion sense. Really.

Anyway, let's get back to the appointment. After checking-in with the receptionist, Sammie and I made ourselves comfortable in the empty waiting room. I found a couch to sit on with a fancy coffee table in front--one covered with magazines like *Time* and *Sports Illustrated* and *Better Homes & Gardens* and other crappy magazines that I couldn't imagine anyone subscribing to except for doctors to put on their fancy coffee tables in their questionably decorated waiting rooms--and watched Sammie examine everything. He looked over the kids' toys and books and playthings and quickly decided they weren't of his caliber. He turned up his nose at them like a dog rejecting generic, kibble dog food. He could be a real fuddy-duddy when he wanted to be, the little snob. It's true.

"Not to your liking?" I said, giving him the stink eye. He looked at me and crossed his arms, defiantly.

"These are for *babies*," he said, pointing to a bead maze on the coffee table, the beads painted in bright, primary colors while the base was covered with cartoon animal and flower stickers. He was right to be offended by it. It *was* for babies, particularly unpretentious ones. I mean, have you ever met a pretentious baby? I didn't think so. Babies will play with anything they can touch or shove in their mouths. Babies are unpretentious as hell. This time, Sammie was the snobby one. He just wasn't having it with the baby toys.

"I see. Want to sit on the shmouch with me?" I said, patting an empty cushion next to me.

"Is it a shmoft and shmooshy shmouch?" he said, perking up a bit. Talking in Shmenglish always seemed to cheer him up. It was my go-to mood changer.

I caressed the cushion with my hand in small circles to the left, then in larger circles to the right. I firmly gripped the material of the couch cushion, examining its texture and all like I was a couch connoisseur, then said, "Seems pretty shmoft and shmooshy to me."

"Great!" He launched himself onto the couch like a football player diving into the end zone in a desperate attempt to evade vicious defenders and score a much-needed touchdown. He rolled up in the fetal position, his feet pressing into the back cushions. "Yeah, seems shmoft to me."

"Are you comfortable?" I said sarcastically, pretending to read a copy of *Time Magazine*.

"Not really." He got up from the couch and shuffled through all the *grown-up* magazines on the coffee table. He couldn't seem to find what he was looking for, nothing fun or entertaining or mysterious or enchanting enough for him. "Do they have any comic books like Spider-Man or Dr. Strange?"

"Do you see any comic books?"

"Nope, no comic books. Do they have any snacks?" he said.

"No, this isn't the grocery store or the Speedy-Stop."

"I know that! They still might have snacks for kids."

"No snacks. Just shots and Band-Aids." And with this, a serious look washed over his face, the blood draining out from his cheeks, leaving chalky, white skin where healthy-looking skin once was. He looked like he had seen a goddamn ghost, what, with his little mouth agape and his eyes wide with fear and his eyebrows perched high into his forehead. He was really cracking me up although, I'm sure, he was experiencing the beginnings of a panic attack.

"Did you say *shots*? Am I going to get a *shot*?!" he said, grabbing my bicep and squeezing the shit out of it. He had a pretty firm grip for a third-grader, I imagined, although no other third-grader we knew had squeezed my bicep before. Good ol' Sammie Boy just seemed pretty strong to me for his age.

"I don't know if you're going to get a shot today. Maybe you will, maybe you won't. It's up to Dr. Dimes."

My response wasn't good enough for him. He released my arm then sprinted around the other side of the coffee table--more than an arm's length away from me, just out of my reach--defiantly standing in a tough-guy stance, his fists pressing into his hips. He glared at me then said, "You didn't say anything about getting shmots. I don't want a shmot."

"But what if Dr. Dimes says you need one?"

"Then I will tell her I don't *want* one." A genuine look of dread appeared on his face and I couldn't help but feel sorry for him, really sorry. My memories of visiting the doctor at his age and refusing the reality of receiving vaccinations from long, pointy needles was still very vivid in my mind. I knew exactly how he was feeling. It was really the worst thing imaginable for him--at this moment. I wanted to reason with him but I knew reasoning wouldn't do me any good. Sometimes, there's just no reasoning with a little kid. Kids can be very unreasonable little creatures. "Daddy, please. No shots!" he said, covering the top of his left arm with his right hand, as if it could shield his skin and muscle tissue from the penetrating, pointy needle.

"Tell you what. If you have to get a shot, and I'm not saying you will, but if you do, then I'll take you to get a donut. How's that?"

This proposition intrigued Sammie Boy. His ears pricked up and a slight smile appeared on his face, one side of his mouth upturned. His stiff stance loosened a bit too, then he said, "How many donuts can I get?"

"How *many*?! How many do you want?"

"Ummm... 12?" he said, his slight smile twisting into a bigger sly one.

"*12 donuts*?!" I said, shocked. I mean, playfully shocked, not *really* shocked. Sammie giggled then sprinted back around the coffee table, leaping onto the couch. He hugged me and giggled some more.

"Just kidding, Daddy. If I ate 12 donuts, I would get constipated real bad and I don't want to get con-stuh-pay-tid."

"Smart boy," I said, shuffling through the shitty selection of magazines, looking for another rag to dismiss. "One donut will be fine for you. Maybe two."

"Two!" he said, inconspicuously slipping his hands between the cushions of the couch (although I noticed) and sliding them along the seams. "I want *two* donuts."

"What are you doing?" I said, watching him rifle his hands deeper, hoping to find something--anything long forgotten by an exotic and mysterious stranger.

"I'm seeing if anyone left anything in the couch," he said, turning the corners of the cushion, his hand like a shark steadily stalking an unsuspecting fish. After rounding another cushion corner, his hand stopped, as if it encountered something completely unexpected. "I feel *something*," he said, then pulled out his secret plunder: a Buck Knife. He looked at it with total disbelief, an illegal-looking weapon in his little, innocent hand. I couldn't believe it either. I snatched it from him as quick as I could.

"Oh no, you can't have *that*," I said, then examined the knife. It was a hunting knife, the folding kind, with a thick, wooden handle and brass fittings, and a notch in the top of the blade to insert a thumbnail to unsheathe it, which I did. The blade was about four inches long, silvery and shiny and obviously very sharp. It snapped solidly into place after unfolding it, straight and long and rigid and dangerous. Sammie was amazed.

"Whoa! It's huge! Can I have it?" he said.

"No," I said. "You cannot." The knife was quite heavy and sturdy, solid and well-made. It had a dangerous heft to it just like any other weapon--a pistol, a rifle, a sword, a battle ax--and I knew without a doubt that whoever was the owner of this knife would have stabbed someone or something with it, if needed for protection. Why else carry a knife like this in his pocket to a pediatrician's office if he wasn't prepared to stick someone with it? Did he intend to stab someone *here* with it, like Dr. Dimes? Maybe he was a jealous ex-boyfriend seeking revenge for a broken heart from a tramp like Dr. Dimes. Or maybe he just used it to open mail and it slipped out of his pocket while waiting for his daughter to finish her annual check-up and get her required vaccinations for elementary school. It was a real goddamn mystery. It's true.

"And why can't I have it? I *found* it. Finders keepers, losers weepers!" Sammie said, defiant again. But I wasn't letting my third-grader take home some random, gigantic, hunting knife that he found between the seat cushions at his pediatrician's office. That would be a poor parenting decision on my part, if I ever heard of one. Right? You know I'm right.

"I know you're proud of your discovery but it's not appropriate for someone your age."

"And why not? I'll be careful with it."

"No."

"Please?"

"No."

"Please?!" he said, raising his voice a few octaves higher, the tail end of the word squeaking out.

"No!" I said, raising my voice, too.

"Then can I have a budgerigar instead? I'd rather have a *budgie* than a knife anyway. Please!"

"What the..." I said, confused at his change of heart and his off-the-cuff negotiating style. I closed the knife and wedged it between my thighs, where it could do no harm.

"So, that's a yes?" he said.

"Now, wait a minute!"

While negotiating with my son between taking home a dangerous weapon or owning a parakeet, a woman's head appeared in a door on the other side of the waiting room. It was a familiar face, pale skin with rosy cheeks, small eyes under thick, black eyebrows, and a full head of jet-black, curly hair: Dr. Dimes. Her shiny, bright-white teeth sparkled through her forced, professional smile, her lips lacquered with bright, red lipstick.

"Good morning!" she said. "How are you doing, Sammie?"

Her voice startled good ol' Sammie Boy. He dropped his hands behind his back, as if he was guilty of something and was caught unexpectedly, and turned to her. I think the idea of receiving a shot was still fresh in his mind and I could see it on his face: the fear. He looked petrified, as if he was witnessing all the kid atrocities in all of kid history right there in front of him. Poor kid. He was paralyzed with fear.

"Good morning, Dr. Dimes. Are you going to give me a *shot*?"

"That's a good question. I don't think so but I have to look at your shot record to be sure. Want to come back with me?"

"Can my Daddy come with me?" he said, turning to me with that pained, little face of his, the fear and anxiety on full display now. He was really playing it up, too, like a real charity case.

"Sure, he can. Let's do this!"

Sammie reluctantly followed her and when I began to stand up, I felt the Buck knife slide down between my legs, handle-first. I was pretty lucky that it wasn't laying in my lap, blade-first. I imagined it sliding down my legs and dropping to the top of my right foot, stabbing through my shoe and into my delicate foot. It was a horrible daydream consisting of a lot of blood and limping and sliced footwear. I quickly folded the knife and slid it into my pocket before Dr. Dimes could see it.

We followed her down a hallway with laminate flooring (the kind that looks like wood) and white walls covered with photographs of all the children that were her patients, thousands of boys and girls ranging from new born infants to kids that looked a couple of years older than Sammie, the photos freezing their cute little faces in time--a time when they were young and innocent and compliant with their doctor's orders. I was hoping to see a photo of Sammie when he was much younger but I didn't see one, too many to sort through as we walked. Dr. Dimes 5-inch, patent red, stiletto heels clicked and clacked on the laminate floor and were very much out of place at a doctor's office. They were what some people affectionately call "Fuck Me Pumps." And when I mean some people, I am referring to hookers or strippers or floozies, not medical professionals. Her pencil skirt was a vanity-size too small, hugging her chunky ass and thighs like a pork sausage casing stuffed with too much seasoned filling. Her white blouse--the top two buttons undone, exposing her jiggly and veiny, large breasts--struggled to stay buttoned by a lone button, precariously hooked in the button hole by its teetering edge. If she breathed in too much or laughed too hard, then I could see that button launching across the hall like a heat-seeking missile. Lucky for me and my poor eyes, I was glad that struggling button held its ground. The last thing I needed to see was my kid's pediatrician's exposed boobs. It's true.

Dr. Dimes glanced over her shoulder at good ol' Sammie Boy and said, "What grade are you in now?"

"The third grade!" he said proudly, the fear of a shot replaced with pride and joy.

"The third grade?! My, how time flies, doesn't it?" she said. I assumed she was talking to me since kids don't really have any perception of time flying anywhere. Kids are always in the present. All they think about is shit like being hungry or boredom or exhaustion or happiness or sadness. The contemplation of time and their place in it is reserved for much later in life, particularly after having their own children. That's when time seems to be sliding into oblivion faster than you can imagine. "I remember when you were much younger, in diapers no-less. Don't you, Mr. Burchwood?"

"Yep, seems like yesterday," I said. And it did just seem like yesterday that my boy was crapping his pants and slamming his face in a plate of pureed green beans and creamed corn and Cheerios and goo goo and ga ga'ing all over the place. Where *did* all that time go? Flushed down the toilet of history, that's where.

"Come over here so I can weigh you," she said to Sammie. She motioned toward a scale and he stood on it. She asked him to take his shoes off and he did, tossing them to me one-by-one in a frenzied manner. Standing on that scale--bright diamonds of canary yellow and baby blue on his cherry red argyle socks peeking out from underneath his Levi's--it seemed like the most exciting thing to happen to him since he found the Buck knife. He stood there at attention like a foot soldier, proud that he followed orders and was dressed to impress. One of his socks had a hole at the tip, his big toe protruding out. "Wow! Seventy-five pounds. What have you been eating? Rocks?"

"Why would I eat *rocks*?" said Sammie, confused.

"Oh, I don't know. To make you heavier than last time?"

"Daddy said he'd buy me twelve donuts after my doctor appointment!" he said, beaming at me.

Dr. Dimes followed with a disapproving look, shaking her head as she scribbled some notes on her clipboard, no doubt writing what a horrible father I was, then said, "Oh, did he? He said *twelve*?"

"Yes! Twelve! And I'm gonna eat them *all*!"

"Maybe one donut, if any at all. Do you know what the saturated fats in donuts will do to your arteries when you get to be my age?" she said, placing a gentle hand on his shoulder and leading him through the hallway.

"Sa-chur-ay-ted what?" he said, looking at her as if she was wiser than all get-out and she was revealing the mysteries of the universe to him. Since when do doctors play dirty against parents? Since the beginning of time, that's when. It's true.

We walked through a winding hallway that transformed from a children's photo gallery to ergonomic work stations built into the walls for nurses and office assistants and drug representatives and whoever else was on-staff. Several women were sitting around, what, trying to look busy shuffling papers and writing stuff down and organizing more papers and shuffling mail and adjusting their chairs, but I knew they weren't doing shit. I knew all the *tricks* to looking busy. I could tell when people were acting busy rather than *being busy* because I was a pro at acting busy. It really wasn't too hard to look or act busy. Managers are easy to fool. You know? Of course, you do. But these people couldn't fool *me*. I knew they were just waiting for me and Dr. Dimes to pass so they could go back to their computer games of Solitaire or paperback romance novels or mobile phone apps or newspaper crossword puzzles or knitting or scrapbooking or whatever they were really doing. But one thing I knew for certain: they weren't doing shit. I knew this for certain.

Once we passed all the slackers, we followed Dr. Dimes to the examination room. Inside, there was a small desk attached to the wall (a stool in front and a chair to the side), an examination table, a small sink with a mirror above it, and a trash can for medical waste. Butterflies were painted on the walls by someone who wasn't very good at painting. I mean, I could tell they were supposed to be butterflies but they looked more like flying insects that had been placed in a microwave for ten seconds--not long enough to kill them but long enough to slightly melt and disfigure them. They looked sad and tired as they sagged above some droopy sunflowers, also looking slightly melted. It was a sad depiction for a sad place for kids. I imagined the pastoral scene was supposed to calm the kids from the terror they were experiencing: half-cooked butterflies freefalling over half-cooked sunflowers. Lame.

"Sit up here," Dr. Dimes said to Sammie, patting the examination table covered with white paper, then sitting at a desk in the corner of the room. The white paper crackled as Sammie wiggled his butt, trying to get comfortable. I plopped into a chair next to the desk. She typed something quickly on the computer then turned her stool to face my boy, crossing her legs and interlacing her fingers around her knees, locking her legs in such a way as to keep her skin-tight pencil skirt from exploding, then she said, "How have you been?"

"Good," Sammie said, smiling suspiciously. "I feel good." His eyes darted back and forth between Dr. Dimes and me.

"Have you been eating a lot of fruits and vegetables?" she said. She typed slowly as she spoke, like a court reporter or stenographer.

"Yes. Tons of them!" Sammie said. He lied. He knew it and I knew it but I didn't say anything, though. I wasn't going to rat him out, not just yet. Dr. Dimes' long fingernails clickity-clacked on the computer keyboard.

"Good! Do you go outside and play every day?"

"Yes. All the time."

"Do you get lots of sleep at night? Do you go to bed at a reasonable hour?"

"What's ree-soh-nay-bull?" Sammie said, scratching his head.

"Do you go to bed early or stay up late?"

"I go to bed when my daddy tells me to."

Dr. Dimes turned to look at me and said, "And what time is that, Dad?" She continued to type as she interrogated us.

"Nine o'clock."

"Oh," she said, typing something. "That's a good bedtime but eight o'clock would be better, if at all possible."

"Sure," I said, knowing full-well that eight o'clock was completely out of the question. At my place with two rambunctious kids, that was practically impossible for me. Even just trying to get them to bed at that time would be a ritual in futility but I wasn't about to be disagreeable. "We'll give it a shot."

"Lots of rest and a well-balanced diet are the most important things you should do for your child," she said, unlatching her fingers to shift her legs. Her gargantuan breasts, covered with a faded green and blue roadmap of veins and capillaries, wanted desperately to escape her blouse but the single button holding it together was doing a masterful job of keeping them imprisoned. The fashion designer of this heroic blouse would be impressed with the shirt's unintended ability to keep the doctor's semi-professional look intact. I thought for sure her tits were going to fly out but they didn't, thank goodness. That would have been really embarrassing for her. And me. It's true. "That should be your priority, Mr. Burchwood."

"My kids are my *priority*," I said before she stood up, ignoring my answer. She approached the examining table.

"Let's see how you're doing," she said to Sammie, checking his eyes, then ears, then throat with one of those all-in-one doctor thingamajiggies: an otoscope. Good ol' Sammie Boy complied with everything she asked him to do, like a good boy, as she looked at his eyes and the various orifices in his head, sticking his pink tongue out or tilting his head when commanded. "Now lift your shirt so I can listen to your breathing."

He lifted the front of his striped t-shirt and exposed his skinny torso--all bones and pasty skin and very little fat. Under the fluorescent lights, his midsection looked like that of a concentration camp victim. She placed the plastic and metal chest piece of the stethoscope around her next to his skin and he squealed and giggled and squirmed then said, "That's cold! It tickles!"

"I'm sure it does. Now, try not to make a peep so I can hear your breathing and your heart beat."

"OK," he said, struggling to contain his outbursts. He really tried his best to not laugh or squeal but I could see it was really hard for him as she touched various places on his chest and ribs and back. Almost as hard as it was for the button on Dr. Dimes blouse to keep it together. That was pretty goddamn hard. Good ol' Sammie Boy was pretty ticklish, though. I knew this for a fact. I was proud that he kept his composure as long as he did. She then raised his arms by the wrists and looked over his skin for what I assume would be weird moles or marks or sores or whatever. Finally, she tapped his knee with one of those rubber hammer-looking things and his leg involuntarily knee-jerked to life. "Ow! That hurt!"

"I'm certain it didn't hurt but I know it feels weird. It felt weird, didn't it?"

"Yes," he said, sheepishly. I think he was embarrassed when he realized that his body could do things without his brain telling it to. I remember having the same realization when I was close to his age. It's a really mind-blowing thing to learn for a kid, how strange and wondrous our bodies are.

"Everything seems in order. He's healthy in every way," she said, sitting back down in front of the computer, furiously typing her medical findings. "Was there anything else you wanted to discuss with me?"

"Are you going to give me a shot?" Sammie said, worried.

Dr. Dimes continued to type some more then stopped, flipping through papers on her clipboard, looking for the answer. "Nope. No immunizations are due at this time. Next year though."

"Oh good," Sammie said, relieved, forcing a smile. He wiped imaginary sweat from his brow then started kicking his legs back and forth. He had nervous energy, I guess.

"And how about you, Dad? Anything you wanted to discuss?"

"Well..." I said, stopping to look at good ol' Sammie Boy then looking at Dr. Dimes, the seriousness displayed on her face contrasting weirdly with the amount of cleavage exposed in her blouse. I had a hard time *not* looking at her tits. They were just RIGHT THERE, in my face. It was difficult not to look even though I knew it was unacceptable for me to look. Why did I have to be in this uncomfortable situation? It was like reverse sexual harassment. "You see, there's this thing... about Sammie. I discovered something about him recently that I wanted to talk to you about." My son sat up straight, a look of shock and dismay on his face.

"Oh, really?" she said. She stopped typing and turned to me-- shifting her legs, knees, and fingers into a different interlocking configuration. "Tell me."

"Well, you see, Sammie has this ability. It seems he can see--"

And without any warning whatsoever, good ol' Sammie Boy leapt down from the examination table and hopped into my lap, quickly covering my mouth with one of his tiny hands and cupping my ear with the other tiny hand, then hissing into my ear, "Daddy! No, don't *say* anything!"

I looked at him, quite surprised by his reaction, almost speechless. Can you imagine that? His eyes darted back and forth, looking at mine, searching for a secret sign that I wouldn't betray him and the things he had shared with me: his visions of the future.

"It's OK, Sammie. Dr. Dimes is here to help and I need to discuss this with her. Would you rather wait outside with the nurses?"

"Can I go weigh myself again?" he said, looking at Dr. Dimes.

"Of course. Just ask the nurses to help you." He reluctantly left the examination room, locking his eyes with mine as he closed the door behind him. That little bugger! Dr. Dimes turned to me and said, "So what did you want to tell me?"

"Well, I know this will sound strange and all but I think my son can see the future." She blinked her eyes a couple of times, a look of bewilderment settling in. I'm sure she had been told a million things about peoples' kids across the gamut like bad behavior to drug abuse to bad grades to hyperactivity to diarrhea to rashes to allergies to constipation but--and I'm certain of this--I'm sure no other parent had told her that their kid could see the *future*. It's true. Who says stuff like that? No one, that's who. "He told me about things he thought would happen and then they happened. I know it's hard to believe."

"I would be lying if I said I wasn't skeptical," she said, unfazed.

"Certainly."

"And, I'm sure you believe what you are saying is true," she said, unlocking her fingers to release the pretzel twist her arms and legs had become while listening to me. I bet she was tired of me by now. I was sure of it. "But I have to be honest here. This really isn't my area of expertise--whether I believe you or not." She began typing some more into the computer.

"I see. But do you believe me? Because I'm telling you the truth."

"It doesn't matter if I believe you or not. My specialty is in general medicine, not psychology or psychiatry or metaphysics or the supernatural. I can look at your son's body and tell you most things related to his physiology but I can't tell you how his brain works, whether he can see the future or not."

"So, you *don't* believe me, do you?" I said, gathering myself and the paperwork needed to check-out at the front desk.

"No, sir, I do not. But that doesn't mean you're not telling me the truth. Anyway, maybe you should take your son to a psychologist or a therapist. There are some that specialize in working with children. But I know we've talked in the past about the possibility that you son is on the autism spectrum, right?" she said, matter-of-factly.

"Yes, but I don't feel he--"

"Kids on the spectrum see the world differently than normal kids, you know?"

"Uh huh," I said, disappointed in the direction she steered our conversation. I mean, like, three years ago we discussed autism but I didn't feel that good ol' Sammie Boy was autistic nor was he on any spectrum of autism or any other type of similar disorder. Sammie was a normal kid through and through. He was as normal as can be--well--except for the seeing the future part. It's true. But I was fed up with Dr. Dimes anyway, what, with her big tits and tight skirt and her know-it-all attitude. It was time for me to go and take Sammie with me. It was donut time.

"But if you want to explore it further, then here's a card for a therapist I know that is great with kids. She's the best." She handed me a business card that I promptly placed into my shirt pocket without reading it. It really was time to go.

"Thanks," I said, getting up for the door.

"Oh, and Mr. Burchwood?" she said, insistent.

"Yes?" I said, ready to leave.

"Make sure Sammie gets and an early bedtime and lots of sleep. Boys his age need *lots* of sleep. LOTS."

"Thanks," I said, disinterested in anything else she had to say.

Then I left the examination room, scooped up my kid from the weigh scale (he was unattended, by the way), and we left together without checking out at the front desk, good ol' Sammie Boy flung over my shoulder, laughing and squealing all the way to my car.

"Daddy, can I have that knife I found in the couch?" he said, giggling and squealing his little head off. He was laughing all over the place. The sun was bright in the cornblue sky, not a single cloud in sight.

"No," I said, opening the car door and setting him in the back seat.

"Please?" he said.

"No," I said, sitting in the driver seat.

"Please?!"

"No!"

"Fine!" he said, folding his arms and glaring at me from the back seat. I could see his little face in the rear-view mirror and he knew it. He stared right into my reflected eyes. "I'd rather have a budgerigar anyway."

"Ummm."

***

There was a time in my life when becoming a famous writer was all I thought about. But those times were gone. I wrote a couple of books that didn't sell very well then my writing career fell off the face of the Earth faster than my initial meteoric rise. After so many bad literary runs, everyone dropped me: my agent, my publisher, my editor, everybody. Then I got divorced, my family was decimated, and my desire to write was gone. Dreams smashed. Marriage destroyed. Goodbye. It's funny how fast something you were once so passionately involved with in your life can simply vanish: a career, a marriage, your dreams. POOF! They say life is a series of ups and downs, good and bad, pain and pleasure. It doesn't sound so cliché when you're getting your own ass handed to you. Life can kick you in the balls so hard--so hard you can't breathe. It's true.

When I finally had the realization that my writing career was over, I placed all the things I possessed from my dead career in a box--notes, manuscripts, letters from editors and my agent, headshots, business cards, unused fancy writing pens, Moleskine notebooks (some new and some used), news clippings, and book reviews. I neatly placed them inside the box, sealed it shut with packing tape, wrote the words "My Writing Career" on the top, and placed it on the floor in my closet next to my box of collectible comics. And there it stayed unmolested until I moved to my apartment where it was placed in a very similar spot on the floor in my new closet. And there it sat for quite a while longer until I accidentally kicked the box with my foot while looking for a pair of pants that I wanted to wear to the Beer:Thirty--an aptly named hole-in-the-wall down the street from my apartment complex. My foot practically went through the side of the box when I kicked it, the cardboard weak from sitting around for so long. I mean, I know I'm strong but I'm not *that* strong.

After pulling my foot out of the damaged box, I slid the box out of my closet into my room and sat on the floor to open it. The box was coated with a thin layer of dust as well as the remnants of dust bunnies and carpet fuzz and insect carcasses, stuck in the packing tape at the bottom corners. It was like I had recovered a long-lost time capsule and I was kind of excited at the prospects of rediscovering the things I had placed inside years before. Would the artifacts still be in pristine condition? Or would they have fallen prey to hungry silverfish or other paper-eating insects? Or maybe it was like my entire writing career was a dream and there would be nothing but blank paper inside the box (that would be weird)? No matter the outcome, I was excited to find out. When I pulled the tape off the top of the box, the ripping sound of the tape tearing from the cardboard called out to my boy, who quickly appeared next to me on the floor. He was all excited and bouncy and hyper and curious like most kids his age. He could barely contain himself, he was *that* excited. It's funny how just opening a box can mesmerize a kid and send them into fits of excitement so intense that it seemed they would lose their goddamn minds. Good ol' Sammie Boy was no different. It's true.

"What's in the box, Daddy?" he said, sitting on his knees and bouncing in place, his lower legs bent and contorted below his thighs in a way that looked almost painful (at least to my old eyes, anyway). "More comic books?!"

"Sorry son," I said, opening the top of the box and folding the flaps down on the side so the box would stay open. "This is only stuff I wrote."

"Did you write any Dr. Strange stories?"

"No, I didn't," I said, rummaging through the box.

"Why not?" he said, looking offended. "Dr. Strange is cool!"

"Yes, that is true. But I didn't write for comics. I wrote novels."

"What are nah-vulls?" he said, his attention turning to the box and what else may be inside.

"So, novels are long-form books of literature."

Just then, he noticed one of my headshots, a photograph taken about ten years early--back in the day when I had slightly more hair on my head, slightly less fat on my gut, a somewhat earnest stare, and a perfect amount of beard stubble. He lunged his tiny little hand into the box, pulled out the 8 by 10 photograph, and said, "Whoa, Daddy! Is that you?"

"Yes, that's me."

"You look so *different*," he said, examining the photograph and the visage of my younger self. He seemed quite shocked for some reason, a reason I couldn't really figure out. To me, I didn't look much different but, to him, it was like I was a completely different person altogether. Weird. Kids definitely have a different perception of things, especially good ol' Sammie Boy. "Look at your beard!"

"Son, that is *not* a beard. I just had a little stubble."

"What is stuh-bull?" he said, really perplexed. He had no idea what I was talking about. But, before I could even get into it with him and explain the difference between a beard and a five o'clock shadow, there was a loud knock on the door. The pounding at the door startled the both of us; my heart pounded as well while Sammie's eyes bulged through his surprised look. Little Jessie screamed from her room then Sammie realized who the visitor was. "IT'S NAT!"

Good ol' Sammie Boy tossed the 8 by 10 photograph of yours truly on the ground faster than my literary agent dropped me from her roster and bolted for the door, hoping to get there first and greet our guest before his sister did. That was another game he played against his little sister: who could answer the door first and find out who the mystery guest was. Whenever someone would knock on the door, the two of them would lose their friggin' minds--pushing and shoving and punching and screaming and crying and complaining--all the way to the door. Usually, once they answered the door and saw who it was, they would immediately lose interest in the guest as if the conquest to answer the door was more important than who was actually on the other side. But this time, the guest knocking on the door was one of their favorite people in the world and they knew it. They had patiently been waiting for her to come over.

"IT'S NAT! IT'S NAT! IT'S NAT!" they both said, pushing and shoving each other.

"I'll get it!" Jessie said, hitting Sammie Boy in the arm.

"Ow! No, I'll get it!" he said, shoving Jessie in the chest and knocking her back against the wall. This flipped a switch in her: the anger switch. Boy, was she pissed! I could see it boil up in her little face. She turned bright red and clinched her little fist, as if to harness all the strength she had, and unleashed a brutal attack on the boy as if she was kicking the ass of an 11-year-old black belt at her dojang who had been teasing her the afternoon before at school. She coiled her leg then kicked good ol' Sammie Boy--right in the gut. He dropped to the floor quickly like a sack of Russet potatoes falling off a kitchen counter. It happened so fast I could barely see the blur of her leg in the air. She was quick as lightning and deadly with a kick. It was a thing of beauty to behold, actually. I felt bad for him, though. Sammie writhed in pain on the floor while Jessie politely opened the door.

"Hi Nat!" she said, letting her babysitter inside our apartment. Of course, once Nat was in the door and saw good ol' Sammie Boy on the floor--wedged in-between the door and the wall--her babysitter duties commenced immediately. She knelt next to my boy before I could get to him. Everything happened so fast.

"Oh, Sammie! Are you OK? I didn't, like, hit you with the door, did I?" she said, propping him up in her arms. She hugged him and swept his hair from his face. Boy, he ate that shit up. Sammie loved the attention, especially from a pretty college student. It's true. Nat was tall (way taller than me) and slender with straight, shiny red hair parted in the middle and a constellation of freckles on her nose and cheeks and arms. In short, she was a stunner.

"Jessie *kicked* me in the stomach," he said, really hamming it up. It was hard to tell if Nat was 'in' on the game but she was always a trooper, always sweet and caring and patient with the kids. I don't know how she did it. I saw right through his little charade but she played along.

"Oh, you poor thing! And *you*," she said, putting her arm around Jessie. "You must have been, like, pretty upset to kick your brother like that, huh?" Nat had them both in her long arms, pulling them close to her.

"Yeah, I got mad," Jessie said, her head drooping.

"Tell you what, you two. If you guys make up then I'll, like, share my bag of Gummi Bears with you. How's that?" And before another crocodile tear could fall from Sammie's eyes or before Jessie's face could get any redder, those two brats were hugging and kissing and begging for Gummi Bears. That was a neat little trick Nat had there, keeping candy handy in case there was a kid brawl or kid argument or whatever. I was going to have to remember that trick for myself. You know? For when Nat wasn't around to breakup their annoying fights. "See! We're all, like, friends again. And how are you, Mr. Burchwood?" she said, standing up, looming over me.

"Better, now that *you're* here," I said. "But you know to call me, Simon. Right?"

"Right," she said, walking into the living room and placing her things on the couch. The kids swarmed around her like bumble bees dancing on blooming honeysuckles. They couldn't contain their excitement. "I always, like, forget. I was raised to be polite to my elders, you know?"

"Your elders?" I said, appalled. "Do I seem that *old* to you?"

"Well, you're, like, not *old* but you are older than me. Right?"

"I guess you are technically right," I said, trying not to show just how much that comment stung me deep down to the nugget core of my soul. It's silly trying not to show how much things affect you on the inside. How do you *hide* those things from people? You hide them by trying to act like a goddamn statue, that's how. "Come back here with me. I was just putting some things away."

I walked back to my bedroom then sat back on the floor, next to the box of memorabilia from my failed writing career. I reached for the headshot of my younger self but Nat got to it first. She picked it up, gawking at it, then said, "Is this you? You look so *different*!"

"Really?" I still didn't understand why I looked so different in the photo to good ol' Sammie Boy and Nat. What were they seeing that I wasn't? Had I changed that much? Did I really look that much older? That was a really, really depressing thought. It's true.

"You look, like, so much *younger* in this photo. And it looks professionally shot, too."

"Yeah, I hired a professional photographer to take that. Pretty cool, huh?"

"Boy, I say. Very cool. Why did you, like, hire a professional to take your photo?"

"I was a writer, once. It seems like a long time ago."

"A writer?! How cool!" she said, beaming and smiling and her green eyes twinkling all over the goddamn place. I've said it before and I'll say it again. Telling people you are a writer brings something out in them that is undeniable: pure envy. I don't know what it was about telling people that I was a writer but, once I did, they would start to tell me about all their hopes and dreams from when they were a little kid of being a writer or a dancer or an actor or a painter or a cartoonist or some creative dream of theirs that was usually squashed mercilessly by their parents. It never, ever failed. "When I was a little girl, I always wanted to be, like, a writer. I read SO many Judy Blume books and Roald Dahl books. I, like, devoured them!"

Before I go on, let me tell you a little about Nat, or as her parents named her when she was born, Natalie Ashley Wellsley. Nat--as me and the kids affectionately called her--was born and raised in an affluent suburb of Dallas, Texas. Sometime around when she was 12 or 13, she sprouted into the 6'2" Amazonian that the kids and I see to this day. Her amateur career as a volleyball player sprouted in junior high as well, something that carried her through high school and into college, a full athletic scholarship in tow at Southern Methodist University (a snooty private university in the heart of Dallas). She managed to graduate from SMU with a degree in science but her promising career as a professional volleyball player was crushed after an Anterior Cruciate Ligament injury so horrific that the current SMU volleyball team still tells the story as a cautionary tale in the locker room (her ACL popped so loudly after an awkward landing from spiking the ball that it sounded like a whip-crack). She moved to Austin not long after graduating SMU with the promise of a job as a lab technician at the University of Texas but a clerical error kept her from securing the job. She settled on babysitting and nanny work to pay the bills, which serendipitously brought her to my little family.

"But you studied science at SMU, right?" I said.

"Yeah, I did. I didn't say, like, that a writing career would have been *practical*. I just *dreamed* of being a writer and a fashionable one at that." She sat down next to me on the floor and prodded through my box of memorabilia, picking up the different paper things--a business card, some newspaper clippings, some ruled pages with handwritten notes on them. She honestly seemed fascinated with the things in my box and, for a brief moment, seemed nostalgic for a time and place that wasn't hers to be nostalgic for. "A girl can, like, dream." She placed all the things back in the box.

"That's true. We all can dream, right?" I said, folding the flaps of the box over the top, bending one underneath the others to keep the top closed shut.

"Now, my dream is, like, to find a full-time job in a lab. That would be sweet."

"I'm surprised you haven't been offered a job in modeling."

"In modeling?!" she said, laughing and wheezing and snickering all over the place. She got a real kick out of that comment, like I was pulling her leg or something. But the truth was, although she was kind of too tall and gangly and awkward at times, her bright red hair and shiny green eyes and freckly, translucent skin had a striking beauty that was unique and otherworldly. I would have to say that I had never seen someone like her. She was a stunner, really. And the best thing about modeling is that no one would have to listen to her say the word 'like' repeatedly, like, a broken record. Sometimes, she said that word at a pace that would have pummeled a prize fighter into submission, if the word 'like' was a right-handed series of jabs to the face. It was maddening to hear her say it sometimes. But, as often times are the case, Southern Belles also possess a level of charm and grace not possessed by normal human beings. It's true. "You have got to be, like, kidding!"

"Well, I wasn't. But that's OK. Just saying." I slid the box back into my closet, pulled out a light jacket to put on, then closed the closet door. Nat had retreated from my bedroom while I was finishing up. I found her sitting on the couch with Sammie and Jessie bouncing on the couch cushions next to her. They could barely contain their excitement to have her with them. It looked like their little heads were going to explode.

"What do you guys want to do while your dad is out?" she said, trying to contain them with her long, thin arms.

"Watch a movie!" Sammie said.

"Play a game!" Jessie said.

"Movie!"

"Game!"

Their volley of words almost turned into a shoving match but Nat was swift enough to preemptively soothe their argument. She smiled at them and said, "How about we do, like, both?" My kids looked at each other, thunderstruck. Their minds were blown. Their mouths were agape. They happily slid down in place next to their babysitter, serene pleasure on their little faces. Nat smiled at their obedience then looked at me. "And you? What are your plans?"

"I don't know. I might just go down to The Beer:Thirty for a drink or two. We'll see."

"Sounds good," Nat said, looking for the remote to the TV. "We'll be here. Say bye to your daddy, kiddos."

"Bye Daddy," they both said, content.

"Bye kids," I said, kissing each of them on the cheek. But when I tried to stand back up, I lost my balance and fell on top of the three of them, landing squarely on Nat. I quickly stood up, fully embarrassed and apologetic. "I'm so sorry!" I said, my arms out trying to put some gentlemanly space between us. Nat seemed more amused than embarrassed.

"Don't worry about it. Go out and, like, have fun!"

And so, I left the apartment, leaving my kids in the able hands of their babysitter, Natalie Ashley Wellsley--the 6'2" ex-volleyball player from SMU, science grad, potential model, and their favorite babysitter of all time. I walked down the staircase to my garage where my Volvo S70 waited for me in the dark. I got in it (it started right up), opened the garage door, backed out into the apartment complex parking lot, and sped around the perimeter of the complex to the exit gate. I sped down the street toward The Beer:Thirty, a hole-in-the-wall I occasionally went to so I could drink a few beers in private away from the kids; sometimes I would think about my life, sometimes I would watch a basketball game or whatever was on TV, and sometimes I would think about what it would be like to meet a woman and possibly date. But something went off inside of me and I didn't feel like doing any of those things. I didn't know what I wanted to do but I didn't want to sit in The Beer:Thirty like a sad-sack mulling over my problems. So, I pulled into the next convenience store I saw, bought a six-pack of beer, got back in my Volvo, and headed back toward my apartment complex.

Once inside the gate, I drove around the perimeter back toward my building. But instead of pulling into my garage, I backed into a parking space across from my building and turned the engine and headlights off. I pulled a beer from the six-pack, opened it, and took a swig. I watched the large, lit window of my living room, the curtains drawn tight, and the silhouettes of Nat and my kids danced across the white curtains like fairies flitting across a misty meadow, carefree and balletic and joyful. I sat in my car and watched the dancing silhouettes well into the night, drinking beer by myself, and enjoying the stillness of my solitude.

CHAPTER

FIVE

FULL
FLAVOR

Chapter Five

Getting my kids ready for bed was sometimes--no, I mean all the time--a feat of ungodly proportions. It was like wrangling cats or making sand castles out of dry sand or containing a flash flood with cardboard boxes or convincing a narcissist to be empathetic or whatever. It seemed like an impossible task *every night*. Each night, as bedtime for the kids approached, I seemed to forget how I got through it the night before, what, forgetting all the things I said or did to get my children to comply with my commands, to do what I asked, and to just get ready for *fucking* bed. I don't want to sound too harsh or come off as being ungrateful for the time with them or anything like that. But I will say this--as much as I love my children--sometimes they drive me bonkers. Hard to believe, right? It's true.

I had quite a list of tasks to accomplish each night and, if the list wasn't complete by the end of the evening, then I felt like a complete, parenting failure. I don't know why really, but I just did if I didn't get all the things done I needed to do. The list of tasks went something like this (though not an *official* list it was very comprehensive): make or purchase a dinner for the kids, feed the kids, clean up after dinner, assist both of them with homework, assist both of them with packing up their stuff for the next day of school, get both of them in the shower (luckily, I had two showers in my apartment--one in the master bedroom bath and one in the kid's bathroom), pick out their clothes for the next day, lay out their pajamas for the night, make sure they brush and floss their teeth, and have a bedtime story or ritual ready, then complete any house-cleaning after they fall asleep. Suffice it to say, I guess I was making up for the loss of the other parent in our lives. You know who I am referring to? Of course, you do. Being a single parent is exhausting and stressful. It's true.

Anyway, on this particular night, it seemed good ol' Sammie Boy and his little sister Jessie conspired against me, or at least it felt that way to me. Neither one was being particularly cooperative and, although all the tasks on my list were being completed, they were completed in such a way that they didn't seem completed at all. Everything was a slog. The kids bickered with each other all through dinner, making our familial ritual less pleasant. Cleaning up took extra-long because the bickering turned into a small-scale food fight; there was shit everywhere to clean up: food on the carpet and the mini-blinds, some spilled juice on the table-top, there was even food shrapnel on the walls. So, rather than try to talk sense into them (impossible to do with elementary school-aged kids) or ask them to help clean up (yeah right!), I carried them each to their respective bathrooms (flung over my shoulders, caveman-style), turned on both showers, and barked at them to wash up for the night.

"No, no, no, Daddy!" Sammie said.

"No, no, no, Daddy!" Jessie said.

"Yes, yes, yes," I said to both.

I closed both doors. While they reluctantly showered, I decided to enjoy a smoke break on the balcony of my apartment--alone. The night air was cool and the sun was setting behind the trees that lined the perimeter of the apartment complex, an assortment of flowering mountain laurels guarded the property from the surrounding streets, some of their canopies white, some pink, and some exploding red. I didn't have much on my balcony--like I've said before--except a wooden bench, a chair, and an old coffee can under it, to throw cigarette butts in. The coffee can--of the Café Bustelo variety, bright yellow and red with art deco lettering for its brand name--was one of a few remnants from the life I lived before I was married, when I was a young man and an aspiring writer just out of college, before I had children, and before my writing career was a spectacular failure. The coffee can, at first, inconspicuously accompanied me from each successive apartment lease to the next, reappearing in a box of knickknacks along with cheap kitchen utensils or stolen office supplies, then reestablishing its place on the balcony or patio of each new abode as the go-to ashtray. Over time, its inconspicuous, magical reappearances morphed into nostalgic reliability; it always seemed to be a part of my life, wherever I went, whoever I was with. It became that thing--that identifiable piece of shambling patio décor--that was all my own. As people came in and out of my life, smoking cigarettes with me on the many patios and balconies of the many shitholes I lived in, the Café Bustelo coffee can was always there. While I was married, the coffee can was relegated to a box in the garage but, after the divorce and moving to my current apartment, it reappeared again like an old friend.

A flood of memories poured into my brain as I lit my cigarette and stared at that coffee can, its exterior colors still bright red and yellow even though the metal seams had succumbed to rust and corrosion and a thin layer of ash and pollen coated its sides. I thought it weird that one of my prized possessions, which hid in the garage from my failed marriage and made it out the other side of a hectic move to a new home, was a rusty coffee can full of stinky, cigarette butts and ashes. As I listened to the water from both showers snake its way through the pipes in the thin walls of my apartment building, I thought of old friends, old girlfriends, old pets, and old smoking sessions. 'What was the point of owning possessions?' I thought. 'What did it mean that something most people would consider a piece of trash held so much significance to me? Why did my life end up where it was at that moment?' When I was in my twenties, I didn't ever imagine being divorced in my forties and living the life of a single parent in a rented, two-bedroom apartment a mile from my kids' elementary school and forced to live two miles from my old two-story house. I contemplated these things while I smoked my cigarette, inhaling deeply as the thoughts of my past raced through my mind, the nicotine-infused smoke penetrating my blood stream. But I didn't have long to myself. Through the blinds in the balcony door, I saw Jessie running butt naked--soaking wet, hair mashed to her shoulders in a soppy mass, her towel in her hand dragging behind her on the carpet--and Sammie crisscrossing in the opposite direction, just as wet and just as naked. I quickly tossed the barely-smoked cigarette into the coffee can and ran inside.

What I couldn't hear outside, what, with the street noise and parking cars and chatty, drunk neighbors and the late evening wind, was their screams of sheer delight. With their lack of clothes came uninhibited joy, the kind of pleasure you might see from a wild animal being filmed from a long distance without any predators around and not a care in the world, trotting alone and nipping at dandelions or something. Sammie and Jessie chased each other across the full length of the apartment, tackling each other in my bedroom, jumping on my bed with wet feet, then initiating the chase again in the opposite direction to their bedroom, both towels dragging across the carpet behind them. I tried to catch them but they were too slippery, their skin slick and shiny like wet seals, and their excited bodies writhing out of my grasp. I finally was able to corral them between the couch and the coffee table, then tossed them onto the couch, tickling and harassing them for not giving me enough time to myself as well as cutting their shower time short.

"What do you think you're doing?!" I said, pretending to body slam them like a wrestler, standing up with my stiff elbow extended, then coming down but not really jabbing them, just pretending. The mock wrestling move made them squeal with delight. "You're supposed to be showering then getting ready for school. Not running around the apartment--naked!"

"Why do we have to shower every night, Daddy?" said Sammie. His question perplexed me enough that I stopped tickling them and thought about it, yet keeping them pinned to the couch with stiff arms.

I thought about it some more, not finding a good answer to his question, then said, "That's a good question, my boy. I guess my answer is that it's good to shower every night."

"But do we *have to*?" said Jessie, as I draped their towels over their shivering, little bodies.

I contemplated her question then said, "I guess you don't *have to* shower every night. Just seems like a good practice."

"What if you're too busy doing homework and forget to shower?" Sammie said.

"Or what if you're too busy hunting ghosts or something?" Jessie said, looking serious as if that was a *real* question worth asking. Kids do that, you know? They ask the most bizarre questions and expect you to take them seriously. But as a parent, you can't condescend your kid's worldview. You have to let a curious kid be a curious kid. It's true.

"I guess if you were *seriously* hunting ghosts and you forgot to shower, then that would be OK. Hunting ghosts is important and time-consuming," I said.

"Yes! It is!" she said, looking at Sammie for validation. He was happy to comply. He liked this line of questioning.

"Ghosts are scary!" he said.

"They *are* scary," I said, drying them with their towels, taking turns with each of their soppy heads, then wrapping them in their towels like burritos. "But tell you what, if you go finish getting ready for bed then we can do some Mad Libs together. How does that sound?"

"Yeah!" they said, in unison, jumping up from the couch and running to their respective bathrooms to finish getting dressed and brushing their teeth and chanting while they brushed, "Mad Libs! Mad libs! Mad Libs!"

Before I go on, let me explain something to you. If you didn't already know, Mad Libs are a kind of word puzzle game that is frequently played as a party game or as a pastime when you're bored while waiting for the bus or something like that. But I don't usually play Mad Libs that way. For a very long time, especially back in my writer days, I used Mad Libs as a way to end writer's block, something I suffered from on a very frequent basis when I was trying to make a living as a writer. If I ever encountered writer's block, instead of suffering like a goddamn idiot, then I would whip out a book of Mad Libs. The nonsensical results of adding random words into the blank spaces of the sentences were a real hoot and it helped my mind unhinge itself from the debilitating effects of the writer's block. Let me give you an example. For instance, Mad Libs may present a sentence puzzle like this:

"Sam _____ his green _____ while he _____ on his _____."

Now, as you can see, there are a dozen ways to complete this puzzle. A proficient writer (like I *used* to be) might complete the puzzle like this:

"Sam <u>drives</u> his green <u>car</u> while he <u>talks</u> on his <u>phone</u>."

Bingo! Pretty simple, huh? And fun! Now, what I've found when I play Mad Libs with other people is that they approach the game as if they were still teenagers, filling the blanks with sexual innuendos or profanities or double entendres that were ridiculous, mildly amusing at best. The last couple of times I played Mad Libs with friends or acquaintances, it was a goddamn disaster. My other junior high buddy, Jason, back in good ol' Montgomery, Alabama, would play Mad Libs like a miscreant, inserting words of such poor taste that he would laugh all over the goddamn place like a maniacal hyena. He would finish his sentence like this:

"Sam yanks his green penis while he masturbates on his hamster." Then he would laugh and spit and wheeze all over the place like he was some kind of comedic genius. Real funny, huh? It's completely idiotic. But that was Jason. He was a complete idiot. It's true.

Fortunately, my kids weren't so asinine like Jason. They played Mad Libs with a childish abandon that was sweet and endearing and innocent. I loved that about them. I entered their room, which they shared together, ready for our bedtime ritual; Sammie's side a shrine to Marvel Comics superheroes like Dr. Strange and Spider-Man while Jessie's side was a shrine to My Little Pony and kittens. It was as if the bedroom was divided down the middle by an imaginary line, perpendicular to a window in the middle of the back wall--Sammie's superheroes ready for battle in the posters on the wall above his black, lumpy, futon bed on one side and Jessie's ponies and kittens in cute poses on the posters on the wall above her pink, poufy, princess bed. Their room suffered from a personality disorder so great that it was hopeless, a schizophrenic job of interior design so catastrophic that I should have been ashamed of myself for allowing to happen. They seemed to be able to live in harmony despite their reluctance to acknowledge the other's presence in the room. It was an adolescent stalemate of wills.

Since Sammie's futon could lay flat like a double bed, we usually used it as our gaming spot since it was comfortable and big enough for the three of us to lounge on. They were both on his futon, lying next to each other in their pajamas with their respective Mad Libs editions before them, a pile of colorful pens and pencils and markers between them, and looks of contentment on their cute little faces. They were ready to play, waiting for me to initiate the proceedings of fun. So I did, telling them that they could each start their own page and that I would recite their finished silly "stories" aloud. It wasn't a contest although I'm sure each of them had a little competitive streak in their hearts. They both scanned the pages quickly, counting how many blanks they each had, their tongues out, their pencils gripped tightly. The only unfair advantage was that good ol' Sammie Boy was a few years older than his younger sister, so his reading and writing skills were a tad higher than Jessie's skills. But, considering they both were in elementary school, the advantage Sammie held was slim at best. Sammie had a slightly better understanding of the grammatical meanings of the words the game called for; Jessie had a little more determination to beat her brother at games in general, just like her determination to kick everybody else's ass in her taekwondo class. They were equal opponents in my eyes, for the most part.

Under each blank in the puzzle was the type of word that needed to be inserted and both kids would prompt me for a reminder of just exactly what a noun, adjective, or adverb was. Sammie said, "Daddy, what's an adverb again?"

"An adverb is a word that modifies a verb, adjective, or another adverb and usually answers questions pertaining to *how?*, *in what way?*, *when?*, and *where?*. Got it?"

"OK," he said, then quickly scribbled a word in the blank.

Jessie looked up and then said, "Daddy, what is a noun again?"

"A noun is the name of a person, place, thing, or idea. Got it?"

"OK," she said, then quickly scribbled a word in her blank space.

Both of them had handwriting that was juvenile and kind of crappy but legible, which was good. I was very proud of both of my children, able to continue doing well in school despite the hardships we all had to endure. I think--if I were in their place at their age--that I would not have dealt well with my parents getting divorced then one of my parents kicking the bucket. My kids, in contrast, seemed to be flourishing at school and in their little lives. Sometimes, a little adversity in your life, no matter how cruel or atrocious, can nourish your soul and help you blossom. It's the shit that fertilizes the flowers. It's true.

Miraculously, little Jessie finished her puzzle first, rising on her knees and slamming her pen on her puzzle book, then said boastfully, "How do you like them apples?!" She danced in place, her hips swiveling, swinging her arms around, and chanting something like a deranged, miniature cheerleader.

"Calm down. Let your brother finish. This isn't a race," I said, placing a calm hand on her shoulder. She was reluctant to dismiss her celebration.

"Yeah, it's not a race, stupid," good ol' Sammie Boy said, irritated with his little sister. He continued diligently.

"Hey! That's not nice!" Jessie said, clenching her little hands into tiny fists of fury. I could tell she wanted to deck her big brother and I knew--if she actually did--that she would clobber him pretty good. But I wasn't going to let that happen. I try to be a good parent, you know? It's true. I did my best to calm the little taekwondo master down.

"To get nice, you have to be nice," I said, hugging my daughter. "Someone important said that but I can't remember who."

"Yes, Daddy," she said, hugging me back, tightly.

Sammie finally finished his puzzle and sat up, cross-legged, handing me his puzzle book, a big smile on his face, then said, "I hope you think it's funny, Daddy."

"Of course, I will think it's funny," I said, trying to be honest. I picked up Jessie's puzzle book then held them both in front of me. "Which one should I read first?"

"Mine!" Jessie said, throwing her hands in the air, like her brother and I had no idea she was there in our midst, as if she was invisible. Sammie rolled his eyes.

"Read hers first," he said, annoyed. "She seems to want it so bad."

"Yes, mine! Read mine, Daddy!"

"OK," I said. "Just *calm down*. Chill." She sat down, struggling to contain her excitement. She was pulsating.

I read her page out loud. Here is what it said:

"The <u>hippo</u> <u>shot</u> out of a <u>cannon</u> while sipping <u>tea</u> and eating <u>cupcakes</u>. He <u>walked</u> <u>home</u> one night after <u>school</u> and ate <u>ice cream</u> for <u>dinner</u>. He <u>threw</u> his <u>homework</u> in the <u>trash</u> and <u>watched</u> <u>TV</u> until he had to go to <u>school</u> the next <u>day</u>."

Little Jessie burst into laughter when I finished, falling back on the bed pounding her stomach with her fists, and kicking her legs like she was in the throes of unwanted death. She got a real kick out of hearing me read her puzzle out loud. She was laughing all over the place. I snickered, too. I thought her attempt at non-sequitur humor was pretty cute for a first grader. Good ol' Sammie Boy was not impressed and didn't laugh at all. He sat there--his arms crossed and his face twisted into pinched disinterest--ready for me to move on. His sister's attempts at humor were just not *that* interesting or funny to him.

"Can you read mine now, Daddy?" he said, a bit of dourness in his tone. It caught me off guard a little bit: his sudden seriousness. I thought we were having fun. I thought wrong.

"Sure Sammie. But do you want to at least tell your sister she did a good job?"

"Good job," he said, as if being forced to eat pea soup and was ready to just get it over with.

"Thanks a *lot*," Jessie said, sarcastically. She seemed genuinely hurt that he didn't find hers funny. It was a little out of character for him and our bedtime ritual.

"Sammie, are you all right?" I said, placing my hand on his shoulder. His demeanor went from dour to distraught.

"I'm OK. I just don't think you're going to like mine."

"And why not? Your Mad Libs are always great, always funny. Can I read it?"

"Sure."

I looked at his page and read it out loud. Here is what it said:

"The <u>man</u> <u>stood</u> in the <u>fire</u> while <u>screaming</u> and <u>waving</u> <u>his</u> <u>arms</u>. The <u>fire</u> grew <u>bigger</u> and <u>stronger</u>. The <u>fire</u> was <u>hot</u> although the <u>fire</u> <u>ate</u> the <u>world</u>. The <u>fire</u> <u>walked</u> and <u>laughed</u> all the way home."

Little Jessie laughed but not because she thought it was funny. She laughed because she felt superior. Then she said, "That one is *so stupid*, Sammie!"

I didn't laugh either. It was too strange and creepy to laugh at and, more than anything, must have meant something. I mean, why would he repeat using the word *fire* so many times? It wasn't like his elementary vocabulary was that bad. Maybe my boy was trying to tell me something. I decided right then and there to find out.

"Jessie," I said, lifting her off the futon bed and onto the carpet. "Can you go brush your teeth?"

"But I already brushed my teeth, Daddy!" she said, stomping her feet. "*Before* the game. I want to play Mad Libs some more!"

"Go brush your teeth again, please. I need to speak to your brother. We'll play some more Mad Libs tomorrow night."

"Daddy!" she said, protesting.

"Just go brush your teeth. Please! Don't make me tell you again."

And that was all I had to say. She stomped out of the room, shaking the plaster off the ceiling in the apartment underneath us, no doubt. Good ol' Sammie Boy sat there quietly, sulking. His arms had slithered themselves around his mid-section, as if he was preemptively protecting himself from an emotional assault. I took a deep breath then said, "Sammie, are you all right?"

"No, Daddy. I'm worried."

"Worried? What are you worried about?" I said, prepared for the worst. I wasn't sure what he was going to say. The apocalypse? Fire and brimstone? What could be on fire? I picked up his Mad Libs book. "This means something, doesn't it?"

"Yes, Daddy," he said, ashamed.

"What does it mean?"

"I don't know, Daddy. When we started the game, all I saw was fire."

"And where did you see fire?"

"In my brain."

"No, son, what was on fire?" I said. He looked down at his lap. His arms gripped his mid-section tighter.

"Not what, Daddy. You mean *who*."

"Who?" I said, confused.

"Yes. You mean, *who* is on fire?"

"In your mind, you saw someone on fire?"

"Yes."

"Who was it?"

"I don't know. I just saw a person on fire. I didn't know who it was. Are you mad at me?" he said, quivering. He looked like he was about to cry.

"No. Why would you think I was mad at you?" I exhaled, involuntarily releasing a sigh.

"For telling you?"

"No, son, I'm not mad at you. But you are being a little vague."

"What do you mean vay-guh?" he said, looking up at me. His face took on a soft color, peachy in hue and tone, as if he was feeling flushed from drinking a warm beverage or sitting in a warm bath. His eyes caught something behind me. He craned his neck up a bit, his eyes peering into the distance, the color on his face becoming a little warmer and brighter. In his eyes, a splotch of orange danced and shimmered in the small pool of black of his pupils. I turned around to see what he was looking at and, through the mini-blinds of the window in his room, an orange glow seeped between the thin, metal slats of the blinds. "Does being vay-guh mean you don't believe me?"

"What the hell?" I said, lunging for the mini-blinds and pulling them open in the middle, looking through the gaping hole of bent slats to see a raging fire on the balcony of our apartment. The wooden bench was engulfed in flames with a pillar of black smoke swirling in a dense, grey knot then racing toward the sky. Sparks popped and snapped then jumped from the balcony, flying to the ground like miniature comets, their mini-comet tails streaking orange through the night air. "Oh shit!" I said, jumping off the futon and running full-speed to my bedroom on the opposite side of the apartment, where I knew I had stored a fire extinguisher--somewhere. Maybe under the bathroom sink. Maybe next to the toilet. Nope! Not anywhere handy. The frustration sent a yelp burping from my chest as I rummaged for it. Maybe it was under my bed. Maybe it was under my dresser. I furiously tore through my bedroom and bathroom before I noticed little Jessie standing in my doorway, the small, red, cylindrical fire extinguisher I was looking for, clutched in her tiny hands to her chest.

"Daddy, there's a fire on the balcony!"

"Yeah, no shit!" I said, grabbing the extinguisher from her. "Stay inside! Don't go near the door!"

"Yes, Daddy!" she said, running off to her bedroom.

I burst through the door to the balcony, the mini blinds on the door swinging wildly and clanking against the edge of the door because they were not attached at the bottom of the window. A wave of heat hit my face and chest, something I wasn't prepared for. I pulled the small hose from the clasp on the side of the extinguisher with one hand and squeezed the handle with my other hand--to no effect, instantly realizing that I really had no idea how to operate the damn thing. I had never used it before or any other fire extinguisher, for that matter. In a panic, I tried to summarize the instructions on the side of the red barrel--while reading and fumbling with the lever and other things that seemed like moving parts--when the extinguishing material exploded from the end of the small hose, getting me in the face and chest in the process, white foam spraying everywhere.

"I got it! I got it!" I said, screaming for someone--anyone--to hear. I pointed the small hose at the fire, focusing on the bench because that's what seemed to be the fuel of it. I stepped to the left and stepped to the right, making sure to cover as much of it as possible with the white, foamy discharge. It seemed to work, my awkward technique with the fire extinguisher. After ten seconds of blasting the fucking thing, the fire disappeared with a final, pathetic pop. Underneath the bench, the Café Bustelo can sat, black and charred, smoke rolling over its top edge. I thought of how I tossed my lit cigarette into that can earlier before running inside to chase my wet, naked children around the apartment. I was such an idiot for doing that. It's true.

While I stood over the smoldering remains, my downstairs neighbor walked out into the grass beneath my balcony, a Chihuahua wearing a red sweater in her arms, and a look of annoyance on her face. She was a rather heavy set woman wearing blue sweatpants and a red sweat shirt, her body the shape of a gelatinous yam, and her hair a curly, black mass that sat on her shoulders in a taut heap. I had only met her once but had forgotten her name. I was really bad with names. I've always been really bad with names. Maybe her name was Bertha or Sally or Jennifer or Guadalupe or some shit like that. The truth is, I had no idea what her name was.

Her little dog yapped as it looked up at me. I was waiting for her to yap too but all she did was ask me calmly, "Is everything all right up there?"

"Yeah," I said. "Just a small fire." I lied.

"Do I need to call the fire department?" she said.

"No, I think I got it under control. Sorry."

"Are you sure?"

"Yeah. Thanks though."

She stood there for an awkward, silent minute or two, scratching her dog's scalp, looking suspiciously at me, then walked back into her apartment without saying goodbye. I was actually glad she was gone and not making a bigger deal about this than it really was. Some people will do that, making big deals out of rather mundane events, or things that are kind of important but really, they aren't. I took care of the fire and that's what really mattered. As I stood there, clamping the small hose back to the side of the fire extinguisher (feeling sort of manly for putting out a fire by myself), I noticed two pairs of eyes watching me through the mini blinds across from the balcony--in the kids' bedroom--and remembered that these pair of eyes belonged to my kids: Sammie and Jessie. I decided to go back inside and assure them that everything was fine.

Once inside their bedroom, they both attached themselves to my waist and squeezed tightly. They were shivering and warm, the damp warmth that comes from stress and trauma.

"Daddy! Daddy!" They both cried. They were distraught and I couldn't blame them. There was a raging fire right outside their window and I'm certain it freaked them out, seeing their father dancing around the fire like a complete idiot, not knowing how to operate the fire extinguisher properly. It must have been a really scary sight from the vantage point of the bedroom window. I hugged them tightly, as tight as I could. Once they felt my embrace, they sobbed freely, without resistance, unrestrained. Sammie looked up at me, his little face covered with tears, his cheeks flushed. He struggled to breathe through his clogged nostrils, more tears welling up at the corners of his eyes.

"I told you, Daddy," he said, burying his face in my side.

"I know you did, son."

"Are you mad at me?" he said, his voice muffled in the material of my shirt.

"No, son. I'm not mad at you."

I held them in my arms for what seemed like an eternity. We eventually laid down on the futon mattress, pulling the comforter over ourselves, and fell asleep together--my little family.

❊ ❊ ❊

My Volvo S70 sped us--me and good ol' Sammie Boy--through the winding, narrow streets near Rosedale, a swanky neighborhood whose homes were mostly built around the 1930s or so and whose local businesses had risen to iconic status, which sat northwest of downtown Austin. It was a pretty cool, quirky little neighborhood with a very desirable location, making it WAY out of my price range, as a normal person with normal income. But it was where the therapist that Dr. Dimes recommended was located, her office inside a building near Jefferson Street and 38th Street. Her name was Dr. Dena Davis, LCSW, BCD, LCDC, MD--with I'm sure a long list of other indecipherable abbreviations, too many to list or give a shit about--and she called herself a psychotherapist. Psychotherapy is commonly referred to as 'talking therapy' and Dr. Davis--as she would clarify to me during her introduction--was really good at *talking*. She could talk the shit out of practically anything, from the mundane definitions of childhood mental disorders to the elaborate descriptions of what she ate for lunch on any particular day. But I'll get into that in a little bit; back to what good ol' Sammie Boy and I were doing: speeding to his appointment in the Volvo.

"We're shmooming to the shmoctor! Shmooming to the shmoctor!" he said, gripping the door armrest and leering out the window, watching the businesses and trees and signs and people at bus stops zoom by, their visages a colorful blur from the speed at which we passed them as well as the refraction of light through the door window. He loved pressing his face to the glass and distorting his view in such a way that it seemed to him that we were going much faster than the speed limit of 35mph. "Why am I going to see the shmoctor again anyway?"

"It's a different doctor."

"Oh! What's this doctor's name?"

"Dr. Davis."

"Is Dr. Davis a boy or girl?" he said, something catching his attention on the sidewalk. "The Statue of Liberty!" he said, bouncing in his seat. In the rearview mirror, I saw the reflection of someone dressed in a styrofoam Lady Liberty costume, performing the moonwalk, holding a sign that said, "BIG TAX REFUNDS!"

"I believe the doctor is a *woman* but we'll have to wait and find out. You never know sometimes," I said, trying to be sarcastic.

"That's weird," he said. He raised his knees to his chest and wrapped his arms around his legs, holding a position that looked like he was pretending to be a hard-boiled egg. I stopped at a traffic light, waiting to turn left through the intersection so we could get in the parking lot of the office building where Dr. Davis' office was. "Is that the building?"

"Yes. Almost there," I said, the light turning green. We turned left through the intersection, then turned in the parking lot. I drove slowly as I looked for a spot.

"And why am I going to see the doctor *again*?"

After I found a spot, I parked, turned off the engine, then turned to my boy and said, "Well, I want to find out just how special you are. Does that make sense?"

"Special? You mean like Dr. Strange or Spider-Man or something like that?!" he said, excited.

"Well, no. I don't know. It's really hard to say. I don't know what to make of this ability of yours to... see things before they happen. Do you understand?"

"Are you mad at me?" he said, sensing my uneasiness with the topic and conversation. Kids are very perceptive, more than most people give them credit for. It's true.

"No, son. I'm not mad at you. Not at all. But if you're special then I'd like to know. That's all."

"That's all?" he said, releasing his legs from the hard-boiled egg position, ready to dart. In the side pocket to his door was his trusty sketchbook, which he quickly pulled from the pocket and pressed to his chest.

"Yes. Ready to meet the new doctor?"

"Yes!" he said, unbuckling his seatbelt, opening the door, and bolting from the car. He cradled the sketchbook under his right arm like a football player, holding it tightly. I quickly followed. Kids are crazy and nobody seems to watch where they're going when they're driving. As a parent, you have to watch out when your kids are acting crazy. They could get smooshed.

He bolted across the parking lot, not looking where he was going, at a speed that was way too fast for my old bones. But I could at least see him and that's all that mattered. He climbed into a landscaped area to the right of the entrance to the building, lifting his arm as if he was going to karate chop the shrubbery, and he made his way in the foliage like an explorer trudging through the Amazon jungle. The bushes shimmied as he shoved his way through them, some leaves and twigs falling here and there.

"Sammie!" I said, worried, rushing over to see what he was doing. I didn't want him destroying anything, which any kid can do when you stop watching what they are doing. Kids can be a real pain in the ass if you stop watching them. They are bound to get into all kinds of mischief if you don't. It's true.

"Yeah Daddy!" he said, calling from below the sea of leaves that spread out across the front of the building, supplying some color and ground cover--no doubt--cheaply and effectively. It looked lovely until my boy rummaged through it like a deranged wolverine. "I think I found something!"

"What?!" I said, worried. Hopefully, he didn't find a dead animal or something like that. Now *that* would have ruined my day. "What do you mean you found something? Just come on out. We have an appointment to go to."

"But I found some treasure!" he said. Loose leaves flew above the shrubbery as he excavated his 'treasure.' I worried that he had found a cover to some wires or pipes or nozzles for the irrigation system or something of the like that would spark the imagination of a young boy who--of course--would want to open something like that and gaze inside, hoping to find treasure or frogs or toys or rocks. "It's in the dirt. It's silver! I almost got it!"

"Please come out, Sammie. We have to get inside for your appointment."

"OK, Daddy. I'm coming. I got it! I GOT IT!" My little, deranged wolverine hacked his way out of the shrub jungle, leaving a few broken limbs behind, unfortunate casualties of his excavation. When he emerged from the bushes, his face red from holding his breath while tearing through the shrubbery, he extended his little hand to me, opening it to reveal a silvery-looking hunk of metal. "Look! I found treasure!"

"Give it to me," I said, examining it. I wiped the dirt from it, some of which was a crusty mud layer that had been there for some time. I immediately knew what it was. Good ol' Sammie Boy had discovered some treasure all right: an old Zippo lighter. "Amazing."

"Can I keep it, Daddy?!" he said, his hands on his hips, his sketchbook shoved into the waistband at the front of his pants. I love how kids just shove things into the waistband of their pants like that was the most practical thing to do. Can you imagine a grown man holding a thermos of coffee at work then shoving it in his waistband when a coworker approached him to say hi and shake his hand? That's a funny thought, isn't it? I knew you'd think it was.

"No," I said, wiping the last of the loose dirt from the old Zippo. Engraved on the front, in big, bold, serif letters was: FULL FLAVOR. Directly above the engraving was a caricature of a flame, almost cartoony in appearance, floating above the obvious advertising slogan like a punctuation mark. The tiny dents, scratches, and patina of the metal told me that the Zippo was quite old--if not ancient--and had been in the dirt for quite some time. I flipped the top open and a tiny cloud of dirt and dust billowed out, some of which good ol' Sammie Boy involuntarily inhaled. I immediately apologized. "Sorry son! Didn't mean to do that." He coughed and wiped the dust from his lips and nostrils.

"Why can't I keep it?" he said, grabbing me by the belt, pulling at my midsection as if he was trying to get me to his height (which was way down there). "It's *my* treasure."

"It's not treasure. It's a lighter, for starting fires."

"Cool!" he said, more excited about his find now, knowing that it was a tool of potential destruction. I slipped the beat-up Zippo in my pocket and placed a gentle but firm hand on his back.

"We have an appointment to go to. Let's go!" I said, leading him inside the building to find an elevator to the second floor. We immediately found one and went up.

On the next floor, Sammie bolted out of the door and immediately ran to the left at full speed, his sketchbook under his arm again. But when I realized from a sign on the wall that he was going the wrong way, I called out to him to come back. "That way," I said, pointing in the other direction. "To suite 218."

"OK, Daddy!" he said, bolting the correct way. He found the door and went in. I soon followed.

Inside, we were greeted by a doorbell and a sparse waiting room-- one couch, a coffee table with some magazines on it, and a fake, plastic tree that looked like a miniature palm tree, bare white walls, a French door with curtains on it--and a window for a receptionist who wasn't to be found. But before I could sit down on the couch, a woman opened the French doors and greeted us.

"You must be Sammie," she said, extending her hand to my son. "You're a fine looking young man."

"Thanks!" said Sammie, all smiles and blushes. He ate that shit right up. Most kids his age do. It's true.

Then she turned to me, extending her hand, and said, "You must be Sammie's father, Simon."

"Yes. Yes, I am. Nice to meet you, Dr. Davis," I said. I shook her hand which was delicate and brittle, like a bunch of tree twigs that had dried through the autumn and were bundled at her wrist. Her skin was very white, almost translucent, and the road map of blue-green veins and capillaries went up her sinewy arm in a pulsing zig-zag of intersections and freeways and toll ways. Her hair was pitch black, as dark and black as the night sky in rural Montana. She was at least 60 but may have been older but I really couldn't tell, to be honest. My mother told me to never ask a woman her age and that advice has stayed with me through thick and thin. I wasn't about to ask Dr. Davis how old she was. That would have been plain rude, according to my mother. It's true. "I hope we aren't late."

"Not at all. Let me take Sammie back to my office to get him comfortable. I'll come back shortly with some paperwork for you to fill out."

"OK," I said. "Sammie, give me your sketchbook."

He handed it to me then she put her arm around my boy and led him to her office down the hall. "We're going to become fast friends--you and me," she said to him.

"OK!" he said, excited.

I sat on the couch, adjusting myself to get comfortable. I could hear them from her office as Sammie ran around, touching this and that, no doubt, asking what this thing was and what that thing was. I wasn't too worried about him and his behavior. Dr. Davis came highly recommended by Dr. Dimes so I had hope that she at least knew what she was doing. But for some reason, I was certain that she never dealt with a kid like good ol' Sammie Boy. He was special. I knew it.

After a minute or two, Dr. Davis came back in the waiting room with a clipboard full of papers and a pen for me. As she sat next to me, my nose was assaulted by her fragrance--a combination of patchouli, some kind of pungent, flowery soap, and a musty earthiness I can only describe as the smell of mold after a hard rain when the hot Texas sun comes out. Her scent was so hard to ignore that I pinched my nose in a nonchalant manner, as if pretending to hold in a sneeze, and tried not to reveal my true motivation for protecting my nostrils.

"Can you fill these out for me?" she said, handing me the clipboard. Holding the clipboard made it difficult to pinch my nose so I suffered in silence. "I understand you have medical insurance, correct?"

"Yes."

"Good. The co-pay will be $50, due at the end of every appointment."

"OK."

"And let me get this straight. When you called... And you were referred by my dear friend, Dr. Dimes?" she said, placing her bony hand on my leg, touching it ever so gently with her twig fingers. I inhaled in short breaths to control the amount of her scent entering my nose. It didn't help so I allowed her scent to molest my nose hairs. Those poor hairs shriveled.

"Yes. She is Sammie's pediatrician."

"Great! Good woman, great doctor. So--" she said, withdrawing her hand then placing it on her forehead. Her head tilted back as if she was searching the deep recesses of her mind for our previous phone conversation. "You mentioned that you believe--and I'm quoting you here--you believe that your son, Sammie, 'can see things before they happen.' What do you mean by that?"

"Well," I said, hesitating. It did sound crazy when she asked in that way--why I called her and all. But I didn't know what else to do or who to talk to about my boy's special ability. I believed deep down in my soul that good ol' Sammie Boy could see the future but I didn't want to come off as sounding *crazy*, especially since I was talking to a psychotherapist. I tried to tread lightly. "I know it sounds crazy."

"Crazy? My business is *crazy*, you see?" she said, chuckling. "Do I think you're crazy? No, I don't. Do I think your son could have the ability to see things before they happen? Who am I to say at this point? It remains to be *seen*," she said, patting the paperwork on the clipboard on my lap. "Can you fill these out for me?"

"Sure," I said, sighing.

"And one other thing: To instill trust in your son, I will tell him that whatever he and I talk about will only be between him and me. I will let him know that I will not be talking to *you* about what he and I talk about during our sessions. Make sense to you?"

"Yes," I said. "Makes perfect sense to me."

"But," she said, standing up from the couch, straightening her posture by pushing back and forth on her hips. "I will call you at a later date to tell you *everything* Sammie and I discuss. You do need to be kept in the loop. Just don't tell Sammie that. OK?"

"You got it."

"Make yourself comfortable. Our session will take about 55 minutes." She walked down the hall to her office and closed the door, leaving me to myself--all alone--in the waiting room.

While I filled out the paperwork, I thought of my junior high friends, Jason and Stanford, who I was friends with when my family lived in Montgomery, Alabama while my father was stationed at Gunter Air Force Base. Jason was pudgy and goofy and all kinds of hyper, like a lot of white kids who drank too much soda and ate too much junk food. He was the one I used to play Mad Libs with, when we were kids. Stanford was a black kid who was skinny and gawky and wore huge coke-bottle glasses that made him look like Urkel before Urkel even existed on TV. He was the one I was telling you about that I believe stole my copy of copy of *The Amazing Spider-Man* #6 in fair condition when we were kids. Anyway, Jason, Stanford, and I were great pals and we would ride our BMX bikes in the wooded area behind the junior high and, this one time, the three of us camped out back there and Jason told us about how his parents forced him to see a therapist because he was having problems in school, bad grades and tardies and having a potty mouth and all. He really hated going to his therapist. He told us it was humiliating and boring and he never really understood *why* he had to see the therapist. He said he enjoyed talking to his friends more than talking to the therapist because he felt like we were *really* listening to him, not pretending to listen to him. I wondered if Sammie would feel the same way as Jason did. I wondered if he would clam up and not say anything at all to her. Good ol' Sammie Boy was really good at doing that sometimes: clamming up. Maybe his new nickname should be Clammie. That's just too good. It's true.

Anyway, the next thing I knew, I could hear the door open to Dr. Davis' office. She and Sammie were conversing and laughing. It sounded like--to me--that the appointment went well.

"You can keep that comic book, if you'd like," she said.

"Really? Can I?!" he said, excited.

"Sure. It belonged to my son but that was many, many years ago. It's all yours now."

"Gee, thanks! DADDY! DADDY!" he said, running up the hall toward the waiting room. He burst through the French doors, a comic book rolled up in one of his hands, the doors slamming against the wall. "Look what Dr. Davis gave me!"

He jumped on the couch next to me and unraveled the comic book, a withered, yellowed copy of the Silver Age semi-classic: The Defenders. It was issue #25 with a cover price of 25 cents.

"I don't know, son," I said, knowing that there may be some collector's value to the early 1970s comic book. I looked at Dr. Davis and said, "Are you sure? I'd hate for Sammie to take something of value from you."

"Of value?" she said, then a deep bellow blurting from her reedy throat. "My son left behind piles and piles of comics and books and board games and trading cards when he moved away to college. That was ages ago. I let my clients have as many as they want and can carry home with them. You'd be doing me a favor."

"Look, Daddy!" Sammie said, pointing at the wrinkled cover. "Dr. Strange is in this one!" Sure enough, Dr. Strange was flying on the cover, blasting some baddies with a red and yellow energy blast from his hand while the Incredible Hulk and Luke Cage pounded some other dumbass baddies with their boulder-sized fists. It was a striking cover, really. I'm certain it caught Sammie's eye, mostly because Dr. Strange was on it but it was a nice fight scene nonetheless. It had that classic Marvel look.

"I see that, son. Did you tell Dr. Davis 'thank you'?" I said, placing a hand on his shoulder.

"Thank you, Dr. Davis!" he said, beaming at her.

"You're welcome, Sammie," she said, patting him on the back. Then she looked at me and said, "Same time next week?"

"Yes, same time," I said, handing her the check for the co-pay.

"Great! I'll talk to you then," she said, then flashing me a not-so-subtle wink. I'm surprised Sammie didn't notice, the way she winked at me and all. As if in slow motion, her wink was as obvious as siren lights on top of a police cruiser in a traffic jam. Fortunately, he didn't notice. He was too enthralled with the cover to his issue of The Defenders #25. She lifted her hand, shaped like a phone receiver from the 1980s, to her face.

"OK, talk then," I said, pushing Sammie toward the door to leave the waiting room, handing him his sketchbook.

"I didn't know Dr. Strange was in a *super group*!" he said, holding the comic book up to my face as we left the waiting room. All the way down the hall, he continued to flash the comic book to me as if I was ignoring him on purpose. Partially, I was.

"Yes, son."

"Can you believe it?!"

"Yes, I read them all when I was your age," I said, pushing the down button for the elevator when we came to it.

"Is there more you can show me?"

"Of course. I would love to," I said as the elevator dinged and the door slid open. We stepped inside.

"Do you have them at home?"

"We can check tonight after dinner. Sound good?"

"Yeah!" he said as the door slid shut.

The elevator took us to the ground floor and we walked back to the Volvo S70 together, hand in hand.

HERE LIES

CHAPTER SIX

BORN SEPTEMBER 1
DIED AUGUST 31

Chapter Six

The fuzzy grass covering the cemetery grounds was lush and green and fluffy and soft, ebbing in waves as the wind gently pushed the blades back and forth in a spring time dance. Good ol' Sammie Boy stood on the curb in front of our parking space, glaring at me, his legs taut with excitement. He was ready to run and was growing impatient, waiting for me and his little sister to get out of the car and accompany him across the great lawn and down the path to where his mother's grave lay. It was a nice day for a visit. The sun shone brightly high up in the pale, blue sky; the only clouds present were wisps of cottony white, like down feathers slowly drifting towards outer space.

"Can we go now?!" he said, performing a jig somewhere between a pee-pee dance and the nervous prance before a competitive 50-meter sprint. He could barely contain himself, the poor kid. He was *that* excited. "What's taking so long?!"

"Hold your horses!" Jessie said, releasing her seat belt in the backseat of my Volvo and looking for her sunglasses in the pocket behind the driver seat in front of her. She had these kid-sized sunglasses that were styled like Oakley Sunglasses (the kind you would wear in the outdoors doing outdoorsy things like skiing or hiking or shooting unsuspecting animals) that wrapped around her head with a bright red frame and polarized lenses that refracted the sunlight in rainbow streaks and flares. She loved them like nothing else she owned except maybe for her taekwondo dobok (that's her uniform, if you didn't know). She wore her dobok and her sunglasses whenever she could but she wasn't wearing her dobok that day. The thing was stinky and dirty and balled up in a wad under her bed. Her sunglasses were usually stuffed in the pocket behind my seat but they weren't there, for some reason. She wasn't going to spend a significant amount of time in the sun without them so she was determined to find them whether her brother was anxious or not. Kids can be real assholes to each other when they don't want to be rushed. It's true. "I'm not going down there without my shades!"

"Since when do you call your sunglasses *shades*?" I said, curious.

"Since last week, Daddy. You know? Forever ago!"

"I see."

"Where are they?!" she said, getting down on the floor board and twisting her body into the tiny space so she could look under the driver seat. She looked like a turtle balled up there on the floor board, most of her arms and legs tucked under her body. Then she sprung up, her arms stretched above her head with her kid-Oakley, bright red sunglasses in her hand, and said, "I found them!"

"Great! Let's go!" Sammie said, tapping his foot incessantly on the curb.

"Wait! I need the flowers, too!" She gathered up the bouquet from the backseat, clutching the bunch of roses, astrids, and baby's breath flowers tightly in her little arms. I helped her out of the car and closed things up while my two kids shoved each other a bit before sprinting across the great, green, fuzzy lawn of the cemetery that separated the funeral home and parking lot from the cemetery itself. They were really looking forward to visiting their mother's grave. Me--not so much. Things had already been hard enough for me but they really wanted to visit her grave so I agreed. Besides, it was a really nice day to be outside, even if we were spending time at a cemetery, although, spending time in a cemetery was depressing as hell. Any time in a cemetery is depressing as hell. Am I right? Of course, I am.

I sped up my pace to catch up with my two little heathens, who didn't seem too concerned with the sanctity and solemnity of the cemetery. They treated the tombstones like pylons on an obstacle course, running around and through them, chasing each other with outstretched arms, attempting to grab each other by the necks of their t-shirts. When I caught up to them--both entrenched in the competitive throws of attempting to best the other at their game of 'catch the monkey'--I stopped them in their tracks. Holding them at arms' length, my intervention snapped them out of their craziness.

"You guys need to show a little more respect," I said, giving them 'the look.' You know? The *LOOK*. That's the look a parent gives their children to let them know that something serious will happen if they don't calm-the-heck-down. That something serious is never said, just implied by a hard squint of the eyes and a pinched grimace, the jaw clinching so tightly that their punishment is never revealed, leaving their over-active brains to assume the worst--the worst in their minds anyway. "This isn't the schoolyard, you know?"

"Of course it isn't, Daddy," good ol' Sammie Boy said. "Our teachers wouldn't let us play in a sim-uh-terry. That would be weird!"

"Then why don't you two *chill*?"

"OK," said Jessie, reaching for my hand as a sign of reconciliation, roughly clutching the flowers with her other arm.

"If you want to play games, then let's read the gravestones as we walk. These people here were once mothers and fathers and sisters and brothers and grandmothers and grandfathers. They were people that were loved when they were alive. We should respect them."

"How about cousins?" Sammie said, looking up at me, really perplexed. "Were any of these people *cousins*?"

"I'm sure some were," I said.

"How about uncles?" Jessie said, chiming in. "Or aunts?"

"Yes, we could rattle off all the kinds of relatives they could be. I'm certain they were all of them--once. Here," I said, pointing at the nearest gravestone. "What does this one say?" I gently pushed Sammie Boy toward the gravestone.

The stone said:

> SACRED
> TO THE MEMORY OF
> JOHN GRIFFIN
> BORN MAY 1, 1827
> DIED AUGUST 13, 1868
> LOVING SON AND BROTHER
> NOW IN THE ARMS OF
> THE LORD

Good ol' Sammie Boy bent over at his waist, getting a better look at the bold lettering carved into the stone, then said "Say-krid to the mim-ree of John Grift-in, born May one, one eight two seven. Then died August thirteen, one eight six eight. Luv-ing sun and bruh-therr. Now in the arms of the Lord! Is the Lord, Jesus, Daddy?"

"Yes, son."

"Why is Jesus a Lord, Daddy?"

"Good question. That's just what people call him."

"Can we read some more graves?"

"Sure."

Sammie and Jessie held my hands as we continued on. They read the names off each tombstone. The simpler names--like Brown or Smith or Jones--they would pronounce with glee, unperturbed by complex syllabic combinations of foreign origins. But when they came across more bizarre or complex names, they would stop in their tracks and slaughter the pronunciation of the names. What did you expect elementary school kids to do with Polish or Spanish names? I mean, some of these names were even hard for me to pronounce, what, with names like Jodorowsky and Feigenbaum and Tousignant and Mazariegos and they would stand there, dumbfounded or stumped, attempting to pronounce the names, scratching their scalps and spitting all over the place with a slobbery stutter. It was cute and irritating at the same time. And forget the occasional Chinese or Japanese name we came across, the inscription etched in the Asian alphabet of the deceased's ethnicity. They would see those foreign letters and just scream with delight.

"This one is in Chinese!" Sammie blurted out, not knowing if the letters were really Chinese or Japanese or Korean. They looked Chinese to me but what did I know? I didn't know shit about Chinese. It's true. Jessie then said, "Whoa! A Chinese one!" Then we would move on, losing interest pretty quick.

Their mother's grave was at the back of the cemetery with the rest of the newer graves. As we walked toward the back, the dates of the deceased moved toward our present time and the surrounding trees became smaller and more twig-like. The trees at the front of the cemetery were massive oak and pecan trees, having grown through the generations to their current, majestic heights. But in the back, closer to where their mother was buried, new trees were planted as new graves were plotted so all the trees were about the height of broomsticks, and not much bigger around than that, too. They were kind of sad in their young state, all held upright by strings to stakes in the ground, the wind whipping their frail trunks around. It seemed they almost were being pulled out of the ground by the gusty, springtime breeze. And none of us--not me, not Sammie, not Jessie-- would live to see them grow into tall, majestic trees. Maybe my kids would be lucky enough to live long enough to see these trees grow, if they stayed in Austin. But who knows if that'll happen? I don't, that's for sure. Nor did I care. No one really knows what will happen in the future. Well, except maybe for Sammie.

"Daddy, are we close yet?" Sammie said.

"We're getting close," I said.

"Good, 'cause I'm getting tired," Jessie said. "This stuff is heavy!" She clutched the bouquet of flowers tightly yet awkwardly, being that the bundle of flowers was just slightly too big for her little arms to comfortably hold, and the fact that she didn't want the petals or pollen of the flowers getting in her face. But she was strong and did her best not to drop them on the ground although the tissue and plastic wrap around the stems of the flowers was becoming a little mangled.

"Want me to hold the flowers?" I said, extending a hand to her.

"Yes!" she said, unceremoniously tossing them to me. The flowers sagged as I examined them, some of the stems broken at right-angles, which made them more perfect for the occasion. After releasing the flowers, my two kids ran a sprint the last of the way, good ol' Sammie Boy in front with his sister very close behind, clutching for the back of his t-shirt. When they reached their mother's gravestone, good ol' Sammie Boy touched it first. Even in a cemetery, both of my kids were competitive as hell.

"I win!" Sammie said, proudly. He danced a little jig to celebrate.

"You pushed me," Jessie said, crossing her arms, pissed off. "You're a cheater!"

"Am not!"

"Are to!"

"Daddy, did you see me cheat?" Sammie said, crossing his arms defiantly.

"I don't know. Why don't you two have a seat?" They both dropped to the grass; a disappointed harrumph slipped out of Sammie's mouth. Both upset with the outcome of their sprint, they sat--cross-legged and cross-armed / criss-cross, apple sauce--staring at their mother's gravestone. "You should say a prayer for your mother," I said.

They both tilted their heads forward and pressed their palms together, reciting something under their breath that I imagined was a prayer or something like that, although I couldn't tell for sure. It's hard to say what little kids say to themselves while they are praying or pretending to pray. But, being that they were children, sitting still too long without moving or fidgeting was practically impossible. I knew at least one of them would stop praying and say something. And good ol' Sammie Boy did. He looked at me and said, "Daddy, do you think Mommy is in *heaven*?"

"That's a good question, son. But I don't know, really."

"But Grandma Moma says all mothers go to heaven."

"Yes, your Grandma Moma says *a lot* of things. But, I don't know. Saying ALL mothers go to heaven is quite the blanket statement. Don't you think?"

"I think Mommy *is* in heaven," Jessie said, her head still tilted forward and her palms still together. "She was the best mommy in the whole world!"

"That's great, sweetie," I said, shifting the weight on my feet, crossing my arms, and looking down the row of gravestones. About ten down was an old man--his bald head underneath a poker visor and his thin arms poking out of a brightly colored Hawaiian shirt--sitting in a folding lawn chair and drinking a glass of iced tea. He stared lovingly at the gravestone in front of him.

"Daddy?" Jessie said, looking up at me, quite perturbed. "Aren't *you* going to pray for Mommy, too?"

"Well..." I said, looking back at her. I didn't have the heart to tell her the truth, the truth being that I would have loved to have been anywhere else at that moment than standing in front of their cheating mother's grave, a woman who broke my heart so severely that I didn't want to pray for her. I wanted to piss on her grave, to tell you the truth. But you don't tell grieving children something like *that*. That would be a pretty selfish thing for me to do. Who would do that? A stone-cold bastard, that's who. But I wasn't a stone-cold bastard. I was a good daddy--at least I tried my best to be a good daddy--and a good enough one to know to keep my mouth shut about their cheating, nut-bag mother. It's true. "I already said my prayer for your mother."

"Then sit with us and say another," she said, patting the fuzzy grass next to her. How could I refuse that? I couldn't refuse that, I tell you.

"OK." I sat in the grass between my children in front of their cheating, lying, crazy mother's gravestone. I glanced over at the old man who was still smiling and sipping iced tea. He looked like he was happy to be sitting in a cemetery, staring at a grave of a loved one. I wished I was sitting in a cemetery, staring at the grave of a loved one. But I wasn't.

"Let's hold hands," she said and we all did. "Sammie, you want to say the prayer this time?"

"OK," he said, tilting his head forward, closing his eyes. I watched him recite his little prayer. "Dear God, please watch out for my Mommy's soul. She was a great mommy and I miss her every day. Let her know we love her and miss her, too. Amen."

"Amen!" little Jessie said. But noticing I didn't say *amen*, she turned to me and said in a stern tone, "Say amen too, Daddy!"

What my kids didn't know was that I didn't want to say amen. I didn't want to remember her in the way that they remembered her. She wasn't a great mommy--to me. She wasn't a great wife, either. She was a cheating, lying, no-good person to me and I regretted every moment with her. Well, I didn't regret that I had children with her because I loved my children. But children are just little miracles so I guess I was grateful to their mother for giving birth to them. That, really, was about it.

"Daddy?" she said, looking at me, concerned. I didn't know what to say at that moment. My head was filled with the circumstances surrounding her mother's death, how she had started dating a car salesman while we were still married, and continued to see him when we separated. I thought of the difficult divorce we went through and the hard feelings I experienced because of the betrayal I felt. But mostly, I thought about the circumstances surrounding her death and how the police called to tell me--a few months after our divorce was finalized--that Sammie and Jessie's mother died in a fiery car crash after a night of heavy drinking with her car salesman boyfriend. They had gone downtown and bar-hopped from one bar to the next, drinking shots of tequila and glasses of wine, downing them with reckless abandon. Supposedly, her boyfriend became enraged when another man hit on my ex-wife, behavior she didn't discourage from the unsuspecting suitor. The two men brawled--punching and kicking and elbowing each other--until the bouncers at the bar threw them all out in the street. The two men quickly truced when a crowd grew around them and my ex-wife and the car salesman reluctantly walked back to his car together, arguing the entire way. The last thing anyone knew was that they drove home but on the way, her boyfriend lost control of the car and it plunged off an overpass and crashed into an embankment, the car exploding and the two dying in the fire, both still buckled in their seats. The police said that their investigation led them to believe that they were so intoxicated that they probably weren't conscious; they probably blacked out and weren't even aware that they were in a crash. What a sad way to die, I tell you. It was a very sad, pathetic way to die. It's true. "Daddy, aren't you going to say *amen*?"

"Do you really want me to say *amen*?" I said.

"Yes," she said.

"OK, then. Amen." I hugged my two children, the two I loved most in the entire world and they put their little arms around my back. They squeezed me tight and I returned their embrace, pulling their shoulders under my arms into my sides. They were the sweetest children in the whole world. They deserved much better than the truth about their mother. They deserved peace. So I didn't say anything about what I was thinking. I just hugged them and loved them. "Who wants ice cream?"

"Me!" they both said, jumping to their feet.

"Last one to the car is a rotten egg!" said good ol' Sammie Boy and, before I knew it, they were off in a full-sprint, down the row of gravestones and passed the old man sitting in the lawn chair, sipping iced tea. He waved at them when they ran by but they didn't notice being too busy trying *not* to be rotten eggs. I began to follow them but noticed I was still holding the mangled bouquet of flowers for their mother. I looked at the flowers then looked at the gravestone. I quickly tossed them on the ground. There wasn't any point in putting them in a plastic vase like the rest of the flowers in front of the other gravestones. Someone was just going to pick them up and toss them in the trash soon, so tossing them on the ground was the quickest way to deal with them. I didn't want to spend any more time there anyway. I was ready to go. Really.

I walked towards the old man and as I got closer, he looked up at me and smiled. In addition to the snazzy poker visor he was wearing on his bald head, he had on a brightly colored Hawaiian shirt, tan slacks, and Birkenstock sandals that were so worn out and old that they looked like they were actually from the 1960s. His build--thin and wiry and bony--propped up the gaudy shirt like a wire hanger suspended in mid-air. He had a pleasant smile, one that was refreshing to see in such a dismal place, and even more refreshing since he still had all of his teeth--yellow and grimy and dingy as could be. He looked like he was having a grand old time, sitting in a crappy lawn chair and sipping iced tea in the back of the cemetery. No one was going to bother him back there, that's for sure. No one in their right mind anyway. It's true.

"Good day to you," he said, nodding at me, lifting his glass of iced tea as if to toast.

"And good day to you," I said, trying to get by him quickly before he could say another word but I wasn't walking fast enough. He was about to trap me with his Southern charm.

"Are those your children there?" he said, lifting his other hand, indicating the direction in which they ran. And like a tractor beam engulfing an orbiting space ship, his charm roped me in; I couldn't escape. I looked off in the distance and watched them run as fast as they could toward the car. They were hauling ass.

"Yes, those are my kids."

"Brought them to see a loved one, I see? Their mother, no doubt," he said, then sipping his iced tea with a loud slurp, punctuating his sentence forcefully. He was an interesting looking character with his thin, bony, hairy arms and big, honking, hook nose and the hazy, brown irises of his eyes swimming in the yellowy area of his sclera, that in most people would be white.

"Yes, that's their mother over there..."

"You must miss her dearly," he said, slurping some more iced tea. "I miss my wife. I miss her so much that I come to visit her every day. It's not so bad sitting here in the cemetery. It's pretty nice most days. Nice and quiet."

"Yes," I said, looking anxiously toward where my kids were. They had disappeared while the old man was talking to me. I didn't see them anywhere. "It does seem rather quiet, now that you mention it. I have to get..."

"You know, when a loved one leaves your life, they can leave a large crater after their passing, like a huge meteor has crashed into your world. Doesn't that seem so?" he said, looking at me with his hazy, yellowy eyes. He seemed like a kind old man, one that I might normally talk to if I wasn't so distracted. I was starting to worry about my kids and where they ran off to. I was hoping they would be waiting for me at the car. That's what most normal kids would do, right? I knew they didn't have the keys to the car so they couldn't cause much trouble. "I really do miss my wife. She was my best friend. Was your wife your best friend too?"

"Their mother was my *ex-wife*."

"I see. Well, then you two must have worked things out in the best interest of your children, I would hope. That's the right thing to do."

"Of course," I said. I lied. That really wasn't what happened. Nothing was worked out between me and their mother, in the best interest of our kids or otherwise. It was all a big pile of shit. The only thing I could say was that I was going to be the best dad I could be. The rest of it went down the toilet. I really hate when people say that, that divorced people should work things out and do things in the best interest of their children. I mean, if people were grown-ups and acted like grown-ups then it would seem that *that* would be something that they could do. But most grown-ups don't act like grown-ups and most people that get divorced act like assholes to each other. They get divorced for a reason and it's not because they want to be friends and be nice to each other and do things in the best interest of their kids. It's because one of them took a big shit on the other one in the form of adultery or lying or mishandling of money or they killed someone or they punched their spouse or they punched their kids or they did any number of diabolical things while being unhappily married to their unsuspecting wife or husband. People don't get divorced because they're friends; people get divorced because they are *not good* for each other. And the truth is, even if I wanted to be friends with Sammie and Jessie's mother, I couldn't be. She was dead. And that was the end of that. It's true. "We did our best, I guess."

"That's good to hear," he said, slurping some more tea and adjusting his poker visor a few degrees to keep the ever-shifting sun out of his eyes.

Just then, way off in the distance, I saw good ol' Sammie Boy running back towards me with his little sister right behind him. He was flailing his arms all over the place, so much so that he looked like a little bird trying to take flight for the first time. He was yelling something but I couldn't make out what he was saying.

"I have to go," I said to the old man. "It was nice meeting you."

"It was nice meeting you too, young man. Hope to see you again," he said.

"We'll see. Might happen."

I started walking in their direction and Sammie's arms flailed and flapped more and more intensely as he ran. The closer he got the more I could see that his face was as red as can be. Something seemed to be wrong so I picked up my pace, turning my hurried walk into a jog. Soon, he reached me but was in such a panic that he bent at the waist and propped himself up against his knees. He was wheezing and panting all over the place. I thought he was going to pass right out.

"Daddy! Daddy!" he said between gulps of air and heavy panting.

"Are you OK? What's wrong?"

"Daddy! Daddy! That man."

"Yes? What about him?"

"That man. He's..."

And just then, a heavy weight pushed down on me like a hot mass of air from above. I knew something was wrong and had a bad feeling about it. It was happening again.

"He's dead."

I turned around to find the old man face-down in the grass, his body sprawled out in front of his wife's grave. I quickly made my way back toward him and when I reached him, I looked down at his frail body--his hands gripping some grass, his arms spread out in such a way that it appeared that he was hugging the earth above his wife's grave. The glass of tea laid in the fuzzy grass, all of its contents spilled out in a small heap. I looked back at my boy, his face bright red and sweaty. He looked like he was about to cry.

"Please don't be mad at me," he said, whimpering.

"I'm not mad at you," I said, putting my arms around him. Jessie ran over and tried to put her little arms around the two of us. We all stood there together--embracing each other--next to the old man lying in the grass. He was on his way to be with his best friend. "I'm not mad at you one bit."

SAMMIE & BUDGIE

✳ ✳ ✳

I sat at the desk in my cubicle at the Texas Commission of Employment and Benefits--staring off into space, my mind far and away from the work at hand, sorting through possible explanations of why and how my son, good ol' Sammie Boy, could see into the future. Just how could he do such a *phenomenal* thing? I racked my brain but I really had no idea. So, rather than work on the long queue of service requests for network access, email issues, and server hard drive space waiting for my attention, I decided to, instead, fuck off from work and sort this thing out, this ability of his, this power that literally was like that of a super hero. I mean, he had been predicting things left and right, things that would happen moments later, events that he could only be receiving from the ether somewhere. Who does that? A super hero, that's who. My boy could one day be a part of a ragtag group of super mutants or vigilantes or crime fighters or whatever. Don't believe me? After what's happened so far, you should. It's true.

On my desk surrounding my computer monitor was an army of miniature monuments made or purchased in my honor by both of my children--little clay sculptures, totems constructed of colorful beads and Elmer's glue, Father's Day pens and medals, origami animals of twisted construction paper, and an artificial rose with maroon, felt petals and Kelly green, plastic stem and leaves, a little dusty from living on my desk for so long. The vision of my mind's eye blurred, returning focus to my actual eyeballs, and I surveyed this army of knick-knacks given to me by my kiddos, particularly a green, coiled snake made of clay, sitting on a pallet of purple--maybe it was an island or a lily pad or an oblong pancake. It was hard to tell. The snake had one red eye, placed carefully and with precision by good ol' Sammie Boy on the right side of the snake's head, and it seemed to stare at me. It was a beautiful reminder of how much my kids loved me, that they put that much work and effort into things that many parents immediately tossed in the trash the minute after their own children gave it to them. I had so many of these lovely items and I had been collecting them for so long, they all had a layer of dust over them like kudzu vine covering a barn in the Georgia countryside. Some even had cob webs, homes to miniature spiders and their brood. I picked up the clay snake and dusted it off, then blowing the remaining dust from its underside onto the carpeted floor of my cubicle. 'What a lovely gift,' I thought. It *really* was lovely. 'Where do these visions of Sammie's come from? His subconscious?' I thought some more as I examined the clay snake.

I set the snake back on my desk and decided to look it up on Google. Who doesn't look things like this up on Google? A damn fool, that's who. I typed this in the search box: *is seeing the future possible*? And what did you know? A long list of links to dubious websites and questionable articles written by--who?--a bunch of whackos appeared on my screen, their blue and green links hovering above the article descriptions like doodled paths by a demented seaman on a pirate treasure map, most likely taking me to the same place as the disillusioned pirate diagram: absolutely nowhere. I scanned over the article descriptions and saw they were written by self-proclaimed precognition gurus, parapsychologist experts, and real professional psychics, all of which I was certain were absolutely full of shit.

Terms like precognition or parapsychology seemed based in science being that they were fancy, scientific sounding words and all, but really they were fancy words for things that scientists thought were bogus but nut bags, whackos, and psychos thought were real phenomena. I mean, precognition is an *alleged* psychic ability to see events in the future but it goes against almost every proven scientific fact, things like antecedence, or the notion that an effect does not happen before the cause and shit like that. Even Aristotle parsed the idea of precognition in dreams and came to the conclusion, after mulling it over for hundreds of pages, that precognition was nothing but a mere coincidence. How about that? If Aristotle thought it bunk, then it must be bunk. Right?

But I couldn't get it out of my head that no matter what I read about precognition and no matter how I analyzed it in my own head--rationalized it, scrutinized it, examined it, considered it, questioned it--the things I experienced with good ol' Sammie Boy were *real.* Maybe once or twice could be declared a coincidence but then he continued to do it. The afterschool counselor, dozens of coin tosses, the lottery scratch ticket, the fire on the balcony, the old man kicking the bucket at the cemetery, he foretold them all. When do you cross the line from coincidence to fact? After it happens three times? Four times? Ten? When do you stop being a skeptic and start *believing?* I mean, this wasn't some bullshit story that some crackpot televangelist was shoving down my throat on late-night TV. This wasn't a tall-tale told by a weathered world-traveler just returning home from a foreign land I had no knowledge of, telling me of fantastical creatures and magical humans and talking animals that he swears existed over there. This was *my* son. And he wasn't just telling me things, I was seeing his ability with my own goddamn eyes. I mean, I saw it all! What was I supposed to do? I can only be skeptical for so long. After a while, after seeing him do this over and over again, I would just have to believe it. Right? You would believe it too if you were me. It's true.

I became so frustrated with my Google search that I decided to get some fresh air. I pushed my leather, executive chair away from my dusty desk. I got up and walked away from the web of unreliable information sources on the internet, walked through the labyrinth of cubicles occupied by my coworkers--some brilliant, some morons--in the Information Technology Division of the Texas Commission of

Employment and Benefits. There was Ryan, all snaggle-toothed and hunch-backed and awkward, the epitome of the nerd stereotype. His technical skills were overshadowed by his unfortunate dingy gums and dirty, crooked teeth. His choppers were in such mangled shape that I affectionately called him Snaggle; and when I say I affectionately called him that, I mean I called him that to *myself*. There was also Melvin, a nerd so tall that he could play third-string backup to a center for a Division IV collegiate basketball team, except that his main skill was talking, not dribbling. He talked so much that I affectionately called him Spellvin, as in he could put you under his spell on account that he talked so much. His monotone stories about his drinking escapades or his outings with his kids or his arguments with his wife or his shenanigans with the ladies in Human Resources were spellbinding. Really. Finally, I walked past Tim, the most annoying guy in my entire division; the guy whose cubicle was repurposed to be his own, personal kitchen away from home. Every morning once he came in from riding the Metro Rail, he would start mixing his breakfast of oatmeal and prepping his pot of coffee and his bowl of sliced fruit and his toast and whatever else he craved, opening and closing the mini microwave door, setting then popping his toaster, pouring water into the coffee pot and starting the coffee maker, and stirring and mixing and clanking his kitchen utensils all over the goddamn place. It was a miracle that he ever got any work done 'cause it seemed that the only work he was doing was cooking then shoving food into his pie hole. And once he was done after an hour of prepping, cooking, then eating his breakfast, he would then sit in his cube belching and farting for another hour. It was infuriating! I affectionately called him Farty McBelcher on account of all his farting and belching. Original, huh? Original or not, it was appropriate as hell.

After walking past my so-called colleagues, I stepped down the stairs at the back of the building, out the exit door, and into the sunlight, a day so bright and luminous that I couldn't remember the last time it was so beautiful outside. The Texas Commission of Employment and Benefits resided in the building directly behind the capitol building of Texas, the largest state capitol building in the entire United States, and they shared a massive 22-acre lawn that contained oak trees, pecan trees, and monuments to heroes of the Alamo as well as Confederate heroes. It really was a sight to behold and it was something I enjoyed on a regular basis, a place to get away from my friendly yet sometimes very annoying coworkers.

My favorite bench sat under a pecan tree on the northeast corner of the great lawn, one with a wrought iron frame and a wood seat as sturdy as the capitol building itself. In the 1880s when the building was constructed, its location in Austin was selected for several reasons but one of the more practical being that it attracted the winds from the Hill Country that came across Lake Travis, providing the building with natural, cool air conditioning most of the year. Most of the time, when I sat on my favorite bench between the state capitol and the building of the Texas Commission of Employment and Benefits, a strong breeze blew across the great lawn, making the sit under the tall pecan tree as pleasant as possible, even in the hot months of summer. This day was no different. As I sat on my fave bench, I watched the canopies of the other trees across the great lawn sway to and fro above me, their branches poking and tickling and intertwining with each other. It was nature's dance. The squirrels and grackles hunted and pecked for pecans, nuts, and food bits left by the visitors, politicians, and government workers that careened across the sidewalks and grass. And I contemplated the power my son possessed.

I may not have been the smartest man in the world, but I did know a little of science and philosophy. I was well-read, you know. I was curious and inquisitive and contemplative of my place in the world and the solar system and the galaxy and so on and so forth. For lack of a better summary: I thought about *things*. Who doesn't think about things? If you don't think about things, then you are a goddamn fool, I tell you. It's true. So I sat there under the pecan tree, in the cool breeze watching squirrels and grackles and politicians and other random people and, for some reason, I thought about space and the sun and the planets and how the planets circle around the sun in such an orderly fashion, spinning and rotating and orbiting to their heart's content--occasional blips like asteroids and comets and meteors flying around and smashing into each other. I thought it strange how atoms looked and acted like miniature solar systems with electrons orbiting around a nucleus of protons and neutrons, building all the things in the world we see and feel and eat and destroy. And if we were made of atoms and we looked out into space and we contemplated things like time travel, made possible by refracting light across great distance, then why couldn't it be possible to see into the future? I mean, just looking at other galaxies through a telescope was a sort of time travel into the past being that they were hundreds or thousands of light years away and their light taking millions of years to reach our eyeballs peering into those telescopes. Our brains were also made of these same atoms that made up this beautiful world that sat in this solar system that careened across our galaxy, across time and space and shit like that. If time travel was possible across space, then surely precognition was possible in our minds? Am I wrong? Maybe. I don't know. It's a lot to think about; a lot to digest and parse and extrapolate. They say anything is possible, right? There are days, too, when I think anything is possible.

I sat there for a good ten or fifteen minutes before I realized that my boss--the kind and amiable and talkative and polite Mr. Healy--had somehow snuck up on me while I was in deep contemplation and sat next to me without detection. I didn't feel him sit down next to me at all; the bench didn't move or squeak or creak one bit. It was as if he floated down from the fourth floor of the Texas Commission of Employment and Benefits on the southerly winds from the Hill Country like a feather, carefully landing next to me and not disturbing my trance-like daydream. I didn't know he was next to me until he said something to me.

"Hey there! How's it hanging, pardner?" he said. I about jumped out my skin, I was startled that much. He scared the shit out of me. It's true.

"Oh! Hi there, Mr. Healy. I didn't see you," I said, my breath hard and hoarse and loud. "You scared me."

"I didn't mean to scare you, my boy. I was just walking around-- going for a stroll, as they say. I saw you and thought you might want some company. Would you like some company?" he said, smiling with the inquisitiveness of a child.

"Sure," I said. I lied. I didn't really want any company but who was I to turn down a visit from my boss? I mean, I did owe him quite a bit for hiring me in the first place. Where would I be without him? Nowhere, that's where.

"Great! You seemed to be contemplating something of great importance. Do you mind telling me what you were thinking about?" He crossed one leg over the other, wiggling his rear end into the bench as if he was going to stay for a while--a long while. He was making himself pretty comfortable, that's for sure. I didn't know if I wanted to tell him what I was really thinking about. He might think I was a kook or something. I mean, you don't just tell people that you believe your son can see the future. That just *sounds* crazy and all. Doesn't it?

"Oh, I was just daydreaming. That's all."

"I see," he said, wrapping his two hands around the peak of his knee--intertwining his fingers in a tight lattice to hold his posture together--as if settling in for a long stay on the bench (maybe hours). I wasn't sure I was prepared for a long visit with him. Who is prepared for a long visit with their boss? A *brown*-noser, that's who. And I was no brown-noser. "And how are your children? What are their names?"

"Sammie and Jessie?"

"Yes! Yes, Sammie and Jessie," he said, untangling his fingers and slapping his knee like a game show contestant smacking a red buzzer to answer the game winning question. "Cute as buttons, those two!"

"Yes, they are cute. Thank you."

"And their mother? How's she?" he said. Then the awkwardness crept in, like a dense fog oozing through the trees of a forest, choking the air. As he looked at me--smiling like a TV news anchor--his dopey smile drooped upside down when he remembered that my kids' mother was no longer on this earth and the time off from work I needed to take the kids to the funeral was systematically approved by none other than himself. I could tell he immediately felt bad about asking that question. Everyone seems to feel bad about asking me that question. It's an uncomfortable topic, just not fun at all. "Oh, Simon. I'm sorry I asked that. Of *course* I knew she had passed away."

"Sure," I said, shrugging it off.

"I'm really *sorry.*"

"It's OK. Really."

"The kids are holding up well, I hope?"

"Yes, as good as can be," I said, gazing up at the sky.

"That's great," he said. He unlocked his crossed legs and wiggled himself upright, as if to get up. "I didn't mean to disturb you. I'll just be on my..."

"No," I said, extending my arm, impeding his ascension from the bench. I felt bad that he felt bad, especially considering I didn't really feel bad at all. In fact, I'm not sure why I gave him any grief whatsoever, intentional or not. I guess I was as shocked as anybody that he even forgot at all. I mean, how can you forget such a gruesome thing? He knew all the details of my ex-wife's car accident. I sat in his office the day after it happened and told him everything in a brief moment of unbridled confusion and confession. I was embarrassed for days after the way I conducted myself. I was hysterical and not for any of the reasons many people thought. I was simply a goddamn mess. "You don't have to go. It's OK. Really. Please have a seat."

"Are you sure?" he said, his posture frozen like a lightning bolt caricature, a zig at the hip here, a zag at the knees there.

"Yes, I'm sure."

He sat back down and wiggled his rear end back into the nooks and crannies it occupied just seconds before, and then he said, "Good! I wasn't ready to go back into that damn building anyway!" We both laughed, releasing the fog of awkwardness into the atmosphere, dissipating into outer space.

"Me neither. I like sitting out here on my break. It's very peaceful."

"Agreed. I like walking the capitol grounds. It is beautiful. Our forefathers knew what they were doing when they designed this. And--yes--peaceful. Sometimes, when I'm walking around, looking at the trees, watching the clouds drift above the tree tops, and the squirrels running around burying pecans, my mind drifts into a trance. Do you know what I mean?"

"Yes. Yes, I do. I guess you could say that when you walked up earlier, I was in a trance, too. I was thinking about the possibility of things."

"This sounds very interesting!" he said, crossing his legs again, twisting back into the contorted pretzel of a posture. "Do tell. The possibility of what?"

A blur of gray and brown caught the corner of my eye and I looked out on the great lawn, my vision locking in on a plump squirrel across the way, in the long shadow of a tall pecan tree, jabbing its little arms back and forth into the tall blades of grass, burying a nut, no doubt. It noticed me watching it and our eyes locked, the stillness of his stare penetrating me. He was neither scared nor worried--just motionless in his observation of me--as if to say, 'I see you, asshole. What? I'm burying my nut. You got a problem with *that*?' As I stared at the squirrel and it stared back at me, I felt the anticipation swelling up next to me and wondered if I should let Mr. Healy in, let him know exactly what I had been going through. I mean, sometimes it seemed like Mr. Healy was my therapist, in as much as he listened to the things I had to say when they affected my job, things that required time off from work. He knew about the time it hurt for me to pee and I had to go see an urologist. He knew about the time a cat of mine swallowed a *long* piece of string then shit it partially out, only to have a turd entangled in the string and dangle behind him as he ran around the house, thinking a predator was chasing him or something, when it was just a turd on a string hanging out his butt. And he knew about the time I ate a sandwich with a moldy piece of bread on it and I had an allergic reaction to the mold. He knew a *lot* of things about me, but I wasn't sure I wanted him to know about my son, good ol' Sammie Boy. I decided to be a little vague about what I was thinking about. I decided to be vague as hell. The squirrel quit staring at me and ran up the pecan tree, disappearing behind a branch.

"I was wondering if seeing the future was possible."

"Seeing the *future*?" he said, his face twisting into thoughtful curiosity. "That's interesting. Why were you thinking about that?"

"Oh, I don't know. My mind just drifted, I guess."

"Well, I will say, that with advances in technology, we've been able to do things like build telescopes that can see so far across the galaxy that they say we are actually looking back in time. So I don't know why we couldn't do something like that to see forward into time. Know what I mean?" I nodded. He continued. "And what would we even use a technology like that for? Spy on our enemies? Or lookout for the disasters for the sake of saving mankind? Would a technology like that be used for good or evil?"

"Well," I said, scratching my head, a little exasperated with the direction he went with my thought. "I wasn't really thinking about technology looking into the future. I was thinking about our own *minds* doing it, seeing things happen before they happen."

"Like a superhero?!" he said, slapping his knee again in that distracting way a lunatic yells at an invisible assailant. "Like a freak in a movie? What was that movie about the guy who was in an accident then could see into the future?"

"I don't know," I said, annoyed.

"You know?" he said, grabbing my arm and squeezing it hard. "That movie with the actor that talks funny? The one with the poufy hair!"

"I have no idea."

"Walken! Christopher *Walken*. That's the guy. He was in that movie--*The Dead Zone*! That's it." He slapped his knee again and shook his head, astonished at the difficulty of remembering the name of that movie. He was worn out. Really. I hadn't seen that movie so I never would have thought of it. Most of the movies based on books by Stephen King were absolute shit. It's true. I avoided them like the plague. "That's the one. He could see the future of that congressman. The one who ruined his own career. Did you see that one?"

"No, I didn't."

"You gotta see it. I love Stephen King movies. I just love them to pieces. They are *so* good."

"OK," I said, looking across the lawn for the squirrel, the one burying his nut a little while before. I didn't see him anywhere. I wished I was wherever he was, far and away from this conversation, attending to other matters like hiding nuts or climbing trees.

"Sorry, I digressed. What I was really wanting to say is that our minds are capable of anything. That's what they say, right?" he said, slugging me in the arm like kindergarteners on a school bus, teasing each other. "We know so much now about space and history and our minds and our bodies and evolution and you name it. People one hundred years ago would be astonished at what we know now. Right?"

"That's true."

"So who knows? Anything is *possible*," he said, releasing his intertwined legs, bouncing to his feet. "All I know is, I gotta skedaddle. I have to take a dump before going back to the office. See ya on the flip side, pardner!" he said, then scurried off quicker than he appeared earlier. Maybe he sensed my lack of enthusiasm for his observations or maybe the gut bomb he was experiencing really was too hard to hold. Who knows? All I knew was that I was alone--again--just like I wanted to be. Too bad my lunch break was over and I had to go back inside to work.

As I got up and walked back toward the building, the squirrel from the staring contest a little while before ran across a branch above me, tearing through leaves and tiny branches and balls of tree moss like he was running for his life. He ran the length of the branch until there wasn't any more branch to run across. Without stopping, he launched into the air, his little forearms extended, his body long and taut like a furry missile. From my vantage point, it seemed like he had made the decision to jump to his death but he knew what was going to happen and where he was going to land. He fell onto a branch of an adjacent tree--the weight of his landing sending tree bark and leaves furling to the ground--and quickly disappeared into the green, bushy shade.

CHAPTER **3** SEVEN

Chapter Seven

Picking the kids up from school could go one of two ways, depending on the weather. 1) It could rain and a car line would form that would stretch three blocks around and away from the school with parents impatiently waiting in their cars to pick up their kids from beneath a small, covered staging area. 2) It could be sunny and I could skip the entire car line nightmare altogether, me opting to stand next to my parked car on the street next to the school. That was the more sane option--the 'standing around and waiting for my kids to come to me' option. Not that I minded having the kids placed directly into my car by a drenched teacher who would rather be downing frozen margaritas with well tequila (that's the cheap stuff, if you didn't know) than assisting ungrateful, grouchy children into their parents' vehicles. It surely was more convenient that way--the car line option. But there was a part of me that preferred that things weren't so *easy* for my kids. Sometimes, I felt, my kids had to suffer a little bit, maybe not a lot but just a little bit of suffering was the right thing to do. I mean, I couldn't be responsible for raising spoiled brats, now could I? Why would I want to inflict that kind of pain onto unsuspecting, potential friends, mates, and coworkers of my children? I just couldn't do it, I tell you. It was like a moral imperative or something. It's true.

So on this particular day, it was hot as blazes outside and the sky was as clear as the cold water in Barton Springs, and I decided right then and there that I would wait by my car on the street. I was pretty certain my kids would find me; that was our routine if it was sunny. If it was raining, then wait for me under the shelter. If it was sunny out, then walk to my car. I usually parked in the same place every time, or somewhere relatively close. Most of the parents were lazy assholes, opting to form the three-mile long car line and wait for their kids in the air-conditioned cabs of their massive SUVs, the chrome tailpipes belching hot-house gasses into the suffering sky. Besides, standing up was good for me. It was a nice antidote to sitting on my ass all day at work.

Every day at 2:45pm on the dot, the school buzzer would ring from loudspeakers--little plastic boxes mounted on brick walls or metal poles, dotted around the main building, the portable buildings, and the playground with the massive black-top--while the principal wished the exiting children a good day and pleaded for them to do their homework as they were instructed by their teachers. I watched the kids trickle out and at first, it was onesie-twosies--a straggler, a punk, a nitwit, a hyperactive, a loner, a booger-eater, and a stinker. Then came the rest, led in orderly single-file lines by worn-out teachers, the classes closest to the main exit leaving last. Cursed were the kids whose classes were closest to the exit; they would have to watch all the other classes leave first while they waited their turn to escape. Torture, I tell you! Both Sammie and Jessie's classrooms were in the middle of the building so they were neither cursed nor charmed. They always came out within the midst of the throng, their faces instantly visible the minute they emerged. Isn't funny how parents can find their children instantly in the middle of a crowd? Like a red marble in the middle of a sand box, I could spot Sammie and Jessie's cute faces without trouble. And whenever they saw me, they would come running, their arms and backpacks flailing about as they ran toward my car.

"Daddy! Daddy!" they said, their cries of happiness growing louder as they got closer. I waved back enthusiastically. It was a sweet, little routine that I enjoyed very much, something that I made sure to enjoy because I knew it wouldn't last forever. All kids outgrow the joy they have when they first see their parents after a long day at elementary school. It was a fact of life. And there is nothing worse than a fact of life taking a dump on the little pleasures you experience with your children. It's true.

"Yeah! School's out," I said. "What do you guys want to do?"

I opened the back door to my trusty Volvo S70 and they both jumped in. Soon after I got in, we were off, maneuvering past the cars, some parking, some yielding. My kids' excitement was palatable. I could feel it in the front seat.

"How about some ice cream?" Jessie said, rubbing her little hands in a greedy fashion. She knew we had ice cream the day before and hoped that I wouldn't have remembered that little bit of information. But I didn't forget things like that.

"We had ice cream *yesterday*," I said. She harrumphed with disappointment. "How about something else?"

"Daddy? Can I ask you a question?" Sammie said.

"Sure, son."

"When was the last time we went to the duck pond?"

That was a good question. I couldn't think of the last time we had gone to the duck pond, a little ritual I started with the kids when they were very little. And when I mean little, I mean *barely walking* little. I racked my brain but I couldn't think of the last time we went so I said, "I don't know. Is that what you want to do today?"

"Yes, Daddy!" he said, beaming at his sister, knowing he won the choice. Little Jessie returned a despondent look to her brother, a ploy which affected him deeply. "But Daddy?"

"Yes, son?"

"Can we get ice cream *tomorrow*?"

"Of course, son," I said, looking in the rear view mirror. Jessie wrapped her little arms around her little brother's head, squeezing tightly.

"You're the best brother *ever!*" she said, swinging his head to and fro, like she was clutching a red, rubber kickball.

"Stop it!" Sammie said, trying to get free, annoyed with her stronghold.

"But I love you, brother!" she said, giggling.

Sammie finally broke free from his sister's clutches, noticed some children on the sidewalk we passed by, and propped himself up on his knees, peering out the rear window. He raised his right hand in front of his face, extended his index finger and thumb, and pinched the air repeatedly as if crushing flies or mosquitos or gnats or some other flying, pestering things in the back window.

"There's that *jerk*, Tommy, and his stupid *jerk* friend, Jimmy. I'm pinching them and pinching them! I'm pinching them so hard that I'm crushing them! I'm crushing their big, fat heads!"

"Sit down," I said, commanding good ol' Sammie Boy to obey. He didn't obey. He continued to air-pinch the bullies, even as their bodies grew smaller and smaller into the distance as we drove away.

"You're always pinching people to death," Jessie said, crossing her arms in frustration. "You never actually *do anything.*"

"I do stuff," he said, embarrassed that his little sister was calling him out.

"Oh yeah? What does pinching from far away do, anyway?" she said, giving Sammie the stink eye.

"It makes me *feel* good," he said, turning back around and sitting in his seat. He smiled, obviously thinking about the bullies crushed between his fingers, their guts and brains all over the place, no doubt. Their bloody carcasses squirted streams of blood as he crushed them--in his mind.

"I'll kick their butts for you," she said.

"Thanks, sis, but that's OK."

"I will. I'll kick their asses! I'm almost a black belt in taekwondo, you know!"

"Jessie!" I said, surprised. "Watch your mouth."

"Sorry, daddy," she said, elbowing her brother. "But I would for my big brother."

"That's sweet *and* disturbing at the same time, but I appreciate the sentiment toward your brother. Let's try to practice some restraint, please. Just because you can hurt someone doesn't mean that you *should.* OK?"

"Fine," she said. Boy, was she mad. I just knew that when she grew up that she would really be able to take care of herself. If she wanted to kick somebody's butt, then she could. I worried for any unsuspecting, oblivious boyfriends in her future. They better watch their steps around her. She'll annihilate any cheating asses for sure. It's true.

"So, to the duck pond then?" I said, quickly changing the subject.

"Yes!" they both said, clapping their little hands.

I sped up the Volvo s70--away from the school and the bullies and the teachers and the principal and the janitors and the lunch ladies and the other, boogery kids--then turned into a small subsection of the subdivision called The Lake at Wells Port (ingenious, huh?). It was named The Lake at Wells Port because there was a small pond in the middle, a man-made puddle created by the developers of the subdivision, in a section of land that naturally collected run-off in pond-like fashion, but whose retaining power was increased by the use of a cement dam. They stocked the pond with fish and turtles and mallard ducks, little creatures that gave the sub-sub-division a modicum of character, something the other sub-sub-divisions didn't have, unless drug dealers in low-rent duplexes is considered character (in some cities, that *is*). And this tiny bit of character made an impression on my children, something that they tucked away deep inside their little souls and cherished. Driving through The Lake at Wells Port engendered nostalgia in their hearts and excitement in their minds. They loved visiting the pond. It was one of their favorite things to do with me.

"Daddy, can I ask you a question?" said Sammie.

"Sure, son."

"Do you think Broken Wing is still there?"

"Good question, son," I said, scratching my head. Broken Wing was an unfortunate duck whose one wing was so crooked and mangled that the duck dragged its busted limb on the ground as it walked around. When it swam, its wing floated at its side like a feathery raft attached by stringy tendons. We didn't know how its wing got in this state but its broken wing gave it a memorable characteristic that gave it its namesake. "I guess we'll see."

"What about Berry?" Jessie said, her curiosity piqued by Sammie's question. Berry was another duck whose caruncles (the red, fleshy, bumpy things on its head, in case you didn't know) were so grotesque and bright red, that they reminded Jessie of a clump of red berries. Hence, she named the poor duck Berry. "Do you think Berry is still there?"

"We'll see," I said, trying not to run off the road and tear through someone's lawn and crash into their house.

I sped through The Lake at Wells Port in an attempt to keep the kids' nostalgia at bay. The sight of certain houses or neighbors or landmarks sent their minds into a tizzy and I wasn't really interested in going back in time with them and reliving our past lives. I just wanted to get them to the pond to scope out some ducks and have a good time. But that was really hard with two inquisitive, hyperactive kids in the car. I couldn't drive fast enough to distract them.

"Look!" Sammie said. "There's Mr. Sebastian. He used to give us candy every Wednesday. He said candy got you over the hump on Hump Day. Remember, Daddy?"

"How could I forget Mr. Sebastian?"

"And look, Daddy!" Jessie said. "There's the curb where I crashed my bike and got this scar on my forehead! Remember, Daddy?" she said, pointing to a small divot in her forehead.

"How could I forget? I see the scar on your forehead every day."

As I zoomed my car around curve after curve, it became apparent that I wasn't going to be able to get through our old neighborhood without driving by our old house, the house we all lived in when my ex-wife was still alive and she and I were still married. While we were going through our divorce, I referred to the house as our Crazy House on account that I almost went *crazy* there. Such a thing it is, to survive a bout with craziness, especially when divorce is involved. Most people don't win that battle. I was lucky to get out of that toxic marriage with even a tiny bit of my sanity intact. Can you believe it? It's true.

"Daddy, can we stop in front of our old house?" said good ol' Sammie Boy with that sweet way he asked me for things. How could I resist that? It was really hard for me to resist.

"I don't know," I said. "We really don't have a lot of time." I lied. We had all the time in the world but there was no point in telling my kids that. Parents end up losing any advantage they have over their children if they start telling them the truth about how things in the world really work. I kept our abundance of time to myself.

"Just for a second. Please!" he said. Then I knew I couldn't resist my children. They both leaned forward and gave me that look, that *look* that melts parents' hearts. You know that look, right? If you don't, then you will--one day.

"Fine," I said.

"Yeah!" they said, bouncing and squirming and jiggling around in the back seat, cheering and laughing. It was an unexpected victory for them and they were reveling in it. I reluctantly let them have the victory if it meant I wouldn't have to drive by the Crazy House again in the future. That was a card I'd hold close for later. I turned right on Mallard Duck Drive--the street our old house resided on--and slowly drove until we stopped in front of it.

"There it is!" they said, unbuckling their seat belts and smashing their faces against the window to look. "It looks so *different*!"

In reality, it looked practically the same as the day I sold it. The lawn was lush and green. The oak tree's canopy was full and leafy. The color of the siding was the same. The shrubs around the covered, front porch were all the same except for one, new addition: a Knock Out rose bush. Its blooms were of such a brightly oversaturated red that they appeared to be exploding in the air. The kids must have been focusing on the rose bush and nothing else about the house. But why would they focus on anything else? I was the one that took care of the front of the house. I was familiar with every inch of that yard and the exterior of the house.

"Nah, it looks the same," I said, dismissing their observation. "Only the rose bush is new."

"Nuh-uh," Jessie said, defiantly. "It looks totally different. I said so!"

"Right, if *you* say so."

"Can we get out and look, Daddy?" Sammie said. "It's been forever since we stopped by."

"No, son, we cannot. It's not our house anymore. I don't want to annoy the new owners."

"How would we annoy them?" he said, confused. "We are a nice family."

"I know we are. But when someone buys a house from someone else, they usually don't want to have anything to do with the previous owners."

"That's weird," he said, sitting back down in his seat. "Remember how the ducks used to walk over to our yard and the mama ducks would lay eggs in the bushes?"

"I sure do," I said as I slowly pulled away from the house. Sammie's question was my way out of this dilemma. "Then we'd have cute ducklings in our yard after about four weeks."

"They were so cute!" Jessie said, oblivious to my driving. My scheme had worked. "Baby ducks are cuter than anything. Cuter than kittens, cuter than puppies, and cuter than babies!"

"Cuter than baby *pandas*?" Sammie said.

"Even cuter than baby pandas."

As Sammie and Jessie debated the cuteness of various baby animals, I drove away from the Crazy House and down the street to the cul-de-sac where the trailhead for the jogging trail around the lake was. I parked the car and unlocked the doors. The kids spilled out the side of the car, still debating about ducklings versus any other baby animal known to man. I walked on the trailhead and the kids followed, eventually seeing their surroundings and where we were. They stopped debating and started walking behind me--silently--taking in the beauty of the pond and the surrounding trees. There was some debate amongst the residents of Wells Port if the lake or pond was really a lake or pond, considering it was called both. I guess if you wanted to get technical about it, it was really a small lake or a large pond. Either way, it was a serene place inhabited by a variety of ducks, geese, cranes and squirrels, even turtles and toads and snakes. Surrounding the lake was a trail for walking, jogging, or biking, always occupied by exercise buffs. There was a pier for fishing and another smaller pier for launching small, non-motorized boats but you rarely saw anyone brave enough to careen around the brown, murky waters in a small dingy or whatever. You'd have to be a real nut to want to float around that murky lake, teeming with swimming snakes and snapping turtles and weird fish. One of those creatures was sure to chomp your balls off if you fell in that yucky water. That's for sure. Surrounding all of this was a combination of oak trees, ash trees, cedar trees, and other indigenous trees I wasn't so familiar with.

The kids followed me for a short ways on the trail at a leisurely pace but once Sammie spotted a turtle sunbathing on a partly submerged tree branch, they tore through the grass separating the trail from the pond at break-neck speed, Sammie in front and little Jessie not far behind him, her arms swinging frantically so she could catch up to him. Nothing got good ol' Sammie Boy more excited and bent out of shape than a sunbathing turtle. He just couldn't resist the goddamn things. It's true.

He knelt in the mud, inches from the brown water that lapped at the muddy shore, and grabbed a two-foot long, somewhat straight stick. He extended the stick in the direction of the turtle, tapping its tip on the surface of the lake, sending tiny ripples toward the turtle in hopes of getting its attention. But the turtle was unperturbed, looking up at the sky. It didn't seem to care one lick that Sammie wanted to touch it or hold it or pet it or whatever his little heart desired to do with the ugly-looking amphibious creature. In fact, the turtle acted like Sammie didn't exist at all, which was far *worse* to my boy than simply ignoring him. Jessie stood behind him the whole time, impatiently wiggling her leg and tapping her foot. She wanted the turtle to look their way as much as Sammie did.

"Daddy! Daddy! It won't look at me!" Sammie said, tapping the water a little more aggressively with the end of the stick.

"It must be busy."

"Busy? Doing *what*?!" he said, looking at me, puzzled. "It's not doing anything. It's just *sitting* there."

"To you, it may look like it's not doing anything but that doesn't mean it's not doing *something*."

"What could it be doing?" Jessie said, placing her hands on her hips and tilting her head slightly--quizzically. "Thinking about a girl turtle?"

"Could be," I said, chuckling. "It totally could be thinking about a turtle girl. Or maybe some turtle philosophy."

"Fill-os-oh what?" Sammie said, annoyed. He stood up, tossing his stick in the grass, and approached me with his hands on his hips just like Jessie. They both gazed up at me, confused, hands resting on their sides. I guess they didn't know what philosophy was or that it was something for a turtle to contemplate. Why would they know that? They were just little kids. All little kids care about is eating, sleeping, watching TV, and playing with their toys. Their place in the universe was none of their own concern. "Turtles don't think about stuff, Daddy.

They just eat bugs and stick their heads and legs in their shell when you pick them up and stick their faces up at the sun to get a turtle tan."

"A turtle tan? That's good. I like the sound of that."

"How can I get it to come over here?" he said, running back to the muddy shore, looking at me then looking at the turtle. I could tell he *really* wanted the turtle to come over to him. What he would do once it did come over to him was a mystery to me though. "I'd do anything!"

"Anything?" Jessie said slyly. "Would you give me all of your *money*?"

"Yes!" he said.

"How about all of your *toys*?" she said.

"YES!"

"How about all of your *comic books*?"

"Ye--" he said, then biting his lip, forcing the pronunciation of that affirmation to cease immediately. "What?!"

"Would you give me all of your comic books if I got the turtle to come over?" she said, her hands on her waist and her right foot furiously tapping. She seemed pretty sure she could get that stuck-up turtle to come over to her. "Because if I can get it to come over then I want *all* of your comic books."

I was surprised at first at the level of wickedness in her tone when she asked good ol' Sammie Boy that question but then I remembered that she was her mother's daughter. As much as I hated to admit it, there was some of that woman's DNA in my daughter. Sometimes, there was a little more of that DNA there in her than I'd like to admit. Talk about a sore subject for me. It's true.

"Well," he said, standing up. "As much as I love my comic books, I *would* give them to you if you could. But you can't!"

"Can to!" she said, defiantly.

"Cannot!"

"Can!"

"Can't!"

"Just you watch me!" she said, storming away from her big brother and looking for something on the ground. I didn't know what she was looking for but she was adamant to find whatever it was that was going to snap the turtle out of its stubborn trance and swim over to them. She approached a thicket of shrubs and bushes, walking around it and peering inside, seeing something. She took a step back, then two steps back, winding up her arms, then she leapt in the thicket, leaves flying everywhere. It was a daring move, one that I surely would not have taken. I mean, who knew what was living inside that thicket? Rabid dogs? Feral cats? Angry birds? She was about to find out. But that little Jessie, she wasn't scared of anything. Bigfoot could be crouched in there and she would dive in anyway. It's true. The bushes and shrubs rustled as she moved around inside. Then after a minute of rummaging, she jumped out of the thicket--her hair tussled, leaves stuck to her shirt, scrapes on her face and arms--holding a wooden, folding ruler, the kind made of a light-colored wood with metal hinges (probably steel or brass or whatever). It was one of those kind of old-school rulers that my grandfather would have had in his tool box or something like that. It was dingy and covered in dried mud. She held it high above her head as if threatening the gods above with it. "I found what I need to get the turtle to come over!"

She ran back to the lake shore and knelt down. She unfolded the ruler and straightened a few lengths of it, probably getting it to about three feet of its six feet or so of length. She extended it toward the turtle who, for a few seconds more, sat motionless. Frustrated, she brought the ruler back in and extended two more sections, getting it to about four feet in length. She slowly extended the ruler and tapped the water. Miraculously, the turtle moved its head, turning its nose towards us. It blinked two or three times then, without hesitation, slid into the water and swam toward us like a miniature motorboat. Little Jessie tossed the ruler at her brother and cheered, then covered her mouth to muffle her excited yelps. Good ol' Sammie Boy stood there--slack-jawed and wide-eyed--in utter disbelief. He couldn't believe his bratty little sister had the magic touch when it came to turtles. I couldn't believe it either, quite frankly. Who knows how to do this stuff anyway? I surely didn't. I wouldn't have bet money on it, I tell you.

"I can't believe it," Sammie said, placing both of his hands on the sides of his surprised face, like one of the characters from a *Little Rascals* short film, witnessing something amazing. "How did you do *that*?"

"I told you I could get the turtle to come over. You owe me ALL of your comic books, big brother!"

"That's fine," he said, stepping to the shore and kneeling down. The turtle swam up to the shore then stopped. It turned its head and stared at good ol' Sammie Boy with its black turtle eye. It sat there, motionless, like a statue. "Daddy, can I ask you a question?"

"Sure, son," I said.

"Can I pick it up?"

"Sure."

Sammie slowly reached for the turtle. He placed his fingers over the top of the shell and his thumb underneath it, slowly raising the turtle off the ground and towards his face. As the turtle got closer to his face, at first it moved its legs as if it was trying to run then it slowly retracted its legs and head into its shell, for safety. Once at a very close vantage point to examine, all of its extremities were tightly pulled in under folds of wrinkly, scaly skin. As Sammie turned the shell where its head used to be, all he could see was the tip of the turtle's beak and part of one eye.

"He's looking at me!" he said, giggling and wheezing at the silly sight of the turtle's one partially revealed eye. "Look!" he said, extending the turtle toward his sister. She too looked at his protected turtle face, giggling as well.

"It looks funny!" she said, covering her mouth to hold in the loud laughter waiting to be released. She didn't want to frighten the reptilian thing, I could tell. She may act tough as nails but she's really soft and gooey on the inside. I promise. "Look, Daddy!"

Good ol' Sammie Boy extended the turtle to me to examine it and I looked at its wrinkly, scaly skin covering most of its wrinkly, scaly, turtle face stuffed inside that crusty, dirty shell. It was cute, for sure, but something inside me told me that I should tell my boy to let it go free. As cute as we thought it was, the turtle was probably scared shitless. I mean, we were four giants compared to its small size, picking it up off the ground and pulling it close to our faces where, I'm certain, it probably feared we would try to eat it or rip its extremities off or something like that. Now, I've had fried alligator before but I would never try to eat a goddamn turtle. That would be disgusting.

"You should put it down, son. It's probably scared of us."

"Why would it be scared, Daddy? We're a nice family."

"I know that but the turtle doesn't know that. It probably thinks you are going to eat it."

"Ooo, gross!" he said, falling to his knees and releasing the turtle into the water. Its legs and head immediately popped out of its shell, flapping and waving to and fro. It disappeared under the brown water in seconds like a scaly submarine. "I would never eat a turtle. That's so gross!"

Jessie laughed a hearty laugh now that the turtle was gone and she couldn't scare it anymore. She grabbed her stomach, trying to contain herself. "I bet if you tried to eat it, that it would *pee* in your mouth!"

"That's disgusting! Why would you say that?!" Sammie said.

"'Cause it's true!"

"Is not!"

"Is to!"

I placed my arms around their shoulders and reeled them into my sides--hugging them tightly. "Let's go sit on our favorite bench under the tree before you two start pounding each other. It's too nice a day for fighting. OK?"

"OK," they both said.

Good ol' Sammie Boy folded up the ruler and slid the thing in his pocket. His sister sprinted across the grass toward the walking trail. As she ran, she said, "Catch me if you can, big brother!"

"I don't want to," Sammie said. We watched his sister run away, her body shrinking as she fled down the trail of crushed, red granite, past runners and walkers and bike riders and dog walkers and baby stroller pushers. She was running like a man-eating beast was chasing her.

"Where do you think she's running off to?" I said, looking at Sammie.

"Who knows?" he said, not caring. We walked across the grass together to the trail--my arm draped across his shoulders, his arm clinging to my waist--then stepped on the crushed granite that was the foundation of the trail. Our feet crunched and crunched as we walked. "Daddy, can I ask you another question?"

"Yes, of course, son," I said, watching the speck of his sister running around the perimeter of the lake, well beyond calling distance. "What's on your mind?"

"Do you ever have dreams?"

"Dreams? You mean, like when I'm asleep?"

"Yeah. You know? *Dreams.*"

"Sure, I do. Sometimes. Not all the time. Every once and a while, I'll remember a dream that I had. Why?"

"Did you know I have dreams *all the time*?"

"Really?" I said, pulling him closer. His sister was out of sight--gone--somewhere passed a group of trees on the other side of the lake. I wasn't too worried, though. The walking trail circled the entire lake. Eventually, she would be right behind us unless she passed out or something. You never know with kids. Sometimes, they are an endless ball of energy. And other times, they run out of energy and unexpectedly drop like a sack of potatoes. It's weird. Good ol' Sammie Boy was worrying me, though. Something was off about him. I wasn't sure what but I could tell. "Are they the same dreams? Or different?"

"Both. Sometimes they are the same. And sometimes they are very different. I'm always in them, though. I'm always in them like I'm in a movie or something."

"Really? And how does that make you feel?"

"Strange."

"I bet," I said, patting his shoulder. "Let's go sit on our favorite bench so you can tell me all about these dreams."

"OK."

We walked together around the first turn of the walking trail then off into the grass toward a tall pecan tree, about twenty feet from the trail. Underneath the majestic nut tree was a wrought iron bench--painted dark green with designs of vines and leaves in the metal--with wood slats in the seat. The tall tree generously shaded the bench as well as generously dropped pecans on and around the bench. There were so many nuts on the grass that it appeared the bench stood on a brown, woven rug. Pecans crunched under our feet as we approached the bench. We sat on the bench, sliding off leaves and pecans so we could get comfortable.

"Tell me more about your dreams," I said, crossing one of my legs over the other, interlacing my fingers around my knee.

"Well, my dreams are always about me. Me and my friend Budgie!" he said, his face lighting up.

"*Budgie*? Who is Budgie?"

"Budgie is my friend in my dreams. He's a budgerigar. You know what a budgerigar is, right?"

"Yes," I said, remembering he had told me quite a few times recently what a budgerigar was. I wasn't about to admit that I forgot who or what a budgie was. Maybe I was getting old or something. But I didn't tell Sammie that. Why would I tell Sammie that? I'm not a fool.

"He's my friend who is a parakeet. We explore together."

"Explore? Where are you in your dreams?"

"I don't know. It's kind of like a desert. Sometimes, there are mountains but mostly there isn't much. We did find a cave and that's where we stay most of the time," he said, interlacing his fingers then resting his hands on his lap. He kicked his legs back and forth as he talked, a nervous kid habit.

"Why do you stay in the cave most of the time?" I said, curious.

"Because of the shadow monster."

"The shadow monster? Sounds scary."

"Yes, he's scary. *Very scary.*"

"So when the shadow monster is not around, then what do you do?"

"We explore. Find stuff and take it back to the cave."

"What kind of stuff do you find?"

Sammie scratched his head as he thought of the stuff he and his bird friend found in his dreams. Something told me he was now editing his story a bit, as kids do sometimes, so they don't say the wrong thing and get in trouble. I thought it strange that he was doing this considering he was telling me about a dream, not something *real*, and he wouldn't get in trouble for telling me--whether it was a lie or not. I didn't say anything though. Why interrupt his cool story?

"Just stuff. You know? For adventures. Knives. Sticks. Coins. Stuff like that."

"I see. Then you take the stuff back to the cave and put the stuff in a chest, like a treasure chest?"

"No, we don't have a treasure chest. My dream isn't about pirates, Daddy!"

"Sorry," I said, smirking.

"I'm being *serious*, Daddy! Serious schmerious."

"I said I was sorry."

"That's OK, Daddy. But I'm telling you about my dreams for a reason. I'm telling you 'cause me and Budgie found something weird. It bothered me."

"Oh really?" I said. This piqued my interest. What could it be? I didn't want him to stop so I kept quiet but right then and there, Jessie appeared out of nowhere, screaming and yelling and grabbing us. I didn't know where she came from but she literally came out of nowhere like a nightmare.

"You're it!" she said, screaming like a banshee. She slapped Sammie on the knee. He didn't take too kindly to that.

"Go away!" Sammie said, irritated, swatting back at her. "I'm telling Daddy something. Something *private*! And important."

"Oh, yeah?! What about?"

"I'm not telling *you*?"

"And why not?!"

"'Cause!"

"'Cause why?!"

"Jessie," I said, trying to calm them down. I didn't want them to start throwing punches or kicking each other or slapping each other or some shit like that. It could happen. Actually, it always happens. One of their feelings gets hurt, then the little fists start flying. It's a predictable escalation of juvenile aggression. "How about you run around the lake one more time? I'll time you. How's that?"

"*Time* me?" she said, smiling. "And what do I get for a fast time?"

"Ice cream?"

"OK!" she said, quickly in her starting position. She was ready to bolt. "Are you ready to time me?"

"Yes," I said. I lied. But she didn't know that. "I'm ready. On your mark. Get set. Go!" And off she went at full speed. I had no intention of timing her or taking her for ice cream. I just wanted a little more time with my boy. We watched her run away. "That gives us a little time. Now, tell me. What did you find?"

"Well," he said, sitting up. "Budgie and me, we walk around in this desert world. There's not much around so we walk and walk and walk. When we find something, it's always special because there's not much to find. When we find something, we always take it back to our cave for safe keeping. We never know when the shadow monster will come and try to get our stuff."

"How frightening," I said, patting good ol' Sammie Boy on the leg. He acknowledged me with a nod. "A shadow monster sounds scary."

"Yeah, the shadow monster sucks. He's always trying to get to us. But when we go in the cave, we're safe. So, we went back to the cave to drop some stuff off and we were sitting by the fire. We like to have a fire going to keep us warm and so we can see because it's dark in the cave. We were sitting there, enjoying the fire and eating a snack, when I saw someone at the back of the cave. It was weird 'cause we had never seen anyone else besides the shadow monster so when I saw someone else, I got scared."

"What did you do?"

"I grabbed a stick I had found and I put it in the fire. I put it in the fire so I had a flame to take with me and Budgie--to light our way. We walked to the back of the cave, slowly and carefully. The closer we got to the shadowy person, the more I could see that it wasn't the shadow monster. It was someone I recognized, someone sitting in a wheel chair. Do you know who it was?"

"No," I said. I didn't have a clue.

"It was *PeePaw.*"

Now, for those of you who don't know, PeePaw was the nickname for my dad, Sammie and Jessie's grandfather--Marvin Burchwood. PeePaw was the name Sammie gave him when Sammie was a toddler. Sammie's mother and I tried to tell Sammie to call my dad *Grandpa* but, when he tried to pronounce it, all he could say was *PeePaw.* And it stuck! My dad--from then on--was forever known as PeePaw. Funny thing was, if you had known my dad when I was younger--like when I was a teenager--then you would know that PeePaw was a funny name to give him considering he was such a cranky, onerous, son of a bitch. He was the crankiest, most onerous, biggest son of a bitch you'd ever meet. It's true. Much later in his life, Alzheimer's Disease would decimate his body and mind into a softer version of himself and then PeePaw seemed to fit more appropriately as a term of endearment. PeePaw was what both my kids lovingly call him.

"You saw PeePaw in your dream?" I said, sitting up, more attentive. Sammie's dream just got a lot more interesting.

"Yes."

"And what was he doing there--in the cave?"

"Well, at first, it looked like he was sleeping. He was bent over in the wheel chair. I could have sworn he was sleeping. I didn't know what to do. I didn't want to wake him up."

"But did you wake him?"

"I looked at Budgie to see what to do. He always gives me good advice. Budgie is my best friend. So I looked to him and he acted like I should wake up PeePaw. So I reached out to touch PeePaw. You know? On his shoulder. And when I touched him, he fell over. He fell out of his chair onto the ground of the cave!" Sammie's eyes opened wide as saucers. I could tell the sight of his grandfather falling out of his wheel chair affected him. What a traumatic thing to witness for a little boy like Sammie.

"Oh no! How frightening. What did you do?"

"Well, I wanted to pick him up. You know? Help him. I got down on the ground so I could try to help him up but as soon as I touched him, he turned to dust. His whole body turned to dust and blew away when I tried to touch him. It was so... weird. Budgie couldn't believe it. I couldn't believe it either."

"I bet. Sounds very strange indeed," I said, rubbing my chin, thinking about my jerk father. The idea of him turning to dust was appealing.

"Do you think PeePaw is OK?"

"Oh, he's fine," I said, sitting back on the bench. I looked in the distance for little Jessie and I could see her running along the jogging trail toward us. She was running at full-speed still, as if a demon was chasing her. Isn't it amazing how much energy children have? I wish I could bottle all of her energy and use it when I really needed it. I always need a boost of energy. Getting older sucks that way. "He's at the nursing home eating tapioca pudding or ice cream or custard or apple pie or something like that. He's all good."

"Are you sure?" Sammie said, looking more worried. "I'd hate for anything to happen to PeePaw. I *love* PeePaw."

"I know you do, son."

"I love PeePaw to *death*."

As soon as he said that, Jessie was upon us, panting and sweating and flustered and bright red in the face.

"Time! What was my time, Daddy?" she said, panting and wheezing all over the place. "Was it good enough for ice cream?!"

"You bet," I said, standing up. I extended my hand to Sammie so he would get up, too. "Let's go get some ice cream, son."

"But what about PeePaw?" Sammie said. He looked really concerned but I wasn't worried about it. It was just a dream, nothing more.

"What's wrong with PeePaw?!" Jessie said. Now she was worried just like Sammie. It was a child-catastrophe.

"*Nothing* is wrong with PeePaw. Sammie and I were just taking about him. Nothing's wrong. It's all good. Let's go get ice cream."

"Yeah!" they both said.

"I'll race you to the car, big brother!" Jessie said, again in her ready position.

"I'll beat you, sis!" Sammie said, then they sprinted towards the car.

"No fair!" she said, following him.

I watched them run off into the distance, their little arms flying, their little legs pumping. Nothing like a promise for ice cream to rile up my kids into a friendly game of "beat-you-to-the-car." I followed them but at my own leisurely pace. I wasn't about to sprint after them. I didn't have the strength or energy to do that. What sane parent does? I reflected on the talk I had with my son and enjoyed the fact that he felt comfortable enough to talk to me about his dream. I was surprised to learn that they were recurring dreams and that he had a friend that was a parakeet. How cute. I wondered how long he had had these dreams. What did they mean? Did they mean anything at all or were they just random stories his brain was releasing while he slept? Who knows. I'd have to look into it. Dreams are fascinating. Dreams are very fascinating, indeed. You can learn a lot about yourself by analyzing your dreams. It's true.

As I walked along the jogging trail, I looked out on the lake at the ducks swimming and the turtles sunbathing and the fish popping their faces out of the water and the people jogging and walking and enjoying themselves. I thought about a time when I believed that this neighborhood would be the place where I would live until the kids left home for college and I would retire there and would live happily ever after until I was old and gray and tired. It's funny how you make these kinds of plans yet they never seem to turn out that way--not for me anyway. Back then, when I was thinking about growing old in this neighborhood, I had no idea that, in reality, I would be divorced way before I ever got old and gray and that my bitch-cheating-wife would die in a bizarre car accident with her dipshit boyfriend. How was I to know all that back then? No one plans things that way. No one, I tell you.

As I walked to my car, thinking about this and that and the other, my cell phone rang. I pulled the annoying device from my pocket and read the digital words on the little screen, the words announcing who was calling. I saw the name of the nursing home where my dad lived in San Antonio, Texas: Autumn Grove. They were calling me about my dad, no doubt, but they never called me unless there was a good reason, either about a bill or something serious, like an emergency. I didn't really want to know so I didn't answer the call. I let the call go to voicemail. I figured if it was important then they would leave a message to call them back. And sure enough, they left a message. I reluctantly listened to the message.

"Please call us back," the message said. A sweet voice on the other end said, "It's about Marvin Burchwood. We need to discuss something with you."

Then I hung up the phone.

Shit.

* * *

Marvin Burchwood. What can I say about retired Army Colonel Marvin Burchwood? Do you think it was easy dealing with a man named Col. Burchwood? Probably not, right? You would be correct. But that clichéd image of a brusque, barrel-chested, buzz-cut block of a military man was a little different from the reality that was my father. My dad was a brusque, barrel-chested, buzz-cut block of a military man on the *inside*; his exterior appearance was closer to pudgy and doughy, a slight man whose internal rage was way beyond anything his external appearance revealed, which was that of a short, Jewish man with a high forehead from a receding hairline and large, metal-framed glasses perched on his straight, thin nose. He was mad about *everything* in his life and made sure to let everyone in close vicinity know it. No one was immune to his rage--not my mom or me--and that's the way it was until my mother unexpectedly passed away from an aneurysm which then segued into his irreversible bout with Alzheimer's disease. In fact, he didn't really take on the PeePaw persona until the Alzheimer's dulled his personality like a jagged rock smoothed over time by the deluge of water from a mighty river. The angry Col. Burchwood I knew as a timid kid was not known to Sammie and Jessie. They just knew him as PeePaw--a forgetful, Teddy Bear of a feeble, old man. He was a force they would never reckon with, only hug and share cookies with. How strange. I never would have imagined *that* when I was a kid. I really thought he would torment me all my life. Life is strange, isn't it? It's true.

Before my mother passed away--a sweet woman named Beverly Burchwood--the signs of Alzheimer's disease in my father were there but not prominent enough to take seriously. My mother had a beautiful soul and nasty Col. Burchwood really didn't deserve such a kind, docile wife. No one expected her to pass away so suddenly like she did, what, with her caring hippy ways and her healthy eating habits and her knowledge of meditation and yoga and all. Not long after she abruptly passed away from the lethal aneurism, my father's health changed quickly. Forgetfulness soon turned into repetitive storytelling to confusion and anger to complete helplessness, as if her passing was the disease's cue to cut loose. After several disappearing acts where he would get in his truck then drive away and not come back, I knew something had to be done. I received several calls from different neighbors that described waking up in the middle of the night to my dad banging on their doors then angrily pissing on their front porches, I really knew something had to be done. But it wasn't until the San Antonio Police called to inform me that my dad had physically assaulted the kind woman I hired to clean his house once a week that I finally did something about it. My dad told the police--who came to his house after the maid called 911 and screamed she was being murdered--that the innocent housekeeper was a witch who had broken into his home and tried to steal the apricot preserves he loved so dearly from his refrigerator. The police were very kind to my dad, especially after they learned he was retired military and perused the military certificates, plaques, and medals that decorated his house. Cops are generally kind to ex-military, no matter how messed up or sick the retirees seem to be. I guess they can relate to the military lifestyle, PTSD, and whatever. The police are simply the military for your city, am I right? Well, that seems right to me anyway. They were the ones to suggest Autumn Grove. 'It's a nursing home for vets,' they said. 'He will be taken care of.'

I called Autumn Grove soon after the attempted murder and they gave me their spiel which was that they were a home for ex-military and, since my father was high-ranking *and* had been diagnosed with Alzheimer's, he was a shoe-in. I moved him in all by myself; my ex-wife was too busy boffing her boyfriend to assist me at the time. Not far outside San Antonio was his new home: Autumn Grove. That was never the place he imagined he would spend his last days. In reality, you never really know where you'll be at the end of your life. No matter how hard you plan, you'll just end up where you end up. Life has a funny way of doing that to you--unraveling in unexpected ways against your best-made plans. It's true.

So, during and after my divorce, Autumn Grove became kind of a destination for me and the kids--a place to get away from the misery I was experiencing in Austin with my separation and divorce--and we spent time with my dad even if he didn't know why there were two whacky kids he didn't seem to know jumping on his bed and calling him PeePaw. Sammie and Jessie just wouldn't accept it when he said he didn't know who they were. They thought he was playing a prank on them. Unfortunately, he wasn't. Unlike when I was a kid, though, he was never mean to them. If there was a silver lining to the Alzheimer's, then it was the dulling of his angry personality. He didn't rage against the people in his life anymore. He only got angry at inanimate objects, like furniture. When his memory would relapse and he became reacquainted with the people around him, the congenial part of his personality would reappear, and he would welcome them with open arms and smiles. Like a record skipping then repeating a delightful chorus to a pop song, he would greet whoever was accompanying him as if he hadn't seen them in years and was happy to get reacquainted with them. Not so with furniture. Whenever he would forget the placement of the furniture in his room (stubbing his toe on the bed frame was a familiar frustrating predicament), his rage would explode from within him and he'd bash and hit the thing like he wanted to destroy it. But he never did this with people; he was Marv to the staff at the nursing home and PeePaw to my kids.

I returned the call to Autumn Grove when we got back to our apartment later that day. The women I spoke to on the phone, Ms. Robyn, was a kind woman and said nothing but sweet things about my dad, Marv. Ms. Robyn explained to me on the day I moved my dad into Autumn Grove that she had retired from a career as a realtor to manage Autumn Grove, something that she knew was her destiny. When I asked her how she knew it was her destiny, she told me, "I just love old people to death. I LOVE THEM!" When I told her at the time that loving my dad would be like loving a cactus, she just laughed and said, "You'll see. I will love your dad, too." If you ever have to put your parent into a nursing facility or assisted living or a hospital or whatever, make sure they have someone on staff like Ms. Robyn. Otherwise, your mom or dad will be fucked. Most retirement places, they don't give a shit about the elderly even though that's their business. Most of those places are really just in business to suck the government benefits dry and steal your loved one's savings, not to take care of their clients. It's true.

Anyway, I asked Ms. Robyn what the issue was. "Do I need to come down right away?" I said, worried.

"Well," she said, smacking her lips, thinking of an appropriate response, then releasing a high-pitched whistle from her pursed lips. "Tell me your definition of *right away*."

"Well, I have two small children to take care of and it's hard to just leave at the drop of a hat. Can you tell me exactly what's going on?"

"He hasn't been eating," she said, matter-of-factly. "Not even the cookies. And you *know* how much he loves cookies."

"Yes, I know. But do you know what is wrong with him?"

"It's hard to say. Maybe he's just done."

"Done? What do you mean by *done*? Like, done *done*?"

"Yes, like done DONE," she said, punctuating with another high-pitched whistle. "But you never know. He may snap out of it. He may smell those delicious oatmeal raisin cookies and get out of this hole he's in. But I don't know for sure. I just know what I know."

"And what do you *know*? If you don't mind telling me."

"Well," she said, smacking her lips again, thinking of another appropriate response, then releasing a high-pitched whistle from her pursed lips. She seemed to do this whenever she had something serious or important to say. It was like her cue: the whistle. Maybe her nickname should be The Whistler. Sounds like a Spider-Man villain, right? "Usually when they stop eating like this--and when I mean *they* I mean the other patients suffering from Alzheimer's--it means they are ready to die. They don't say it but that's what happens. Usually."

"Usually?" I said, repeating her word.

"Usually," she said, then went silent. I sat there with the phone in my hand in a state of shock. You are never really prepared to hear someone say the end is near for someone you love, even if they are in a rest home and you know the end is coming. It still doesn't prepare you to hear someone *say* it. "But you never know."

"Never know what?" I said.

"You never know. He may come out of it."

"Really?"

"No," she said, matter-of-factly. She was really good at that, speaking matter-of-factly. It's true. "When can you come down here?"

"Well," I said, thinking, perusing my mental calendar. "This weekend coming up, it is a three-day weekend. That might work."

"Might?" she said, bewildered. "I'm not joking here, Mr. Burchwood."

"Simon. My name is Simon. Please call me--"

"Simon," she said. "Figure it out. I'll be here. I suggest that you be here soon. Your dad needs you."

"OK," I said.

"Good day," she said, then hung up the phone.

Later that day, after leaving work then picking up the kids from school then getting home then freaking out from the stress of it all, I told the kids that we would be making an impromptu, emergency trip to San Antonio the next day to visit PeePaw. They screamed with delight. I didn't have the heart to tell them *why* we were visiting PeePaw--just all of a sudden--out of the blue. They were just happy to be going on a road trip to visit him and all. It had been a while since we visited him--something I felt quite guilty about for some time--but when you have little kids, you really can't feel guilty about things outside of your immediate purview. When you're a parent, you have enough on your plate as it is. You can't really worry about anybody else besides your own children. (And your spouse if you're lucky enough to still be married. Who stays married these days anyway? Nobody, that's who.) Besides, I didn't really like my dad, not *personally* anyway. I mean, he was my dad and all, but not a very good one in my personal opinion. What can I say? He was kind of an asshole to me for a lot of years. It's hard overlooking that, you know? Of course, you do.

I tried packing some bags for the imminent trip but the kids were being real pains in the butt. I mean, I had asked them to bring some things they wanted to take on the trip so I could put them in the bags but, instead of being practical and helpful, they were dragging all the toys from their bedroom into my room where I was packing. They brought in action figures and baby dolls and comic books and MadLibs books and markers and coloring books and sketchbooks and whatnot and so forth. Then they were throwing them on my bed, creating a makeshift pile of crap. They were driving me crazy. I pleaded for them to take their irrelevant things back to their room but they pleaded with me in return that they needed *all* of their things for the trip. Sammie, in particular, said he needed his sketchbook and pencils and pens and markers with him so he could draw his cartoons. I decided right then and there that I was going to need help for the evening. Out of complete desperation, I called in the babysitter: Nat. Maybe she could help keep the kids distracted so I could pack. I gave her a buzz on my phone and--thankfully--she answered.

"I don't mind coming over to watch the kids. I'm not, like, busy or anything. I was just watching TV," she said, sincerely.

"You don't mind?"

"Not at all. I'll be right over!"

"Thank you so much," I said. "You don't know how much I appreciate it." Then I hung up the phone. I couldn't believe my luck. Every parent needs that go-to person to help them from going bananas because of their insane children. For a lot parents, it's their spouse or their partner. But for single parents like me, it's just not that easy. I didn't have many people to call to help me out with my kids when I was in a bind, not many people I trusted anyway, like friends or family or coworkers, especially not my coworkers. But I trusted Nat so I guess she was *my* person. She was a godsend, really. It's true.

In a matter of minutes it seemed, there was a loud knocking on the door. Sammie and Jessie lost their little minds. They ran and answered the door--letting Nat inside--excited and shocked that she was there to hang out with them so unexpectedly. They just couldn't believe it. What a surprise! Their little minds were blown.

"Yeah!" they both said, screaming and running circles around Nat as she tried to walk to the couch to drop her things. They swarmed her relentlessly but, instead of being annoyed, Nat giggled and smiled. I think she liked the attention from the little creatures.

"Thanks for coming on short notice," I said, gratefully.

"Not a problem," she said. Sammie and Jessie were climbing all over her as she sat on the couch, like two monkeys careening up a banana tree. It didn't faze her at all, though. She was a real pro, I tell you. "Why are you, like, going to San Antonio again?"

"My dad. He's not doing well."

"PeePaw! We're going to see PeePaw!" Sammie and Jessie said. They just blurted it out like Nat knew who PeePaw was. They were a couple of heathens, what, with no manners or social skills or common decency, particularly when adults were trying to have an adult conversation. It was a little annoying, to say the least.

"And PeePaw is, like, your dad?" Nat said, looking at me, confused. She tried to keep her composure while the kids were climbing all over her.

"Yeah, the kids call him PeePaw."

"That's cute," Nat said. She seemed really sincere about that, too. Amazing.

"Anyway, if you can keep them busy while I pack, that would be great."

"Of course," she said. She looked at the kids and exclaimed, "Who wants to watch a movie?"

The kids screamed with joy. They had a ritual of making microwave popcorn for any movie, no matter what time of the day or the day of the week or who they were watching it with. The mere suggestion of a movie sent them into a frenzied panic for microwave popcorn. This time was no different. They both raced into the kitchen, tearing through the pantry for a box of microwave popcorn. Finding an unopened box, they ripped it open and fought over who was going to place it in the microwave and start the timer. That was Nat's call of duty.

"I guess I better go referee this, like, popcorn situation," she said, smiling then heading to the kitchen to breakup their disturbance. She was a godsend, I tell you. She lumbered into the kitchen, her tall, alabaster frame towering over my two, little monkeys. She reached down into the adolescent melee, pulling the bag of popcorn from their desperate grasps. As she placed the popcorn in the microwave and set the timer, their frenzy subsided as they watched the microwave inflate the popcorn bag.

I immediately went back to my room to pack for the trip. Without the kids disturbing me, I could get it done in a matter of minutes. I went into my closet, pulled a suitcase out, and started throwing things in it--pants, shirts, socks, underwear, shoes, and a belt. I could hear the microwave ding, so I knew that the movie would be starting soon, and it had gotten noticeably quieter since Nat went to control the movie / popcorn situation. The next things to pack were in the bathroom so I went in there and got the necessities--toothbrush, toothpaste, floss, deodorant, hairbrush, allergy medicine, fiber pills, pain meds for headaches, nail clipper, a razor, some shaving cream, and so on, plus stuff to cover my stink. For years, I used a dopp kit for my toiletries but the last one I had burst open when the zipper jammed, a wad of hair lodged in the zipper's teeth. I tried to force the zipper open and ended up ripping the side off of it, sending my stuff flying. I never got another dopp kit. I was just too busy with life, I guess. I had a brown, paper sack--the kind the kids would use to take their lunch to school--so I put my bathroom stuff in it. While stuffing the bag, I noticed Nat was standing next to me, appearing out of thin air like a ninja, looking puzzled as I put my stuff in the brown paper sack. She was so quiet that I didn't notice her coming back into my room.

"What are you *doing*?" she said, her hands on her waist, her head tilted to the side as if examining something so puzzling that she couldn't put heads or tails together of what exactly she was witnessing.

"Packing."

"You put your toiletries in, like, a brown, paper *bag*?"

"I don't have anything else to put them in and if I put them in my suitcase with my clothes, then they might leak all over them," I said, exasperated.

"I have something you can use. Just got it today but, like, I don't need it. Hold on," she said, quickly leaving my bedroom. I stood there, looking at the brown, paper sack, thinking how pathetic I must look to a fashionable younger person--like a bum with a 40oz bottle of malt liquor wrapped in a similar brown, paper bag from a dingy, convenience store. Pathetic. Isn't it funny how sometimes you can inadvertently look like the biggest idiot in the world to someone else in your life? I did feel like the biggest idiot in the world. It's true. A moment later, she came back in my room and said, "Here, use this."

She handed me a small, canvas, tote bag covered in painterly flowers of orange and yellow and pink, fluorescent green leaves, a shiny, gold zipper, and a pink ribbon looped in one corner of the bag. And to be honest, it was the furthest thing from looking like anything even near *manly*, or even in the vicinity of manliness. It was the girliest-looking little bag I had ever seen in my entire life. Jeez.

"What am I supposed to do with *this*?" I said, confused.

"You should put, like, your stuff in it. Your bathroom stuff."

"Instead of in a dopp kit?"

"Yeah! It's great, sturdy, and, like, *fashionable*. It was given to me FREE at the salon for spending more than $50 on hair products. I don't really need it, though. I have plenty of little tote bags. Keep it! You don't even have a dopp kit."

"I don't know," I said, skeptical. "It's not very..."

"Very *what*?" she said, looking at me like I was being totally ridiculous for not wanting to put my shaving stuff in a pink, flowery, free salon bag. Who wouldn't want that? "It's way better than a brown, paper bag!"

I really didn't know what else to say. What looks better: a brown, paper sack or a pink, flowery bag? Seemed like a stalemate to me. But what did I know?

"How are the kids?" I said, realizing that Nat was hanging out with me instead of watching the kids. I peered around her lanky frame to see if they were destroying anything but I didn't see them.

"Oh, they're fine. Mesmerized by the movie! You know how they get when a movie comes on?"

"That's true." I reluctantly unzipped the salon bag.

"You don't mind that I hang out with you, do you? You seem, like, lost."

"I feel a little lost, actually. I was caught off-guard with what's going on with my dad. I wasn't expecting it, I guess," I said, looking around my room at the pile of junk my kids brought in as well as half-packed bags of clothes. I was a mess.

"Who does expect something like this?" she said, placing her hand on my shoulder. "Let me help you."

"That's very nice of you but you are helping me--just being here with the kids."

"That's cool. But they are, like, busy watching a movie," she said, her face lighting up. "Tell me something that relaxes you. Maybe it'll help you."

"Relaxes me?"

"Yeah, like, I take a bath with Epsom salt to relax. What do you do to relax?"

"I'm not taking an Epsom salt bath right now!" I said, embarrassed, chuckling at the notion of sitting in my bath tub instead of packing. "That would be ridiculous."

"No, silly. What relaxes *you*, not me."

"Oh. Hmmm, let's see," I said, thinking. "When I need to relax, I sneak out on the balcony and smoke a cigarette."

"Really?!" she said, looking surprised then disgusted, her nose and mouth scrunched. "Cigarettes are, like, gross."

"Right. Bad habit, I know."

"But if that's what relaxes you, then... by all means. To the balcony."

I felt a smile slide across my face, the kind of smile elicited from the recognition from someone that even if something you enjoy is bad, it's still good. I opened the drawer of my nightstand and found a pack of smokes and my Zippo lighter, then said, "Let's go!"

We made our way from my bedroom through the living room, even walking in front of the kids while they watched whatever Disney animated movie they were watching. It didn't matter which one it was, really. They were so mesmerized by it that they didn't even notice us walking between them and the TV. I mean, they noticed our forms-- the mass of our bodies blocking the animated characters on the screen--but we were just three-dimensional objects obstructing their view. They craned their necks to look around us. We continued out the door to the balcony, the metal mini-blinds clanking against the door as we closed it.

Outside, Nat stared at the charred remains of my wooden bench and the burnt Café Bustelo coffee can underneath it. On the balcony floor, a black, charred area of singed cement spread out from under the bench like a pitch black, circular, shag rug. On top of the burnt bench lay a brand new seat cushion, a light crème color with a forest green pattern of bamboo plants sewn into the material--a cheap replacement I found in the grocery store seasonal section. The smell of burnt wood and cement still lingered in the air, a slight aroma that distinctly smelled of charred, man-made materials. Nat couldn't believe her eyes. It appeared something horrible happened yet no one was concerned enough about it to clean up the mess. I surely wasn't.

My cheap, lazy fix was to buy a new seat cushion then pretend like the accidental, cigarette butt-blaze didn't happen. As far as I was concerned, it didn't--until I had to explain myself.

"This doesn't look good," she said, lifting her hand to her face to either cover her mouth and nose because of the nagging feeling of disbelief or to keep the aroma of burnt furniture and coffee can from entering her innocent nostrils. I couldn't figure out which it was. It was probably both.

"It was an accident," I said, opening the pack of cigarettes, fumbling to get one out. They were wedged in the pack like sardines. "I threw a lit cigarette into the coffee can and it caught on fire."

"On fire? Like, you could have burned the building down--*fire*?"

"Yeah," I said, lighting a cigarette. She couldn't hide her displeasure that I was smoking in her presence but she didn't tell me to stop either, which I respected and appreciated a lot, so I took a drag. She was now an accomplice to my bad, secret smoking habit. "The fire could have been bad."

"And Sammie and Jessie saw the fire?"

"Yeah, freaked them out," I said, taking a drag then exhaling a rather large plume of smoke into the evening sky.

"I bet."

"I felt really bad about it, too. Like exceptionally guilty. It made me feel like a bad parent. I've been feeling that way a lot lately, too."

"Like, you're a bad parent?" she said, then sat down on the new bench cushion. A little air escaped from the seams of the cushion like a slight fart. Nat giggled. She patted the cushion for me to sit down so I did.

"Yeah," I said.

"You're not a bad parent. I promise. *I've* seen bad parents. Like, really!"

"Like how?" I said, continuing to smoke, curious.

"You don't even want to know. It's bad. But you, you're one of the good ones. I promise."

"How do you know for sure?"

"Because your kids tell me things and I listen to what they have to say. Your kids adore you, whether you believe it or not. They, like, *love* you to death."

"Really?" I said. I played coy a little although I knew my kids loved me. What parent doesn't know that? Well, I guess if you're one of those kinds of parents who doesn't give a shit about being a parent, then you wouldn't know. But if you have even an inkling of the desire to at least *want* to be a good parent, then you *know*. How could you not know? I mean, the love just pours out from children. It's unconditional. Most kids adore their parents unless they are psychos. Kids will overlook a whole litany of bullshit as long as they receive a little love from their parents. Kids are easy to please. It's true. "I try my best."

I leaned back on the bench and finished the cigarette, the two of us sitting in silence. I turned my head to look into the door window, my two kids sitting on the couch, mesmerized by the movie they were watching. The popcorn in their bowl was gone--some stray kernels on the couch and on the floor--but their gaze to the TV was strong. When the cigarette extinguished itself from lack of tobacco to burn, I leaned forward then dropped the cigarette between my legs into the burnt coffee can underneath the bench. I placed my head in my hands, heavy from the stress of the things to come.

"It must be hard, like, taking care of kids while you're in a crisis, by *yourself*," she said, placing her hand on my back. Her touch startled me. I wasn't expecting it. I mean, who would expect like that, a 20-something they didn't know very well to just touch them? I didn't expect it, that's for sure. It was nice, though. It had been a while since someone--anyone--had laid a hand on me.

"Yeah, learning to be a single parent has been tough for me. Thinking about how this weekend will be with the kids and me having to deal with my dad... Well, it's been stressing me out."

We sat in silence for a good 30 to 45 seconds, the breeze blowing on the balcony from the west, a breeze that had traveled from the Hill Country then over Lake Travis and finally to my apartment complex. The breeze was cool and crisp and dry.

Nat shifted in her seat, changing the configuration of her crossed legs, then said, "Well, if you need some help, then I don't mind going with you guys. I don't have, like, anything planned this weekend. And I could use the extra money."

I was shocked, really. I mean, her suggestion came out of nowhere, just out of the blue. I didn't think of asking Nat to go on the trip with us. Why would I think of that? It had never crossed my mind but it made total sense. I mean, the kids absolutely adored Nat. She was the cat's meow to them. But would it be weird asking her to tag along with us? I had to think it through. After I got over the initial shock, I said, "Would you really want to help me? If so, I'll get an extra room at the hotel so you have some privacy."

"That would be great. I'll just need to go home and get some things for the trip. You know? Like, a change of clothes."

"Of course," I said, sitting up. "Get whatever you need. You sure you don't mind?"

"Not at all. I should let the kids know that I'm going with you all, though," she said, standing up. I stood up, too, to be polite. It's not polite to stay seated when someone stands up in front of you, especially a young woman. I didn't want to be rude.

"Of course." I opened the door and she stepped inside, ducking under the low-hanging door frame. She was so tall. I stood there on the balcony, watching her tell the kids about joining us on the trip, their burst of excitement that led to jumping and bouncing on the couch, the screams of happiness, the cries of joy. Little did I know how close we would all become on this trip, just from this quick, spur-of-the-moment decision.

The shit was about to hit the fan, as they say.

It's true.

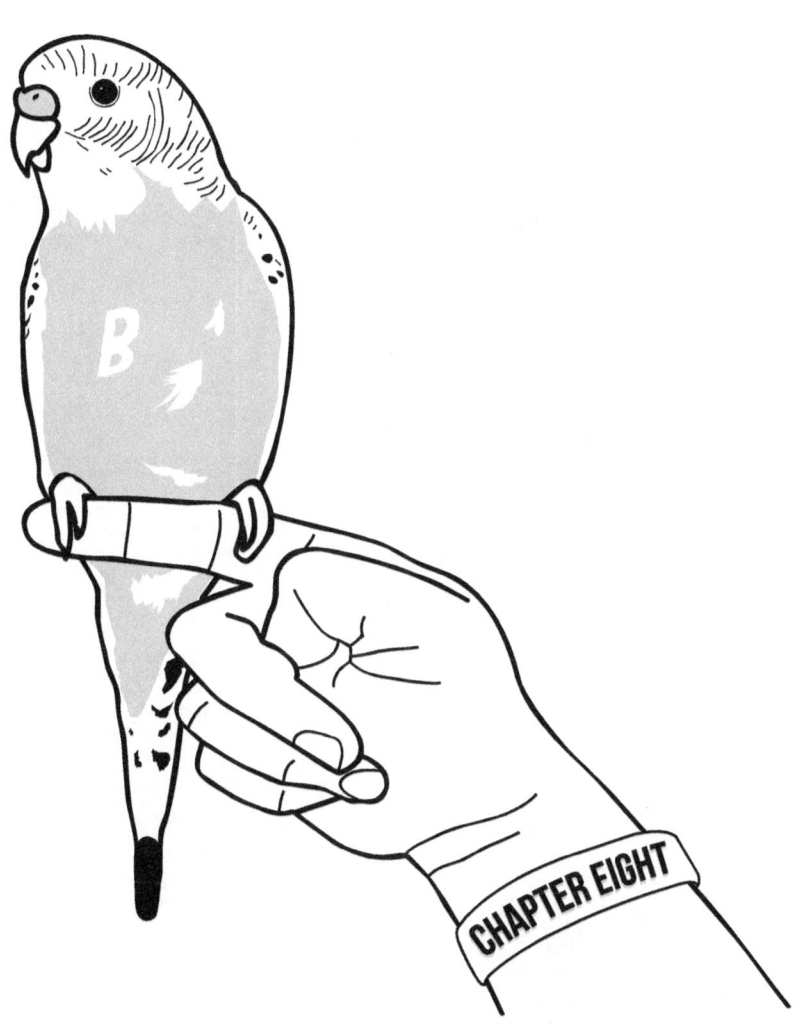

CHAPTER EIGHT

Chapter Eight

Taking the kids out of school was--and always is--a royal pain in the ass. Really. I mean, I had to call or email teachers and therapists and administrators. There was also the after-school stuff i.e. more therapists and coaches, etc. The list was endless. And it's not just good ol' Sammie Boy. I had to deal with little Jessie's people, too. It's enough to make me want to check out as a parent. It's way too much work sometimes. If I wasn't so in love with my kids, then I would have quit being a parent a *long* time ago. Too much administrative bullshit. It's true.

I spent the morning of the day we were supposed to leave for San Antonio to visit PeePaw emailing Sammie and Jessie's teachers, explaining why they would be absent from school. I emailed Ms. Fox, explaining to her as well why my boy would not be seeing her for speech therapy. I imagined how she would respond if we were speaking in person, in her heavy, German accent. 'Zat vill be fine. Your son is a fery shpecial boy. A good boy. A hardverkink boy. He is one of my favorite shtudents!' I always got a kick out of speaking to Ms. Fox. Her accent just got to me--in a good way. I had to also cancel an appointment for an annual checkup with Dr. Dimes for little Jessie as well as letting her taekwondo master know that she would be missing a tournament that weekend, an opportunity for ass-kicking all the little martial artists in our district. The hardest email to write was to Dr. Dena Davis who had suggested earlier that we meet on this day--the day we were leaving for San Antonio--to further discuss Sammie and some of the things she felt she discovered about my boy. She had a way about her that was so overly aggrandizing and overtly self-important that I found it difficult to disappoint her or alter schedules and appointments or do anything in any way that seemed as if I wasn't complying with her direction or advice. But I will say this, the more she dived into the machinations of good ol' Sammie Boy's psyche--or what she thought was in his little psyche--the more I felt she was off-target. I mean, I know she's a professional psychotherapist and all, but it didn't really seem that she knew what the fuck she was talking about. I guess it's part of the field to make grand observations about her patients' minds but it seemed to me that I just knew my kid *better* than she did. I was reluctant to continue taking Sammie to see her but I was also reluctant to cancel appointments with her, too. I was in between a rock and a hard place and it made for constipated communications with her. It was just awful.

The one person who I had a feeling *might* hold up everything but didn't was Nat. Like a trooper, she showed up to my apartment promptly at 8:00am with a backpack over her shoulder, a purse in her hand, and a smile on her face. Of course, Sammie and Jessie lost their minds when they saw her at the door, again. Why wouldn't they? It was their standard reaction. But Nat, she had this way about her--this way she made herself up with her hair and her makeup and her clothes and her accessories and all--that obviously took some time to put together. I figured (and I'm not trying to be sexist here at all, although I guess it's kind of sexist, but it's inadvertently sexist) that she would be late. But she wasn't. And not only was she *not* late, she was ready to go. And without any knowledge at all on my part, she was going to turn out to be a perfect travel companion, which is unbelievable if you ask me. I'm not the easiest person to get along with as well as to travel with. I have tons of friends to attest to this fact. It's true. And I guess I was being a little sexist earlier. I didn't mean to be. Please, let's keep that between ourselves and not tell anyone else, especially Nat. OK? I'd appreciate it. Thanks.

"Is everyone ready for a road trip?" she said, the kids buzzing around her like ecstatic bees on wild flowers. "I'm ready. Are you ready!?"

"Yeah!" they both yelled then ran to their room.

She smiled then closed the door behind her. It still amazed me just how tall she was, every time I saw her. I was like an elf standing next to her. We made for an extremely odd-looking pair, literally the Odd Couple. "How are you?" she said, looking down at me.

"Good. Stressed but good. Just got done letting all the folks know who need to know that we are leaving town. You know? Teachers and such."

"Good for you. Being, like, responsible."

"Somebody has to be responsible, right? Want some coffee before we go?"

"Sure," she said, walking into the living room and plopping on the couch, then tossing her backpack on the carpeted floor. She began to lift one leg over the other in an attempt to get somewhat comfortable in a cross-legged position but good ol' Sammie Boy came speeding out of the kids' room, gripping a small, plastic bag in one hand and his sketchbook in the other hand, then jumped on her lap. He really caught her off-guard, I could tell by the way she reacted. She released a high-pitched squeal then said, "Sammie! Be careful."

"Sorry, Nat! Want to see what I'm bringing on our trip?"

"Of course," she said, then watched him as he dumped the contents of the small, plastic bag onto the coffee table. It seemed everything that he had been collecting for his entire life was in that bag: a popsicle stick, a quarter, the buck knife, the Zippo lighter, a Dr. Strange comic book, the folding ruler, a rubber ball, a pencil, and other knick-knacks from so many different eras in his life that it would be difficult to explain them all. None of his crap was of any importance to our road trip though (except maybe the comic book which would provide some pretty good entertainment while we were in the car, but I was pretty sure he had already read that particular issue). I'm sure Sammie had his reasons. Little kids always have their own little reasons for why they collect the things they do and why they would want to take the entire collection everywhere they went. Right? Their little reasons usually didn't make any sense to anyone but them. "Wow! That's a lot of stuff," she said, amazed.

"I need ALL of this stuff!" he said, waving his arm across the top of the coffee table like a game show hostess, as if to say, 'Look at these fabulous prizes!'

"You do?"

"Yes!"

"And what's in the sketchbook?"

"Oh, my very important drawings and cartoons. Want to see?"

"Sure!"

"How about the clothes I asked you to pack?" I said from the kitchen while I poured Nat a cup of coffee. I can't imagine a morning without coffee. Can you? I didn't think so. Even if I had to drink black coffee, I would. That's how much of a coffee addict I was. I took Nat the cup of black coffee then said, "I don't have any milk or cream but I did add sugar. Is that OK?"

"Yes, thank you," she said, accepting the coffee then setting the hot cup on the coffee table. She turned to Sammie. "Did you pack your clothes like your father asked?"

"Maybe," said good ol' Sammie Boy, hamming it up all over the place. He was really good at that, hamming things up, especially when he was guilty of something. I could tell he hadn't packed his clothes; I could tell by the look on his little face. Guilty! Parents just know these types of things about their children but I didn't say anything. I decided to let Nat handle it.

"Go finish up so we can go," she said, attempting to sip the coffee but it was still too hot to drink. She set the coffee cup back on the coffee table and didn't pick it back up again. A wasted cup of coffee, I tell you. Sammie quickly shoved all of his trinkets into the plastic bag, put his sketchbook under his arm, then ran to his room. He was excited to leave for San Antonio, the exact opposite of how I was feeling. I dreaded this trip for more reasons than one. But I was glad Nat was going with us so she could help me. I really needed the help, if you didn't know. I was a mess--a big, fat mess. She turned to me and said, "You, too. We need to, like, hit the road."

I agreed and went into my bedroom, gathered my bags, then set them by the door leading to the garage. Soon after, Sammie and little Jessie pulled their little wheeled suitcases to the door, too, and we all stomped down the stairs to the garage where my trusty Volvo S70 sat waiting. I popped the trunk and everyone tossed their bags in there. Sammie and Jessie hopped in the back seat. Nat sat shotgun. Before getting in, I said, "Gotta lock up. Be back." So I ran back up the stairs to my apartment.

Inside, I walked over to the front door to lock it. As I turned the lock, I thought of all the things I would possibly have to deal with in San Antonio concerning my father. What if he was dying? What if he died while we were there? Was I prepared for that? Where would he be buried? Did he even want to be buried? What if he wanted to be cremated? I became overwhelmed. My head sagged forward, lying against the back of the door. In the reflection of the chrome door knob, I could see my face--twisted and discolored and elongated and distorted--a bizarre facsimile of my face. How I looked in the reflection was how I felt on the inside: twisted up. But before I fell into despair, I could hear my children screaming for me to come back to the car. They were impatient and ready to go.

"Daddy! Daddy!" I heard them yelling from the garage. I pulled myself together and locked the door. I quickly looked around the apartment to see if any lights were left on (none were) then I was out the door to the garage, locking it behind me. I bounded down the stairs, two steps at a time, then hopped in the front seat of the Volvo.

"Everybody ready?!" I said.

"Yeah!" they all blurted out.

I started up the Volvo then we were off, backing out of the garage then closing the garage door, out of the complex parking lot, down the main street past the convenience store, past the dumpy bar called the Beer:Thirty, past the street we usually turned on to go to the elementary school, toward the interstate highway that would take us to San Antonio: I-35.

Road trip.

The funny thing about going on a road trip with kids is that the most exciting part of the road trip--for them--is the first ten or fifteen minutes of the trip. That's it. Out of the entire trip, no matter how long the trip is or where the destination is, the most exciting part of all is the starting part. In that short period of time, nothing is as exciting as the *idea* of the road trip. To a kid, it just *sounds* so amazing! Fun! Adventure! Unknown places! Who will we meet?! What will we see?! And then, after the first ten or fifteen minutes, the boredom sets in. The monotony of the scenery along I-35--the flat, grassy areas between towns followed by the identical strip malls and outlet malls with their Chili's restaurants and McDonald's fast food and their Best Buys and Walmarts and Targets and Old Navies and their Starbucks and convenience stores and whatever--was stupefying. When my kids realized that the trip was not going to be instantaneous, that's when they asked the universal question, the question that every kid asks their parents when they begin a road trip. "Are we there *yet*?"

"Not even close," I said. The kids slumped into the back seat, sighing and harrumphing. It was going to be a long trip, I could tell, seeing them sunken in their seats with their arms defiantly crossed. Determined not to let their little attitudes ruin the trip, I turned to Nat and said, "Have you ever been to San Antonio before?"

"Oh, yes," she said, smiling that big, pearly white smile of hers. "My dad used to take us to Sea World when I was a kid. We'd drive down and stay in a hotel, go to Sea World and see Shamu, hangout for a few days and, like, go eat Mexican food."

"Sounds fun," I said, trying to keep my eyes on the road. It was hard having a conversation without *looking* at Nat. I tried my best to not crash while I talked to her, watching the road and all. "That was before, like, everyone found out that Sea World was mean to their killer whales. You know?"

"Because of *Blackfish*?"

"What is that?"

"That's the documentary movie that shed light on how killer whales were treated in captivity at places like Sea World."

"No, I never saw it. I just read about the killer whales on, like, the *internet*. It's a shame how they were treated. I would never go to Sea World again."

"I see."

"Not even if my dad asked me to go. I would never go again." An uncomfortable silence set in the cabin of the Volvo, like a thick stench, noticeable yet debilitating. I peeked in the rear view mirror and noticed that the kids had subsidized their boredom by drawing and playing video games--Sammie probably drawing new cartoon adventures in his sketchbook and Jessie probably playing *Street Fighter* or *Mortal Kombat* or some violent fighting game like that on her Nintendo. Nat eventually continued, "Would *you* take your kids to Sea World?"

I felt like an unwitting trap was being set in front of me and I wasn't sure how to proceed. I mean, San Antonio wasn't a million miles away but it was far enough that if I answered incorrectly then it could be a really, *really* long road trip. On the one hand (playing Devil's Advocate here, which is something I love to do), there was a lot more to do at Sea World than only go to the Shamu show. I mean, there was a water park and rides and roller coasters and other animals that didn't mind living at Sea World--like the penguins and the fish and the dolphins and the Clydesdale horses and the water-skiing squirrels--which didn't seem to offend the rest of the world as much as killer whales living in captivity at an amusement park. And their summer pass was a good deal, too good for a lot of people to pass up for summer entertainment for their kids. But I also could see the ethical dilemma that consumed Nat because she obviously loved animals and I didn't want to hurt her feelings. Who wants to hurt their babysitter's feelings? Nobody, that's who. I proceeded cautiously, not telling her we owned season passes, and said, "I would never take my kids to Sea World ever again."

"That's good," she said without hesitation, peering out the window, watching the suburban sprawl morph into the downtown landscape of Austin as we drove by. I could see her face in the reflection of the window. Nostalgic thoughts had taken hold of her, I could tell. "I remember driving through Austin on those trips to Sea World. Sometimes, my dad would take us to this barbeque place in Austin. It was a kind of, like, a famous place. At least that's what my dad used to tell us."

"Do you remember what it was called?"

"Nope. Not a clue. Wish I knew. But I remember the part of Austin where the exit was. Whenever we got close to that exit, I knew we'd be eating barbeque soon."

"Daddy?" said Sammie from the backseat, interrupting Nat. "Can I ask you a question?" He unbuckled his seatbelt and leaned forward on the front seats, his little arms draped around the headrests. Nat turned to look at him while I kept my eyes on the road.

"Sammie! Why did you take your seatbelt off?" I said.

"But I have to ask you a question. It's important!"

"OK. But make it fast then get your seatbelt back on."

"Are we going to be stopping any time soon?"

"No. We have to get to San Antonio in good time. Why?"

"Because I have to go to the bathroom. Bad," he said, panting as if it was hard work holding the urine in his bladder.

"Really bad?"

"Really bad," he said, a look of pain on his face in the rearview mirror. "It's an *emergency*."

"But we just got on the road not too long ago."

"I'm sorry, Daddy," he said, sulking into the backseat. His sister did not console him. She continued to play her Nintendo as if nothing was happening. Nat felt badly for the little dude. She felt *really* bad for him, I could tell by the sound of her voice.

"Let's pull over," Nat said, setting her hand on my shoulder. "I'll take him to the bathroom."

I could feel her hand through the material of my shirt. It was weird having her hand on my body but I didn't say anything to her about it. I didn't want it to be an awkward thing. Do you know what I mean? I'm sure you do. Of course you do. Anyway, I said, "Are you sure? But we literally just got on the road."

"I don't mind," she said, turning to Sammie Boy, a sweet smile on her face. "I probably need to go, too." She winked at Sammie--as if telegraphing a secret message or something--and he winked back to her. I scanned the highway for an exit and, fortunately for Sammie's bladder and for my sanity, there was one coming up in less than a mile. I maneuvered the Volvo S70 to the right lane and followed it to the exit and onto the access road of I-35. Before long, we stopped at a convenience store so Sammie could take a leak.

I parked the car and Nat got out, followed by good ol' Sammie Boy. I watched them both walk through the entrance of the convenience store together, his little hand in her hand. By this time, Jessie noticed the car was parked. She looked around confused, as if she had awoken from a bad dream and didn't know where the hell she was or if the world around her was real or still a dream. She rubbed her little eyes with her little fists then said, "Where are we?"

"I stopped 'cause your brother had to go tinkle."

"Tinkle?! But we just got on the road!" she said, tossing her pink Nintendo on the seat, unbuckling her seat belt, and leaning forward. "He's always causing problems, Daddy!"

I chuckled when she said that. It was pretty funny, really. Kids can be little comedians sometimes, especially when it involves joking about their pesky siblings who do annoying things to them all the time. It's true. Even though Sammie and Jessie loved each other, they also loved to tease each other any chance they got. This was little Jessie's chance to unleash her frustration with her big brother.

"*Always*?" I said, matter-of-factly. That was a bit of a stretch but I played along.

"Always! He *always* has to pee. He probably has a world record in peeing."

"Really?"

"Really!"

"And what do you base this on?"

"'Cause he's always asking to go to the bathroom. At home. At school. At restaurants. In outer space. Everywhere!"

"Sounds time consuming."

"It is, Daddy. It is," she said angrily, crossing her arms, her face twisting into pure annoyance as she gazed out the window, her mind rummaging through a catalog of very annoying events she had to endure from her brother, no doubt. "He's like a *girl*!"

Now, I was surprised by this comment considering that it came from *my* little girl. Not that little Jessie acted anything like a girl. In fact, acting like a girl was the last thing Jessie did. More than anything, she had the spirit of a boy trapped in a girl's body. I wouldn't be surprised if when she was older that she enlisted in the Marines or played an extreme sport or turned her love of taekwondo into a professional career or something along these lines. She was tough as nails and I didn't expect that to go away with age. If anything, I expected her to get tougher and tougher with age. I turned to look at my tough-as-nails daughter and said, "But you're a *girl*, sweetheart."

"No, I am not."

"You're not? Then what are you?"

"I'm a *warrior*," she said, a sly grin sliding cross her face. "And don't you forget it!"

"All right. All right. Calm down, killer," I said, looking in the window of the convenience store, trying to see if I could see Nat. I didn't see Nat or Sammie, for that matter. Sammie must have been setting another world record in peeing. "You should be nice to your brother."

"I'm nice to him!"

"Your brother... he's special, you know?"

"Special?" she said, then giggling hysterically as if that was the funniest thing she had ever heard. "Special sauce maybe!"

"Ha ha," I said, dryly. Little Jessie fell into the backseat, laughing at her own joke at Sammie's expense. He wasn't there to defend himself and, even if he was, I doubt he'd have much to say in return. Sammie wasn't very good at zingers or witty comebacks or any of that kind of stuff--mean or otherwise. He was way too sensitive for that. When I said he was special, I wasn't kidding. But soon, I saw Nat's head appear through the glass and Sammie's next to hers. It was a weird sight at first--their two heads floating behind the glass together as if they were part of the same body--until I realized that Nat was carrying my little boy in her arms. I immediately knew something was wrong. I jumped out of the car, ran to the store entrance, and swung the door open for Nat. She passed my little boy to me, his arms wrapping around my shoulders, his legs wrapping around my waist. I held him close to me, so close that I could feel his heart pounding. I knew something was wrong, I just didn't know what exactly.

"You all right, buddy?" I said. He nuzzled his face into my neck, his whimpers barely audible.

Nat's face was covered with concern, wearing her distress and confusion like dollar store makeup.

"Sorry to scare you Simon but Sammie said he, like, saw something but he wouldn't tell me what that meant," she said, worried. "I heard him crying in the bathroom so I went in there to get him. I thought maybe someone was in there with him--scaring him--but he was, like, by himself."

"Yeah," I said, looking around the convenience store for any onlookers. The clerk behind the counter watched us, mostly 'cause we were standing in front of the entrance. Maybe he thought we were going to steal something. Who knows? But all I knew was that I knew exactly what was going on with good ol' Sammie Boy. And it wasn't good. "Well, this happens sometimes."

"What do you mean?" she said, confused. The store clerk was getting irritated now with our standing in the entrance. He started waving his hands all over the goddamn place like he was directing an airplane to land or something. He looked like a big ol' dufus, waving his arms like that.

"Either come in or go out. You're blocking the door!" he said.

"Sorry," I said, indicating to Nat to follow me outside. Walking back to the car, Nat closely followed me, close enough that I could feel her arm touching my arm. Sammie gripped my neck tightly as I walked. "Well, you see. Sometimes, Sammie has these--" And right then, Sammie released my neck then forcefully placed both of his hands over my mouth tightly, as if sealing every bit of air in there. I couldn't speak, a muffled couple of words trapped in my mouth, tripping over my tongue.

"Daddy! No, don't *say* anything!" he said, hissing in my ear. Nat could hear him, though. She was caught a little off-guard, I could tell. I looked at her and she looked at me and we stood there in a momentary lapse of uncomfortable silence. It was weird, as if time stood still. "*Please*!"

"OK," I said. "Sorry, son." I squeezed him tightly, giving him the type of hug I know he craved, that comfortable, firm hug kids need so they know you are being sincere. We stood there for a moment in our embrace then I opened the backdoor of the Volvo and placed him inside. "Put on your seatbelt," I said to him. He complied then I closed the backdoor.

"Everything all right?" Nat said, still looking quite concerned.

"Yeah," I said, sighing. "I'll tell you about later. OK?"

"Sure," she said.

I smiled at her, then winked. That was my signal that we should go. So we hopped in my trusty Volvo S70 and drove away--just like that. A quick stop so my kid could take a leak turned into quite the awkward moment.

It's true.

***

When I was a kid, my parents used to love going on long day trips around Texas on the weekends and they would drag me along with them. Living in San Antonio at the time made it easy for us to go to different destinations in Texas because San Antonio was almost centrally located, with easy access to many freeways and interstate highways to get us where we were going. And being that Texas was such a large and geographically diverse state, there were--and still are--a lot of beautiful and unique landmarks and state parks and country towns and big cities and amusement parks and so on and so forth. I mean, Texas was a massive state, bigger than many countries in Europe, even. It's a pretty goddamn big place. It's true.

One of the things that used to capture my imagination as a kid when we drove around were these billboards that I would see on the side of I-35 or I-10 that advertised these fascinating, titillating, and sometimes dangerous sounding places: Inner Space Cavern, Natural Bridge Cavern, Aquarena Springs, Enchanted Rock, and more. The thing about these billboards was that they had spectacular headlines and out-of-this-world illustrations, something that sparked the imagination of a kid like me: a brainy and nerdy and curious and imaginative kid. For instance, Inner Space Cavern was a cave located in Georgetown, Texas. It was discovered by the Texas Highway Department in 1963 during the initial construction of I-35. There were many large openings to the cavern during the Ice Age, and several skeletons of prehistoric Ice-Age animals had been found in there. So, by the time the late 1970s came around (the era of the great Burchwood family day-trips!), the geniuses who oversaw the cavern came up with this brilliant advertising campaign of depicting saber-toothed tigers on their billboards with headlines such as "Come See Where this GREAT PREHISTORIC BEAST was Discovered!" or "Innerspace Caverns: Burial Site of the Vicious Saber-toothed Tiger!" Can you imagine what this billboard did to the brain of a child like me? My brain exploded!

But here's the thing: our car zoomed by these signs at top speed. There wasn't enough time for me to contemplate what they were saying or for me to ask thoughtful questions to my parents about what they meant. All I knew was that image of the saber-toothed tiger was burned into my brain and I had to go to Inner Space Cavern. Every time I saw that billboard, I asked my dad to take me. And Colonel Burchwood always--I mean ALWAYS--said no. It didn't matter how many times I said please or if my mother pleaded with good ol' Marv to appease me once and a while because I was a good boy and deserved a treat every once and a while or whatever. He was a mean ol' bastard, that Colonel Burchwood, I tell you. Crusty and as cantankerous as can be. It's true.

The reason I tell you all this is because I was pretty sure that we would soon see one of these billboards on the way to San Antonio for our emergency visit to see the crusty ol' bastard, Retired Colonel Burchwood. After we got back in the Volvo S70 and sped away from the convenience store, good ol' Sammie Boy calmed down and continued drawing in his sketchbook while his sister played her Nintendo. I took a peek at what he was drawing; he was drawing more cartoons of him and his imaginary pet bird, Budgie. But he and his sister were nice and quiet. It was like the incident in the convenience store never happened, except that it did and I didn't really get a chance to tell Nat what the hell was going on. I mean, in some ways, it would have been nice to give Nat the full-disclosure about my son. She was helping me and all with the kiddos. In theory, it seemed like the right thing to do. But sometimes, things that seem like the right thing to do in theory really aren't the right thing to do in real life. Do you know what I mean? Of course, you do. Besides, I figured if there was a right time to tell her about my son's ability to see the future, then I would take the opportunity to do so. That was not the right time to do that.

So, back to the billboards.

I was pretty certain we would see a billboard that would blow Sammie and Jessie's minds. Most of the ones I saw as a kid were long gone, replaced by boring advertisements for gas stations and outlet malls and fast-food restaurants and local politicians and shit like that. But there was one that was still around: the Snake Farm. It was a road-side attraction that still existed, a remnant of that long-gone era of country, small-town spectacles that used to mesmerize the ignorant locals of New Braunfels as well as the travelling tourists from across the state who didn't know any better, or were just bored. It was one of those places that as a kid I desperately wanted to go to but my parents never took me. Maybe, this would be a bonding experience that I could have with my own children--bridging the gap between my childhood and their own--and also allow me that opportunity to do something I never was able to do as a kid. I looked over at Nat to see what she was doing. She was quietly gazing out the window, enjoying the serenity of being away from her usual routine, her elbow propped on the door's armrest, her hand supporting the weight of her head.

I touched her arm which startled her. She placed her palm over her chest, where I imagined her heart to be, attempting to calm herself and keep her heart from pounding out of her chest. I felt pretty bad about it, startling her that is. Then said, "Didn't mean to scare you."

"It's OK," she said, catching her breath. "I was, like, deep in my own head just now."

"You know what?"

"What?" she said, sitting up, curious, fixing her hair where she thought she may have messed it up even though it wasn't messed up at all.

"There's something coming up that I want the kids to see. What are they doing?"

She slowly turned her head to look in the back seat, trying hard not to disturb them. She quietly reported back to me. "They are both doing their thing, playing games and drawing."

"So, do you think they can hear us?"

"Nah," she said, whispering, still primping her hair. Young women like Nat love to primp their hair. It's part of their self-esteem, self-care thing. Nat was always fixing her hair. It was just her thing, too.

"I want them to see this billboard coming up. Do you think you can get them to watch?"

"What billboard?"

"You'll see," I said, grinning. "It's gonna be great! I promise."

Nat reached in the backseat and touched each of the kids' knees. They slowly lowered their diversions, a look on their faces as if they were in a deep trance. I could see their glazed eyes in the rearview mirror. They looked like little zombies. It's true.

"Hey guys! Keep your eyes open. Something is coming up that your dad wants you to see," she said, cheerily. Sammie and Jessie shook their heads, shaking off their self-induced hypnosis. Being that Sammie was on the passenger side, he leaned over slightly to get a better look out the window. Jessie had to unbuckle her seatbelt to get closer to his window, placing her hands on Sammie's lap to prop herself up. Sammie didn't like this very much and began to protest.

"Hey! Get off me!" he said, trying to push her hands away.

"I'm trying to see, too!" she said, resisting his attempt to remove her hands.

"Fine! Only for a minute."

"Fine!"

Nat looked at me then rolled her eyes. She was used to this routine from these two, I could tell, but it didn't seem to faze her. She was a professional, I tell you. After about ten seconds of silence, I could see the billboard in the distance, the same billboard that had been in the exact same spot for at least 35 years: the Snake Farm. Just seeing it again gave me the chills like it did when I was a kid.

"Look, kids!" I said, pointing to the billboard. "What does it say?"

"Snake... Farm?" good ol' Sammie Boy said, then I heard a tiny gasp under his breath. He perked up then said, "What's a *Snake Farm*?"

"Yeah, Daddy!" Jessie said, chiming in. "What's at the Snake Farm?!"

"I don't know. I've never been to the Snake Farm. But I've always wanted to go," I said, sighing.

"I've always wanted to go, too," Sammie said.

"You've never even seen the sign before, dummy!" Jessie said, slugging Sammie in the arm.

"Have too!"

"Have not!"

"Have!"

"Not!"

"OK. OK!" I said, exasperated. Sometimes, just sometimes, their bickering sucked the joy out of life. I found myself taking deep breaths to deal with the unexpected onslaught of stress. "Calm down, you two. Would you both like to stop there and check it out?"

Nat gave me a concerned look. She pointed to her wrist as if she was wearing a watch and said, "We have to be in San Antonio for your dad. Remember?"

"I remember," I said, a little annoyed that she remembered. "But I want to experience this with my kids. We won't take long. OK?"

"OK," she said. "Put your seatbelt back on Jessie."

Little Jessie politely obeyed her babysitter--leaning back in her seat and putting her seatbelt back on--then I navigated the Volvo S70 to the far right lane, approaching the exit ramp. Once we exited and were on the access road, the small compound of white, stucco buildings quickly approached us. I slowed the car down and turned into the gravel parking lot. We had made it.

"Is this *it*?" Sammie said, worried.

"What a dump!" Jessie said.

Boy, was she right. Instead of the world-class, magnificent facility of exotic, wild animals and endangered species that the billboard promised, the sad compound looked more like an abandoned motel from the 1950s that hadn't seen a visitor since 1959. The compound consisted of three, white stucco buildings--all with dilapidated window screens, sagging and rusted window-unit air-conditioners, chipped and yellowed lead paint that once was white but was now the color of mucus, over-grown thorny shrubs, and mushy agave cacti--with a gravel parking lot that sprawled across the front of all of them. There was a foreboding feeling in the air since my Volvo S70 was the only car in the parking lot. No one else was as excited to see the Snake Farm as I was--neither my kids or anyone else in the state of Texas for that matter. We had the place *all* to ourselves.

"Is it, like, open?" Nat said, skeptically.

"I'm sure it is. Let's go check it out."

"Are you sure, Daddy?" Sammie said, skeptical too. "It looks haunted!"

"It'll be fine," I said, turning the engine off and unbuckling my seatbelt. "And look! There's a pet store and a taxidermist, too. How exciting!"

"What's a tax-er-der-mist?" Sammie said, all cute and confused at the same time.

"It's part of their very strange business model," Nat said, laughing. "Who puts a farm and a pet store, like, next to a taxidermist?"

"I don't know but I've always wanted to visit the Snake Farm. Ever since I was a kid! Who wants to go with me?"

A collective groan was released from the mouths of my three, reluctant participants. It was a sad, lifeless groan but I didn't let that deter me. I was determined to go inside with my kiddos, excited or not. We got out of the car--the hot, Texas sun baking our arms and faces-- and walked across the parking lot, the gravel beneath our feet crunching as we stepped on it. The passing cars on the highway created a collective hum similar to the crashing waves of the Gulf of Mexico on the sandy shores of Port Aransas, Texas. It was hypnotic. As we walked toward the entrance, I looked back to see all the cars passing by, not concerned or curious at all about the Snake Farm like I was. Maybe they all knew something I didn't know or maybe they just had somewhere better to go. I wasn't sure. The kids walked through the front entrance of the Snake Farm and I followed them.

Inside, the bright sun had constricted my pupils and it took a good twenty seconds for my eyes to adjust to the dark interior. While I stood there--my kids in front of me and Nat next to me--a hissing sound could be heard, low yet steady, and very ominous. I imagined a pit in the floor with poisonous snakes in it, their long, limbless bodies slithering over each other, and their mouths opened with fangs exposed, ready to snap at any human limbs they could lunge at. But instead--once my eyes adjusted to the darker interior of the Snake Farm lobby--what I found was a teenage boy sitting on a wooden stool behind a grimy glass counter with a rickety cash register sitting on top, and he was inflating balloons with a helium tank. It was a weird sight to see, this young kid who wasn't a day over 17 with his red "Snake Farm" polo shirt and his red baseball cap with "Snake Farm" emblazoned across the front of it in bright gold, bold letters--all by himself. After he inflated each balloon, he tied a colored ribbon to cinch the opening then released the balloon to the ceiling, where dozens congregated, impeded from flying to outer space by the ramshackle, stained ceiling above us. He had a name tag on his shirt that simply read: Juan. For all intents and purposes, "Juan" was white as can be (just so you know), not Hispanic by any means. But to be fair, you just never know about someone's true background, although he didn't come across to me as a "Juan," more like a Buford or a Cleetus.

He seemed rather surprised that we were there in the first place as if he had expected to *not* interact with anyone at all, all day, every day. After releasing the balloon in his hand, he said, "Can I help you?"

"Yes, we're here for a tour," I said, looking around, hoping to get a glimpse of the exotic animals we were about to see. "Do we have to buy tickets?"

He continued dutifully blowing up balloons and releasing them to the ceiling. There must have been thirty or more balloons up there, dancing around the brownish water stains in the ceiling tiles. "Tour? What do you mean a *tour*?"

"You know? To see the snakes."

"Snakes?" he said, confused. As he blew up the next balloon, I turned to see Sammie and Jessie mesmerized by the balloon's expansion as it filled with helium. "Do you mean *snake*?"

"Snake?" I said, looking around. I had this weird feeling like I was being filmed or something for a televised practical joke or a blooper or a reality TV show or something. That's what I get for growing up watching five hours of TV a day. "This is the Snake Farm, right?"

"Yep."

"And you have snakes at the Snake Farm, right?"

"Well," he said, standing up then pulling up his sagging jeans. "We have one snake. Her name is Meryl, as in Meryl Streep. She's back there." He pointed to a door at the back of the building.

"You only have *one* snake?" I said, surprised.

"Yep, just Meryl. And she's getting old. We may not have her around much longer. Then we'd have *no snake*," he said, chuckling. He thought that was pretty goddamn funny, I could tell, because he was snickering and wheezing and laughing all over the goddamn place. One of his job duties at the Snake Farm must have been comedian and we were his captured audience. Great, just great. "You want to see her?"

I looked at my kids and Nat and gathered from their nods and stares that they were willing to follow me to see the one and only snake at the Snake Farm, something that I thought was completely preposterous for a tourist attraction like this. I mean, you can't consider yourself a *farm* of animals if you only have one animal. Right? That's what I thought.

I nodded then "Juan" stepped out from behind the glass counter. He was thin and lanky and close to my height, his red ball cap getting him almost there. His worn jeans were a tad too short, revealing green argyle socks with yellow and brown lines from beneath his high-water, denim, end seams. He walked with a slight limp, the type of gangsta limp that an inner-city, hip hop kid would implore at da club on a Saturday night when thinking the ladies were watching him as he strolled to the bar for whatever was on special. We followed "Juan" through a door at the back of the room, into another room, one that was also sparsely furnished or decorated, except for a wooden table at the back with a single aquarium on it, the table sitting between two windows with saggy, dusty, aluminum blinds. Next to the aquarium was a small, red sign that said "Meryl" in gold letters. That must have been their official color motif: red and gold. Fabulous! Inside the aquarium lay a snake, thin and grey and lifeless. We gathered around the table, peering at poor Meryl through the dirty glass, who looked five minutes away from death. There were a few crickets in the tank, too, and I imagined they were her lunch. But instead of eating them, poor Meryl allowed the little buggers to hop inside the tank, unimpeded, like a cricket gymnasium. They used her snout as a diving board to the small dish of water at the opposite side of the sad aquarium from her.

"Feast your eyes. Behold!" our hip hop host said, grinning. "Meryl the snake!"

"What's wrong with it?" good ol' Sammie Boy said. He leaned closer, peering through the grimy glass of the aquarium with inquisitive eyes, his hand resting between his brow and the glass. "It looks like it's *dead*."

"She's not dead. I don't *think* she's dead," he said, leaning over then rapping the glass with the knuckle of his index finger. Meryl's pointy tongue slid out of her mouth in slow motion but the snake was otherwise motionless and stiff. The poor thing looked like it had had it with "Juan's" knuckle. I bet she'd have bit him on the face if she could have, sinking her fangs into the hollow sinus cavity behind his big nose, injecting any poison she could muster into his big, fat, annoying head. "See! Not dead."

"This sucks!" little Jessie said, crossing her arms defiantly. "This is the worst snake farm *ever*!"

"I have to, like, agree with her. Very disappointing," said Nat, standing behind all of us a few feet away. "This isn't much of a farm at all."

I looked at my family and the babysitter and ascertained that they weren't mad at me at all for bringing them to the Snake Farm. They seemed genuinely disappointed with "Juan" and the sad showing of Meryl the near-death snake and I could tell by how they all stood back from the sad excuse for a roadside attraction, looking around the even sadder room for an easy escape, hoping our hip hop tour guide wouldn't rap the glass of the aquarium again. Meryl was certainly a sad sight, not worthy of being put on display for unsuspecting tourists to leer at, expecting a freak show or something. I think, more than anything, Meryl was waiting to be put out of her misery or, at least, released into the brushy area behind the building so she could slither away then die peacefully--alone.

"Are there any more animals to look at?" said Sammie Boy, looking around in hopes that some animal--any animals--would appear. He probably would have been happy with a pill bug or a silverfish or a roach or something crawling across the floor. Kids are easily entertained like that; it doesn't take much to please them. It's true.

"Well," said "Juan," putting one of his hands in his back pocket and using the other to cock his baseball hat upwards, his sweaty, creased brow revealing itself. "The only other animals we have are in the pet store. And the dead ones at the taxidermist!" He started laughing again, like a hyena, sniffling and wheezing and hacking all over the place. He really thought he was something else, something funny. He wasn't even remotely funny, just annoying as hell.

Sammie turned to me, his whole face aglow with animal possibilities, his eyes shimmering with renewed hope, and said, "Can we go to the pet store, Daddy?"

Jessie caught his enthusiasm--like the flu--grabbed my shirt too, and said, "Daddy, please! Can we go?"

I looked at Nat and she returned a concerned look, pointing to her wrist again as if she was pointing to her imaginary watch whose hands were imaginarily turning in time, an obvious reference to the fact that we were on this road trip for a specific reason, which wasn't to look at animals on the side of the road. We were supposed to be going to visit my dad--grumpy ass, retired Col. Burchwood. You thought I forgot about that? Well, I didn't. But obviously, I wasn't in the biggest hurry in the world to get to San Antonio. Don't judge me. OK?

"We should, like, go soon," Nat said, reinforcing her wrist / time pointing / observation thingy. "Don't you think?"

I looked at my kids and demonstrated to her their excitement for the pet store, then said, "But look at them? They're excited." Nat rolled her eyes. I turned to "Juan" then said, "Is the pet store open? Can we go in?"

"Hold on," he said, reaching for his belt and unclipping a walkie-talkie. "Let me buzz Olaf."

"Who is *Olaf*?" I said.

Instead of answering me, he pressed the button on the walkie-talkie and said, "You back from break?" His eyes caught mine then he glanced at the walkie-talkie, his eyebrows rising, requesting some patience. After ten or so seconds of crackling and hissing, an answer came through the ether.

"On my way! Be there shortly!" said Olaf, through the tiny speaker of the walkie-talkie.

"Juan" smiled then said, "Follow me."

My kids yelled hooray and we all proceeded to follow our hip-hop tour guide to the front of the Snake Farm building, through the front door to the gravel parking lot outside. He walked to the front of the adjacent, dilapidated white building and stood on a small, cement pad at its front. The entrance was covered by a locked, screen door with a small sign hung on it. The sign said, "Be Back!" Next to those words was a yellow Sticky Note with these additional words handwritten on it: in 30 minutes. There was no indication of when the 30 minutes started or where Olaf had gone or what he was doing. For all we knew, Olaf could have been doing anything.

"Juan" looked off into the distance, the brim of his baseball hat keeping the bright sun from blasting his eyeballs out of their sockets.

I had this nagging question that kept at me and I wanted to know the truth. So, I said, "Is your name really Juan?"

He smiled, shook his head, then said, "Why, yes it is. Do I not look like a Juan?"

I was caught off-guard a little by his answer. I wasn't expecting him to say yes. I didn't really know what to say actually. I felt like a complete idiot. "I don't know."

"How is a Juan *supposed* to look like?"

An uneasy smirk appeared on my face, revealing a level of uncomfortableness that I wasn't ready to express to someone I had only known for less than an hour. Don't you hate it when someone catches you in your own bullshit? Yeah, I *love* that. I looked in the same direction as "Juan," hoping that Olaf would instantly appear to save the day and let us in the pet store, away from the uncomfortable feeling I was wading through. I didn't see anything or anyone yet in the distance. Sammie and Jessie were making the best of standing outside, both of them chasing each other in an infinite loop of the game Tag. Once one tagged the other, their game reversed and their circle of fun rotated the other direction. Nat spent her time looking at her phone, scrolling through pictures of puppies or kittens or shoes or something like that.

After a minute of this uncomfortable standing around, I finally noticed a plumb of dust rising in the distance, a tan-colored cloud coming up from the shrubs and cacti, accompanied by the sound of an engine, buzzy and high-pitched. I could make out a helmeted figure on an all-terrain vehicle, zig-zagging back and forth, making its way in our direction. The closer it got, the louder the engine got, revving faster when it jumped from the ground, more dust flying when it landed in the dirt. The sight of the all-terrain vehicle caught the kids' attention and they stopped playing Tag. Sammie stood on a parking space curb, shaded his eyes with his hands, then said, "Look, Daddy!" He couldn't believe his little eyes.

Before we knew it, the all-terrain vehicle and its rider were on the edge of the gravel parking lot, jumping a small hill then landing in the gravel, sending a wave of tiny stones and sand and dust toward us. The rider turned off the engine, dismounted, then approached us after taking his helmet off, leaving it on the seat. As he walked toward us-- who I could only assume was Olaf--he took his backpack off and unzipped it as he walked. Then, stopping next to "Juan," he handed him the contents of the backpack: a liter of Big Red soda, a pack of Marlboro Red cigarettes, a package of Cheetos, and a lottery scratch-off ticket.

"You owe me $2.50," Olaf said, annoyed. "And an extra ten minutes on my break tomorrow."

"You got it," said "Juan." "These folks would like to go in the Pet Store."

"No problem. Sorry for the wait, folks. Everyone needs a break from work every once and a while. Am I right?"

"Yeah!" said Jessie, excited.

"Do you have birds?" said Sammie, curious.

"Do we *have* birds?" said Olaf, pulling a large key ring from his jeans pocket, maybe with 50 or so keys on it of various shapes and sizes. He found the key he was looking for, unlocked the door, opened it, then said, "You'll have to see for yourself."

Inside, we escaped the hot sun for the air-conditioned tranquility of the pet store. The choir of animals sang, eagerly waiting to be adopted or purchased: puppy barks, kitten mews, bird chirps and whistles, fish aquarium hums, and so on and so forth. The smell was undeniable: cedar chips, puppy poop, kitty poop, fish food, tank water, you name it. The pet store was jam-packed with cages and tanks and aquariums and pens and boxes and stacks of pet food of all kinds and racks of pet supplies and toys and the like. It was in stark contrast to the Snake Farm, the solemn mausoleum of Meryl the Deathly Snake-- sad, pathetic, and simply not fun at all.

The kids squealed for joy as they careened through the store, looking at one animal for a second or two before moving along to the next excited animal. Jessie and Sammie held hands and they blazed through the store. Olaf got a kick out of seeing their excitement before sitting on a wooden stool behind a similar glass counter to the one in the Snake Farm. Unlike "Juan's" pile of crap from whatever convenience store Olaf had come from, he opened a single power bar, one made of granola and dried fruit, taking a large bite then chewing it thoroughly, like a cow chewing its cud.

Nat and I stood in front of the glass counter, watching the kids as they hurried up and down the aisles of pets and supplies. I leaned on the glass counter then said, "How long have you worked here?"

"Oh, man," he said, his mouth full of granola and dried fruit. Bits and pieces flew from his lips as he talked. "Since I was a little kid. Our dad owns the pet store and the Snake Farm. Normally, he would be the taxidermist on duty but he's on vacation right now. He's in Corpus Christi."

"Your dad is the taxidermist next door?"

"Yup," he said, finishing the power bar then tossing its wrapper in the trash. "It's weird not having him around. Been nice and quiet."

"I see," I said, looking at Nat. She was still perusing her phone, now looking at photos of clothes and shoes and purses. She wasn't interested in what Olaf had to say, at all. Nat was funny that way. She could come off as aloof, whether she intended to or not. She was just that way sometimes.

But before I could continue my scintillating conversation with Olaf the granola-spitter, Sammie started screaming from the back of the store, a high-pitched squeal like you would hear a kid make on Christmas morning, an ear-splitting tone that was pure joy.

"Daddy! Daddy!" he said from the back of the store.

Nat and I abandoned Olaf. In the back of the store, we found them sitting on the concrete floor, Sammie across from little Jessie, a small bird perched on his index finger. The bird was mostly light blue with some grey and yellow feathers on his head, speckles of black dots scattered across his body like pepper grounds. Sammie had the biggest smile on his face that I think I had ever seen in his entire life. In fact, he was so gobsmacked, I thought he might pass out.

"Wha cha got there?" I said, bending down on one knee. The little bird turned its head to look at me. He looked completely at ease on my boy's little finger.

"Daddy, you won't believe it," he said, so consumed with joy and astonishment that I thought he was going to cry. "I found Budgie!"

"Who is Budgie?" I said before immediately regretting that question. Of course I knew who Budgie was. How could I not?

"Look," he said, raising his hand with the bird on it. "He has a letter B on his chest."

I took a closer look at the parakeet's chest and, sure enough, there was a little splotch of white feathers that--if you looked hard enough and with the right amount of imagination--looked a lot like a capital letter B. It's true.

"Wow, Sammie, I think you're right. It does look like a letter B."

"Can I keep him? Please!" Sammie gave me a look of sheer helplessness and despair, as if we didn't take the cute little bird then he would become suicidal or something like that. I wasn't sure what to do. I was really conflicted.

"Sammie, we can't take the bird right now. We're on our way to see PeePaw. Remember?"

"But Daddy," he said, tears welling up in the corners of his eyes, desperation soaking through the brown of his irises. "I'll do anything. We have to take Budgie! He's my best friend!"

Crap. I mean, I had Sammie on the verge of tears with his dream bird perched on his finger, Jessie also about to cry by osmosis, Nat looking at me like I was crazy for giving in to my son's desperate pleas, and Olaf the pet store clerk peering over a dog and cat collar display, granola crumbs stuck on his lips, a puzzled look on his face. What was I to do? I was in a tough spot, I tell you.

"Sammie," I said, gently. "Put the bird back in its cage, son. We have to go visit PeePaw."

"But Daddy--" he said, tears detaching themselves from the corners of his eyes, leaving wet trails of pain and disappointment and suffering on his cheeks.

"Maybe on the way back home, we can stop here again."

"But what if someone else buys him?!" Sammie said, desperate. "I couldn't live with myself if someone else bought him, Daddy!"

I was caught a little off-guard by this last plea. I mean, kids can be pretty dramatic about stuff, especially when they want toys or candy or cake or something like that. But I knew Sammie was pretty sincere about wanting to take this little bird home, I could tell. It just wasn't the right time to consider taking a pet in the car. But I didn't know how to articulate that to my boy. I was at a loss for words. Can you believe that? Me at a loss for words? I looked to Olaf for advice.

"I can hold that parakeet for you, not let anyone else buy him."

"Will you?" Sammie said.

"Sure," he said, smiling. "Let me get you a marker and a piece of paper so you can write your name on it for me." Olaf disappeared for a little bit then reappeared next to us on the floor, a Sharpie in one hand and a 3 by 5 card in the other. "You'll have to put the bird in his cage so you can write your name down."

Sammie gently placed the parakeet back in its cage and closed the door. Budgie--as Sammie called it--sprung onto the side of the cage, like a magnet to metal, at the closest possible point to Sammie, and stared at him with his little bird eye through the metal bars, as if to say, 'Are you coming back for me?' Their bond was undeniable. Sammie then took the marker and card from Olaf and scribbled his name on it, in tall, thick letters: SAMMIE. He slid the card in the front of the cage, at the bottom behind the bird seed holder. Sammie wiped the tears on his face on the front of his t-shirt then stood up, looking up at Olaf, then said, "Take care of Budgie. We'll be back soon."

"OK," said Olaf, smiling.

Sammie smiled too. I think he felt better knowing that there was a sign on Budgie's cage, declaring to the world in definitive, dark letters that the bird was his. And I felt better knowing that I had at least a couple of days to figure out if we would be taking a parakeet home to Austin with us. Sammie leaned over to the bird cage, puckering his lips and making kissy noises. "Be back, Budgie. I love you," he said.

With that, we all said goodbye to Olaf and left the pet store. We got in the Volvo S70 then drove away. The rest of the way to San Antonio was pretty quiet, as quiet as four people in a car could be after a sad farewell like that.

It's true.

Chapter Nine

San Antonio, Texas. Do I need to say more? When people say San Antonio, most people think of these things: the San Antonio Spurs basketball team, the Alamo, the River Walk, Sea World, and Mexican food. To most people *not* from San Antonio, it would seem to be the ultimate tourist destination with plenty of thrilling sights to see and exceptional food to eat. I mean, San Antonio has the best Mexican food in the world, even better than in Mexico! It's true. But to the people that live and work in San Antonio--except for following the Spurs-- most of these things are simply things to avoid. The River Walk? Tourist trap. The Alamo? Meh. Sea World? Killer whale concentration camp. To a lot of people who grew up in San Antonio, that town really meant mostly one thing: military bases. Randolph Air Force Base, Kelly Air Force Base, Lackland Air Force Base, Fort Sam Houston, and Camp Bullis--thousands of families lived and breathed military life in San Antonio and my family was no different. When Retired Army Colonel Marvin Burchwood was on active duty, he was stationed at Fort Sam Houston, an army base in the heart of San Antonio, where he worked in manpower, and our family lived in a suburban home in Northeast San Antonio. My father went to work, my mother stayed home, and I went to school: the perfect military family.

Nowadays, whenever I drive south down I-35 from Austin into San Antonio, I get that nostalgic pang driving through the unchanging landscape of storage facilities, massive mega-churches, chain family restaurants, cheap motels, truck stops, and the skating rink where I learned how to roller skate in the first grade. San Antonio never seemed to change--ever. Driving this stretch of interstate highway was, literally, like going back in time for me. This time, I marveled at the state of suspended animation that we were driving through; time literally seemed to me to stand still.

"San Antonio never changes," I said, out loud to myself. No one else seemed interested in my astute observation, not even Nat--who was sound asleep in her chair like an albino spider monkey with its arms and legs wrapped tightly around its torso--or the kids, who were still playing their Nintendos or drawing in their sketchbooks in the back seat, oblivious to where we were. In the rearview mirror, I could see Sammie and Jessie doing their thing, and my boy repositioned himself as if he had heard me say something but nothing of consequence.

"Are we there yet?" Sammie said, not looking up, disinterested in the outside world, drawing in his sketchbook.

"We're in San Antonio, son."

"We are?!" he said, tossing down his pencil, then looking out the door window. His excitement soon faded. "It's boring *here*. Are we close to where PeePaw lives?"

"Kind of."

"Let me know when we're *really* close to where PeePaw lives. OK?"

"Ok," I said, looking back at the highway then glancing at Nat. She was snoring, a light, rhythmic snore that mingled nicely with the hum of the air conditioner and the road noise. Her head laying against the door panel, she was drooling a bit, a droplet on the armrest still attached to her lower lip by the thinnest strand, like the remnants of a spider web. It seemed physically impossible to me for someone of her height to sleep in the awkward position she was in but, in spite of my astonishment, she was sound asleep. I mean, she was out cold. I thought for a moment to wake her up and save her neck from the impending, severe crick it would receive from sleeping in such a bizarre position, then decided otherwise. Sleep would be good for her, I thought. It was going to be a long weekend. I just knew it.

After a few more minutes of driving, I found the exit we were supposed to take to get to the appropriately named Autumn Grove, the nursing home where my father lived. I wasn't too worried about missing Ms. Robyn since I knew she practically lived at Autumn Grove and, even if she wasn't there, I knew they would call her in if I requested it. She was just that kind of lady--dedicated and loving and open-hearted and dependable. I took the exit then turned right at the next intersection. This part of San Antonio's heyday was definitely somewhere in the mid 1970's but was experiencing a renaissance of late. Several of the 70's styled buildings had been refurbished, painted a more modern color scheme which accentuated their disco quirkiness, but many had been knocked down completely and replaced with buildings with a more arts & crafts style, creating a mishmash of tans and maroons and browns and greens that was at least slightly more appealing than mold and rust and mildew--all for the sake of progress.

Before I knew it, the great lawn of Autumn Grove appeared, the monolithic sign with its namesake mounted right behind the curb to the road. On the other side of the sign was the driveway to my dad's nursing home. I turned onto the driveway and saw the buildings of Autumn Grove in the distance, several hundred yards away, past the great lawn with walking trails and gazebos and park benches and pecan trees and magnolia trees and a duck pond. It was an elderly person's paradise or, at least, that's what the brochures would have you believe. It certainly seemed that way by its appearance. I slowly proceeded up the driveway towards the buildings housing the retirees, when all of a sudden--out of the blue--the engine to my Volvo S70 cut off as well as all electrical power. All the lights on the dash just went dark. Confused, I didn't know what to do while my car slowly stopped in the middle of the driveway, not even halfway to the main building. And like an antidote to the malaise my family suffered from, the lack of motion woke up Nat from her sleep and startled my kids from their gaming and drawing.

Nat rubbed her eyes as she sat up, then wiped her wet cheek with her hand, then said, "Where are we?" She was confused not only because she had slobber on her cheek but because we were not moving.

The kids, too, asked the same question. "Yeah, where are we?" Sammie said, concerned.

"Yeah, Daddy. Where?" Jessie said.

"We're at Autumn Grove," I said. "Well, almost."

"Why are we parked here?" Nat said, looking around. We all watched a long-haired dachshund run across the length of the great lawn to its owner, an elderly woman sitting in a motorized wheel chair. When the dog reached her, it jumped into her lap, then she proceeded to drive toward us, her chair wobbling as it ran over the dark green, Bermuda grass. Her smile was big and wide and a shiny yellow. Her hair was thin and silvery, strands of it dancing away from the rest of her styled hair helmet. The dachshund yipped and yapped as she got closer to my car. "We have a visitor."

I rolled down Nat's window using the button in my door. The elderly woman pulled as close as she could without dropping off the curb at the edge of the lawn. A sticker was affixed to her purple, polyester shirt. The top part of the sticker said, in bold font print, "My Name Is." Underneath that in neat, cursive handwriting written in black marker said, "Bernice."

"Are you having trouble with your automobile?" she said, her long-haired dachshund yipping and yapping, too. The dog's barking clearly irritated Bernice, who seemed quite confused as to what to do about the dog's bad behavior. She tried to muzzle the dog but it was too allusive for her hands to grasp.

"I guess so," I said, loudly. "It just shut off on me."

"Are you here to visit a resident?" she said. Her dog continued to bark at such an irritating rate that Bernice raised her hand--shaky yet determined--then actually clamped the little bastard's mouth shut. It continued to at least try to bark, the muffled noise accompanied by its little dog tongue protruding between its dog lips. "Sorry for all the noise."

"My dad lives here. Colonel Burchwood. He's retired Army." Her face twisted in contemplation, scanning the rolodex of her mind with the name, trying to put it with a face. I realized as I watched her rack her brain that maybe they didn't know my dad by such a formal name. Maybe they knew him informally so I said, "His first name is Marvin. Some people call him--"

"Marv!" she said, excited. The dachshund was determined to yap some more but Bernice held onto its snout as best she could. "Oh, Marv is such a fun man. So sweet and gentlemanly."

Whoa! What was this? I wasn't used to hearing my father described with these glowing terms of endearment, with such gushing and complimentary words. How strange it was to hear him called these things. Maybe, just maybe, we were not talking about the same person. Maybe, she was confusing him with another, different Marv, one who was a good father and sweet to his family and a social butterfly that played Bridge with the gang and sipped brandy from a glass snifter and laughed at everyone's jokes and was always willing to lend a hand to a friend in need. Certainly, she wasn't referring to my father: the asshole. It was all very confusing.

"Maybe you're thinking of someone else. My dad is--"

"No, there's only one Marv in the whole place. I'm certain of it. Such a friendly guy. And such a looker, too!"

"I see. That's good to know," I said, looking at my kids, perplexed. They gave me shrugs in return, confused like I was, mainly because they didn't know who this lady was and we were still stuck in the middle of the driveway. It was awkward. Plus, she was kind of drooling over my dad, which was gross.

"But you *have* to know, Marv isn't doing so well. I imagine that's why you are here, to see him. Am I right?"

I nodded. The dachshund in her lap, quiet now, sat stiffly as if trying to hold back a bowel movement, its face constipated and oblique. He was a sight to see, I tell you. "I need help with my car, though."

"If you can get it closer to the building, then I'm sure Tony will help fix it."

"Tony?" I said, confused.

"He's the handyman. He can fix anything." The dachshund suddenly escaped from her grip and released a series of yips and yaps that almost sent Bernice tumbling to the grass. She tried to grab his snout again--her hand still shaky but quick--but he eluded her, jumped down in the grass, and tore off toward the duck pond to chase some birds milling about the lawn for seeds or grubs or bread crumbs or whatever. "Maybe I'll see you later at dinner," she said. She turned her motorized wheel chair and pursued her little monster, which was running around the perimeter of the pond in a frothy rage. As she drove away, she extended her arm into the arm and waved--a slow deliberate wave--like the Queen of England or a holiday parade queen.

I examined the faces of my passengers, all confused by what just transpired, and offered a suggestion. "Want to push the car?"

"Push, like, *this* car?" Nat said.

"Yeah!" said Sammie and Jessie, quickly opening their doors and ejecting from the back seat as fast as they could.

"If you help them push, then I'll steer the car as close to the parking lot as possible."

Nat wore her apprehension on her face like the wrong color lipstick for the occasion. It was clear she didn't want to push the car but--as far as I could tell--she didn't really have a choice. I mean, the kids were back there trying to push already and she was the *nanny*. It was official; she had to help push.

"Fine," she said, sluggishly getting out of the car. The three of them discussed a quick plan of action at the back of the car. I could feel the three of them pressing on the trunk of the Volvo. She called out, "On three! One! Two! Three!"

As they pushed, the car reluctantly drifted down the driveway toward the main building, slowly picking up speed as the driveway dipped down a slight incline. The Volvo picked up enough speed that it got away from the kids and, as it sped toward the parking lot, I thought for a second that it might make it the whole way. I could see the three of them in the rearview mirror, waving and cheering as the car sped away from them. But as the driveway continued up towards its inverse, the Volvo quickly slowed down almost to a stop way faster than I expected. I pulled the wheel to the right and got the car as close as I could to the parking lot, but not close enough. It lurched to a stop when I hit the curb about twenty feet away from the nearest parking space. Well, it was really close enough. Nat and the kids ran to the car, then stopped, stooped over, hands on their knees, panting heavily.

"You almost, like, made it," Nat said, her hand on her chest, breathing heavily.

"So close," I said. I heard the whir of a small, electric motor in the distance and turned to see what it was. A golf cart appeared, out of nowhere, with a stalky Hispanic man driving. He was wearing a white jumper and a baseball cap, also white, his face serious as if he was ready for business, his grip of the steering wheel firm, his back erect. "Must be Tony," I said.

He parked next to the Volvo, the electric motor of the cart dying the instant he released his foot from the gas pedal. He hopped off the cart and stuck his landing on the asphalt, his fists pushing his hips in place, his legs locked into stiff cylinders, and his gaze intense. He looked at me then the car then the perimeter around the car and, it appeared, he already knew the answer to the question he was about to ask.

"Having car trouble," he said, serious, not a question but a declaration.

"Yes," I said, intimidated.

"Any ideas?" He peered at the hood of the car like he had X-ray vision, seeing the problem at a microscopic level, inside the wires, inside the hoses, inside everything.

"No."

"Of course not," he said, matter-of-factly. "Leave the key with me. I'll fix it." He extended his hand for the key.

"Are you sure?" I said, dangling the key then clinching it. "I don't want to be any trouble. I can call a wrecker or a tow truck."

"Why would you do that?" he said, puzzled. "I said I can fix it. I'll have it ready to go by the time your visit is over."

"Really? 'Cause that would be great, actually."

"Really. It's my job. I fix things." I handed him the car key and he returned a smile that, without a doubt, exuded the confidence and where-with-all of someone who knew exactly what he was doing with exactly the skills he had in his toolbox. As I would find out in time, Tony really could fix *anything*. He was just one of those types of men who could do that, take anything apart and put back together in working order without any trouble at all, like he was just born to do that. There weren't too many men like him around anymore and--if there *were*--I didn't know who they hell they were. Most people I know don't know how to fix shit and that's the truth. "You'll find Ms. Robyn inside the entrance. Just ask for her at the welcome desk. She'll help you the rest of the way."

"OK."

"Have a nice visit," he said, slipping in a quick, kind smile before returning to serious mode.

I gathered my brood and we walked toward the entrance. In front of the building was a covered, circular drive with a number of rocking chairs and padded benches around the perimeter of the driveway, potted plants and flowers and succulents between them, a water fountain to one side and a bird bath on the other. Parked under the cover of the entrance was a long, white limousine, its windows tinted pitch black, an antenna for satellite radio on top, shiny chrome wheels at bottom--the tires glossy and spotless--and the name "Autumn Grove" stenciled on the side in bold letter of burnt orange and oak brown and forest green. It was certainly staged as an elderly person's paradise and there were many places--hospitals and care centers and clinics and retirement homes--that had a similar faux-coziness that betrayed the crappiness of the stark, cheap reality inside. But Autumn Grove was different which was why I put my dad, retired Colonel Burchwood-- PeePaw--there. This wasn't any fake bullshit. It was the real deal, inside and out.

Inside, we huddled then took in the welcome den. The smell of fresh, baked goods hung in the air, music from another era quietly played through speakers in the ceiling, and a few residents sat and chit-chatted with each other on leather couches. The den (I called it a den because that's exactly what it seemed like to me rather than a welcome area or lobby or whatever else a business would call the area by the entrance) was exquisitely furnished with an eye for comfort as well as style, two over-sized leather couches faced each other, a coffee table of sturdy, carved dark wood in between them with cups of coffee and plates of cookies on top, two matching leather sitting chairs on each end, and an elderly couple sitting on one couch together, their eyes locked on each other, their laughter hardy and carefree. It did not feel like the lobby of a business; it felt like a home. Sammie and Jessie were overwhelmed by it all. Nat's face lit up as she looked around.

"I could, like, really live here," she said, her mouth agape with wonder and a little bit of jealousy. "It's *way* nicer than my place."

"Me too!" said Sammie.

"Cookies!" said Jessie. She bolted for a small table just past the welcome desk, a large serving tray with an assortment of cookies and muffins and slices of cake on top, with stacks of paper coffee cups and a thermal canister of what I presumed was coffee next to it--regular not decaf was probably the octane. No need giving old folks decaf; they needed the caffeine to keep them human. Sammie followed close behind her to help inventory just how many sweet things they were going to devour.

"This is nicer than any apartment complex I've ever lived in. It's, like, luxurious," Nat said, still amazed. I wasn't surprised by it anymore. What do you expect to get for $4,000 a month? The residents had it all: a limo, fresh-baked goods whenever they wanted, around the clock dining, comfy places to sit and talk, and nice living quarters. It was a retirement paradise.

"Yeah, it's nice, huh?" I stepped over to the welcome desk which, at that moment, was unoccupied. On it were stacks of brochures about the kind of life you would expect your parents or grandparents to get if you decided to place them in the loving hands of the staff at Autumn Grove, as well as some ballpoint pens with the name "Autumn Grove" on them, and a shiny, stainless-steel table bell. I pressed the button on the bell and it dinged a soft, pleasant note. The elderly couple on the couch looked our way, smiling, pleased that there were visitors in their midst. For a quick moment, a picture of my parents appeared in my mind--next to the actual scene in front of me--and I imagined my parents sitting there on the couch, together, in the welcome den, talking and laughing and eating cookies and drinking coffee, in the autumn years of their lives that was never to be. This daydream was abruptly interrupted by Sammie and Jessie, arguing over who would first try the baked treats, each elbowing the other, jockeying for position. I ignored them, not giving any credence to their petty argument, and held Nat back from breaking up their argument. It was the right move because Ms. Robyn appeared behind the welcome desk, all smiles and open arms, as usual.

"Simon Burchwood!" she said, making her way around the desk to hug me, tightly. She held her embrace longer than most people, like a loving aunt who hadn't seen her favorite nephew in a decade and missed him dearly. I caught the look on Nat's face, a look of warmth and happiness usually reserved for the sight of a pile of newborn kittens or some other cute thing like that. It was a little awkward, to be honest. She released me a good ten seconds later but held on to my arms, pulling back and getting the full view of me. "It's been a little while, hasn't it? Since I saw you last?"

"Yes, Ms. Robyn. It has."

"And why is that, my boy?" she said, putting her hands on her hips, standing sternly. "Have you been too busy to visit us? And visit your dad?"

"Well--" I said but she interrupted me.

"Do your kids want some cookies?" she said, looking at Sammie and Jessie. Of course good ol' Sammie Boy and little Jessie heard this and went insane. Why would they *not* go insane? They were little kids. That's just what little kids do.

"Yeah!" they said, taking a treat in each hand then running back over to me. Ms. Robyn embraced them, smiling at them and touching their cheeks and messing their hair and looking into their eyes, gazing at them.

"Boy, are they cute," she said, blushing. "All children are cute. But yours are especially cute!" The kids beamed at her, lovingly, in awe, as if she were Santa Claus or the Easter Bunny or the grandmother they wished they always had. It was cute to see. Then Ms. Robyn placed her arm around my shoulder, pulling me closer to her, and said, "Are you ready to visit your dad?"

"Yes."

"Good! Let's go. I think he knows you are coming. Follow me!" she said. As she said this, she released me then placed her arm around Nat's waist and pulled her close. Nat was too tall for the 'around the shoulder' thing. She was like an Amazon warrior, really--tall, way too tall for most people. I imagine the person she ends up with as a life partner will be tall, too, a giant, even. It's true. "And who is this beautiful young woman?" Nat started beaming and blushing and rolling her eyes all over the goddamn place, too, just like my kids did. I had never seen her so embarrassed before. Her face was the color palette of a nectarine: reds and pinks and oranges. It was a sight to see. She and the kids must have been in need of some attention pretty bad. They were just absorbing it all in like sponges that had been deprived of water for years.

As we followed Ms. Robyn and Nat out of the welcome den, I marveled at just how nice a facility it was. Even calling Autumn Grove a facility didn't do it justice. It was a residential complex, nicer than most apartment complexes you've seen, I guarantee it. It's styling and quality of construction was something closer to a resort with its crown moldings and deluxe baseboards and pristine carpet and eye-catching color scheme. As we traversed down the first hallway, what struck me most was how happy all of the residence were--elderly couples walking hand in hand, talking, laughing, generally in a splendid mood, smiling at us, winking, waving. Sammie and Jessie gladly waved and winked back, enjoying the attention from the residents who, it seemed, were glad to see children in their hallways. Old people love children usually--unless they are jaded or sick or insane--at least that's what I've noticed. It was a rare day when an old person was not happy to see my kids, so rare that I can't even remember the last time an old person was mean to them. How could they be mean to them? They are so goddamn cute. It's true. As we walked, Ms. Robyn was really laying it on thick.

"Have you ever considered modeling?" she said to Nat, pinching her butt. That startled Nat and she turned to look back at me, a look of surprise on her face. I gave her the thumbs up but I don't think that made her feel any better. She seemed to take it in stride. A second pinch in the butt turned her around. "You could make a killing at modeling. Look at your legs. They go on forever!"

As we traversed down the hallway, I noticed decorations on each of the doors to the apartments, things like hand-made wreaths of dried leaves and flowers in the shape of hearts, framed photos of loving families mounted next to some of the doors, some apartment numbers replaced with fancier, custom-made numbers of carved wood or molded bronze, and welcome mats with intricate woven designs or salutations painted on in large, bold letters like 'WELCOME' or 'HOME IS WHERE THE HEART IS.' It was obvious to me that the residents loved living here, that it was a home and not the last place of refuge for the helpless like a traditional nursing home or state hospital or insane asylum or someplace like that. I suddenly felt a sense of pride in my choice of home for my dad, something that I hadn't felt before in an unsolicited way. As I watched my kids run, waving at my dad's neighbors, Nat with her arm draped across Ms. Robyn's shoulder (I guess Ms. Robyn finally got her to let down her guard), and door after door of happy residents, it seemed my dad was in a good place.

Ms. Robyn turned her head to me then said, "Almost there. Just around the bend." She fished in her pockets and pulled out a large key ring, seemingly too large to fit in the form-fitting slacks she wore, and she searched for the key to my dad's place. Ahead of them, Sammie and Jessie continued to run, that is, until Jessie tripped and fell, sliding across the carpet 'Pete Rose' style, on her stomach with her arms stretched out in front of her. The fall startled her but she didn't make a noise until she stopped sliding. Nat released Ms. Robyn and knelt to pick up Jessie, tears streaming down her red face but she was the opposite of sad. Boy, she was furious.

"Are you OK?" Nat said, worried.

"Didn't hurt!" Jessie said, crossing her arms defiantly, her face maroon with embarrassment and anger.

Ms. Robyn found the key she was looking for then said to Jessie, "How did you know to slide into the correct door?" Jessie shrugged and didn't seem to care. "Here's your grandpa's home."

Ms. Robyn slid the key into the lock and the rest of us gathered around her, as if waiting to see what would be revealed behind the door, like it was some kind of surprise we weren't expecting to see. As she turned the key then the door knob, the door seam released a sound like a vacuum-sealed package taking in air after being slit open. She slowly pushed the door open and we followed her inside. The short entry way led us to the living room where my dad laid, on a hospital bed in the middle of the room, surrounded by a number of medical machines and other pieces of important looking equipment, all seemingly hooked up to my father by what looked like dozens of wires and tubes and straps. A large TV was mounted to the wall and on it, some daytime talk show hosts mimed congeniality but it was mute or the volume was turned all the way down. My dad looked pale and grey--like the color of a cheap piece of butcher meat that boiled in a pot of water too long--and he laid motionless as if sleeping or unconscious, his eyes barely closed, his skin wilted, his hair tussled. And accompanying my father was someone who I presumed to be a nurse, a fit woman whose skin was the color of a roasted coffee bean, her hair shiny and straight, her outfit styled somewhere between workout clothes and hospital scrubs. She sat on a stool and was reading a weathered copy of *The World According to Garp* by John Irving. She was chuckling as we all gathered around my father: retired Colonel Burchwood, PeePaw, my dad.

She looked up at us and said, "Have you ever read this book?" We all shook our heads. No one, it seemed, knew the world according to Garp. "That Jenny Garp is crazy!" she said, slapping her knee then laughing all over the goddamn place like a woman possessed, like she was privy to something all of us should know but sadly didn't.

"Everybody," Ms. Robyn said, smiling. "This is Sharice. She is..."

"I help Marvin," Sharice said, quickly interrupting Ms. Robyn.

"Yes, that's right. She assists your father with all of his medical needs: shots, pills, bandages--"

"And even sponge baths!" Sharice said, giggling and snickering. "He's crazy about his sponge baths. Yes, he is! He loves them more than anything except maybe his scotch on the rocks. He likes that, too, almost as much as the sponge baths. But the baths, he likes those most. Yes, he does!"

Sammie and Jessie and Nat all looked at me, befuddled, almost disturbed. I wasn't sure what their deal was. I mean, Sharice was a little... different, but, knowing how much it cost to live at Autumn Grove and just how nice a home it was, I doubted that her ability as a nurse was anything but stellar. To me, she just seemed a little *eccentric*, that's all. Who was I to judge, right?

"This is Colonel Burchwood's family," Ms. Robyn said, introducing all of us. She put out her hand, flat yet firm, in front of her like a game show hostess, pointing at me. "This is Simon, his son."

"Oh, I've heard *a lot* about you, son! Nice to finally put a name with a face." She put out her hand for me to shake and I reluctantly shook hers. She had a firm grip like a football player or a wrestler or some type of athlete. She about pulverized my hand with her tremendous grip.

"OK," I said. I didn't know how to respond to that. What had she heard about me? That was a strange thing to say. It's true. And my hand, she just about crushed it. "This is Natalie or Nat, as we call her." I gestured to Nat with a similar hand signal to Ms. Robyn's game show hostess move. Nat and Sharice exchanged a burly handshake, as burly as two women could muster.

"And these are the Colonel's grandchildren," Ms. Robyn said, quickly chiming in, placing her hands on the backs of Sammie and Jessie, easing them forward so Sharice could see them clearly. "This is Jessie and this young man is Sammie."

As soon as Ms. Robyn said my boy's name, my dad--retired Colonel Burchwood or PeePaw as my kids called him--opened his eyes and turned his head in our direction, his yellow teeth revealing themselves from behind his parched lips. Man, he did not look good. He looked about three steps from the grave. Really. A hiss slipped through his dingy teeth, faint and airy and musty.

"Sss... Sammie?" he said. "Is that you, my boy?" He extended his withered arm from under the bed sheets--wrinkled and grey and sinewy with white, wiry arm hair on his fore arm--and his knobby-knuckled fingers slowly unfurled for the touch of my boy's hand. Sammie reached for him, grabbing his forefinger with his tiny hand.

"Yes, PeePaw?" he said, nervous. "Are you OK?"

"Come closer, my boy," my dad said, low and raspy and weak. "Come closer so I can see you."

"I'm right here, PeePaw," he said, gently stepping closer to the bed. He was barely tall enough to see him once next to the bed but he did the best he could, using his other hand to grab another of PeePaw's fingers, pulling himself as close as he could to his grandfather. "What is it?"

"It's time," PeePaw said, low and faint. I understood the words he said--barely--and so did Sammie but I don't think either one of us knew what he was talking about exactly. PeePaw slowly curled his fingers, cupping Sammie's hands, softly, like he was holding a small bird's egg. Sammie didn't pull away or try to free himself from PeePaw's gentle grasp. In fact, Sammie leaned closer, propping himself up on his tip toes. "Come closer."

"OK, PeePaw," Sammie said, turning his head to give my dad his ear. "What is it?"

PeePaw lifted his head ever so slightly from the pillow, craning his head just so, to get his lips as close as he could to Sammie's little ear. As his lips touched Sammie's ear, he whispered something--speech that was completely inaudible to me--that made Sammie giggle and smile, covering his mouth as if embarrassed, like a fart slipping out during class or something. I looked at Sharice and she stood there, smiling and nodding, not saying anything. Did she know what my dad was whispering to good ol' Sammie Boy? I didn't know. But once my dad was done whispering to Sammie, Sharice clapped her hands as if to shoo us off.

"Now, I know y'all came a long way to see Marvin but it's time for his medicine, then his sponge bath, then his dinner. Go on, now!"

"Excuse me?" I said, confused.

"My Mr. Marvin is on a tight schedule. I run a tight ship," she said, placing her copy of *The World According to Garp* in the back pocket of her pants, coming around her side of the bed to where Sammie stood. She peeled my dad's fingers apart, releasing my boy, who came running to my side, hugging me around the waist. "How about you come back in a couple hours?"

"A couple of hours?" I said, still confused. Was she kicking us out so soon? I looked at my dad to see if he had anything to say about it but he just laid there, looking me straight in the eyes, but his look was dead, vague, empty. It was like he was looking right through me, like he didn't know me at all, like a stranger passing me on the street, looking in the direction of their destination, miles away. I looked at my kids and Nat and could see that they all looked tired, depleted, worn out. Maybe a little rest would be good; maybe we just needed some space. "I guess we'll go check into the hotel," I said. "Maybe we'll just come back early in the morning."

"If you say so," Sharice said, reaching for a small table on wheels, which on top sat a plastic tub of medications and sponges and bandages and stuff like that. She rummaged through them all as if looking for something important, something indispensable. "We'll be here."

"Well," Ms. Robyn said, appearing from the perimeter of the group, like a ghost from a fog. "Maybe tomorrow morning is best although I would stress that you get here as early as possible. That would give us some time to talk about--things of an urgent matter." She placed her hand on my shoulder, gently. "How about 8am?"

"I think we can make that," I said, gathering my two kids. I winked at Nat and she snapped out of her spell, as if I was a hypnotist awakening her. The entire visit was somewhat weird, stranger than I expected, but maybe I was just tired or hungry or something. I placed my hand on Nat's back, directing her in front of me. She corralled the kids and we all left my dad's apartment.

In the hallway, Sammie and Jessie immediately ran away like two prisoners in an impromptu jailbreak. They ran at top speed for where, I didn't know. Maybe they wanted to go outside and run around the pond with the dachshund; maybe they wanted to run back to Austin. Nat, like the good nanny she was, quickly followed them, although they were fast little buggers. As I walked, Ms. Robyn put her arm around me and embraced me as we walked. She really was a sweet lady and I could tell that she felt a lot of empathy and sympathy for the family members that came to visit their loved ones.

"You know, I'm worried about your father. I'm worried that he won't be here much longer," she said, putting her head on my shoulder. "It's just a feeling I have."

"I see," I said. "He does seem kind of out of it. When he looked at me, it seemed like he didn't recognize me at all."

The hallway opened up to reveal a gathering area, a place where a lot of folks were playing a game like Bingo or something, a conductor was calling out numbers and the players were doing something to pieces of paper in their laps. They all seemed to be having fun, still full of life, a long way from death's grasp. Maybe they had ten years left; maybe five years left. Who knew, really.

"It's just something you'll need to be prepared for when it comes. You know what I mean?"

"I know what you mean. At least he has Sharice. She seems like a good nurse."

And with that, Ms. Robyn stopped in her tracks. She looked at me, consumed with guilt or remorse or something, one of her boney hands covering her mouth.

"Nurse?" she said, confused. "You don't know?"

"Know what?" I said, also confused.

"Sharice isn't your dad's nurse. She's your dad's girlfriend."

Girlfriend? Did she say, 'My dad's girlfriend?'

Well, shit.

***

My Volvo S70 was the only car left in the parking lot--its driver-side door wide open, a plate of chocolate chip cookies left on the passenger seat, a note taped to the steering wheel on yellow-lined paper written in red marker that said, 'I fixed your car - Tony,' a roll of duct tape on the dash--and it looked like it had been to the car detailing place. You know? The place where they wash your car and wax it and vacuum it out and shit like that. I'm not sure what Tony fixed but it seemed that his magic weapon was duct tape. I considered for a moment sending one of the kids back into Autumn Grove with Tony's magical duct tape but I knew we'd be back early in the morning, so I left it sitting on the dash as a memento, as a reminder, as a decoration. When the universe provides you help, then you let it happen. It's true. So, the duct tape stayed on the dash where I found it.

"Can I have some cookies?" Sammie said, as the kids climbed in the back seat, buckling their seat belts.

"Of course, my boy," I said, buckling my seat belt. Nat passed the plate to the back seat, Sammie's little hands outstretched and quivering with excitement. Kids with cookies are happy kids and parents with happy kids are happy parents. Nat looked a little wiped out, though, like she had been carrying bags of sand up four flights of stairs. I felt bad for her. Really. "You doing OK?"

"Yeah, I'm fine," she said, buckling her seat belt as well. "It's just been, like, a weird day."

"I agree," I said, starting my car. And guess what? It started--and amazingly well, too. What Bernice said was true; that Tony really *could* fix anything. I was going to have to remember to bring him a breakfast sandwich or breakfast tacos or a dozen donuts or some kind of gratuity the next morning. You gotta repay kindness with kindness. I really believe that. "Let's go check-in to the hotel then chill out."

"Ok," she said, leaning back in her seat, her head lying heavy against the head rest. In the reflection of the window, I could see that same blank stare she occasionally wore on her face, similar to the stare she had on the ride down from Austin. I wondered what she was thinking about or if she was even thinking about anything at all. I wondered if she was contemplating her place in the universe, if she thought about what she would be doing next year or the year after or the year after that. Was she saving money for her retirement? Did she have health insurance? Did she have someone to love: a man or a woman? I wasn't really sure which type of partner she would have because I didn't have that kind of intimate knowledge about her. Who has that kind of intimate knowledge about anyone, really? I wondered if I should even ask her what she was thinking but, with a little more contemplation, I decided I just shouldn't say anything at all. Maybe, just maybe, she needed a break, so, I gave her one. We all could use a break every once and a while. Right?

As I drove all of us to the hotel--the kids in the back seat devouring cookies, Nat in the passenger seat staring out her window, the car running well--all I could think about was what Ms. Robyn told me on the way out of Autumn Grove about Sharice. 'She's your dad's girlfriend,' she said. Girlfriend. My dad had a girlfriend. My infirmed dad--weak and withered and grey and dying--had a *girlfriend.* What the fuck? Not even I--much younger than my gimpy father and in better health and with a job to boot--had a girlfriend. How was this even possible? It was almost too impossible to comprehend and even more bizarre after Ms. Robyn pulled me aside and told me the circumstances surrounding their courtship. Here's what she told me.

After apologizing profusely for what she was about to tell me and, apologizing some more because she thought I already knew this information, she described in great detail the routine Autumn Grove maintained under the direction of my father, Retired Colonel Marvin Burchwood; Marv to the other residents; PeePaw to my kids. Even though my father first arrived at Autumn Grove with a diagnosis of Alzheimer's Disease--a diagnosis certified by three separate specialists and medical practitioners--there were times when he displayed acute lucidity and specificity concerning his own personal care. For example, a few days after he was first admitted--by which time I was already long gone and back in Austin--he appeared in the front office of Autumn Grove with a list of demands and instructions for his stay, moving forward. Like back in the day when he was in command of a team of soldiers, he stormed in Ms. Robyn's office with a handwritten list, written in ball-point pen on a legal pad. He required a steady supply of liquor, particularly scotch or whiskey, with an occasional cigar, particularly Puerto Rican ones. He demanded to be taken to the race track--Retama Park, a horse track just outside of San Antonio--to bet on the horses at least once a week. Also, he insisted on being driven to The Gentlemen's Club--a strip club not too far from Autumn Grove--also once a week, where, after Bernard the limo driver parked, he would push my dad to the entrance in a wheel chair and then PeePaw was whisked away by the staff of the strip club to a private table in a secluded area inside. Bernard was given strict instructions to return for my father in two hours and wait for him to be wheeled back to the entrance by the staff. The Gentleman's Club was where, supposedly, he met Sharice: his 'nurse.' Can you believe this? I almost couldn't believe it because it was almost too good to be true and, like being forced to drink water from a fire hose, too much to consume all at once. How do you drink from a fire hose? You don't. You just get blasted in the face. And there's nothing worse than getting blasted with new, salacious information about your sick father. It's true.

But then, Ms. Robyn said to me, there were the other days when my dad was not so lucid and, in fact, entrenched deeply within his disease. On those days, he was not his normal self and, without warning, would sometimes become quite violent, as was the case for some patients with Alzheimer's Disease, particularly at night. Many times, he would wake up in the middle of the night--screaming his head off and throwing stuff around his room--and when the night staff arrived to assist him, he would throw punches and bite them and fight with them as if they were demons from his nightmares come to life. 'It was awful,' she said. 'Truly awful.' Of course, a facility like Autumn Grove trained their staff to deal with patients like my father but it was still a difficult situation for everybody. Nobody wanted to get hurt, whether it be patients hurting staff or the other way around. Ms. Robyn and the staff took it all in stride and took care of good ol' Marv the best they could, regardless of these violent episodes.

Then, one day out of the blue, Sharice came back from The Gentlemen's Club with Marv, in the limo. When Bernard was helping Marv out of the car under the covered, front drive of Autumn Grove, Ms. Robyn was waiting for him when Sharice hopped out of the limo, dressed in a way that immediately told Ms. Robyn that she was an employee of The Gentlemen's Club, all bedazzled and overly made-up with glittery makeup in hues of red and purple and pinks--bright enough to illuminate the darkest of back alleys--and smelling of cheap perfume and cigarette smoke and stale beer. It was a strange scenario that did not have a precedent or protocol at the retirement home. But with her frequent, regular visits and insistence from my dad that she be the one to help him with his care, Ms. Robyn eventually and reluctantly relinquished much of the staff from helping retired Colonel Burchwood, except in the direst of circumstances or emergencies. Besides, she said, he had plenty of money to pay her. When she told me this, I was a little confused.

"Plenty of money?" I said, quite perplexed.

"In the trust fund," she said, reluctantly.

"Trust fund?"

"Oh boy," she said, covering her mouth. "You don't know about the trust fund, either, do you? What have I done?"

"I don't know anything about a *trust fund.*"

"I shouldn't have said anything. I'm sorry. I've broken a sacred trust." She buried her face in her hands, her breath sputtering from either a panic attack or anxiety or both. I didn't know what to do.

"I'm glad you told me," I said, placing my hand on her shoulder which startled her a bit. "I need to know about these things."

"I still shouldn't have said anything but I've just been so worried about your father." She dropped her hands, her face red from being concealed, her skin flush with embarrassment and stress. She looked like she wanted to be somewhere else, anywhere but at Autumn Grove talking to me about my philandering father.

"I know," I said, consoling her. She was on the verge of tears. I could tell that she really cared about her clients a lot, my father included. She was the perfect person to manage Autumn Grove. I mean, who decides that they believe managing an old-folks home is their calling in life? An angel, that's who. It's true.

Anyway, as I was rehashing all this while driving to the hotel, I was interrupted by good ol' Sammie Boy from the backseat of the car, his mouth full of half-chewed, chocolate chip cookies, tapping my shoulder with his little, slender index finger. Kids have a way of doing that--interrupting your thoughts at the wrong time and all. Sammie was a real pro at that.

"Daddy, can I ask you a question," he said, spitting out bits of cookie and chocolate while he talked.

"Sure, son. Go ahead."

"Can I have the tape?"

"What tape?"

"That tape--*there*!" he said, his finger emerging from the back of the car and pointing to the roll of duct tape on the dash--the one left by Tony the Fixer--his index finger so taut that it bent downward at the middle knuckle.

"Sure," I said, reaching for the duct tape. In the time from when Tony left it on the dash earlier until then, the roll of tape adhered itself slightly to the vinyl dash, making it a tad more difficult to pick up than expected, like pulling a snail reluctantly from a wood plank. The sound of it coming unstuck from the vinyl dash attracted the eyeballs of the others in the car, all watching me. "Why do you want it?"

"For my collection!"

"Collection? Collection of what?" I said, handing him the roll of tape.

"My collection of survival stuff. For me and Budgie," he said, grabbing it, then sitting back down.

"For you and Budgie? Really?"

"Really!" He was as overjoyed as can be. Kids love collecting that kind of stuff. Weird, right? They get pleasure out of stockpiling things that most adults don't give a shit about, things like random rolls of tape and stranded paper clips and empty water bottles and dilapidated cardboard boxes and old razor blades and sticky popsicle sticks and anything he could get his hands on really. It was almost like he was a hoarder--my sweet, little hoarder. I'm not sure what he meant by survival stuff. Should I have taken that literally or figuratively? Was he saving up for the apocalypse? Or for recess at school? I'd have to dig deeper another time.

We drove a mile or two before finding the Motel 6 where I had a reservation for two adjoining rooms--one for me and the kids and the other for Nat--the configuration I thought best for the four of us. I mean, I could have reserved just one room and I'm certain we could have made it through with two double beds and a roll-away bed for Sammie and Jessie but, as much as that sounds doable and all, there wouldn't have been very much privacy for any of us. The kids probably wouldn't have cared but I'm certain Nat would prefer a modicum of privacy, even for twenty minutes, to take a shower or put up her feet or sleep undisturbed or whatever. If there was one thing I was certain of, most women like their privacy. It's true. Trust me on this one, OK?

The Motel 6 where I made the reservations was in the process of being remodeled--as the customer support lady told me over the phone while making the reservation and she assured me that it wouldn't affect our stay--so I wasn't surprised to see construction vehicles and construction materials and construction workers in the parking lot as we turned in. I was reassured by Vicky--the dedicated Motel 6 employee over the phone--that the corporate motel chain was determined to upgrade their image to a more appealing traveler destination for lodging than what people previously thought Motel 6 to be: the motel of choice for pimps, prostitutes, drug dealers, unscrupulous transients, and murderers. Their new goal--if I understood this properly--was to attract business travelers and, more specifically, middle and upper-middle class families with lots of kids and pets. That was their goal, anyway. A pretty modest goal, in my opinion, and they were starting in the right place with a little family like mine. Vicky just wanted to reassure me that even though there was quite a bit of construction and remodeling going on, that our stay was still going to be pleasant, enjoyable, and serene. That's right: *serene*. That's the exact word she used. That's a funny way to describe an overnight stay at a corporate hotel chain. That's like calling a frozen dinner *exquisite*. What an awkward word choice. Maybe her dream was to be a writer, too; it seemed possible, the way she talked and described things.

The reality was that the Motel 6 was a simple, beige, rectangular building with dark brown, tinted, square windows in a symmetrical pattern, without a lick of decoration or adornment or fanciness at all. The only break from this simple design was a tiny, covered, circular drive, the place where guests could park briefly to check-in, jutting from the side of the beige rectangle, haphazardly attached by stucco and caulk and metal flashing, like a child's attempt to construct a monument from the pieces of a cardboard box and random art supplies. I parked the Volvo S70 in that precarious place and informed my brood that I would check-in and get the keys to the room. I asked Nat if she could stay with the kids in the car and she said, "Like, of course." I shut off the car and ran inside.

I noticed right away that the reception area was dual purpose: a lobby for guests to check-in or ask questions to the right and a dining area for an all-you-can-eat breakfast of cereal and oatmeal and frozen waffles and bland fruit that was served every morning promptly at 6 o'clock, to the left. No one was in the dining area (since it was closer to dinner time and the hotel didn't serve all-you-can-eat dinner) but music serenaded the empty tables anyway, contemporary country music playing from speakers mounted flush in the ceiling. A small hallway that began where the check-in desk ended revealed a window at the other end of the hall, the glass foggy from humidity on the other side and a sign posted underneath the window that read, 'SWIMMING POOL,' and the pleasant sound of children playing and laughing could be heard. If any sound in this building was something close to serenity, then the sound of children playing and laughing was probably it. I made my way to the reception desk to check-in.

As soon as I placed my hands on the desk, the hotel clerk appeared from a side office, as if out of thin air (POOF!), short and rotund, her face seemed familiar to me although I couldn't make out which singer or movie actress or TV star she certainly reminded me of. Her hair was mostly sculpted in a business-like fashion except for a few strands that broke free from the auburn, hair-sprayed dome, the renegade hairs slithering through the air, like seaweed pulled back and forth by an undercurrent, as she walked toward me. Her dark blue business suit cried "mostly serious" and the single button holding the jacket together strained to keep its composure. She wore a gold name tag that read, "B. Smith."

"Can I help you?" she said, not smiling, not pleasant, not anything.

"I'd like to check-in."

"Your last name?" she blurted.

"Burchwood."

She typed something on a keyboard in front of her, the keys covered with a dingy, once-clear, rubber protective covering that was supposed to be replaced periodically, but never was. Why place a temporary, rubber, protective covering over a keyboard then *never* replace it? I fixated on that conundrum. "First name: Simon?" she said. When I confirmed, she typed some more. "Check-out is at noon tomorrow. Breakfast starts at 6am. The pool is open until 10pm." She slid two key cards on the desktop to me, the Motel 6 logo emblazoned on them in red and blue.

"Thank you," I said, taking the key cards.

"Enjoy your stay," she said, turning unceremoniously to walk back to the side office: her cave, her chamber of solitude.

Right then and there, I knew who she reminded me of: movie actress Anne Ramsey. She was the cantankerous, homely actress who played the momma in the movie *Throw Momma from the Train*. I knew she reminded me of someone I recognized and I had to ask her if she was aware of the unfortunate likeness she had to this actress.

"Excuse me!" I said, leaning on the reception desk. "Can I ask you a question?"

She stopped in her tracks and turned to me, her face as grim and sour and shriveled as Anne Ramsey's face, put off that I stopped her from doing what she was going to do in that side office. What was she going to do in there? Maybe sip some gin? Maybe take a valium? Possibly, take a nap? I didn't really know.

"Yes?" she said, irritated.

"Has anyone ever told you that you look like the actress from the movie--"

"*Throw Momma from the Train*?"

Stunned, I didn't know how to respond. Sometimes, when you think you have some insight into something, you really don't. You're just as annoying and irritating and socially awkward as the next person. "You've seen it?"

"No, never seen it," she said. She turned and continued to the side office. I heard a succession of clicking noises and then a small plume of smoke billowed from the office, the smell of maple syrup and chemical cleaner with it. I looked at the key cards, both nestled in a paper envelope, the numbers 47 and 49 written on the inside flap of the envelope in black marker. I slid the key cards into my pant pocket and returned outside, where Nat and my kids were waiting in the car. Bob Marley was playing on the stereo when I got in; *Three Little Birds*, I think. The kids loved that song.

"All good?" Nat said.

"I think so," I said, starting the car and driving to the back of the building.

At the back, the parking lot was mostly empty, and on the building was a sign indicating which room numbers were on which floor. It appeared number 47 and 49 were on the fourth floor: the top floor. The kids in the backseat were so excited that they could hardly contain themselves. When I parked the car, they quickly gathered up all of their belongings and were out the car doors, chasing each other around a cigarette receptacle by the back entrance to the building. Nat and I got out of the car and gathered the bags from the trunk, and fortunately, there weren't too many of them. Locking up the car, we approached the back entrance, the key cards in my hand, and Nat tried to corral good ol' Sammie and little Jessie, although they were quick little buggers and weren't going to let her easily corral them. I opened the door, unlocking it with the key card, and propped the door open for my family. The two kids quickly ran inside, running for the elevator down the hall.

"Hold the elevator!" I said, calling to them, and they did once the door slid open, both propping the door open with their little bodies. Nat and I got in the elevator then they did, too. Sammie looked at me for direction, then I said, "Press number four." And he did. The elevator door slid shut and carried us to the top floor. Once there, the door slid open again and the two banshees stormed out, yelling and screaming as they chased each other to who-knows-where they were going. They had no idea where they were going or what they were doing. They were just adolescent energy incarnate. "Look for rooms 47 and 49!" I said, calling to them again.

"They're, like, so excited," Nat said, smiling. "It's, like, they think we're on a vacation."

"I wish we were," I said, holding the elevator door so Nat could walk out, releasing a sigh from my mouth so heavy that I thought I'd trip over it. Nat was so tall that she had to duck her head as she stepped out of the elevator. We headed down the hallway toward the kids, who were both dancing and pointing to a doorway toward the end of the hall. "Our rooms," I said, imagining that they had discovered them the way they were dancing and pointing like that. They were acting like a couple of wild animals--hooting and hollering and pointing and jumping around, making a racket. I handed Nat the key card for room 49 and, when we got there, she opened the door to her room and I opened the door to ours: me, Sammie, and Jessie.

Inside our room, the kids jumped on one of the double beds then jumped back and forth between the two double beds. They were screaming and laughing and having a good time trying to catch each other. I didn't feel like telling them to calm down like any other parent would have. I mean, they were pretty loud and obnoxious and all but I didn't care. I was just glad we made it that far--all in one piece: no disasters, no food poisonings, no cuts or bruises, no hurt feelings, and my dad still alive. The room was sparsely furnished and the maroon comforters on the bed blended in perfectly with the maroon curtains on the windows, which melted into the maroon and green and beige carpet, a fragmented pattern weaved into it like a Fourth of July explosion in a night sky. There were the two double beds the kids were jumping on, a night stand between them with a business phone and brass lamp on it, a table masquerading as a desk in the back corner, and a waist high dresser with a TV on top. The walls were bright white as if the paint had just dried the day before and, above each headboard for the beds, were framed photos of rural, Texas landscapes composed of fields of bluebonnets, sunflowers, longhorns, and rickety barbed-wire fences: stereotypical Texas bullshit.

Sammie suddenly stopped jumping on the beds, then said, "Daddy? Can I ask you a question?"

"Sure, son," I said, setting the bags I was carrying on the dresser. Jessie continued jumping on the beds, jabbing her brother whenever she could.

"Stop it!" he said, defending himself with an elbow, landing a blow.

"Daddy! Sammie elbowed me!" she said, angry, her face red.

"You two cut it out," I said, blandly. I wasn't in the mood to referee them. I was too tired. "What did you want to ask, Sammie?"

"Daddy? Where's Nat?"

"Nat?" I said, unzipping the bags and pulling clothes out to put in the dresser. "Nat is staying in the room next door."

"Next door? How are we supposed to *see* her?"

I stopped unpacking my clothes and turned to my boy, both hands falling to my waist, anchored into my sides. "Open the door here and knock on the other door." I pointed to the locked door which adjoined the two rooms, the one between the dresser and the bathroom. Good ol' Sammie Boy stared at the door, confused, not knowing that a lot of hotels have adjoining rooms for large families. He jumped off the bed while his sister continued to bounce around. He unlocked the door and slowly opened it to reveal another door without a door knob. He stared at the door for a moment as if examining a portal to another dimension (it probably seemed like that to him) before stepping closer, then lightly knocking on the door. He leaned closer to listen. We could hear footsteps on the other side then the click of a deadbolt, unlocking the door. It slowly opened, Nat standing on the other side, a big grin on her face.

"Surprise!" she said, then laughed.

"Nat!" the kids said. She came into our room. Jessie lunged from the bed and wrapped her arms around Nat's thighs. Sammie wrapped his arms around her as well and they clung tightly to her as if they were afraid she would disappear again. Fortunately, she did not disappear.

"Did you guys miss me or what?"

"Yes!" they both said.

"I was only gone for, like, a minute," she said, rubbing their backs, consoling them. I continued unpacking our bags and putting things into the dresser. "What do you guys want to do? Get dinner? Go to the pool?"

Sammie and Jessie released her waist and looked at each other. By the looks on their faces, I knew they came to a unanimous decision without even discussing it. "Pool!" they both said, then running around Nat like she was a maypole. "Pool! Pool! Pool!" they continued to chant.

"Well, I didn't bring a bathing suit," she said, pushing some hair that had fallen in front of her face while she looked down at the kids encircling her. "But I can put my feet in the water while you swim. Do they have their bathing suits?" she said to me.

"No, but they can swim in those clothes. I know they won't care."

"We don't care! We don't care!" they responded.

"I'll put my feet in the water, too. Maybe we can have a pizza delivered. Kill two birds with one stone."

"Great!" Nat said. "Let me get my purse." She walked to the door that adjoined the rooms, bent over, and placed a trash can in front of the door, to keep it propped open.

When she went into her room, the kids followed her, finding two more beds to jump on. Nat got a kick out of that, seeing the kids happy and enjoying themselves. She grabbed her purse and we locked up the rooms. We took the elevator back down to the first floor. As it opened, we saw the first evidence inside the building of construction. There were drop cloths on the floor and blue painter's tape outlining the door frames of all the hotel rooms on the first floor but there weren't any workers around, their tools and protective equipment abandoned on the floor. We walked down the hall and around all of the construction equipment, as if making our way through an obstacle course, the kids blazing fast, Nat and I at a slower pace.

Once we found the door to the pool, I opened it and watched my family go in. I looked to the lobby to see if anyone was around but there wasn't anyone in there--not one soul. It was still deserted like before. I didn't see any sign of B. Smith, either: the momma thrown from the train. She must have been in the office sleeping or smoking or whatever it was she was doing earlier when I interrupted her. I closed the door behind me.

The pool was in an enclosed room with a couple of tables around it, a trash can, a bin with fresh pool towels, and a container for used pool towels. On one wall was mounted a long leaf skimmer and a round flotation device. The kids immediately jumped in the water without thinking about it, as most kids were prone to do. Nat sat by the stairs that dipped into the pool, putting her feet in the water, then sat on the edge, her tall frame hunched over, her knees jutting up toward her shoulders. She patted the cement, indicating for me to see with her, and I did, after taking off my shoes and rolling up my pants. The water was warm and balmy, the smell of chlorine hanging in the air, thick and dense enough to make your eyes tear up. The kids stood in the shallow water on the other side of the pool, splashing each other in their faces. The pool wasn't very deep because they were standing up with the water at their chests, maybe three feet deep.

"Want me to call and order a pizza?" she said, reaching into her purse for her cell phone.

"Maybe in a bit," I said. I watched her continue to rummage through her purse, looking for something, not her phone but something of some importance it seemed. Finding what she was looking for, she pulled out two, small bottles of liquor, like the kind you would get on an airplane--one yellow and one red--both bottles the hue you'd see in the glow of a neon sign. She offered one of them to me, the red one, colored like liquid death. "What's this?"

"Something to take the edge off," she said, the side of her mouth upturning to a sly smirk.

I read the label on the bottle. It read, "Fireball."

"What do you have?" I said, curious what her piss-yellow bottle contained.

"Tequila, I think. Cheers!" she said, holding up her tiny, yellow bottle, the urine-like liquid splashing around inside. We tapped the plastic bottles together, as if toasting, then she opened hers and downed the liquid in one swift motion, the flavor of her drink causing her face to twist and contort. Her body shook with relief after she swallowed. I cracked the top to my bottle then took a whiff. The foul scent burned my nose but, rather than be a party-pooper, I drank the foul, red liquid in the spirit of togetherness. The fake cinnamon-flavored alcohol burned my throat as it descended all the way down to my poor stomach, its splash into my gut immediately causing my bowels to revolt. What had I done?

"That was... good," I said, wiping my lips with my forearm then handing her the empty bottle of death.

"No, it wasn't!" she said, laughing. "That was, like, disgusting." She threw the two empty bottles back in her purse.

On the other side of the pool, the kids tossed a worn-out volleyball back and forth to each other, in an impromptu game of 'hot potato,' releasing the ball as soon as their hands touched it as if the ball had been soaking in the garbage of the cafeteria at their elementary school. The kids were having fun, though.

"Have you had any luck finding a better job?" I said. She seemed distracted, like she had something weighing heavy on her mind, something burdensome. She seemed that way most of our trip, too.

"No, nothing promising. I'll just have to keep looking. You see--"

"You just have to keep trying. Something will come along."

"Yeah," she said, sighing.

"I had a hard time, too, after college. You know?"

"Simon?" she said, wrapping her arms around her long legs, her body in the form of an egg.

"Yes?"

"I have something I have to tell you. I've debated this--to myself--over and over and over. I just wasn't sure if I should, like, say anything to you about it."

"It's OK," I said, nervous. What could she have to say to me? It seemed like she was about to cry. I didn't want that. Nat crying during our trip was *not* part of the plan. "You can tell me."

"You see... I'm sorry about Jessie."

I looked over at little Jessie, seeing her playing with her brother, then looked back at Nat, confused. I said, "Excuse me?"

"No," she said, her head lowering, her forehead laying on her knees. "Your ex-wife, Jessica."

Now, in case you forgot, or maybe I didn't tell you. I don't remember. The kid's dead mother, my ex-wife--the cheating, lying, drunken mess--was also named Jessica, just like my daughter. I know, that's weird. But that's the way it was. Little Jessie was really Jessie, Jr., a small Jessica, a mini-me as they say, Jessica the Second. But even knowing that, it was easy for me to get confused when someone only said the name Jessie without being a little more specific. I mean, little Jessie was right there in front of us. Why would I assume that Nat was referring to my ex-wife?

"Oh, I see," I said, straightening my back, sitting up. "What did you want to tell me?"

Nat sat for a moment, deep in contemplation, mulling something through her mind, probably negotiating the best way to tell me what she needed to say. I could see it: the machinations of her thought processes. The kids continued to play, splashing around the pool, laughing, screaming, not a care in the world.

"I saw her once--out--with a man, another man, not you, before she died. I was out for a night of drinking with some friends. We were downtown, bar-hopping, going to clubs, drinking. I was in this, like, bar, I don't remember which one, and I was drinking with my friends, when I saw her." She scratched her head and seemed nervous.

"Go on," I said, curious.

"I saw her, like, with a man. They weren't standing far from me. They were, like, as close as the kids are now, maybe ten feet away. She clung to the man, her arms were around him, she would grind up against him. It was obvious to me that they were *together*. You know?"

"I see," I said. I knew my ex-wife was a cheat but it was strange hearing someone else report her bad behavior to me, like seeing someone you know on TV. It was weird. "Did you talk to her?"

"Oh, no, no, no! I didn't talk to her. That would have been, like, *awkward*. I just watched. I knew it was her. I was certain of it. I just watched her and that man."

Little did Nat know that I already knew that my ex-wife was a cheat but, still, I didn't say anything. I didn't interrupt her story. I let her continue.

"Go on."

"Later that night, she eventually left with that guy. She didn't see me or anything. But, the next time I babysat your kids after that, I mentioned to her that I saw her out downtown not long before. And she looked, like, *shocked* that I had said that. She told me something, like, that she never went downtown. Ever! That barhopping downtown was for losers or something like that. And I just knew that she was lying. She was lying to my face."

"Mmm hmm," I said.

"And then you walked up and she turned to you and said that, too. Do you remember?" I thought about it, looked back in time in my mind, and remembered, acknowledging that I remembered that night. "She said that going downtown sucked and you agreed. I didn't say anything else about it. She quickly changed the subject, like, to what to do with the kids. And that was it. I never said anything else about it, until now."

She reached out and grabbed my hands, holding them tightly. I looked at her--her face grim and sad and flushed--and realized that she was having a very difficult time with this, that she held onto this memory with a lot of trepidation and resentment and remorse. I felt bad that it was eating her inside. As we sat there, my hands in hers, for the first time I felt a release from within me, a release of emotion and anger and sadness and an acknowledgment of the pain I felt, the pain Jessica--my ex-wife--caused me. Nat knew the pain I felt.

"Thank you for telling me," I said.

"For, like, the longest time, I didn't know if I should say anything to you about it."

"What made you decide to tell me?"

"Well," she said, releasing my hands from hers, then placing her hands on the cement behind her, leaning back, extending her legs out into the warm, pool water. "The last time I was at your apartment to babysit, after the kids went to sleep, I was looking around your place. And I realized, like, that there weren't *any* photos of your ex-wife around, not one. I looked around the living room and your bedroom and the kids' bedroom. Not one. Then I knew that you probably knew..." A tear appeared at the corner of one of her eyes, clinging to an eye lash. "And I felt so bad that I knew, too. And I just, like, wanted to say sorry." The tear released itself from her eyelash and streamed down her face, then dropped on her shirt.

I leaned over to her, stretching my arms out, inviting her for a hug. She hugged me tightly, crying a bit. I cried, too, grateful that I had a friend like her. It was nice being acknowledged. It was just nice, period. "Thank you for telling me," I said.

Nat pulled back, wiping the tears from her face. "I just wanted to say I'm sorry. I feel really, like, bad about it."

Then, all of a sudden--out of the blue--good ol' Sammie Boy started screaming all over the place. He was screaming and yelling and waving his arms, like a duckling flapping its wings to get its mother's attention. He climbed a ladder at the other side of the pool and ran toward us, his arms in the air like he was swatting at a swarm of locusts or bees or something like that.

"Sammie, don't run around the pool!"

"Daddy! Daddy! Daddy!" he said, frantically. He slowed his pace to a speed-walk, the way kids do when you tell them to not run on the wet cement around a pool, his arms swinging stiffly at his sides. They could slip and fall and split their heads open, you know? Of course, you know; everybody knows that. Jessie followed him, speed-walking as well. "Daddy! I have something I have to tell you."

"Yes, son. What is it?" He was hysterical. His eyes were as wide as saucers.

"Something is wrong!"

"What's wrong?"

"Something is wrong with PeePaw!"

And that was the end of our time at the pool. Just like that: over. We didn't even get a chance to order the pizza. There was no time to order a pizza anymore, anyways. It was getting late. The kids were going to have to settle for whatever we had with us, candy bars or potato chips or something like that. Sometimes, your kids have to take whatever they can get and, sometimes, whatever they get is candy for dinner. Making parental decisions can be hard.

It's true.

Chapter Ten

A Sammie and Budgie Cartoon in TECHNICOLOR

Chapter Ten

When I was a little boy, I received very few signs of genuine affection from my father--almost none. Colonel Burchwood was not the warmest of fathers, to say the least. Hugging my father when I was a little boy was a lot like hugging a cactus--no matter how careful I was, it was not going to be a pleasant experience and I was going to get hurt. His rough facial hair *and* prickly demeanor seemed to be an impenetrable fortress around his heart, a small, secluded place I rarely got to see. To make things worse, instead of talking like a normal person, he used military terms and slang all the time when speaking to me (not that military folks are abnormal; but they use some terminology that is very specific to their profession that not many people know about). When I was acting out--just as any little kid would do--he would call me things like a dittybopper (a word to describe soldiers marching out of sync with a cadence) or a football bat (an individual, or way of doing things, that was particularly odd) or an oxygen thief (a harsh term for someone who was useless or talked too much). In other words, he spoke to me--not as his kid--but like I was his soldier, someone under his command, a subordinate, a grunt. You can imagine how fun that was for me. Not very fun at all, I tell you. It was like I grew up in a goddamn boot camp. It's true.

So, you could imagine my surprise when I witnessed a loving bond develop between Colonel Burchwood and my kids, Sammie and Jessie, when they were little tikes. It was almost like I was witnessing the impossible become possible--the discovery of alien worlds, experiencing time travel, the cure for cancer! I certainly didn't see that coming from him, the surly Colonel, becoming PeePaw, hugging my kids and telling them he loved them and supporting them the way I had always dreamed he would support me--as his child and son--but he never did. That's like your school bully becoming your best friend or your rapist becoming your supportive spouse. Weird. It was a lot to take in. I know, that's a little much. I'm not trying to offend you; just making a point. Are we still good? Good.

Anyway, Sammie's vision about PeePaw while at the pool left him distraught, almost inconsolable, for a few hours, so much so that we never had any dinner or went anywhere else or did anything else. We holed up in the hotel rooms. We *hunkered* down, as they say in the military. Sammie convinced me to call Autumn Grove to check on PeePaw and I did call quite a few times late into the night. But no one answered, not once. I just got the answering service, which was weird because they were supposed to have someone on-call 24 hours a day, seven days a week, 365 days of the year. Maybe someone on their staff called in sick or had a family emergency or something important.

Maybe they were hungover. Or maybe, they decided not to go into work at all and drink all night long instead--drowning their sorrows in cheap beer and tequila shots and frozen margaritas--and quit their job the next morning like some people are inclined to do, in a blaze of glory to no one else but themselves. Sammie didn't seem to understand *why* no one was answering the phone at Autumn Grove. It seemed to his little mind that someone *should* answer the phone, in case a family was trying to get a hold of their family member, just like we were with PeePaw. I promised Sammie that we would wake up at the crack of dawn, quickly eat some breakfast at the all-you-can-eat breakfast bar, then zoom over to Autumn Grove as soon as we could.

"We can't dillydally, Daddy. OK?" he said, very sincere and serious.

"OK," I said. "We won't *dillydally*. I promise." I was serious, too. Who *dillydallies*? Nobody in the modern world dillydallied. That's slang straight out of a 1930s slapstick comedy.

"We have to get to PeePaw as soon as possible. He *needs* us."

"Are you sure about this?" I said, skeptical. "He's never needed us before."

"He does this time. I promise!"

Like I said before, we didn't eat any dinner but that didn't mean I didn't feed my kids at all. I mean, sometimes my parenting skills can leave little to be desired but I didn't want them to go to bed without *any* food. So, I gave Sammie a fistful of coins that I had scooped out of the ashtray in the Volvo S70 (European cars have lots of ashtrays) and instructed him and little Jessie to run down the hall to the vending machine and buy themselves a snack. Anything. Sammie looked at me with some trepidation, as if I was setting a trap for him.

"*Anything*?!" he said.

"Yes, anything," I said.

Sammie grabbed his little sister by the hand and led her out the hotel door and down the hall. I stepped out into the hall to watch them run for their evening snack, holding hands the entire length of the floor, and stopping at the vending machine to peruse their choices. Sammie loaded the machine with coins, all of them clunking loud enough for me to hear, and they each made their choice. As their snacks descended to the holding tray, they cheered and cheered--their arms raised triumphantly, jumping up and down, their fists clinched high--as if they had won the lottery. They ran back holding hands, back into the room, then jumped into their bed, ripping the wrappers off their snacks and devouring them.

At this point, to be able to wake up early required an early bedtime. So, I informed Nat and the kids that it was time to brush their teeth and go to bed, otherwise, there wouldn't be any getting up early. And they all did. In our bathroom, Sammie and Jessie brushed and flossed their teeth, washed their little faces, and put on their pajamas.

I assumed Nat had a similar routine since we could hear her in our room; the sound of water flowing freely--in the sink and in the toilet--camouflaging whatever routine she had. When Sammie and Jessie were done, they both ran into Nat's room to hug her. They caught her off-guard and she squealed delightfully then chased them to their double bed in our room to tuck them in. She really was good with the kids: attentive, loving, and kind. She pulled the covers up to their little faces and tucked them in like little burritos.

"Time for bed," she said, pinching their cheeks and pushing their hair from their faces, so they could see her. "We have a long day tomorrow."

"Do you think PeePaw is OK?" Jessie said, her voice cracking a bit from the stress of the unknown.

"Hard to say. We'll see," Nat said, smiling at her, then looking at Sammie. "What do you think?"

Sammie stared back at her, a look of apprehension on his face. His eyes turned to mine, trembling, attempting to hold back tears. Then he said, "It's not good."

"Well," Nat said, kissing them both on the cheek once more. "We'll see in the morning. Good night. Try to, like, get some sleep."

"Good night!" they both said, then Jessie pulled the covers over both their heads. They giggled but otherwise, stayed still.

Nat smiled at me, stepped closer, then said, "Good night to you, too." She threw her arms around my neck and hugged me, which caught me off guard, her tall, lanky frame bending down to embrace me. I wasn't expecting that at all. "Hopefully we can get through tomorrow in one piece."

"I hope so," I said, placing my arms on her back. She smelled of lavender and cocoa butter. "Thank you."

"I'll see you in the morning," she said and went into her room. She turned off the light in there but didn't close the adjoining door. In our room, I turned the light off in the bathroom and got into my bed. For a good 30 or 40 seconds, I couldn't see a thing. The room was dark--pitch black like the night in the countryside where there aren't any city lights or buildings or cars or anything except wide open spaces--so dark you can't even see your hand in front of your face. The only sound in the room was the hum of the air conditioner and an occasional honk from a passing car outside. Every sixty seconds or so, the air conditioner's compressor would switch on, increasing the pitch of the hum almost to a squeal. I noticed, too, when my eyes adjusted to the darkness, the contours of the room becoming clearer, the fixtures in the ceiling and on the walls delineating. The flashing green LED light of a smoke detector assured me that it was in compliance, ready for action.

I laid there in my bed, staring at the ceiling, my arms across my chest like an Egyptian mummy, my heart beating inside my chest. A lifetime of images flipped through my mind like a Rolodex filled with grainy Polaroid photos, images of my father from the little kid perspective of a 10-year-old Simon Burchwood, peering up at him from down low, the sadness I felt from being ignored strangling my heart, still present. Little Jessie sniffled a bit (probably from seasonal allergies), which soon turned into the low cadence of night breathing, which eventually turned into the low rumble of adolescent snoring. I turned my head in the direction of the kids' bed and noticed good ol' Sammie Boy, the top half of his little face peeking out from under the covers, staring up at the ceiling, too; not able to sleep because he was nervous about tomorrow or from eating too much goddamn candy before bed or something. He didn't notice me looking at him. Abruptly, he'd cover his face again, as if discovered by some imaginary night monster, then slowly peeked out again to see if the monster was gone. He repeated this routine quite a few times without noticing me before--out of the blue--jumping out of bed and onto his feet. He tiptoed quietly, like a mouse, across the room to the door that joined our room to Nat's room, then disappeared into the darkness.

'What the hell is he doing?' I thought to myself. I tell you, kids do the most unexpected things. They really are unpredictable little creatures that do unpredictable little things like eat their own boogers in front of others or put their fingers where they shouldn't like in electrical sockets or pee in the bath tub when their siblings are in there, too, or go into someone's hotel room without asking first. It was borderline creepy what he was doing. It's true.

So, I decided right then and there to spy on him, like any good parent would. I made sure I had my shorts and a t-shirt on and tiptoed to the door as quietly as I could so not to disturb little Jessie from her sound sleep. As I got closer to the door, I noticed a glow emitting from Nat's room, which became brighter as I reached the door frame. I slowly peeked in, trying to be as quiet as possible, when I noticed a Looney Tunes cartoon on the TV--Sylvester the Cat and Tweety Bird--with the black and white cartoon cat debating with the tiny yellow bird, declaring 'Sufferin' succotash!' while raining saliva onto Tweety. Sammie and Nat giggled together as they watched the classic cartoon in the dark under the covers of Nat's bed. Knowing that I wasn't going to disturb anyone's sleep or privacy, I decided to intercede.

"What's going on in here?" I said, standing next to the bed, looking at the TV then back at Sammie and Nat, trying to be quiet about it. I didn't want to wake up little Jessie.

"Come watch with us, Daddy," Sammie said, patting a spot next to him. "It's Looney Tunes!"

"I see that. Was Nat OK with you invading her space?"

"It's fine," she said. "I don't mind at all. I couldn't sleep anyway."

"Me neither," I said, sitting next to Sammie on the bed. My little boy patted the pillow next to his, inviting me to lie down, with me on one side of the bed, Sammie in the middle, and Nat on the other side. The part came in the cartoon where Granny discovered Sylvester attempting to consume Tweety only to be swatted by her broom. The three of us laughed even though we knew what was coming from Granny. Who doesn't know that part is coming? It's a classic.

Sammie placed his hand on my stomach and said, "Daddy, can we adopt Nat into our family?" I was a little surprised by the sincerity in his voice. He sounded as serious as serious can be.

"She has her own family, son," I said, whispering, patting his hand.

"But they aren't *nice* to her," he said.

We laid in the bed, watching a succession of other Looney Tunes characters--Bugs Bunny, Elmer Fudd, Foghorn Leghorn, the Road Runner, the Coyote, Daffy Duck--like three enchiladas in a bed wrapped in sheets and a comforter and a blanket, until the darkness crept into my eyes and the night fell over my consciousness and my sleep consumed me.

※ ※ ※

I am walking through a desert vista, the sky and ground painted in the pastel palette of Van Gogh: bright, vibrant, disturbed--the color of things like when you squint your eyes tightly then open them wide. I walk with the confidence that I know where I am going, although I have no idea where I am located or where I am going. I walk. I walk into the desert vista, the darkness of night behind me, getting smaller as I go forward, falling away like a black rock tossed off the top of a building. The baby blue clouds in the effervescent pink and yellow sky drift then lunge then drift, like a school of fish swimming in tandem with the current of the wind. I see a cliff up ahead. I walk to the cliff.

At the edge, I look down. The desert vista continues below, thousands of feet below, miles below my feet. I impetuously step out into the air, expecting to fall to my death; it's so far down. The fall will be long and torturous and excruciatingly slow. My foot leads my descent, down, then instantly touches dusty ground. I continue to walk, barely missing a step, just a slight stumble then steady again. I walk and walk. The clouds swim. I see birds, flying in a formation of a V, then a W, then a Y. I sense that the sky is where I'm supposed to be. I am a bird. I need to fly. I walk still. I see a cliff up ahead. I walk to the cliff. I walk off the cliff and continue to walk, again. It continues, on and on and on, the clouds drifting, the birds flying, the cliffs keep coming. I am a bird. Why am I walking? This is bullshit. I *need* to fly.

I look down. My feet are bird's feet, scaly and grey and lanky, the claws at the end of my toes scraping the ground as I walk. My arms are wings. My vision is long and deep and clear as a bell. I can see forever. I still walk. I want to fly but I cannot fly. I see a cliff up ahead. I walk to the cliff. I want to fly off the cliff. I walk off the cliff hoping to fly but I walk, on and on.

Am I dreaming?

I walk.

Am I *dreaming*?

I like to walk. I like to dream. But I want to fly.

I walk some more, goddamn it. I see a cliff up ahead. I walk to the cliff.

At the edge, stands a flag pole. A flag waves at the top of the pole. The flag is grey and frayed at the edges and long and proud as can be. It dances with the clouds, waving in tandem with them as they swim through the pastel, baby blue sky. I walk to the flag pole then look up. It is tall and stretches above me to the clouds. I can reach it if I try, I just know it. I raise my arms. My arms are wings, remember? The feathers of my wings are grey with blue and white and yellow, splotchy and scattered throughout. Can I fly? I know I can fly. If I flap my wings hard enough, I will fly to the sky. I want to touch the flag. It waves at me. It taunts me. It beckons me to fly.

'Come to me,' it says. 'Fly, goddamn it.'

I know I can fly.

I have wings.

I can fly.

Am I dreaming?

No, I am flying.

Goddamn it, I can fly to the sky and grab that flag. I am flying. The flag trembles because it didn't think I could really do it. I fly at the speed of sound, up the flag pole, to the sky. I grab the flag. It wraps around my wings, around my body, around my mind.

It wraps around all of me until the darkness creeps back. I have the flag and the flag has me. It is dark.

* * *

I woke up in the enchilada bed, alone. Nat was gone and Sammie was gone, too. I was wrapped up in the sheets and the comforter and the blanket as if I had barreled down a hill and entangled myself in the bed linen, rolling up into a big, fat burrito. The TV watched over me, some morning show I was not familiar with on the screen, a man and a woman speaking gibberish to each other, laughing at each other's lame jokes. In the glow of the TV, I unwrapped myself from the bedding, noticing that my arms were not wings at all, they were in fact my chubby, hairy, original arms. I was dreaming. Again. About what? I didn't know. Can I fly? Not in this lifetime. Was I glad to be awake? Hell, yes.

Next to me, laying on the comforter, was a sheet of paper ripped from good ol' Sammie Boy's sketchbook, a cartoon of my son sleeping next to his snoozing, avian friend: Budgie. I examined the black lines of the cartoon and the shape and form of the two characters, giant Z's floating next to them, indicating that they were sound asleep. Sammie must have drawn it after I fell asleep or early this morning before I woke up. I didn't remember him drawing in his sketchbook the night before. The last thing I remembered before the bizarre dream I had was watching Looney Tunes, Sylvester the Cat and Tweety Bird arguing about something ridiculous as they were prone to do, like how Sammie and Jessie argue with each other about trivial things like who gets to open the door first. My kids could be cartoon characters in their own right. It's true.

I noticed some movement coming from the bathroom and assumed it was Nat. Hopefully, she was brushing her teeth or washing her face or something like that. I decided to let her know that I was awake. I didn't want her coming out of there assuming that I was still asleep or wasn't there, particularly if she wasn't dressed. That would be weird--very weird.

"Good morning," I said, out loud. No response. The commotion in the bathroom continued. "Hello?" I said, louder this time.

"Daddy!" I heard from the bathroom. Then, little Jessie came running out and leapt on top of me, like a preying mountain cat--quick, fast, and ruthless. She knocked me down, back into the enchilada bed. "I didn't know where you were when I woke up. Everybody was in this room. *Why* didn't you tell me you were going to sleep in Nat's room with Sammie?"

I sat up and placed her next to me in one swift movement. My head hurt, a lot, on the back of it where my neck met the bottom of my skull. It throbbed the more I thought about how much it hurt.

"I didn't know we were going to sleep in here. It was a surprise."

"Surprise?" she said, annoyed. "Not to *me*, it wasn't."

"I'm sorry. Where are the others?"

"Sammie is brushing his teeth in the other room. Nat went down to see if they are still serving breakfast. It's kinda late, you know?"

"What time is it?" I said, rubbing my forehead.

"Nine o'clock, I think." She kissed me on the cheek then jumped out of bed. "I have to finish brushing my teeth!" she said, then ran back into the bathroom. "You should get ready, too! Maybe they'll have waffles!"

"You're right." I stood up, tossing the comforter and sheets onto the bed, and went into the other room, taking Sammie's cartoon drawing with me. In the bathroom, good ol' Sammie Boy diligently brushed his teeth, leaning over the counter to get a better look in the mirror.

"Good morning, son," I said. I dreaded the guilt trip I would receive for sleeping so late and not waking Sammie up early, as I promised.

"Good morning, Daddy," he said, his words jumbled in a mouth full of toothpaste suds. After a few more strokes of his brush, he stopped then turned to me, a look of bewilderment on his little face. "You were making weird noises in your sleep last night." He giggled.

"I was? What kind of noises?"

"*Weird* noises. You must have been dreaming!"

"Yeah, maybe."

"Do you remember what you were dreaming about?" he said, then spitting into the sink and brushing his tongue before rinsing his mouth with water from the faucet.

"No, I don't remember," I said. I lied. I remembered all of it. How could I forget it?

"I love dreaming!" he said, running out of the bathroom to the bed. His clothes were laid out neatly for him. Nat must have laid them out; my boy would not have done that all by himself. "That's when I get to have adventures with Budgie." He stripped off his night clothes then dressed himself in athletic shorts and a striped t-shirt--his favorite outfit. "Cool, huh?"

"Yeah, pretty cool," I said, going into the bathroom to brush my teeth. In the mirror, my reflection looked back at me. Boy, did I look like shit. I looked like I was hung over or, worse, a middle-aged loser. I examined my gut--round and hairy and white as Styrofoam--my hairy arms, my balding head, at least I had pajama pants on. I still had Sammie's cartoon drawing in my hand. I could see it in the reflection of the mirror. "I like the cartoon you drew of you and Budgie."

"Thanks, Daddy," he said, putting his shoes and socks on.

As I searched for my tooth brush in the bathroom, I heard the door to the room open. I closed the door to the bathroom most of the way so Nat couldn't see my dilapidated, middle-aged body.

"They're serving breakfast for, like, thirty more minutes," she said, the room door slamming behind her. "Everybody ready?"

"Yeah," I said, not finding my toothbrush. I grabbed Sammie's soggy toothbrush and applied some toothpaste to the bristles. "I'll be out in a minute."

I closed the bathroom door all the way to ensure that Nat wouldn't see me without a shirt on. When I turned back around to face the mirror, I noticed my clothes--clean, fresh clothes--hanging on a hook on the back of the door. Pleased, I brushed my teeth, washed my face, applied some deodorant and a tad of cologne, and got dressed as fast as possible. We didn't have much time to eat before leaving for Autumn Grove.

When I emerged from the bathroom, the three amigos were standing there, by the door, ready to go. Nat was particularly striking in grey yoga pants, a purple athletic shirt, and flip-flops, a small, white purse strung over her shoulder. Her long, red hair was perfectly done, not a strand out of place, parted down the middle. Her form-fitting clothes accentuated her height, which was already above normal to begin with. I felt like a tiny person next to her even though I was 5' 10," at least. She was an Amazonian compared to my dumpy self. It's tough to feel manly next to a woman much taller and in better physical shape than yourself. It's true.

"What took you so long, Daddy?" good ol' Sammie Boy said, annoyed. "We need to eat and go see PeePaw."

"Yeah, and before they run out of waffles!" Jessie said, ribbing her brother.

"All you care about is waffles! What about PeePaw?!"

"I care about PeePaw, too!"

"Do not!"

"Do too!"

"Last one there is a rotten egg!" Jessie said, stiff-arming Sammie then running out the door and down the hallway. Her brother followed as quick as he could, protesting about things not being fair and that she cheated and for them to start over and so on and so forth. Nat chuckled then shook her head. I followed her out the door and down the hallway. Except for construction sounds seeping up through the walls from the first floor, the fourth floor was relatively quiet and seemed uninhabited by any other families or business travelers or people in general. The long, beige hallway with the muted beige carpet and the white baseboards stretched out in front of us. I was surprised to not see anyone else around, particularly since *free* breakfast was being served downstairs. Maybe the breakfast was not as good as we hoped or as good as advertised. Maybe, being FREE was the only good thing about it. The kids impatiently waited in the elevator, Sammie holding the door open by leaning his full weight on one side and waving his arms.

"Hurry, Daddy!" he said, straining to hold the sliding door open. "It's heavy!"

Nat and I entered the elevator and stood in the rear. Jessie assumed the role of elevator operator, pressing the first-floor button. The door slid shut; the elevator descended; the country music played quietly.

When the doors dinged and opened on the first floor, I expected to see hungry families or travelers or workers making their way to the dining area for the free breakfast but there was no one--not a single soul. Even the construction noise floated in air as if being piped in through the speakers in the ceiling: faint, muffled, as if from far, far away. The reception desk was vacant, too. Ms. B. Smith must have been hiding in the back, under her desk, sucking on an e-cigarette or a vaporizer or whatever she was puffing on yesterday that smelled of maple syrup and chemical propellant. It was a weird scene straight out of a suspense movie, there in the lobby of the hotel. Where was everybody?

The kids rushed to the back of the dining area where the buffet was setup, a cornucopia of crap that would make most adults shiver awaited us in all its lukewarm, prepackaged splendor. But to Sammie and Jessie, it was absolutely delightful. There were plastic dispensers of colorful, sugary cereals, danishes and muffins wrapped in cellophane, ripe bananas with large black spots and dull, red apples, heated pans of scrambled eggs and leathery strips of meat that I assumed was bacon or something similar, an aluminum vat of oatmeal, a small refrigerator with rows of strawberry yogurt and cartons of 2% milk that we could see through its glass door, and stacks of plates and plastic cups. But none of this was quite as magical or delightful or divine as the appliance that awaited us at the end of the buffet: the waffle-making station. The kids ran directly to it like bees to sunflowers, then they danced their little, excited, bee dance. They knew what was going to happen and I did too: the waffle apocalypse.

"Waffles!" they screamed, jumping up and down and making a spectacle. "Waffles! Waffles! Waffles!"

"I see that," I said, not as enthused as they were for electronically ironed bread.

"And look, Daddy! The waffles will be shaped like Texas!" Sammie said, entranced, admiring the waffle iron's resemblance to our home state. "That is so awesome!"

"Can we make waffles?!" Jessie said, her hands clinched as if praying to be absolved.

"Sure," I said, pulling a chair out from one of the dining tables for Nat to sit in. She blushed, caught off guard by my gentlemanly gesture, then sat down. I sat next to her. "Are you going to have one, too?" I said to her.

"No," she said. "But I might have, like, an apple."

"I might have some coffee."

"That's an excellent idea," she said, placing her purse on the dining table.

The kids manned the waffle making station. There were two irons at front--both shaped like a miniature Texas--and a tall, batter dispenser in the back with two varieties of batter: regular and blueberry. I imagined the blueberries to be fake, little blue specks of sugar and food coloring interspersed in a goopy blend of inexpensive ingredients and preservatives. The dispensers had photos of children on the front, looking happy and excited. I knew my kids wouldn't be excited after the raging case of diarrhea I was certain they would both be infected with later in the day. But sometimes, parents have to look past these observations and insights. It's no fun raining on a kid's parade all the time. Sometimes, you just have to let the kid get rained on. It's true.

Sammie and Jessie each filled their batter dispenser cups with the yellow goop--Sammie got regular and Jessie got blueberry--then poured it in their respective irons. When they clamped the irons shut, the handles spun the irons on a hinge--180 degrees--so the waffles would cook evenly. A timer with red, digital numbers on each iron began to countdown from two minutes. Good ol' Sammie Boy counted aloud as the seconds descended: 59, 58, 57, and so on. As he patiently counted, I retrieved a cup of black coffee and the best-looking apple for Nat. I was back at the table before Sammie was even close to finishing his countdown.

"22, 21, 20!" he said. He was so excited. He could hardly stand it.

I leaned over to Nat and whispered, "It looks like he's going to pee his pants." She giggled. His countdown continued into the final minute.

"49, 48, 47!"

"I can't wait!" said little Jessie, equally as excited.

Through the excruciating final seconds, the kids jumped up and down, and when the buzzer finally went off, they excavated the waffles from their irons using some plastic tongs, slathered maple syrup on their breakfast, and ran over to our table. They began devouring their breakfast before their butts settled in their seats.

"Are they good?" I said, curious. Both kids nodded in the affirmative. I continued to drink my coffee even though it was boiling hot and the little liquid I could swallow was bitter and weak. There really was nothing worse than a bad cup of coffee, especially in this setting. I mean, how hard could it be to buy at least a half-decent variety of medium blend coffee and brew it correctly? It really wasn't that hard. Nat didn't seem too enthused about her apple, either. It sat in front of her, abandoned. It really was a pathetic excuse for a piece of fruit: dull and askew with a filmy coating of--what?--I didn't know. "Not hungry?" I said to her.

She politely shook her head.

"Daddy, can I ask you a question?" said good ol' Sammie Boy.

"Of course."

"When are we leaving to go see PeePaw?"

"When we're done eating our breakfast."

"Then we must eat faster!" he said, stuffing his mouth with large chunks of waffle. Jessie's eyes widen with disbelief as he stuffed his mouth like a determined squirrel preparing for a tough winter, his cheeks inflating to an obscene size.

"Don't choke yourself," I said, folding my arms, casting a disheartened stare. He didn't heed my warning and continued to eat at a god-awful pace.

"When do you think we'll be back?" said Nat.

"I have no idea," I said. "It might take all day."

"That's fine. I was just curious."

"Isn't it weird that there isn't anyone else around," I said, peering around the dining room and the lobby for someone--anyone.

"I was thinking the same thing," Nat said. "It's, like, we're the only people here."

Just then, as if on cue, a door at the back of the dining room opened, and out from a utility room came Ms. B. Smith--the hotel receptionist--a plume of smoke rising to the ceiling from behind her head, wearing the same thing as the night before except for a clear, plastic apron strapped to the front of her body, as if she had worked all through the night, a trash bag in one of her hands, the other hand wearing a bright yellow, latex glove. She hobbled over to one end of the breakfast buffet, the end opposite the waffle making station, and began unceremoniously dumping the breakfast items in the trash bag. She lifted the bowl of bananas and apples and tossed the fruit in the bag then dropped the empty bowl back on the buffet, hard. She picked up the tray of little cereal boxes and, without examining them or even looking at them, tilted the tray into the trash bag, the little boxes of sugary cereal sliding to their demise. Soon, the trash bag was heavy enough that the bottom of it touched the linoleum floor. She attacked each station of the buffet, discarding the food as if it was contaminated, while dragging the garbage bag behind her. Sammie and Jessie were horrified, to say the least. They looked on--mouths agape, eyes wide-- with disbelief and concern.

"What about the waffles?" said good ol' Sammie Boy, a tinge of sadness quivering his voice, one of his cheeks filled with his bready breakfast.

"Looks like the waffles will be toast," I said, nonchalantly.

"How do waffles become *toast*?" said Jessie.

"They don't," I said. "It's a figure of speech. It means they are done for."

"What if I want seconds?" said Sammie, puzzled.

"Do you want seconds?" said Nat.

"Who doesn't?!" said Jessie.

"Well, now's the time," I said.

The two kids launched from their chairs and lunged to the waffle making station to make a second round of waffles before Ms. B. Smith unceremoniously tossed the waffle batter into the trash bag as well. Watching my two kids attempt to make a second round of waffles before the batter saw its doom was like watching a housewife on a TV game show compete in a timed round for a brand-new washer and dryer set that she desperately wanted. The tension was palatable. They really hungered for a second helping of those Texas-shaped waffles. Ms. B. Smith didn't miss a beat, though. She continued trashing the remains of the breakfast like a machine: an unrepentant terminator.

"All that food, like, gone to waste," said Nat, placing her hand over her mouth as if witnessing a car accident.

As I watched Ms. B. Smith dump the food, I wondered if my dad, retired Colonel Burchwood, was even thinking about us at all. Was he thinking about all we were going through to go visit him? Did he realize the amount of effort it took for me to get the kids out of school, pack for this trip, bring along Nat, and align all the things needed to leave Austin and drive to Autumn Grove in San Antonio, just to see him? Did he ever think I would find out about Sharice and his weekly trips to the Gentleman's Club in the Autumn Grove limousine? Did he worry what I would think or if I would allow it to continue if I ever found out? The older I became, I still was no closer to understanding my father, who he was, or what motivated him. He was an enigma to me, pure and simple, the shadowy figure that followed me through life, lurking in the background, threatening to cause trouble. Strange how someone can have so much influence over your life, isn't it? Very strange, indeed.

When the kids saw Ms. B. Smith toss the remnants of the oatmeal from the scalding, aluminum vat into the trash bag, they knew the waffle station was next. Fortunately for them, the countdown for the waffles alerted them to take their waffles and they quickly dashed back to the table. Not long after, Ms. B. opened the front of the waffle batter dispenser, pulled out the two bags of waffle batter, and tossed them into the trash bag. She unplugged the waffle makers then dragged the trash bag back into the utility room, closing the door behind her, not saying a word to any of us. The breakfast terminator was gone.

"Bizarre," said Nat, pulling a compact mirror from her purse and completing the touch-up job on her face.

The kids dove into their second round of breakfast while I reminded them that it was time to go visit PeePaw. They quickly shoved a few forkfuls of waffle in their mouths then slid their plates off the table to toss in the trash and, just like that--in one swift motion from breakfast to trash to the exit--we were out the door, all four of us, into the sunlit parking lot. We found the Volvo S70 parked in the rear of the parking lot, where I had left it the night before.

And this... this is where things get a little bit fuzzy for me.

If you've ever lived through a catastrophic event, then you know that sorting through the pieces of your memory for the sequence of events that explain the truth of that moment is as difficult as if someone tossed the pieces of a puzzle onto the ground then asked you to put the thousand pieces of the puzzle back together as quickly as possible. I remember getting in the car and driving to Autumn Grove. I remember hearing the kids cheering in the back seat about seeing PeePaw. I remember looking at Nat's face in profile and thinking that she had a perfect nose--small, freckled, straight. I remember the procedurals of traffic--the stopping, the turning, and the passing of cars. I remember seeing duct tape flapping in the breeze from the seam of the car hood. The duct tape was grey and its edges frayed, the white threads of the tape undulating like the legs of a centipede, the tape flapping in the wind like a miniature flag. And I remember (I know this will sound very strange to you but I'm telling you the truth) looking at the seat of Sammie's shorts and thinking to myself, 'Why am I looking at Sammie's butt?'

Isn't that funny?

So strange what happens during a car crash.

I didn't hear a thing. Or, the crash was so loud that it blew my hearing out. I don't know.

No one really explained it to me in detail.

No one really explains *anything* to you in detail when you really want them to.

Life just happens then you are left to sort it out the best you can.

Life is strange. Really.

It's true.

YANKEE CANDLE®

America's Best Loved Candle

CHAPTER ELEVEN

Fête scintillante

with pure, natural extracts

NET WT 22 OZ (623g)

Chapter Eleven

When I opened my eyes, the first thing I saw was a curtain covered with cartoon animals, hanging in front of me, about 8 or 9 feet away, jungle animals, I think. There were monkeys and parrots and wild cats and butterflies and ants and whatever else the graphic design company that created them could think of that lived in an imaginary, cartoon jungle. The animals appeared to be living together in a harmonious state that only existed in the imagination of an underpaid, overworked, graphic designer in Cleveland, Ohio--the farthest place in the world from a real jungle. The animals had stupid-looking, dopey faces and they grinned and winked at each other as if they knew something I didn't know, which was a pretty silly notion, if you asked me. But I didn't give a shit because you never give a shit when the narcotic warmth of morphine flows through your veins, the level of comfort being somewhere near that of a baby being swaddled in a warm blanket by its mother while breastfeeding. That's pretty goddamn comfortable if you ask me. Right? You know I'm right.

But honestly, I didn't know I had a morphine drip plugged into my arm either at the time, now that I think back on it. I didn't know anything but that I felt pretty goddamn good and any worry or apprehension about not knowing where I was didn't exist. When you're in that state, in a hospital after a traumatic event, nothing is normal, nothing is as it was, the repetitive loop of everyday life broken, the routine sameness destroyed, with a nurse delivering the liquid complacency via an intravenous drip. That's the miracle of modern medicine and, particularly, opioid narcotics. You want to talk about modern miracles? Painkillers are modern miracles of the highest order. They're like magic. It's true.

The rest of the emergency room I laid in was *not* as festive as the cartoon animal curtain, drab in its utilitarian whites and beiges: a desk mounted on the wall with a metal stool in front of it, some machines with small, digital screens, waste disposal bins on the floor and also mounted on the wall (biohazard stickers decorating those, the skull and crossbones were not as charming as the dopey, cartoon, jungle animals), posters of human bodies severed in half, their bones and arteries on display like windows of merchandise at the entrance of a department store, and jars of swabs and tongue depressors and the like. I examined the room with the aloofness of someone who had seen this room before--like a million times--and the idea that I had never been in this room before didn't strike me as unusual or anything. In fact, the notion that I didn't know the whereabouts of my children or Nat the nanny didn't seem to concern me at all, either. I was both concerned and unconcerned at the same time, a middle of the road complacency leading to I-Don't-Care-Ville. Actually, if anything at all, I seemed more concerned that I had a rock-hard erection while I laid under a sheet as thin as cheese cloth than the whereabouts of my family. Boy, I was feeling pretty damn good and there wasn't much else I cared about. Ahhh... morphine drip.

After a few moments of marveling at the erection I had, the curtains to the room slowly opened and a woman appeared, a short, stocky woman, who looked quite a bit older than myself, maybe in her late 50s, going about her business in a professional, nurse-like manner. She came into the room and closed the curtains, then walked around my bed, doing this and that to the machines, opening and closing drawers, unconcerned that my erection propped the sheet up like a New England maypole in springtime.

"I'm sorry," I said, my speech slurred as if I had consumed five margaritas then five beers then five more shots of an unknown concoction served by a malicious bartender but without all the aggression that comes from being drunk off your ass from alcohol. I was drooling, too.

"Excuse me?" she said, still not looking at me, still busy doing something administrative, something nurse-like, like a real, medical professional would do.

"I said I'm sorry for... you know?"

She sat down at the desk and typed something on the computer. She typed fast and furious with purpose. She must have taken typing class in high school or at the community college or wherever she got her medical training. I never took typing class in high school. When I typed, I typed with two fingers like two sandpipers pecking coastal sand for unsuspecting mollusks. My typing skills were ridiculously amateurish for someone who had once attempted a career as a writer. It's true.

She continued to type. I continued to drool.

"I'm sorry for the..."

She finally turned to face me, a serene smile on her face, unfazed by my inappropriate sexual response to the drugs.

"The erection?" she said, matter-of-factly. She didn't seem to care one bit.

"Yes, ma'am. *That.*"

"It's OK," she said, returning to the computer, her professional data entry continuing. "I've seen it all here at the hospital. I've seen much worse. I've seen things you wouldn't believe. An involuntary, bodily function is the least of my worries."

I looked in the direction of my boner and it was gone, miraculously, although the sensation of it remained, like a phantom limb. It was odd, feeling the blood pumping through my crotch to an invisible erection. Was I imagining it before? Did she think I was *crazy?* I watched her type, her shoulders shimmying back and forth, like a keyboard player in a funk band. She seemed to be enjoying herself and I watched her as if I was an audience member of said funk band, enjoying the band while sipping a cold beer. She had a kind face--round and tan, crow's feet protruding from her eyes above blushed cheeks--and her auburn hair styled in a fashion that some men do, cut close above the ears, parted to the side, and set in its feathery place with hair gel. She wore earrings with large, glimmering crimson-colored stones, either rubies or garnets or something like that, maybe a gift from her husband although she wasn't wearing a wedding ring. And on one cheek, four very dark freckles configured in a trapezoidal shape that reminded me of a constellation.

"What is your name?" I said, shifting my body so I was laying on my side, the arm with the tubes inserted into it comfortably placed on the side of my body facing up. "If you don't mind me asking?"

She continued to type. "My name is Juanita."

"Juanita," I said, absorbing all the syllables to that Spanish name then regurgitating the name slowly, my tongue thick and heavy and swollen. "Wah-*nee*-tah."

She giggled. I was still drooling like a fool.

"What's so *funny*?" I said, a tingling sensation washing over my body, starting at my scalp then rippling through all the hairs on my body all the way down to my toes.

"You. People. People on drugs. It never gets old."

"What never gets old?" I said, curious.

"The silliness from the morphine. It never gets old."

"Morphine?" I said, surprised. "I'm on more-*feen*?"

"What do you think is being pumped into your arm?"

I tried to sit up but the weight of my body was too much to lift. I rolled onto my back and peered up at the ceiling, my torso sinking heavily into the scratchy linen of the hospital bed. Most of the ceiling tiles were bright white except for one tile with a corner of it stained the color of bog water--brown and festering with microbes that would give you diarrhea. They always say that the one place you don't want to be if you don't want to get sick is in a hospital. Do they say that because hospitals are filled with sick people? Or is it because hospitals are built on the backs of the sick and the financial strain it puts on suffering families? Or is it because hospitals are not as sanitary as they claim to be? I didn't know.

"Are you married?" I said, still examining the ceiling tiles. The clickity-clack of the keyboard halted abruptly.

"I'm a widow," she said. "My husband passed away last year."

"I'm sorry to hear that. How did he die?"

"Cancer."

"Cancer. It's always can-*cer*. Yessir," I said, my lips smacking.

"Mmm hmm," she said, the keyboard clickity-clacking some more.

"Do you have children?" I said. I rubbed my stomach because it felt good rubbing my stomach. It felt good rubbing myself all over.

She abruptly stopped again, rolled on the stool closer to me, then extended my arm, the one without all the tubes stuck in it. She wrapped my bicep with a blood pressure gauge, cinching it tightly with velcro. The pressure of it was almost too much to take but it didn't bother me at all, either. Narcotic drugs are a miraculous thing. Right?

"I have two grown children, a son and a daughter."

"I have two kids, too! A son and a daughter! I love them so much. They are *sooo* awesome. I wish I knew where they were. Do you know where they are?"

"No, I don't. But I can look into it, if you'd like. Do you want me to ask around?"

"Whenever you have time," I said. "You seem very busy."

She giggled some more. She thought that was pretty goddamn funny, I could tell. I can be pretty goddamn funny when I want to be. Sometimes. The Big Dipper constellation of freckles on her cheek slowly spun to life and as I observed its rotation, I marveled at it, spinning slowly. One of the freckles was darker and fuzzier than the others.

"I'm always busy," she said, pumping the blood pressure gauge to life. She didn't seem to mind that I was staring at her and the unusual, astronomical event that was on display on her face.

"I'm curious," I said, enjoying the sensation of her hands touching the skin on my arm. "Before your husband died, did you enjoy being married?"

She stopped pumping the gauge and it hissed as the air retreated from the arm strap. She sighed then said, "That's a very personal question."

"I know," I said, not ashamed.

"Aren't you more concerned about your own state of being at the moment?" she said, the velcro screaming as she tore it apart, removing the blood pressure gauge from my limp arm. "117 over 82."

"Is that good?!"

"It's fine," she said, hanging the blood pressure gauge on a hook on the wall next to some other medical contraptions. "The doctor will be in soon to talk to you."

"But--"

"Yes?" she said, opening the jungle-animal curtain then waiting for my response. A smirk appeared on her round face.

"Was your husband good to you?"

The smirk transformed into contentment, then she said, "He was amazing. The best husband I could have ever wished for. The doctor will be with you shortly."

She disappeared behind the jungle-animal curtain, pulling it closed. The curtain swayed back and forth momentarily, then as it stopped, the jungle animals sprung to life in a hallucinatory dance of fornication, copulation, and jubilation. There were monkeys humping lions, bees kissing ants, elephants molesting zebras with their predatory trunks, and snakes penetrating orangutans in their rear ends. It was a goddamn jungle orgy! Now, don't start judging me like most people like to do, getting on their goddamn high-horse and pontificating about what is right and what is wrong about the world and its love affair with narcotics and such. People love to get on their goddamn high-horse. It makes them feel superior to the rest of us and people *love* to feel superior to everyone else. It's true. I got a kick out of watching the intra-species love fest on the curtain. It brought me great pleasure, so much so that I didn't notice the doctor slip into the room. He was a sneaky bastard, that doctor. He snuck in so stealthily that when I finally noticed him, I almost jumped out of my bed. He scared the shit out of me.

"Good afternoon," he said, all calm and professional and courteous. I yelped when he said that, like a little girl, like a scared little child. How embarrassing. "I'm Dr. Yang and I'm here to discuss what happened to you and your family. Are you aware of what happened?"

I thought about his question like the ancient philosophers pondered the intricacies of life, except I had nothing in there--inside my head. My mind was like an abandoned well and his question was like a pebble being dropped into it, yet never landing at the bottom. His question was swallowed by the abyss of my intoxicated mind.

"Aware of what?" I said, shifting uncomfortably in the bed.

Dr. Yang was a good-sized man, maybe six feet in height with 230 pounds or so of chubbiness hanging on his big-boned frame. His light, clear skin and thin, pink lips contrasted nicely with a dark brown, tiny mole near one of his eyebrows, three wiry hairs protruding from it like crabgrass invading the well-manicured putting green of a pristine golf course. He moved with the deliberateness of a sloth--slow, meticulous, and determined. What was with all the moles on the hospital staff, huh? It was a question that would prod at my curiosity for the rest of the day.

"Aware of what happened to you today?" he said.

"*Today*? What happened today?"

"Mr. B--?"

"Are *you* aware that there is a hairy mole on your--"

"Sir, I know that the morphine drip is easing your discomfort effectively. I can tell by the way you are communicating with me, which is fine. It's doing what it's designed to do. But I need to ask you to try to at least focus on what I am telling you. Can you at least try to do that?"

I will say this about Dr. Yang. He was a goddamn professional. It's true. No matter how stupid or dopey or foolish I was, being under the influence of morphine and all, he never lost his composure. He just sat there--stern and serious and stoic--like a professional doctor should, unfazed by all the stupid things I let slip out of my stupid mouth. That's the way all doctors and nurses should be, particularly in times of trauma. Serious as hell.

"I'll try," I said, holding back laughter the best I could. I couldn't help it. It was all just so goddamn funny.

"Excellent. Now, the car accident your family experienced was serious and I'm afraid to say that some of the family members are in grave condition, as well as... there was one *fatality*."

"Fuh-tal-eh-tee? Is that what you said?"

"Yes," he said, then sat there silently, his eyes turning to his lap where his hands laid, fingers crossed. "I'm sorry to inform you that a little boy did not make it."

"Little *boy*?" I said, the words dribbling from my lips with the consistency of mud. Muddy words and drooling lips. "Fay-*tull*?"

The pleasant sensation that had intimately swathed my body was replaced by a cold chill that raised goose pimples and stiffened my body hair into miniature icicles. Why was there a blackhole in my memory? How could I *not* remember such a severe car crash? Was I going insane? Did I kill my son?

"Yes, sir. But fortunately, the other passengers survived but some have worse injuries than others. We're looking at--"

"Is my son *dead*?" I said, finding the strength to sit up and place my hand on the kind Dr. Yang. "My Sammie?"

"I'm afraid so." Like a water pipe bursting, the tears from my eyes and boogers from my nose ran in a gush of unexpected ferocity but the good doctor seemed to be prepared for this. He patted my back gently, pulling some Kleenex from a coat pocket. He really was a great doctor, I tell you, prepared and whatnot. "I really hate delivering this type of news, Mr. Burnstein. It's a part of my job that I never get used to."

I cried and cried and cried for my little boy, the best son in the entire world, the cutest kid, the most loving boy. I just couldn't believe it yet it must have been true. I mean, there was the good Dr. Yang, embracing a stranger, telling him the unfortunate news about the death of their child. Good ol' Sammie Boy's short life flashed in my mind: the day he was born, the day of his first word, the day he first walked, many more milestones, the first day of school, the first time riding a bike. Everything. Then I thought of his mother and, even though I carried so much hate in my heart toward her, I saw her sadness, her broken heart, her spirit crushed, and it obliterated me. Then I wondered, 'How would I explain this to little Jessie?' What was I going to say to her? How was I going to mend her little broken heart? I cried and cried and cried, embracing Dr. Yang with my cold arms. I held him tight and firm. Then, after weeping some more, I thought, 'Burnstein? Who the fuck is Burnstein?'

"Did you say *Burnstein*?" I said, sniffling, wiping my face on his white coat.

"Why, yes I--" Dr. Yang pulled away from me, then pulled a folded sheet of paper from his doctor coat. He read the paper, examining the dense lines of data on it, then looked at me, bewilderment on his face, then a look of condolence.

"You are Mr. Burnstein, correct?"

"Burchwood," I said, sitting up in bed. "Simon Burchwood. My name is *Burchwood*."

"F-f-fuck," he said quietly, stuttering under his breath but completely audible to me. If there was ever an appropriate time in a professional setting to say *that* word--the F word--then this was it. He quickly stood up and, realizing his extreme error, immediately left the room, the curtain flailing behind him as he retreated. I wondered what he was doing or where he was going. Was he running around like a waiter in a panic who had just delivered the wrong order of food to a large table of hungry customers? Was he looking for Mr. Burnstein or was he looking for my family? Was good ol' Sammie Boy all right? Was my family even in a car accident? I didn't know the answers to any of these questions. But one thing I did know was that the high from the morphine was completely gone. I sat in my emergency room, alone, only the blips and bleeps of the electronic medical equipment to keep my company. Even the dopey jungle animals on the curtain had stopped humping each other, the somber weight of the air killing all hallucinatory magic they were experiencing. Time stood still and I wasn't sure how long it was that I sat there, alone, not knowing the whereabouts of Nat and my kids. But before I knew it, good ol' Sammie Boy and little Jessie and Nat were all in the tiny emergency room-- screaming, cheering, and crying.

"Daddy!" my two little kids exclaimed, jumping up in the bed with me, their little arms wrapped around my neck and shoulders, Nat standing close by teary and blush, with a band-aid on her forehead and a scrape on one of her freckly cheeks. I embraced my children, filled with so many different emotions. It was like I was in a dream.

"I'm glad everybody is OK!" I said, choked up. I extended a hand to Nat and she held it, then I pulled her to the bed. The four of us embraced each other, weeping heavily. "Are you OK?" I said to Nat. I could feel her nodding--her body quivering from crying--and I was content with her non-verbal response. There really wasn't much else to say in that moment. Still feeling the slight effects of the morphine (though it wasn't an enjoyable feeling anymore), I was content in that moment of just being alive, and being with my family.

I never felt more alive in my entire life than during those few minutes, hugging my family, all of us crying, all of us holding onto dear life, the breath in my lungs vibrant and effervescent and full.

Your life never seems as precious as in the moments of a realization that it could have been over--forever.

It's true.

***

Dr. Yang was pretty goddamn embarrassed, so much so that he said he would make things right. And boy, did he make things *right*. After telling all of us that he recommended that we stay one night in the hospital so he could observe us and our injuries, he set us up in a room that might as well have been a goddamn hotel suite. It was large and comfortably furnished, what, with couches and pull-out beds and an armoire with a TV and a round dining table and tastefully chosen framed watercolor paintings and shit like that. You see, all the regular hospital rooms were full but many of the *maternity* rooms were vacant for whatever reason and Dr. Yang was determined to make up for his monumental, administrative blunder--a real fuck up, if you ask me-- and treat us with the dignity and respect we deserved. Well, we didn't actually deserve *that* more than any other patients in the intensive care unit but I liked at least thinking that we did. Sometimes, I'm telling you, it's nice to be pampered.

While we were moving into our new hospital room for the night, I soon discovered that of the four of us, Nat and Jessie were practically unharmed. As I said earlier, Nat had a band-aid on her forehead and a scrape on her cheek but the rest of her was in good shape. Same for little Jessie--practically normal. That tough little girl had a black eye and a bruised ego. That was about it. Both girls were in good shape considering the severity of the car accident, according to Dr. Yang. The worst damage was sustained by yours truly and good ol' Sammie Boy. It seemed from what the emergency responders said was that at the point of impact--when the other car slammed into the back of my Volvo S70--Sammie launched from the backseat, our heads crashing together while he was mid-air, and he landed head-first into my lap. My trusty Volvo went off the road and down an embankment, stopping in a ditch. When the EMTs ripped open my car door, they found the two of us in the driver seat clinging together like the two fish in the astrological symbol for Pisces, two fish swimming the complimentary configuration of yin yang. In fact, we knocked our heads together so hard that the emergency room staff reviewed our injuries through CT scans, results to be given to us later that night by Dr. Yang himself. Sammie's little head was wrapped in gauze and bandages, his hair spilling out the top like the contents of an over-stuffed taco. My fat head was wrapped in bandages, too. We were a pair of Twinkies, to say the least; two concussed heads with brains of mush. It was a miracle that we were alive at all. A goddamn *miracle*. It's true.

We settled into the maternity room with the belongings we had, which was practically nothing, and made ourselves at home the best we could. There was one bed, which I was lying in, and a couple of roll-away beds wheeled in by hospital staff, which Sammie and Nat occupied. Little Jessie insisted she slept on the hide-away bed in the couch for some reason, which I was certain was as hard and lumpy as a rock like most hideaway beds. She stacked the cushions of the couch in a neat pile on the cold, tile floor, pulling the folded mattress from the guts of the couch all by herself. As typical of most Type A personalities, Jessie insisted she prep her bed all by herself, even though it was obvious she was struggling with getting that folded mattress out of the bowels of the couch without assistance from an adult. When Nat attempted to assist her, she said, "I'll do it myself!" with a bark and a hiss that was dreadful, if not downright frightening. Nat left her to do it all by herself. Wise move on Nat's part. She's a pretty smart cookie.

The belongings we had were practically the clothes we had on our backs, except for good ol' Sammie Boy, who had all of his prized possessions including the buck knife, Zippo lighter, popsicle stick, a quarter, a Doctor Strange comic book, his sketch book, and other trinkets and treasures he had been collecting for the past few months. He had all his crap spread out on the round dining table like a vendor at an art bazaar, his things neatly positioned and grouped as if to dazzle potential customers, or to at least impress the hospital staff. Nat was lying on her cot, staring at the ceiling, her purse underneath her crossed-arms like a mummy waiting for the cover of its sarcophagus to be sealed up for eternity. Little Jessie kicked and punched the couch as if her violent blows would convince the couch to give up its mattress in a more congenial fashion. It didn't. The couch held onto its springy innards with conviction and determination like an oyster protecting its pearl from a pesky deep-sea diver. When Dr. Yang returned to check on us, he got a kick out of little Jessie's temper tantrum. He thought her fit was quite amusing.

"Did you watch *The Little Rascals* when you were a kid?" he said, sitting on my bed next to me, his clipboard resting on his lap. "Your daughter's persistence reminds me of the one they called Spanky, the leader of their gang. Did you watch them?"

"Yeah, sometimes," I said, sitting up. Using a remote control, I maneuvered the top-end of the bed to prop up with the push of a button and, once in the position of my liking, I could sit up with the assistance of the mattress. "They would show *The Little Rascals* on Saturday mornings along with *The Three Stooges* and *The Marx Brothers*."

"Those were hilarious! I just loved those old black and white shorts," he said, flipping through some papers on his clipboard. As I watched him rummage through the papers, I hoped that he was actually looking at papers pertaining to me and not some other patient who was a father with a last name starting with 'B.' He read through a few things then set the clipboard back down on his lap. "I want to apologize for earlier. I am extremely sorry for confusing you for *another* patient, which I'm sure seemed unprofessional and inconsiderate on my part. But let me assure you that I have the proper paperwork *now* and will do everything in my power to keep it that way."

"OK," I said, shifting in place. My lower back was sore and the stiffness I felt down there was making its way up to my neck and head.

"Do you accept my *apology*?"

"Of course. I don't really have a choice, do I?"

"I guess not," he said, slightly aggravated by my answer. But what else was I going to say? I was in a spot, wasn't I? I really didn't have a choice but to trust him. "The hospital is busier than usual today. I'm not certain why. Just a fact. Do you have any questions for me?"

I looked over at my family: Nat on her cot staring at the ceiling, Sammie at the table organizing his trinkets, and Jessie wrestling with the couch. I couldn't help but wonder most about my boy, Sammie with his head wrapped in gauze and bandages looking something like a patient in a 1950s horror film. Would the accident affect his mental abilities? How was I going to explain that to the doctor? I sat there for a moment contemplating my dilemma, my vision blurring as my thoughts tumbled on themselves inside my head.

"Well?" the doctor said, impatiently rapping his fingernails on the clipboard.

"How bad is my son's head injury? He has quite a few bandages on his head."

"Well, I'm still waiting for the results from the CT scan. It's really hard to say without that."

"You see, my boy..." I said, hesitating to go on, worrying if what I was about to say would sound crazy or batshit or hysterical or what. Nat stopped staring at the ceiling and sat up on her cot, her purse on her lap. Sammie stopped organizing his things and set his eyes on me. Jessie finally pulled the folded mattress from the couch, its stiff hinges and springs squealing to life when its folded legs popped in place and propped the mattress up on the tile floor. It lunged out of the couch, quick and fast like a cat unexpectedly barfing up a hairball. Fff-ack!

"I did it!" Jessie said, excited. But when she realized I was talking to the doctor, she quietly sat on her bed, crossing her legs with her arms on her knees. "Sorry."

"What *about* your boy?" Dr. Yang said, turning his attention to me. "Is there something I should know about your son?"

Right then and there, as if jumping from a burning bed, good ol' Sammie Boy leapt from his chair, sprinted across the maternity room, then jumped in my bed. He placed his hand over my mouth, muzzling what I was about to say, what he knew I would say about him: our secret.

"Don't say it, Daddy!" he said, hissing in my ear. "Please, daddy. Don't."

"Sorry, Sammie, but I have to. I have to tell the doctor."

Sulking, good ol' Sammie Boy descended from the bed like Gollum retreating beneath the Misty Mountains and lurched back to the round table where his precious belongings waited for him. As he played with his things, I told Dr. Yang everything I knew about my son, his special cognitive abilities, and his ability to see things before they even happen. I told him about the afterschool counselor, the scratch ticket, and the fire on my balcony. I then told him about the old man in the cemetery and the connection my son had with my dad, Colonel Burchwood. I told him everything like a P.O.W. spilling the beans after hours of ruthless torture, telling him every detail about my son's miraculous ability to see the future. As I told him everything, Dr. Yang returned a glance somewhere between skeptical and quizzical, not leaving room for unbiased interpretation. He interlaced his fingers on his lap, steadying himself for the barrage of questions he was about to unleash on my unsuspecting and fragile psyche. He then crossed his legs as most pompous know-it-alls do, wrapping his hands around the propped knee, his body wound up in a state of complete denial.

"Now, let me get this straight... you think your son can *see* the *future*?"

"Yes," I said, as sure of my answer as I was sure my name was Simon Burchwood.

"I see," he said, looking down at the clipboard on his lap, rifling through the clipped papers, looking with persistence for something that maybe he didn't see before. "The future, huh?"

"Yes. Yes!"

"And this is something you can prove with absolute certainty?"

"Well," I said, wondering exactly how I would do *that*, proving it. How would I go about convincing Dr. Yang that I wasn't a nut bag? I looked over at good ol' Sammie Boy, who at this point, had his face in his hands, and I could see the red of his flushed cheeks pressing into his palms.

"Maybe, I should order additional testing for you, Mr. B--"

"Burchwood! My name is Simon Burchwood!"

"Yes, Mr. Burchwood. Thank you for reminding me. I think the trauma of the accident--"

"I can prove it," I said, throwing the bed sheet off my legs. Dr. Yang quickly stood up and stepped out of my way as I hopped out of my bed and hobbled to the round table where my son sat, embarrassed. I placed my hands on good ol' Sammie Boy's shoulders, squeezing them firmly. "I can prove it with a game."

"Daddy, no!"

"Sammie, show him how we play Thump. You know? The game you like?"

"I don't want to," he said, lying his head on the table and covering it with his arms, as if shielding his head from rain drops or hail or even gamma rays from outer space.

"Do you have the quarter with you?"

"Yes," he said, reluctantly uncovering his head. He reached into the mass of belonging he had on the table then held up a quarter. I nodded then he pushed the rest of the things on the table to the side, giving him room to thump the quarter. Dr. Yang joined us at the table as I directed Sammie with what to do.

"Now, do your thing. Guess which side will come up."

"But Daddy--"

"You can do it, son. Don't be embarrassed," I said, patting his back.

He propped the quarter up on its side on the table top with his little index finger, George Washington's profile revealing itself, flashes of light reflecting off its silvery surface. He cocked his other index finger, ready to thump the coin so it could spin on its side along the surface of the table. He took a deep breath then said, "Heads."

He flicked the edge of the coin with his finger and it spun like a dreidel, drifting out to the center of the table, wobbling on its edge as it spun in a circle. We all watched: me, Dr. Yang, Nat, and Jessie. And as it toppled over, there was a collective gasp, as we waited for the result of the spin. I knew that Sammie would prove me right. I just knew it. But when the coin stopped tap-dancing, it revealed the opposite of what he said.

"Tails," Dr. Yang said, dryly.

But I didn't want to be proven wrong so I insisted that Sammie try again. And again. And again. And each time, he guessed wrong, at least five times in a row. Before Sammie could get off a sixth try, Dr. Yang interrupted him.

"That's not necessary," he said, writing something on his clipboard. "I think you all could use some rest. Your family has been through a lot today. We can visit again in the morning." Then he abruptly left the room.

Sammie, dejected and embarrassed, picked up the uncooperative quarter, examined both sides of it, then placed it with the rest of his things. I stood behind him, placing my hands on his shoulders, and said, "Sorry, son. We tried."

"Sorry, daddy. I didn't mean to disappoint you."

"You didn't disappointment me, son. If anything, I'm very proud of you for trying. Maybe next time."

"Maybe," he said. "I don't know."

"Me neither," I said, limping back over to my bed then sitting on it, pulling the thin sheet over my legs, hairy and white like Bratwurst sausages. "Maybe I'm going crazy."

Nat stood up, placing her bag down on her cot, then crossed the room to my bed. She sat down next to me, a look of concern on her face.

"I just realized, like, maybe we should call the nursing home and let them know what happened. You know? With the accident? We did come down here to, like, see your dad and all."

PeePaw. I completely forgot about my dad. He was the reason we were in the car before the accident, the reason we were in this mess we were in at the hospital. Well, not literally the reason, but we *were* on our way to see him. The fuzziness of my memory was not serving me well. I didn't know what to do or what to say and I could sense that Nat saw that on my face.

"Do you want me to call Autumn Grove for you?" she said, placing her hand on mine. The instant the skin of her palm touched the top of my hand, the floodgates of emotion opened inside me and the tears burst from my eyes and I cried and cried like I hadn't cried in a long, long time. I cried like a baby in the arms of my kids' nanny. It felt good to cry, I ain't gonna lie. So I did. I let it all out right then and there in the maternity ward of the hospital somewhere in San Antonio, Texas.

✳ ✳ ✳

Later that night after crying like a little baby for a good ten or fifteen minutes in Nat's arms, me and my little family settled into the nightly routine of the hospital, one where any number of nurses and technicians and doctors and cleaning staff just barge into your room wanting to look at medical equipment screens or ask you questions like 'How are you feeling?' or 'How is the temperature in the room?' or 'Do you want anything to eat?' or 'Is the screaming next door bothering you?' or to take your pulse or to check the level of intravenous bags or to take food trays away or whatever. Forget trying to get some *sleep* in a hospital because it just isn't going to happen. A hospital is the last place you should go if what you need is a good night's sleep. In that sense, a hospital is more like a torture chamber or an insane asylum than a place to heal because of all the noise and the racket and poking and prodding and squeezing and pricking going on. It's true. On top of that, every moment you stay in a hospital gives you a greater chance of catching something that will actually kill you like a staph infection or a virus or pneumonia or whatever creepy ailment may be floating around in the air, like an evil fairy biding its time so it can swoop down your throat and viciously infect you. Is that what you want? If not, then stay the hell away from hospitals.

And like any good family would do, my kids and Nat made themselves at home in the maternity room as soon as all the medical funny business slowed down. At one side of the room, Nat and little Jessie setup a makeshift taekwondo dojang complete with a yoga mat that Jessie found behind the couch as a floor mat, some couch cushions and random pillows as punching and kicking bags, and an aluminum walking cane with its handle removed as a fighting staff. Nat didn't really know any of Jessie's taekwondo routines but it didn't matter. She was a good sport and allowed Jessie to pummel her regardless of her inexperience as a martial arts instructor. In the middle of the room in front of the bed I was lying on, good ol' Sammie Boy had spread out a blanket on the floor and laid all his things on it. From my vantage point in the bed, if I leaned over to one side or the other, I could see one of his arms or legs moving about on the floor, moving things around on the blanket. I wasn't really sure what he was up to but he was being quiet so I didn't mind so much. But then, after a few more moments, the sound of paper ripping and crumpling came from his play area in front of my bed. I knew then that he was up to something.

"Sammie? What are you doing?"

"Nothing, Daddy."

"But I hear something down there. Are you tearing paper?"

Nat and Jessie were engrossed in their made-up taekwondo routines. They didn't bother to see what Sammie was doing. But I knew he was up to something. The sound of kids tearing paper is not a good sign. Ever.

"Daddy? Can I ask you a question?"

"Yes, son, after you tell me what you are doing."

"I'm opening a *present.*"

"A present?" I said, sitting up in my bed, craning my neck to get a better look at my boy. I couldn't see him, though, and decided to just get out of bed and sit down on the blanket with him. I had one machine attached to me with a wire clamped on the end of my index finger (checking my pulse, I think) but the wire was long enough for me to stand up, walk to the end of the bed, and sit down next to my son. My relocation to the floor caught Jessie's attention.

"Daddy?! Are you OK?" she said, panting from kicking and punching the pillow Nat was holding. "Why are you out of bed?"

"I'm fine. Just want to see what your brother is doing."

"He's not doing *jack,*" she said, turning to Nat to continue the barrage on the innocent pillow with her fists of fury. "Like *usual.*" Her fists flew as Nat braced herself. But she was wrong; Sammie *was* doing something. It was just something she didn't care about.

Sammie was holding a small box with red, green, and white plaid wrapping paper, an oversized glittery, gold bow on top with matching ribbon tied around it, some of the paper on the side ripped off, exposing a brown, cardboard box underneath the wrapping paper. I was confused as to where he got the gift and I didn't have any idea how it got there, in our room, in Sammie's little hands. Maybe I was still high from the drugs. I didn't know.

"Where did you get that?" I said.

"I found it."

"Where did you find it?" I said, my eyes squinting to examine his response, scanning his face for signs of the truth.

"Over there behind the TV," he said, pointing to the armoire where the TV resided, on the other side of the room.

"Is it for you?"

"I don't know. There wasn't a tag on it. Can I open it? I bet it's for you."

"Let me see it," I said, extending my hand. Sammie reluctantly gave me the gift, his head lowering as I examined the gift-wrapped box. He was right; there wasn't a name tag on it. And not knowing or caring who was in the room before we arrived, I handed it back to him. "Sure, open it."

Sammie's face lit up like a Christmas tree as he took the gift back, ruthlessly ripping the gift wrap off it, plaid bits of paper flying everywhere. Once the brown cardboard box was completely exposed, Sammie examined it for a place to open it. Seeing that is was sealed

with tape, he reached in his myriad pf things for the Buck knife--
unsheathing it from its wooden handle--and he slit the tape. When
you're in the hospital, most of the things you worry about as a parent-
-like your kid wielding a knife--are thrown out the window. It's true.

"Please don't cut yourself," I said.

"I won't, Daddy. I promise!"

Opening the box, something wrapped in white tissue paper was
wedged inside. Sammie turned the box upside down, giving it a slight
shake, and the gift slid out onto the blanket, the weight of it creating a
noise like the sound of a large rock landing on cement.

"What is it?" I said, watching Sammie unwrap the tissue paper. It
looked to be made of glass, yellowish and shiny.

"Who would give a jar as a present?" Sammie said, giggling. He
handed it to me. "Jar Shmar. What a silly present!"

"It's not a *jar*," I said, turning the gift over, exposing the label, so
Sammie could get a better look at it. "It's a candle, one of those candles
you buy at the mall, the ones that smell like pumpkin pie or cookies
or whatever."

"Cookies!" he said, lowering his head to smell the candle, hoping
it smelled like baked goods. The word 'cookies' caught the attention of
Nat and Jessie (of course) and they stopped sparring so they could
check out anything related to cookies. They came over to the blanket
and sat down with us.

"Did you say *cookies*?" Jessie said, all smiles.

"It doesn't smell like cookies, Daddy," Sammie said, disappointed,
his little nose scrunched up.

"No, what does it smell like then?"

"It smells like the beach."

I raised the candle to my curious nose and good ol' Sammie Boy
was right. It did kind of smell like the beach, what, with the scent of
pineapple and coconut and sand and weathered wood and the humid
wind blowing to the beach from the salty Gulf of Mexico water, with
an undertone of an unknown aroma that was slightly unnatural and
artificial, like burnt plastic.

"I wish we had cookies," Jessie said, sulking. "All we have is this
stupid candle."

"Can I light it, Daddy?" Sammie said.

"How are you going to do that?"

"I have a lighter. Remember?" Sammie reached into his little bag
and pulled out the Zippo lighter he found a couple of weeks before.
Sammie's kleptomaniac behavior seemed justified now that he had a
use for the Buck knife and the Zippo lighter that he serendipitously
found while running errands with me. He opened the Zippo lighter with
two hands--unlike a biker or punker or hipster who would open it with
a single-handed fancy trick--and he awkwardly lit the candle. The
initial flame grew tall from the candle wick like a toddler stretching in

bed after a long night's sleep. Once the flame settled into a smaller, compact size, its glow illuminated our faces like a campfire would, our cheeks and chins shimmering in oranges and reds and pinks. "Can I turn down the lights, too?"

"Sure, I don't see why not."

Sammie leapt up and ran to where the light knob perched on the wall to the left of the door to the room. He stood on his tippy toes and turned the knob--one way at first then the other way--until the fluorescent lights dimmed to an acceptable level, then he quickly returned and hopped in my lap. I really wasn't expecting that. He wiggled his butt until he was comfortably in place. Not to be outdone, little Jessie hopped in Nat's lap, performing a similar butt wiggle, a look on her face beaming victory. Sammie reached up and placed his hand on the back of my neck, pulling my head down, so I could hear him better, then he said, "Daddy, tell us the story about the time you saved my life!"

"What time was that?" I said, honestly confused. I wasn't really sure what he was referring to and a disapproving sigh escaped from his little mouth, originating from where his broken heart resided deep in his little chest. He pulled harder on my neck and told me in my ear the event he was referring to. It really wasn't a life-threatening event but I agreed to tell it anyway. "Oh, right. The time you stepped on a rusty nail and I had to take you to the emergency room?"

"Yeah!" he said, releasing my neck, smiling approvingly at the others. He loved that story.

"Not again!" Jessie said, rolling her eyes. "It's so gross!"

"Is not!" Sammie said.

"Is too!" Jessie said.

"Not!"

"Too!"

"All right, you two. Does *everything* have to be an argument?"

They both crossed their arms in defiance but it didn't stop me from telling the story. One time, not long after moving into our apartment, I took the kids to a house party thrown by an acquaintance. I don't remember why I was invited but I do remember the details: a coworker's house party with food and drinks and games and pets were allowed and it was kid-friendly. That description hit all the checkmarks for me so I made a bean dip and threw the kids and the bean dip in the Volvo S70 and we went to the party. When we arrived, there were quite a few people there already with their own children and their own dip creations and all the kids were running around like banshees and there were dogs running in packs, corralling the kids like they were a herd of meandering banshees. When I found the hosts, I introduced my kids to them. The hosts were Christina and Margaret, two old-school lesbians who had been together for 30 years, and the party was an anniversary celebration for them at their house. They insisted that Sammie and Jessie enjoy their backyard because they had a water balloon station, a game of ring toss, and a trampoline. The kids accepted then ran off while I looked for a place for my bean dip to sit amongst the other mystery dips. The one named Margaret, by the way, was my coworker.

"You thought it would be safe for kids in the backyard. Right, Daddy?" Sammie said.

"Yeah, I thought it would be safe in their backyard."

And that part was true. There were so many kids around with their parents doing their helicopter-parenting thing that I assumed my own kids would be OK. Why would they *not* be OK? It was a family-friendly party for god's sake. So I wasn't worried at all when they ran off. I was just concerned about finding a place for my bean dip and wondered if there were any single ladies around that weren't lesbians, which sometimes can be a tall order at a party thrown by lesbians, but I thought it worth a shot.

"That's weird, Daddy!" little Jessie said. She giggled in Nat's lap, covering her little face with her little hands.

I found a dining area near the kitchen with a table covered in potluck dishes: dips, casseroles, bowls of chips or crackers, stubby carrot and celery sticks, salsas, pickled vegetables, breads, cakes, pies, and shit like that. As I looked for a place to sit my bean dip, a woman introduced herself to me. Short, petite, and blonde with blue eyes, she told me her name was Elizabeth and she asked me how I knew Christina and Margaret. Before I could get two words out or figure out if she was single and *not* a lesbian, I heard Jessie screaming from the kitchen. I quickly set the bean dip on the table and ran into the kitchen.

"It was pretty bad. Wasn't it, Daddy?" Sammie said, looking up to me from my lap.

"Yes, it was pretty bad, son."

There, I found Jessie in a hysterical state of panic and Sammie standing still and quiet, with a pool of bright, maroon blood under his right foot, both feet still in the rubber flip flops he wore to the party. The kitchen was empty. I quickly picked Sammie up in my arms, blood pouring from the bottom of his right foot. The flip flop dropped to the floor, covered in my son's blood, which made Jessie scream some more.

"What happened?!" I said, frantically.

"The nail," he said, weeping. "It stuck in my foot when I tried to see the dog."

"What the--" I said, confused. But there really wasn't time to ask questions. There was blood everywhere--on me, on my son, on the floor. It was like something out of a horror movie. "We have to go. NOW! Come on!"

I ran out of the kitchen with my son in my arms, little Jessie close behind. I could feel her behind me trying to grab my waistband but had a hard time doing that; I was moving too fast for her to grab it. We ran past Elizabeth then Christina then Margaret and a number of other women I hadn't met yet, me apologizing as I past each stunned partygoer, all of whom stood there dumbfounded, like they were in the *Twilight Zone* or something. It was a very bizarre scene. It's true.

"Then what happened?" Jessie said, enthralled.

"I put you guys in the car and I drove to the emergency room."

I drove as fast as I possibly could to the closest hospital, running several stop signs and stop lights along the way, amazed that I didn't get pulled over by a cop. All the while, little Jessie screamed from the backseat and good ol' Sammie Boy wept in the front seat. Although he was crying, he wasn't making a lot of noise like his sister, who was just freaking out in the backseat.

"I thought my big brother was going to die!" she said, still looking guilty that she couldn't keep herself together. Nat put her arms around her while she sat in her lap, rocking back and forth to comfort her.

"I know you did. I know," I said.

On the way to the hospital, I surmised from bits of information between screams and sniffles and gasps for air that Sammie had decided to get a peek at a dog in a neighbor's yard, so he stepped on a pile of wooden fence planks that laid next to the fence to get a better view. While standing on the pile of wooden planks, a rusty nail protruding up from the top one, sliced through the rubber sole of his flip flops when he stepped on it, and the nail penetrated his skin and carved through his flesh--between his tendons and bones and veins and capillaries--according to the doctors at the hospital that X-rayed his foot. The doctors at the hospital said he was lucky to have not damaged the tendons or bones in his foot. But for safe measure, they gave him a tetanus shot, some antibiotics, and soaked his foot in a solution made from iodine.

"You *saved* my life, Daddy," said Sammie, turning around on my lap to hug me. He squeezed hard, as hard as he could with his little arms, around my neck.

"It really wasn't a life or death situation, son," I said, hugging him back, patting him on the back.

"It was to *me*," he said, wiping tears from his cheeks. The "nail incident" was definitely a traumatic experience for my little boy, I could tell. It seemed to affect him more deeply than I imagined it would at the time. I mean, I knew it would traumatize him but not to the point where he thought he might *die*. That's pretty goddamn traumatic, if you ask me.

"It was scary!" Jessie said, looking up at Nat. "It was a good thing you weren't there."

"I bet! You must have been, like, very brave to help your dad and brother."

Little Jessie's face lit up with embarrassment, her cheeks turning bright red, her eyes twitterpated, her forehead flushed. She placed both hands on her cheeks and looked at me, then said, "Daddy, can Nat be a part of our family?"

"What?!" Nat said, astonished.

"Yeah!" said Sammie, agreeing. "She's like our big sister!"

"Yeah!" said Jessie. "Like the big sister I never had!"

"That's very sweet of you two," Nat said, fumbling for words. "I already have a family, though."

"But they suck!" Jessie said. "You told me yourself."

"True. They aren't very nice to me sometimes."

"See! Daddy?" said Jessie, clasping her hands together as if praying to G-O-D himself, praying for some kind of miracle or something.

"You mean, like adopt her?" I said, confused. "But she's an adult. I can't adopt an adult. Can I?"

Nat fell backwards onto the cold, tile floor, laughing a deep, guttural laugh, her arms across her stomach. Jessie turned and threw herself on Nat's belly, giggling hysterically, attempting to tickle Nat as she flopped around on the cold, hospital floor. And as Sammie and I watched them, my arms around my son, holding him close to me on my lap, there was a knock on the door. It then slowly opened and a face appeared, the face of an attractive woman, her skin the color of a roasted coffee bean, her hair shiny and straight, her outfit familiar, sporty yet professional. She was someone I wasn't expecting to see at that particular moment, someone close to my father.

"Excuse me, everyone. Can I come in?" she said. I quickly realized who she was since we met her only the day before, PeePaw's friend: Sharice. She was wearing the same or similar outfit, one that was somewhere between workout clothes and hospital scrubs, maybe blue before or green. I couldn't remember exactly. In one arm, she cradled something in a brown, paper bag. In the other hand, the worn copy of *The World According to Garp*. "I'm sorry for disturbing you."

"Of course, of course, come on in," I said, standing Sammie up from my lap, his arm intertwined with the wire from the medical machine attached to me. As he tried to untangle himself, he inadvertently pulled the wire, detaching it from me. The wire and clamp slithered across the floor but I didn't bother to fetch it. I figured the machine had compiled enough medical data and deserved a break. "Please have a seat."

"May I?" she said, walking toward our makeshift camp site. She stepped on the blanket then sat down, setting the brown, paper bag next to her. "That's a nice camp fire you got there."

Sammie stepped back on the blanket and the two of us sat back down. Once my boy was comfortable in my lap, he said, "Thanks! I made it myself."

"Well then, you're welcome. Your grandpa would be proud."

"How is my dad?" I said, curious.

"Well, that's why I'm here. You see... he passed away early this morning. Really early."

And with that, a heavy silence fell on our camp site, a melancholy cloud of shock and disbelief so dense that no one spoke or said a word, just four mouths agape. Nat, in particular, looked quite surprised. Sharice placed her hand on my knee as if to steady me.

"Passed away?" I said, the words difficult for me to pronounce.

Sammie turned his head to me and said, "PeePaw is *dead*?"

And before I could answer my son, Sharice said, "Yes, dear. Your grandpa is dead. He died peacefully in his sleep."

Both of my kids began to cry the way kids do when something upsets them but they don't understand the depth of their sorrow, their weeps starting small and sniffly, then turning to staccato gasps for air and boogery bawling. I didn't know how to take the news of my father's demise myself. More than anything, I felt like I was having an out-of-body experience, me watching a poor bastard receiving some sour, unexpected news in a nonchalant way from someone he didn't know. Nat didn't say anything, her arms around Jessie, hugging her again, comforting her. It was all just too much to take. I mean, there aren't any rules for how to process some bad news like that. You just have to absorb it and process it the best you can, preferably by not making a fool of yourself. I did the best I could to stifle all my emotions deep down inside. I'm pretty good at that, when I want to be. It's true.

"He died?" I said, clutching for words. I didn't know what else to say. And before I could say anything more, Sharice pulled something from the brown, paper bag, something that looked like a shiny vase except that it had a tiny lid on top instead of an opening where you would shove some cheap, grocery store flowers. She set it on the blanket next to Sammie's campfire candle, the orange light from the tiny flame illuminating the shiny vase, flashes of red and orange and yellow dancing on the sides of it. I could make out a design of Asian origin, something like a dragon or a serpent or something like that, clinging to the side of the vase with its sharp claws, its tail slithering down the length of the vase. "Early this morning?"

"Yes, he did. And he had instructions to be cremated immediately after being declared dead by a medical examiner, which by the way, happened a *lot* faster than I thought it would. It's amazing what well-documented estate planning can do. And prepayments! I came straight here from the funeral home."

"Cremated?" I said.

Rather than reply with words, Sharice's eyebrows raised like two caterpillars preparing to spar, then she tilted her head in the direction of the vase--or rather the dragon-adorned urn--sitting on the blanket next to the candle. I watched the light dance around the dragon on the side of it. It really was a dragon, I was absolutely sure of it, or at least that's what I told myself, or some kind of prehistoric reptile like a proto alligator or crocodile or komodo dragon. If that was the case, then it really was a dragon.

"That's the Colonel, right there," she said, plainly.

Well, shit.

THE LAST
SHMAPTER

The Last Shmapter

Sharice drove a Cadillac Escalade--a massive, shiny, black and chrome tank with tinted, black windows and a license plate that read 'QUEEN-B'--and she was proud of the fact that it was ordered especially for her by my father, retired Colonel Burchwood: PeePaw. When exactly he ordered it for her, she never did say but I assumed it was a somewhat recent purchase. The Caddy Tank seemed brand-new; there wasn't a scratch or ding or scuff on it, anywhere. But more importantly, it was decked out with every conceivable upgrade and feature including but not limited to: black leather seats, a sunroof, custom stereo and speaker system, onboard computer, running boards, chrome wheels, interior wood trim on the dash, leather trim wherever else possible, shag carpet floor mats, and on and on. Its price tag must have been in the upper 5-digits, nearing 6-digits. And I bet that Caddy Tank barely got five miles to the gallon, a hideous reality, if you asked me. She drove that thing with the careless abandon that rivaled the giddiness a 12-year old experienced driving a tricked-out go-cart on a closed circuit at an amusement park. She was laughing and cackling all over the goddamn place, drinking overly sweetened, overly caffeinated coffee from a bedazzled, pink, aluminum coffee tumbler. But before we go any further about how my family and I ended up in the Caddy Tank with Sharice, my father's "nurse," let me back-track just a bit.

After Sharice's surprise visit with my dad's ashes in an urn with a dragon on it, the next morning was rather uneventful and anti-climactic. Dr. Yang released us from the hospital with little fanfare, probably because the injuries that Sammie and I endured were deemed *not significant* enough to keep us in the hospital, or rather, there weren't enough injuries to bill the insurance company for; you can't bill for treatment of bumps and bruises, I guess. So, Dr. Yang instructed us to see our primary care physicians back in Austin--Dr. Todd for me and Dr. Dimes for my son, good ol' Sammie Boy--and to contact him only if our primary doctors had any questions.

"It's better to recover in your own home," he said. "No need to stay here in the hospital longer than necessary."

"Thanks, doc," I said.

He nodded then left. I never saw Dr. Yang again. But don't worry, I didn't cry over it.

As for my trusty Volvo S70, it was not drivable. It was smashed. Totaled. The details of our car accident were still a mystery but one thing was for sure: my car was destroyed. A police officer came to take a statement at some point while I was intoxicated from all the morphine. I don't remember that part, to tell you the truth. But that's

OK because I'm not comfortable around police officers anyway. Any conversion I'd have with a police officer would just lead to self-incrimination from my being nervous as a goddamn mouse in the clutches of a demonic house cat. It's pretty stupid, if you ask me, my demeanor around officers of the law. They just make me nervous, that's all. But my trusty Volvo was demolished and that's where Sharice came in. When Nat called Autumn Grove the night before--to talk to Ms. Robyn, to ask about my dad, and to tell her what happened to us--our phone message was relayed to Sharice because (as we would soon find out) she was now the executor of my father's estate. Weird, huh? Well, at least I thought so. I had no idea that Sharice even existed until this week let alone had some control and decision-making power over some things that would affect my future.

So here we all were--my little family--strapped into the Caddy Tank: Nat and Jessie in the third row, good ol' Sammie Boy and the urn in the middle row (the urn had its own goddamn seat), and Sharice and I in the front seats. She insisted that my father would have wanted her to drive us back to Austin, although I would beg to differ. My father just wasn't the caring type. He wouldn't have cared how we got back to Austin. It's true.

"Your father was such a *caring* man," Sharice said, pontificating between sips of sweet coffee from her bedazzled tumbler, driving the Caddy Tank north on the access road to I-35, the interstate we needed to take to get back to Austin, Texas: our home. "He *loved* to take care of people. Yes, he did!"

"Really?" I said, looking back at my son, who was drawing in his sketchbook, a smaller set of bandages on his head. Nat and Jessie were playing a quiet game of patty-cake way back in the third row. I turned back around and watched the Caddy Tank merge into the thick traffic. "That's not how I remember him at all. He wasn't the caring type when I was a kid."

"People change, especially when they get older. Yes, they do! Mr. Marvin was such a sweet man to me. Very sweet!"

"How so?"

Sharice shifted uncomfortably in her driver seat, setting the tumbler into a cup holder in the middle console that separated our two seats. She looked off into the distance like a weary sailor watching the dark, misty walls of a hurricane fast approaching an unprepared boat. She licked her lips then said, "Now, I'll tell you how I know your father, how I met him and all that, but... you have to promise not to *judge* me."

"Judge you?" I said, confused. I wasn't the type to judge anyone, not to their face anyway. I left all my judging in my *mind*, where it was safe and sound. "I won't judge you. I promise."

"That's good because people like to judge me whenever they find out about my *real* life. And I'm done with being judged, if you know what I mean? Yes, I am."

"Sure," I said. But I lied. I didn't know what the hell she was talking about but I went along with it anyway. Real life? What did that even mean anyway?

"Good. 'Cause you see, I ain't *really* a nurse. I work at da club. That's where I met your father."

The second those words came out of her mouth--*da club*--I remembered what Ms. Robyn told me about my dad's weekly requests: the scotch, the race track, and the strip club. I immediately knew *da club* was meant to be The Gentlemen's Club, the place where my father insisted on going on a weekly basis in the Autumn Grove limousine. I thought about his feeble body hunched over in the wheel chair, the limo driver then pushing him inside, but now I knew Sharice was waiting for him inside da club.

"Yeah, I know about that."

"You do?!" she said, shocked. "How did you know about that?"

"Ms. Robyn told me the other day. She told me everything."

"Ms. Robyn told you, huh? That bee-yotch!" she said, snickering, her lips releasing a snick-snick-snick as she shook her head. "She never could keep a secret."

"Was it supposed to be a *secret*?"

"Well, people be judging. Your dad didn't like people judging him and neither did I. That's all."

"So, you were a stripper at the club? That's how you met my dad?"

"Oh, hell no! I wasn't trying to be no stripper. I was just a waitress. Served drinks and all. But that's how I met your father. When he first came in, da club was pretty empty. There weren't very many customers or dancers during the day. The doorman pushed him to one of my tables. And when I asked him what he wanted to drink, then we got to talkin'."

As I listened to her tell her story, I watched the traffic dissipate as we left the city limits of San Antonio, Texas. I looked back at my son who was in a deep, artistic trance; he wasn't paying attention to us at all, drawing what looked like a bird flying through the sky with a star above it, his tongue wagging as he interpreted his imagination through his pencil to the page. Nat and Jessie, meanwhile, were playing a new game that involved tickling.

"What did he talk about?" I said, turning back to Sharice.

"Mostly, he just talked about being in the military, his work, the men he commanded, and stuff. He loved to talk about being in the military. Yes, he did!"

"Did he ever tell you about my mother? Or me?"

"Of course, he did," she said, reaching for her coffee tumbler. But there was desperation on her face, I could see that. It was there behind the thick mascara and bright red lipstick. She was keeping something from me, I could tell, by the way she fumbled for her words. "But mostly, he talked about the military."

"I see," I said, disappointed. She was just validating what I already knew without saying a word; he didn't talk about me or my mother. I wondered what my mother would have thought about all of this: The Gentleman's Club, Sharice and her Caddy Tank, the life my father led after she passed away, his downward spiral into the clutches of Alzheimer's Disease, and his final resting place in an urn with a dragon on it. How strange.

"That first day, he left me $100 for a tip. One hundred bucks! I felt like I didn't deserve $100 for doing nothin' but listen to an old man talk about the military. But then, he kept coming back. And when he came back he asked for me. Can you believe it?"

I couldn't believe it, actually. I couldn't believe any of it, to tell you the truth. It was almost too much for me to take, really. Here I was, in a humongous, gaudy, sports utility vehicle bought by my dead father for a cocktail waitress in a strip club. How did this happen? What cosmic circumstance allowed this to be? Was my father messing with me? Did he even worry about what I would think when I found out? Did he even think about me at all? Didn't seem so, did it?

"No, I can't," I said.

"And each time he asked for me, he would tell me these long stories, then he would leave bigger tips. $100 turned to $200 and to $300. It got to be pretty crazy. Cray-cray, yes it was!"

"Did you ever question why?"

"I did. I did! I would say, 'Mr. Marvin, why you so crazy?' And he would just smile. He wouldn't say nothin'."

"And that's it? He never told you?"

"Well, he eventually did. He told me one day that I was the only person who *really* listened to him. He said nobody did. Nobody! It was just so sad. I felt so bad for him. He was so nice to me, tipping me so much and all."

"I see," I said, perturbed. Nobody listened to him, huh? What a crock of shit. Really. Crock. Of. Shit. Who did he think he was fooling? Nobody, that's who. But I have to admit, it was strange listening to Sharice retell my father's confession to her, his feelings that no one listened to him, whatever that meant. Was she saying that my father had *feelings*? How weird.

"One day, he came in da club with another man. A dude he called Mark, his lawyer. He had a briefcase with him. And when they sat down at the table, this dude Mark sat his briefcase on a chair next to him. So, when I went to get their order and all, they asked me to sit down. And that's when your father asked me to be his executor."

"What?" I said, astounded. It just couldn't get any weirder. It's true.

"And I said, 'Executor? I ain't trying to be no executor!' I didn't even know what an executor of an estate was. But he insisted that I do it. He said there wasn't nobody else to do it. He said you were gone and your momz was dead. And I believed him, you know? And he said he wanted me to take care of him at the rest home and that he would buy me whatever I wanted so I would do it. And I said, "Whateva?' And he said, 'Whatever you desire.' So, I said OK. And you sitting in it. What I wanted. Yes, it is!"

The Caddy Tank was the price to pay to take care of an old man in a rest home. What a bargain. My dad would have had to pay me a LOT more than that, which was probably why he said I was gone. Go figure. Maybe it was the Alzheimer's Disease that convinced him I was gone even though I wasn't. How did he think he got into Autumn Grove in the first place? I guess he forgot about that, too. Alzheimer's disease is a real son of a bitch. It's true.

"And the rest of his estate?" I said, curious. "Did he leave me anything? Was there anything for my children?"

"I don't know for sure. We'll know once his estate goes to probate," she said, matter-of-factly. "Could be somethin'. Could be nothin'. Could be somethin' for nothing," she said in a sing-songy voice.

"I see," I said, looking to the horizon, thinking of being home with my kids in our own world, away from selfish grandparents or witless 'nurses' or obscenely expensive vehicles and all.

"I'm sorry," she said, gulping more coffee. "I don't know what else to tell ya at the moment. But I do have something for you from your father."

"Really? For me?"

And just then, Sammie started screaming and hooting and hollering all over the place. He was pointing and shouting and pointing some more like the world was about to end.

"Daddy?! Daddy?!!" he said, bouncing up and down in his leather captain's chair. Most of his art supplies fell to the floor as he flung to and fro in his seat. "Look!"

"What is it?" I said, looking in the direction he was pointing.

"Over there! The pet store! Look!!"

Sure enough, there was the pet store from the other day, the one next to the Snake Farm. I wasn't as excited this time to see the Snake Farm like I was before, mainly because we already paid a visit to that dump and it wasn't all it was cracked up to be. But I could see why Sammie was excited. He did make a promise to the little bird to go back and here we were, as close as can be.

"Can we go? Please?!" he said, begging, his hands together in a desperate prayer, squeezing so tightly that his hands shook.

Sharice was confused, not understanding what all the ruckus was about, not knowing about our previous trip to the pet store, and Sammie's painful separation from the cute, little bird in the store. But when I asked her to pull off the highway and go to the pet store, she didn't seem to mind at all. In fact, she seemed happy to do it, not complaining one bit.

"My pleasure," she said. "Let's see what this baby can do!" And with that, she immediately jerked the steering wheel and the Caddy Tank careened off the highway, onto the shoulder, the gravel on the side of the road pelting the underside of the Escalade like hail pummeling a hot tin roof. The rest of us screamed like little girls, even my tough tomboy little girl screamed like a little girl. Then without hesitation, Sharice steered the Caddy Tank to the grassy embankment on the side of the highway, the shiny, black behemoth barreling down the incline of grass and weeds and bluebonnets and Indian paintbrushes to the access road below. We held onto whatever we could with all our dear lives--me holding the armrest of my door while everyone's belongings flew around the cabin--except for Sharice, who was cackling like a goddamn hyena. At first, I thought she was absolutely insane (who *wouldn't* think that?) then realized she was just an adrenaline junkie. It took a simple request like exiting the highway for us all to find that out. Lucky us. "Hold on, little homies!"

The Caddy Tank approached the access road like an avalanche, hitting the road's gravelly shoulder with the full force of its four, metallic tons. When it bounced from the shoulder onto the asphalt road, many of its interior decorations and modifications and accessories popped out of their places--moldings and trimmings and chrome things and leathery touches and knobs and the like. It was as if an aging socialite fell down the stairs and unhinged her beautiful artifice: fake eyelashes, fake nails, tooth veneers, hair extensions, high heels, and a lacy push-up bra flying everywhere. Sensing that we weren't having as much fun as she was--mostly because we were all screaming our brains out--Sharice stopped the Escalade, dust and dirt billowing around her expensive gift from my father, sitting still in the road.

"That was so fun!" little Jessie said from the back. I turned around to find her propped up on her knees in her seat, some of her hair standing on end from the electric charge in the air. "Let's do it again!"

"Your father doesn't seem too happy about it," Sharice said, a tinge of guilt on her face. "Girls just want to have fun like my home girl Cyndi Lauper say. Am I right?"

"Are you insane?" I said, irritated.

"Not the last I heard but it's always a possibility. Life is crazy. Yes, it is!"

"Do you think you could get us to that pet store without killing us all?"

"Of course. I'm sorry. Just thought it would be fun," she said, pulling the shifter into drive, then slowly driving up the access road to the bridge which would take us over I-35 and back down the southbound access road. As we moved down the road, the detached accessories and modifications in the Caddy Tank flopped around like the long ears of a blood hound, all dopey and droopy and shit. It seemed to irritate Sharice to no end knowing that her impetuous decision to have a little fun caused her precious vehicle to hemorrhage internally but she remained a trooper, driving us to save the parakeet.

I peeked back at Sammie as we approached the pet store and his eyes gleamed at the prospects of rescuing the budgerigar from the clutches of the evil pet store owner, I could see it on his cute, little face. And Jessie sat up behind him, her arms draped across the top of his chair and wrapped around his upper torso, a sweet smile on her face as she supported her big brother. It was moments like this that caused my heart to flutter with the love and joy only parents understand, the warmth that emanates from the spaces between the atoms that make up my body.

"Daddy, can I ask you a question?"

"Sure, son. You can ask me a question."

"Do you think he'll still be there?"

"The parakeet?"

"Yeah, the parakeet. But he's really a budgerigar. You know how to tell the difference, right?"

"I trust you."

"Are we buying a bird?" Sharice said, worried. "Because birds kinda freak me out."

"Yes, if he's still there. Is that going to be a problem?"

"As long as it don't fly around in my ride, I'll be fine. I don't like birds. No, I don't! They nasty."

Good ol' Sammie Boy giggled when Sharice said that, as if what she said was completely ridiculous and acceptable at the same time. Kids are like that, though. So naïve, so innocent.

"I'll make sure he stays in his cage," Sammie said. "It'll be OK."

Sharice pulled the Caddy Tank into the gravel parking lot we parked in a few days before, stopping in front of the three stucco buildings: the Snake Farm, the taxidermist, and the pet store. And like the last time we visited, our vehicle was the only one in the parking lot, sitting alone in the lot of gravel and rocks and dust. Olaf's all-terrain vehicle was parked next to the pet store, though--the screeching two-stroke vehicle resting serenely like a wolverine taking a nap--and I remembered what it was like watching him barrel toward this complex of stucco and lost dreams, like a grifter riding across a post-apocalyptic dreamscape looking for his next con. Were we his next con? Probably.

"Looks like nobody home," Sharice said, an observation that, most of the time, would have been astute but I knew someone was home.

"The pet store clerk is here. That's his ride," I said, unbuckling my seatbelt. "Let's go, kids."

"Yeah!" they said, unbuckling their seatbelts and fumbling from their seats to open their doors. The kids and Nat spilled out of the Escalade. Sammie and Jessie ran to the pet store entrance, holding hands, then went inside. Nat quickly followed. Sharice and I weren't in quite the same hurry, maybe because we were older, our hips and joints less agile. We eventually made our way into the pet store.

Inside, behind the glass counter like before, sat Olaf, gnawing on a power bar of some sort, looking relaxed and quite possibly stoned. A cacophony of pet sounds filled the air. And once my eyes adjusted to the darker interior of the cave-like pet store, I noticed that Olaf recognized us from our previous visit, a slight smirk appearing on his face.

"I *knew* you'd be back. I just knew it!" he said, sitting up and adjusting his pants, bent out of shape from sitting down for too long. I smiled then tilted my head toward the back of the store, as if asking, 'Are the kids back there?'

"Yeah," Olaf said. "They went straight for their bird."

Sharice and I navigated through the maze of pet food and supplies, finding the kids and Nat in the back of the store, sitting on the floor in front of the cage we had labeled with a sign during our last visit. Perched on Sammie's index finger was a parakeet that was mostly light blue with some grey and yellow feathers on his head, speckles of black dots scattered across his body, just like I remembered. Sammie had the little bird close to his face, inviting the bird to get friendly, which it did, gently nibbling the end of Sammie's nose with its dull beak and rubbery bird tongue. Jessie got a kick out of watching the parakeet nibble Sammie's nose and leaned in for a closer look. Sammie scolded her for getting too close while Nat did her best to keep the peace between my two kids.

"Daddy, can we take him home?"

"I don't know. We need to ask Sharice. It *is* her car."

Sammie slowly stood up, the little bird gripping his index finger with its little bird feet and flapping its wings, and looked up to Sharice.

"Can we take this budgerigar home with us in your car? I promise to keep him in his cage and not let him out and fly around."

"Oh heavens, no! He won't be flying around in my car. You gotta keep it in the cage or it stays here. OK?"

"Yeah!" Sammie and Jessie said, jumping up and down, Sammie almost letting the parakeet lose. But it held onto his finger, flapping its wings as to not lose its balance and grip, keeping his place.

"You should put him back in the cage if we're going to take him home with us,' I said.

"You really don't mind, Daddy?"

"No. I don't mind at all."

Sammie gently placed the parakeet in the cage then latched the cage door shut. I picked up the cage and walked with it to the counter, the bird looking confused and restless. His whole world was about to change in an instant, and ours too. I paid Olaf a small sum for Sammie's happiness, something like $40 for a parakeet, a cage, and all the accessories and a small bag of bird seed. Olaf thanked us then we were all out the door, on our way back home with a new family member: Budgie the parakeet.

Outside, the sunlight was bright and blinding. The parakeet flapped incessantly, trying to stay on his perch, trying to stay upright instead of at the bottom of the moving cage. Sammie, seeing the bird's frustration, quickly opened the door of the Caddy Tank opposite where he was sitting, the door next to the chair with the urn of PeePaw strapped in it. Sammie looked at me, confused and frustrated.

"Oh no, Daddy! Where are we going to put the cage?"

"That's a big chair, son. We can make this work. Hold the cage for a minute," I said, handing it to him. He and the parakeet commiserated while I unbuckled the seatbelt holding PeePaw's urn in place. I positioned the urn to one side then took the cage from good ol' Sammie Boy and placed it next to the urn in the massive, leather captain's chair. The seatbelt securely snugged both the urn and the cage in place. "See! No problem."

"Thanks Daddy!" Sammie said, hugging my neck then climbing in the Caddy Tank. Jessie and Nat followed soon after, climbing into their seats in the back.

As I closed the door, Sharice leaned over to me and whispered, "You're a nice daddy. If it was me, I wouldn't let my kid take home no parakeet. Birds are a disgusting mess. Yes, they are!" Then she leaned in even closer. "But you're a better parent than I would ever be. That's for sure. Let's get you home."

The rest of the ride back home to Austin, Texas was pretty quiet. Nat and Jessie fell asleep in the way back while Sammie lovingly looked at his new pet. That bird didn't make a peep the entire way home. It just gazed at Sammie with one eye like a pirate, the way birds do since their eyes are on either side of their heads. Sharice didn't say much else either while she drove. It seemed she preferred listening to 1980s rhythm and blues than chit-chatting with a honky like myself, who really didn't know her very well, and any signs of being an adrenaline junkie like earlier were squashed and never appeared again. She drove as if she was on her way to church: calm, serene, and ready for atonement. While the songs of Peaches and Herb, Earth, Wind, and Fire, and Diana Ross played softly--Sharice singing along like people in church do, not knowing all the words but knowing all the melody--I was lulled into a daydream while watching the suburban sprawl of the different towns between San Antonio and Austin, towns like New Braunfels, San Marcos, Kyle, and Buda. As I watched the same stores and businesses whiz by in each city--McDonald's and Home Depot and Target and Starbucks and Burger King and Wal-Mart--time seemed to stand still and I thought about moments in my life where things didn't seem so stressful, like when I was at the pond with the kids or something like that, watching them run around the shore, skipping stones on the water, chasing ducks, and laughing and playing. That's all I thought about the rest of the way back home.

* * *

When we pulled up to our apartment building, it seemed like we had been away from home *forever*. Sharice parked in the driveway in front of my garage then turned off the Caddy Tank, its engine dying quickly and without hesitation. Nat and Jessie were still asleep in the back, snoring quietly--Jessie's head in Nat's lap, Nat's head lying gently on Jessie's back. Sammie was ready to take his parakeet up to his room. The bird's cage, without my knowledge, had unbuckled itself from the seat and floated over to Sammie's lap. How Sammie had done this, I didn't know but it was a marvelous trick--a marvelous sleight of hand--something out of the playbook of Dr. Strange for sure. Or maybe I was just daydreaming, too intoxicated with my own thoughts to notice. Either way, Sharice was ready to help us out. Her door was open the moment the Caddy Tank fell asleep.

"Is this the right place?" she said.

"Yes, home sweet home," I said, unbuckling my seatbelt. Sammie had opened his door, too, and the commotion woke the two girls up, their arms intertwined and wrapped around each other. Little Jessie stretched her little arms above her head and rubbed her eyes with her little fists then said, "Are we home?"

"Yes," I said, getting out of the Escalade along with Sharice and Sammie. The parakeet flapped in the cage as Sammie stepped onto the ground. I walked over to the garage door and opened the cover to a keypad on the wall which would unlock and open it, if I entered the secret code properly. I punched the number combination of 3-2-7-8 which, if you could correspond those numbers with letters on a phone keypad, spelled the word F-A-R-T. That's pretty much the code to all my devices and accounts and things that require a 4-digit code: F-A-R-T. That was the best way for me to remember the code. Childish? Of course. The garage door opened slowly and clumsily, clunking up the metal rails.

"Want me to help you with your things?" Sharice said, smiling.

"What things?" I said.

"Right, right. You don't have much with you."

"I appreciate the offer, though," I said, handing good ol' Sammie Boy the keys to our apartment. He took the keys and placed them in his mouth since his arms were full (sketch book under one arm, sack of his precious trinkets under his other arm, Budgie's bird cage in his hands). He ran through the empty garage and began the ascent up the stairs to the entrance, his feet stomping the entire way up.

Nat and Jessie soon followed him, both groggy. Nat said, "I feel like I've been asleep for days. Let's go upstairs, girl. I have to, like, pee really bad." Nat and Jessie entered the garage then stomped up the stairs, too.

I turned to Sharice, who then outstretched her arms like a long, lost aunt begging for a hug from a reluctant and suspicious nephew.

"Come and give your Aunt Sharice a hug, sugar!"

"OK," I said, reluctantly. I leaned in with one shoulder, attempting to give a quick 'good game' hug, but Sharice wrapped her arms around me and squeezed the shit out of me--a crushing bear hug--lifting my feet off the ground.

She pulled back, smiling as if to say 'Wasn't that amazing?' then said, "Hold on! I have something for you. Yes, I do!" She ran over to the Caddy Tank and opened the driver door. She leaned inside and rummaged in the middle console for something then returned to me with a pad of paper and a pen in her hand. She quickly scribbled something on the pad then ripped the top page off, handing it to me. On it, there was a phone number, hers I assumed.

"Thanks," I said.

"You never know. You may need to call me. And, once I'm done settling the estate, I may be calling *you*. Here!" she said, handing me the pad of paper. "Write down your address and phone for me."

I scribbled my pertinent info on the pad and returned it to her, the ball point pen under my thumb.

"Take care of yourself. And for what it's worth, thanks for taking care of my dad."

"Your father!" she said, a look of genuine shock on her face, both of her hands cradling the sides of her face. "I almost forgot about your father!" She ran back to the side of the Caddy Tank, this time opening the door behind the driver door, rummaged back there, then returned to me with a shiny object in her hands: the urn. She handed the cold, ceramic death jar to me. It was heavier than it appeared, a little heft from the fact that it was filled with my dead dad's ashes. "Your father wanted you to have this. He definitely wanted *you* to have it. Yes, he did!"

"Thanks," I said. I was trying not to be sarcastic but I was having a hard time with that--a really hard time. "I know exactly where I'll put it."

"OK. Bye now! I gotta get back to S.A. I got shit to do!"

"Goodbye."

After giving me one more quick hug, Sharice climbed into her massive Escalade--awaking the sleeping beast that my father gave to her because she was willing to listen to his bullshit--and drove away, the bass from the stereo system wafting in the air as she disappeared from the apartment complex parking lot. I watched until the Caddy Tank vanished beyond my sight, behind the buildings of a neighboring apartment complex.

I looked at the dragon-adorned urn, it's glossy surface reflecting the afternoon sunlight, a menacing scowl on the magical lizard's face, a look not unfamiliar from the disapproving look my late father gave me when I was a disappointing child. I decided right then and there to name this dragon Marv, after my father: that asshole.

"Come on, Marv," I said, walking through the empty garage, closing the garage door, then ascending the stairs to my apartment. "I have the perfect place for you."

Inside, I set the urn on my coffee table and checked the answering machine. Its little green light flashed urgently; its LED displayed the number 7, for the number of messages. I played the series of worthless phone messages from IRS scam artists to non-profiteers to salespeople to prank callers until I reached the last message, one from our renown psychotherapist, Dr. Dena Davis, good ol' Sammie Boy's therapist.

She said, "Good day, Mr. Burchwood. Dr. Davis here. I'm calling to see when we can meet and discuss your son, Sammie, and the spectrum of the various conditions I believe he suffers from. But rather than get into too much detail about it over the telephone, because privacy concerns keep me from divulging more, please return my call so we can setup an appointment to discuss it further." The tone of her voice was swathed in the grave concern of a real professional. Obviously, she took my son's condition seriously as well as the privacy of a third grader. How interesting. Do third graders care about their privacy? I don't think so. But I appreciated her professional temperament and demeanor. "You have my number. I look forward to hearing from you. Good day. Take care."

When her message was done, the answering machine clicked and whirred, the LED number reset to zero, the green flashing light disappeared, and a robotic voice said, "*End* of messages." I could hear Nat and the kids from the bedroom, talking and moving and hopping on beds. I imagined the meeting with Dr. Davis, her arms gesticulating as she described the *spectrum* in layman's terms, her eyes rolling in the back of her head searching for simple explanations for a caring father like me to understand, and forcing a smile to soothe my worries and concerns. And as I stood there daydreaming, Nat emerged from the kids' room, ready to leave.

"I need to, like, get going. I know we didn't plan on what was going to happen but--"

"Nat," I said, very apologetic. "I'm sorry. You know, if I could have controlled what happened on this trip so you wouldn't have gotten hurt, I would have."

"I know," she said, placing her hand on my shoulder. "It wasn't your fault."

"Who can predict something like that happening?"

"Like, nobody," she said, rolling her eyes.

"Exactly. But I appreciate all the help you've given me. My kids love you. *I* love you. Well..." I said, a little embarrassed with the word choice. I mean, I love Nat like she's my kid but I don't love, *LOVE* her.

Let me just make that clear because that would be kind of pervy and all. It's true. "You know what I mean. Right?"

"I know what you mean," she said, smiling. "Let me know when you would like for me to help with the kids again."

"Oh! How about Tuesday, late afternoon? Jessie has taekwondo practice and I have something I'd like to do with Sammie. Can you take her to taekwondo practice on Tuesday?"

"Sure. I can do that."

"Great! See you then."

"See you then," she said, pulling the strap of her bag to the top of her shoulder while going for the front door. "Goodbye." Then she left, closing the door behind her, like a ghost slipping away.

I could hear the kids in their bedroom so I decided to check out what they were up to, probably no good, like most kids are when their parents aren't around. My kids were no different. I mean, they were sweet on the outside but downright mischievous on the inside. Leave them alone for more than 10 minutes and the apartment building would certainly be burnt to the ground. I walked through the living room and past the urn on the coffee table--Marv the Dragon's red eyes glaring at me--to the kids' bedroom. I slowly poked my head in to see what they were doing. Little Jessie was quietly playing her portable Nintendo on her bed, her pink, over-the-ear headphones blocking any noise from the outside world. She looked content to be home.

Good ol' Sammie Boy, on the other hand, sat slumped over on his bed, staring down at the bird cage on the floor. The poor parakeet looked mortified--hopping around in that cage as if escaping his prison was not an option--as it stared back up at my son for a little compassion or some bird seed, at least. I thought after the tearful goodbye at the pet store then the cheerful reconciliation on the way back to Austin from one of the worst trips in our entire lives that my son would be absolutely in love with this... *this* budgerigar, as he liked to call this type of bird. I mean, he had been begging me for a budgerigar for as long as I can remember. You remember, right? I know you do. He had been begging me for a bird *forever*. Now, he looked like he wanted to give up his dream of being a budgerigar owner. It looked like he didn't want to be a bird owner at all, not even with a prized budgie. It was almost too much for me to take. I had to sit down and figure this out. So, I sat on the bed next to my boy and put my arm around him.

"What's the matter, son?" I said, pulling him close to me. "Are you upset about something?"

"I don't know," he said. "I guess it's nothing."

"Seems like *something* is bothering you. You look down in the dumps."

"Dumps shmumps," he said, kicking his feet to and fro as they dangled off the bed, one on each side of the cage. I think that little bird didn't know what the hell was going on. It hopped back and forth as each leg swung by the cage, as if trying to dodge from being kicked or crushed or punted across the room. I knew for sure that Sammie wouldn't kick the bird's cage but it almost seemed like he didn't care if he kicked the cage or not. He was definitely in a weird mood. I could tell. Parents can tell these things about their children. It's true.

"So," I said, fishing for a question to ask. "Did you name your new bird Budgie like you said you would?" Sammie didn't answer but continued to kick his legs. His little hands laid on his lap with interlaced fingers. "Well, did you?"

"No," he said, quietly. "That's not Budgie."

"What do you mean, it's not Budgie? Sure, it's Budgie. You said so yourself."

"No, Daddy, it's not Budgie. *The* Budgie. That's just a parakeet. It's not my friend."

"What do you mean?" I said, confused.

"It's just a dumb ol' parakeet. It doesn't do *anything*. It just hops around in its cage. It probably would rather be somewhere else than in my room with me. It doesn't *act* like Budgie at all. It's just dumb."

"I see," I said, looking at the dumb ol' parakeet, Sammie's reluctant new pet. It sure looked dumb all right, hopping around in the cage like it was insane, slamming against the sides of the cage then falling to the bottom, seeds and feathers launching from the cage and sprinkling the carpet, then flying back up to its perch and starting the insane routine over again. I never was a fan of birds as pets. They're filthy and smelly and weird with the way they stare at you with one eyeball, peering into your soul with that unblinking, black eye. Birds are pretty creepy, I tell you, and usually not very friendly. But Sammie had been pretty persistent about getting a budgerigar. When the opportunity presented itself for me to buy him the one he wanted, I never imagined his hopes and dreams would curdled so quickly like this. Go figure. "Well, how is Budgie supposed to act?"

Sammie stopped kicking his legs back and forth and sat straight up, a serious and attentive look appearing on his face. The dumb parakeet even stopped flapping around its cage and looked at us with its dumb, black eye, cooing and panting while it sat on its perch, happy with its reprieve from the dangerous, kicking legs.

"Well," he said, his face lighting up. "Budgie is heroic and brave and strong. He goes with me on adventures and protects me from danger. He's a real friend, not a dumb ol' bird."

"I see."

"So, I can't name this bird Budgie 'cause he's not the real Budgie."

"I guess you're right. Maybe we should think of a different name for this parakeet. One that suits him better."

"Yeah," he said, sulking again.

"So, the *real* Budgie goes on adventures with you and protects you, huh?"

"Yeah."

"In your dreams?"

"Yeah."

"But you want a *real* Budgie in real life, too?"

"Not really," he said, his still-legs reverting to jimmy-legs, the kicking motion reinitialized. "I don't need a *real* Budgie in *real* life."

"And why is that?"

"Because I have you," he said, looking up at me, a sweet little smile on his sweet little face. "Because you protect me and you go on adventures with me."

"I do?"

That's when my boy put his arms around me and hugged me. Then Jessie noticed the hugging and jumped off her bed--tossing her portable Nintendo on the way--so she could get in on the hug action. The three of us embraced each other: a father and his two, lovely children. It was a very, very sweet moment and I'm not going to screw it up by giving you additional commentary about it so... let's move on.

After we hugged for a few minutes, I instructed Sammie to find a place for the bird cage in their room and to think of a name for the bird--any name but Budgie--since it now was a part of our family, whether it wanted to be or not. And I told both of them to relax and chill out in their room since we had such an eventful trip to San Antonio. They seemed more than pleased to appease me and did what kids love to do--play in their room. I closed the door to their bedroom behind me as I left.

I decided right then and there that I deserved a cigarette so I found my hidden pack of smokes, grabbed my trusty lighter, picked up my dad's urn from the coffee table, and made my way to the balcony. Outside, the charred remains of my wooden bench and the burnt Café Bustelo coffee can awaited me. The black spot on the cement where the can burned fanned out from under the bench like a cheap rug. I sat on the bench and set the urn on the cement floor next to the coffee can. What a pair! I had a realization as I lit my cigarette that both the coffee can *and* the urn had the same purpose: to hold ashes. Both held ashes of things that held some consequences to my life.

As I smoked the cigarette, I thought of my father. He used to love saying these things to me, these whacky things that had some significance to him at whatever random moment it was he decided to tell me, things like, "You need to be useful, son!" or "You need to have a purpose, boy!" He would always pontificate while he forced me to do chores around the house, like I was his slave, while he sat on his ass, sipping beer or drinking coffee, barking these slogans while I raked leaves or cut the grass or swept the garage or took out the garbage. He was a real bastard that way because he didn't help me with these chores. He just wanted me to do them by myself, to teach me a lesson. I don't know what his lesson was, really. It just always seemed to me that he wanted me to do all the work so he could sit on his ass. I think he just wanted to be in control. It's really easy to be in control of a kid when you're the parent; just bark orders at them and threaten punishment if they don't comply. It's much harder to gain their respect by setting a good example. When I became a parent, I decided that I was going to set the good example and *not* bully my kids. That was my hope, anyway.

So, as I smoked my cigarette and reminisced about my father, I decided it was time for Marv to make himself useful. I pushed the burnt coffee can away then took the lid off the urn. After setting the lid on the bench, I ashed my cigarette into the urn, the cigarette ash resting on top of my father's ashes, their color slightly different. As I stared at my new cigarette ash receptacle, an immense feeling of pleasure rushed through my veins along with the nicotine. I had not felt as happy as I did that day in a very, *very* long time.

"Make yourself useful, dad!" I said, out loud, to no one but myself, and my father's ashes.

It was one of the greatest comebacks I had ever uttered in my entire life. My dad would have been furious at me.

It's true.

***

When Tuesday came around, I picked up Nat in the rental car my auto insurance got for me: a three-door, miniature Nissan. The car looked like toy, like some kind of robotic beetle-bug with donuts for wheels. It was a ridiculous color of blue, bordering on nauseating, like the color of a blueberry Slurpee. And the large, round headlights and plastic grill with upturned sides made the goddamn thing look like it was grinning, although I don't know what it was smiling about; it was a pathetic excuse for an automobile. It should have been ashamed of itself. Nat got a real kick out of seeing me drive that stupid, little car, probably in the same way kids get a kick out of seeing their parents fumble through their favorite video games or wear their style of clothes in an attempt to be hip. When she got in the little car, she was laughing and wheezing and giggling all over the goddamn place, slapping her knees and all. She just couldn't get over it. And she could barely fit in the car herself. Her long limbs folded in front of her after she put her seat belt on, like a gigantic praying mantis wearing a tank top and shorts sitting in the passenger seat twisting and contorting to fit in the small space.

"This is, like, the kind of ride a college student would get from their parents!" she said, laughing some more, trying to contain the laughter by covering her mouth. "It's like a go-kart!"

"Very funny. I didn't really have a choice of the *type* of car I could get. This is just what the insurance company gave me. All right?"

"That's fine," she said, giggling some more. "Just sayin'."

"At least I have a car to use."

"True. And you'll be getting a new car soon. Right?"

"Yep. And look at you. You barely fit in here. Who should be laughing at who?"

"Shut up!" she said, then giggling.

Turns out, according to my auto insurance company, the model and year of Volvo I owned had a recall for a component of the electrical system that could potentially turn off the engine while the car was driving--something I wasn't aware of at all--and I found this out the hard way, of course. I was very conflicted upon learning this information, considering how much I wanted and loved that stupid car. Sometimes, things you dream about just don't turn out to be as great as you hoped. In fact, sometimes things you really desire turn out to be nothing more than big piles of shit. It's true. Be careful what you wish for 'cause it just might potentially bite you in the ass.

"Well, the car will be new to me," I said, stopping at a stop sign, then turning right toward the kids' elementary school, good ol' Wells Port Elementary. All the other parents were maneuvering to and around the parking lot, jockeying for position in the car line so they could pick their kids up as soon as possible. As I stepped on the accelerator, the go-kart emitted a sound like mouse flatulence, sputtering and squirting noxious gas from its rear end. It was so embarrassing. "My car wasn't worth more than $10,000. I can't get a new car with that unless I want a car like this *thing*. And I don't want a car payment."

"No doubt. Car payments blow."

"Exactly."

But rather than wait in the car line, I parked on the street that ran next to the school, so we could wait for the kiddos, and just in time, the school bell rang and the kids poured out of the school like a tsunami. Keeping the engine running, we waited in the car.

"I appreciate you going to taekwondo with Jessie today. I promised Sammie that we could have some time together and I thought this was the perfect time to do it."

"It's not a problem," she said, smiling. "I'm, like, glad to do it."

"Then Sammie and I will pick you guys up after practice and we can all go grab a bite to eat. Sound good?"

"Of course."

Before we knew it, my kids attacked the door handles, trying to get in the little blue insect mobile. Nat and I opened the doors then reclined the front seats, allowing the kids to hop in the back seat.

"This car is so *small!*" Jessie said, crawling through the tiny space between the driver seat and the back seat.

"This car should be in *The Wizard of Oz*! A tiny car for the Munchkins!" Sammie said, climbing behind Nat's seat. Nat and I popped the seats back upright and got in the car. "You know. Munchkins Shmunkins!"

"Everybody buckle up," I said, putting the car in gear and tearing off, the miniature car screeching like a mouse in the grasp of a hungry cat.

I drove around the perimeter of the school, around the playground at the back of the school, to the street on the opposite side, the street that led to the strip mall where Jessie's taekwondo dojang resided with Master Lu and the other junior black belts inside, all waiting for Jessie to show up so they could try to kick each other's little asses. I pulled into the parking lot and parked right in front of the entrance to the dojang. I got out of the car to let Jessie out, and Nat too.

"I'll be back in an hour and a half or so. OK?"

"OK, Daddy!" Jessie said, hugging me around the waist. Nat came around and grabbed her hand, then the two girls went inside. I hopped back in the car.

"Ready to go, son?" I said, buckling my seat belt.

"Yeah!"

I put the screeching go-kart in drive and we tore off. Good ol' Sammie Boy decided the day before that he and I needed some Daddy / son time and I agreed, knowing that it had been a while since he and I had spent some quality time together. Especially after what happened in San Antonio, it just seemed like the right thing to do. So, when I asked him where he wanted to go to spend time with me, he replied, "My favorite place!"

We drove down the road leading away from the strip mall then I quickly turned right on Mallard Duck Drive--the street our old house resided on--and slowly drove until we stopped in front of it, so our little routine could play out again.

"Does it look the same?" I said, initiating the routine.

"It looks so *different*!"

"Nah, it looks the same," I said, just like the time before and the time before that. But even though it may seem like a routine that would get old, it never got old to me. I loved playing this game. I loved being a dad. "Maybe the grass looks different but I don't think so."

"I miss Mommy," he said, his voice trailing into a whisper. "Do you miss Mommy?"

"Sometimes," I said. I lied. But he didn't need to know that. It was just a little, as they say, white lie. Sometimes, a little white lie is better than a big, fat lie. Well, maybe that *was* a big, fat lie but I wasn't about to tell him that. Parents don't have to tell their kids *everything*, you know?

"I bet she's happy now," he said, a little cheerier.

"I hope you're right, son."

I drove away from the *Crazy House* and down the street to the cul-de-sac where the trailhead for the jogging trail around the lake was: Sammie's favorite place. I parked the car and unlocked the doors. We got out of the go-kart-mobile and Sammie started sprinting--full speed--toward the lake. He was running like his life depended on it, his little arms flailing, his little legs trucking. Have you ever had a pet dog who--whenever you open the front door--sprints out the door and down the street like a slave running for freedom? That's how Sammie was running, like for his freedom.

"Come on, Daddy!" he said, calling back to me. I was just standing there like a bump on a log, watching my boy run full-speed toward the lake. "Maybe we'll see that turtle again!"

I locked the rental car and followed after him, stepping onto the jogging trail then walking parallel to his running path, me on the jogging trail and my son on the shore of the lake about fifty feet away. He was having the time of his life, yelling and screaming and laughing and whooping it up and looked like he might fall in the lake since he was running so close to the water. But he didn't fall in although he did dunk one foot in the water, purely by accident. He attempted to jump over a large tree root protruding from the dirt and, when he lunged over the root, his right foot clipped the root, sending him off-balance to the water, where his left foot immersed itself in the cold lake. That didn't stop him though; he just kept on trucking.

"Meet me at our bench, Daddy!" he said, waving at me to follow him.

"All right!" I said, yelling back. "Meet you there!"

As he ran from the shore through the grass and up a slight incline to the jogging trail ahead of me, I remembered the first time I brought good ol' Sammie Boy to this lake. He was probably 2 or 3-years old, just a little tyke, a small guy who could walk but wasn't fast enough to keep up with my full-stride, so I strapped the little guy into a jogging stroller and pushed him around the lake. And although I was too much of a fat ass to jog, I wasn't fat enough to speed walk around the lake. So, one day, I pushed him around the lake and this expression appeared on his face that I had never seen before: pure joy. It was as if I had released him in Candy Land or in Willy Wonka's factory or some equivalent of a child's fantasy world. It was sensory overload for good ol' Sammie Boy. He watched the birds fly across the lake and skid into the water. He watched the turtles pop in and out of the water. He watched the squirrels run amok for nuts and bits of food. He watched the frogs and toads hop across the jogging trail. He watched the dogs of our neighbors run and fetch for sticks, even if the sticks were tossed into the water. He just couldn't get enough of the lake. When we were done walking around the lake and about to head back to the house, he turned to me and squealed, 'AGAIN! AGAIN!' Like I said, he couldn't get enough of it. And ever since that first walk around the lake, he had this expression that I affectionately called *Lake Face*, a look of pure joy and excitement that only a mention of a walk to the beautiful body of water could illicit. It really was the cutest thing. Really. I defy you to tell me of something cuter because there isn't anything cuter than that. It's true.

I snapped out of my daydream to see Sammie still ahead of me, sprinting toward a curve in the jogging trail that followed the lake to the left, and taking walkers and joggers and runners to where our favorite bench resided, a good twenty or thirty feet passed the curve, in the grass, at the right of the jogging trail.

"Come on, Daddy! The last one to the bench is a rotten egg!" he said, calling in the distance. I began to run after him but only long enough for him to believe I was actually going to *run*. Once he turned around and commenced sprinting himself, I eased back into my leisurely stroll. 'I will get to the bench eventually,' I thought. There really was no need to hurry and ruin my enjoyment.

As I walked further, I thought of a time when Sammie--a little bigger then than when I used to push him around the lake in a jogging stroller--watched a man toss a stick into the lake then the man's dog jumped into the water after it, swimming toward the floating stick in the middle of the lake, a good thirty or forty feet away. The dog diligently swam after the stick but Sammie was horrified. Good ol' Sammie Boy thought the dog was swimming to its doom and, in an effort to be helpful and save the dog, he jumped into the water as well, to swim after the dog and save it. The dog didn't slow down or even notice Sammie until it reached the stick and turned around to swim back to the shore with the stick in its mouth. When it reached Sammie, about halfway to the shore, the dog slowed down enough for Sammie to grab its collar and get pulled back to the shore by the heroic dog. I ran to see if my boy was OK. And as we stood there on the lake shore--the dog shaking its fur free of dingy, lake water and me clinging to my son--all Sammie could say was, 'I saved the doggy, Daddy. I saved the doggy.'

I snapped out of this daydream to find myself at the curve of the jogging trail. Sammie reached the bench way before I even got to the curve and he was dancing his little victory dance, knowing full-well that he had crushed me in his running competition.

"I win! I win!" he said, dancing around the bench.

When I reached the bench, I sat down and watched him celebrate a little longer.

"I beat you! I beat you!" he said, gloating. "I beat you sooo bad!"

"You sure did. My legs are too old to sprint after you around the lake," I said, patting the space next to me on the bench, inviting him to sit down.

"You're not old, Daddy. You're a spring chicken!"

"I'm a fall chicken."

"Chicken shmicken!" he said, sitting down. He kicked his feet back and forth, as kids do when they have too much nervous energy. If there was a way to store up that adolescent, nervous energy and use it to rejuvenate adults, then I would be a millionaire. It's true.

"Do you remember that time you jumped in the lake and swam after that dog?"

"Do I?" he said, excited. "I saved that doggy!"

"You did. I remember. That was awesome."

Then something caught Sammie's eye in the grass. He jumped off the bench and knelt on the ground, picking up a shiny object from between some blades of grass. He held it up for me to see.

"Look, Daddy. A quarter!"

"I see that," I said, holding out my hand for him to give it to me. He did, placing it in my palm.

"Flip it, Daddy. I'll guess heads or tails."

"Are you sure?" I said, skeptical. "I don't want to upset you."

"You won't upset me. No one is around and I can guess it for you."

"OK," I said, flipping the coin then catching it. "Heads or tails?"

A smirk appeared on his face, one that was borderline sadistic, telling me that my boy already knew the answer.

"Heads."

"Of course it is," I said, then opened my hand to reveal what we both knew. Heads.

"I told you!" he said, pumping his fist quickly, but his celebration was short-lived. "Hey Daddy? Do you remember the time Jessie fell and cut her knee and you carried her all the way home?"

I went through the Rolodex of child injuries in my mind and, not remembering that one, then said, "Of course I do. I..." Before I could continue down the imaginary path, I did remember this particular incident, the one where Sammie and Jessie were chasing each other and Jessie slid on the crushed granite of the jogging trail and fell down. The scrape on her knee wasn't really that bad but it bled profusely, as skin scrapes sometimes do. It looked more horrific than it really was, actually. "Yes! I do remember that time. Your little sister was pretty freaked out."

"Good thing you had that little first aid kit with you in your pocket."

"Yes, good thing I was prepared."

"You're a great daddy, Daddy," he said, kicking at a more furious pace.

"Thanks, son."

"Want me to guess heads or tails again? I can guess it every time."

"All right," I said, and we went through the fateful routine several times, four or five at least with this shiny quarter, the one he found in the grass, and good ol' Sammie Boy guessed every coin toss. I realized, right then and there, that I was never going to tell anyone about my boy's ability to see the future. Well, I had tried to tell a few people in our lives about his special ability but I decided that I wasn't going to tell anyone else. What would be the point? No one would believe me anyway. I mean, all it would do would cause us problems and I didn't want that. Our life wasn't the plot of some sci-fi movie, where a stressed out parent somehow finds contacts with the FBI or the CIA or some government agency that claims they want to study the child for the good of the world but really want to overthrow the Russians or counterattack mutant superheroes or some shit like that. So, rather than have more problems, I decided to just keep my goddamn mouth shut. I placed my hand on my son's shoulder and smiled at him. He smiled at me, too.

"Daddy? Can I ask you a question?"

"Sure, son."

"Where do you go when you die?"

"That's a good question," I said, searching for the best way to answer his question: the eternal question. Where did he come up with this stuff? Was he studying existentialism at school? Or philosophy? Or religion? I didn't know. "People have been wondering about that question for a very, very long time."

"Some of the kids at school say that when you die, then you go to heaven. But I don't know if I believe them or not."

"Why don't you believe them?"

"Well, because the kids that say when you die you go to heaven also say that mommies get pregnant when daddies go peepee inside them."

"Wha?!" I said, flabbergasted, not expecting the change in conversation from the philosophical to filthy, adolescent garbage. "Kids at school tell you this?"

"Yeah, some do. But they're stupid. Mommies don't get pregnant that way 'cause peepee is bodily waste. Babies aren't made from waste."

"Very true. That's not how procreation works."

"What is pro-cree-ay-shun?" he said, confused.

"That's a fancy word for how babies are created."

"Oh," he said, looking out across the lake. He stared at the reflections on the water, the ducks swimming in formation, then his legs stopped kicking back and forth. He stared and stared without saying a word, a look of astonishment on his little face. I had seen that look several times before, the look when he saw things, then told me, then they came true. Was it happening again? I placed my arm around him as he continued to stare at the lake.

"You OK, son?" I said.

"Daddy?"

"Yes."

"I see something. I see you. I see you standing in front of a lot of people, reading something."

"Oh yeah? What am I reading?"

"I don't know but it is making the people happy. They are smiling at you. They are watching you. There are a lot of them. Hundreds. A bunch. And when you're done reading, they all stand up and clap. They are clapping for you. They are cheering for you, like people do at a football game or something. They love you."

"Oh really? I wonder what that means?"

Sammie shook his head then snapped out of his trance. He looked at me with his sweet little face, all flush and embarrassed and confused. I could tell that he couldn't make heads or tails about what he 'saw.' Or maybe he did and just didn't want to say too much. It's hard to say. I surely didn't know.

"Maybe you're reading them one of your stories. Maybe you're going to be a famous writer some day!"

"Oh, I doubt that," I said, scoffing. "I'm pretty sure that *that* is not going to happen."

"Never shmever," he said, giggling. "You should write a book about me and Budgie. Call it *Sammie and Budgie*. And I'll draw the pictures."

"That's a great idea!" I said. It really was a great idea and only someone like my son could suggest such an idea to me and have it *not* sound like absolute bullshit. I mean, kids are great at bullshitting. It's one of their super powers. But they are also great at dreaming. That's where adults suck, the dreaming part. Most adults lose that ability when they start working full-time and are drained of any free time to dream. Sad, so sad. "We should do that."

"Yeah!"

"We can start when we get home tonight."

"Wait! I have an even better idea!"

"Oh yeah, what's better than writing and illustrating a Sammie and Budgie book?"

"Playing a game called Sammie and Budgie!"

"I don't know that game," I said, leaning back on the bench and crossing my legs. "You'll have to explain it to me."

"OK. So, I'm Sammie, *of course*. And you're Budgie. And we team up to save people from the evil sludge monster. It lives in the tallest mountain in the world. It lives inside of it and eats lava for breakfast. The lava burns its stomach and makes it mad."

"Oh yeah? And where is this mountain with an evil sludge monster inside of it?"

Sammie looked around our immediate vicinity and spotted a pile of dirt and gravel about thirty or forty feet away, near a pecan tree, left by a landscaper or construction crew, no doubt, for a project at a later date. It was certainly a size of pile that a boy Sammie's stature could climb.

"There!" he said, pointing at the pile of dirt. "There's the great mountain where the sludge monster lives. Come on! Let's go get him!"

Sammie jumped off the bench and ran full-speed toward the dirt pile. "Come on, Daddy! I mean Budgie. Come on, Budgie!"

I stood up and followed my son to the dirt pile, although at a more leisurely pace than his.

"Coming!" I said.

I watched him traverse up the dirt pile, clutching at handfuls of dirt as he scaled it all the way to the top. Once he had some good footing, he pounded his chest then raised his arms in a victory pose. "V" for victorious.

"Watch out, sludge monster. Sammie and Budgie are here to save the day!"

That's right. Sammie and Budgie were there to save the day from the sludge monster. Or any monster. Or any problem. That's what family was for. That's what our little family was for.

And I thought about Sammie's original idea some more, the idea that he and I should write a book together, one called *Sammie and Budgie*. I would write it and he would draw it. And the more I thought about it, the more it sounded like a genius idea. I mean, think about it. A father and son write and illustrate a book together? What a marketing hook. It's genius!

So, this was the impetus for me to come out of my retirement, my self-imposed retirement, my writing retirement, and write again. Be a writer again. Follow my dreams again, the dream I had of becoming a famous writer. It took being a father to see that *that* was always my dream too, as well as the dream to be a father. A good father. No, a great father. I tried my best to be a great father. I know I had great children so I must have been doing something right. And the title of the book?

SAMMIE & BUDGIE

It was a great title. I couldn't have thought of one better myself. That boy of mine was a genius, I tell you. My little genius.

It's true.

The End

About the Author

Scott Semegran lives in Austin, Texas with his wife, four kids, two cats, and a dog. He graduated from the University of Texas at Austin with a degree in English. He is a writer and a cartoonist. He can also bend metal with his mind and run really fast, if chased by a pack of wolves. His comic strips have appeared in the following newspapers: The Austin Student, The Funny Times, The Austin American-Statesman, Rocky Mountain Bullhorn, Seven Days, The University of Texas at Dallas Mercury, and The North Austin Bee. Books by Scott Semegran include Sammie & Budgie, Boys, The Meteoric Rise of Simon Burchwood, The Spectacular Simon Burchwood, Modicum, Mr. Grieves and more. He is a Kindle bestselling author.

Books by Scott Semegran

If you enjoyed this book then check out the novel **The Meteoric Rise of Simon Burchwood** by Scott Semegran. On his way to New York to celebrate his impending literary success, Simon Burchwood is the prototypical American careerist. But a quick detour to Montgomery, Alabama to visit a childhood friend sends Simon on a bizarre journey, challenging his hopes and dreams of becoming a famous writer. **The Meteoric Rise of Simon Burchwood** is a character study that delves into the psyche of a man who desperately tries to redefine himself.

Is Simon pompous? Yes. A jerk? Yes. Will you like him? Absolutely! "The book is told entirely from Simon's viewpoint. Simon is not a very likeable guy; as a matter of fact, he is a self-centered, pompous jerk. But for some reason, it's pretty fun to be inside his head, mainly because he is an inadvertent, oblivious jerk... you will learn Simon's views on smoking, cleanliness and going to the bathroom, just to name a few. There were times that I laughed out loud... A very good novel that was humorous throughout." -- 4 1/2 Stars / *Red Adept Reviews*

The Meteoric Rise of Simon Burchwood was selected as one of the "5 Best Summer Indie Beach Reads" by the editors of *IndieReader*. Their verdict: "An ambitious, enjoyable read with a superb ending that changed my interpretation of the entire text."

"A clever and surprising twist... cutting observations of the writerly demeanor." -- *Kirkus Reviews*

Buy it today!

* * *

Want more Simon Burchwood? Then get the next novel **The Spectacular Simon Burchwood**. Recently divorced and his writing career in shambles, Simon Burchwood's life is a complete disaster. He reluctantly finds work as a computer support technician and resigns that his career as the next great American novelist will never come to fruition. When he learns that his ex-wife abruptly moves to Dallas with his children, he embarks on a crazy road trip with a nerdy coworker and a hitchhiking punk rock girl and discovers the inspiration he desperately needs for his new literary masterpiece. Take another trip with the one and only Simon Burchwood.

Praise for **The Spectacular Simon Burchwood**:

"The author is quite funny and some of the quips are great. Simon can be hilarious and great to read about in his recaps and memories." –- 3 Stars / *So Many Books, So Little Time*

"Simon is starting to understand something, and his luck literally changes. Semegran handles this quite deftly; even though Simon keeps warbling his "It's true!" declarations at a great rate, the reader does not tire of them, because, well, some of them ARE true, and we see the progress he is making in getting a grasp of what life is about, albeit in his own ham-fisted way." –- 4 Stars / *The New Podler Review of Books*

Buy it today!

* * *

If you enjoyed this book then check out **MODICUM**, a collection of short stories, musings, and cartoons by writer / cartoonist Scott Semegran. The book explores such themes as suicide, parenting, religion, masculinity, the apocalypse, and, most importantly, erections. It's guaranteed to make you laugh, cry, and pee your pants (hopefully, not at the same time).

Praise for **MODICUM**:

"Funny, sweet, dark, and sad, Scott Semegran's comics and short stories create a wholly convincing world of love, loss, and fear. His light touch with heavy subjects is a gift, and his forays into silliness are a delight. I can't tell if his kids should read it as soon as possible, or never." - Emily Flake, cartoonist and author of *LuLu Eightball*

"Hilarious, poignant, twisted... and those are just the stories. Scott Semegran's cartoons bring an added one-two visceral punch to a powerful collection of work." - Davy Rothbart, author of *The Lone Surfer of Montana, Kansas* and publisher of *FOUND Magazine*

Get it today!

* * *

Mr. Grieves started as a poke at human nature through the use of talking, narcissistic animals. It has evolved into a full-on assault to your funny bone. Where else will you find rats fighting over cubicles, camels worrying about aging, a parrot talking to aliens, and a lonely water snail longing for a friend? Welcome to the world of **Mr. Grieves**!

Praise for **Mr. Grieves**:

"An animal or plant — or maybe even an ovum — talks. Sometimes to itself, but more often to another of its kind. The idea is simple, but the execution is smart and almost always funny in Scott Semegran's collection of 140 four-panel comics drawn between 2004 and 2008, **Mr. Grieves**." -- Reviewed for *IndieReader* by Andrew Stout

Get it today!

***

Boys is a collection of stories about three boys living in Texas: one growing up, one dreaming, and one fighting to stay alive in the face of destitution and adversity. There's second-grader William, a shy yet imaginative boy who schemes about how to get back at his school-yard bully, Randy. Then there's Sam, a 15-year-old boy who dreams of getting a 1980 Mazda RX-7 for his sixteenth birthday but has to work at a Greek restaurant to fund his dream. Finally, there's Seff, a 21-year-old on the brink of manhood, trying to survive along with his roommate, working as waiters and barely making ends meet. These three stories are told with heart, humor, and an uncompromising look at what it meant to grow up in Texas during the 1980s and 1990s.

"The writing is sharp and unpretentiously thoughtful, and since each of the main characters finds solace in companionship, this is an affecting literary depiction of the comforting power of friendship. Each of the stories can be read on its own, but taken together, they make a coherent, thematic whole, skillfully produced. An endearing collection that deftly captures the need for youthful fellowship." -- *Kirkus Reviews*

"Verdict: With nary a dull moment, Scott Semegran's **Boys** features short stories filled with unexpected nuances that draws readers right into the heart of his well-developed characters." --*IndieReader*. 5 Stars. IR Approved.

Get it today!

***

Find Scott Semegran Online:
https://www.scottsemegran.com
https://www.goodreads.com/scottsemegran
https://www.twitter.com/scottsemegran
https://www.facebook.com/scottsemegran.writer/
https://www.instagram.com/scott_semegran
https://www.amazon.com/author/scottsemegran
https://www.smashwords.com/profile/view/scottsemegran

Mutt Press:
https://www.muttpress.com